Steel Eyes

Melissa Price

Bella
BOOKS

2015

Bella Books, Inc.
P.O. Box 10543
Tallahassee, FL 32302

Printed in the United States of America on acid-free paper.

First Bella Books Edition 2015

Editor: JoSelle Vanderhooft
Cover Designer: Judith Fellows

ISBN: 978-1-59493-445-2

About the Author

Melissa is a novelist, who in the absence of her computer or a pen, isn't too proud to write in crayon or spray paint. A retired Doctor of Chiropractic and a lifelong guitarist, she also co-wrote the authorized biographical screenplay, *Toma—The Man, The Mission, The Message*. Her novels include *Steel Eyes*, *The Right Closet*, and her work-in-progress *Skin In The Game*. While her house is in Phoenix, Arizona, Melissa *lives* between some un-named exotic Caribbean island and Paris's Left Bank.

Dedication

Dedicated to the memory of Chick and Nancy Price, and Andréa Price Goldsmith, to whose effervescent artistry I remain beholden.

Acknowledgments

To every rescue dog and cat who sat by me or on me late into the night while I wrote, even when I wasn't bribing them with treats.

I am immensely thankful to Bella Books, Jessica Hill, and Karin Kallmaker, without whom this book would not have become what it has.

Thank you to my editor and friend Jacob Shaver whose love and blue-pencil-tactics have made me a better writer; to Oana Niculae whose writing inspires me, and to Suzann Brent who introduced me to real magic. Thanks to Catherine Coulter from whom I learned to "strip search" my work.

To the memory of the musician and authors whose influence is always within reach: Michael Palmer, who said we would meet again on the *Times* bestseller list; Ray Bradbury for his sage advice, and French author Pierre Bourgeade; the iconic Les Paul who instructed me to "Keep Pickin'" when he signed the guitar that became the inspiration for the guitar in this story. (I'm still pickin', Les.)

Thank you to Lee and Ellis Weinrebe-Reeder, Dr. Pam Stalzer, Robert Scanlan, Linda Lane, and Dr. Richard and Elaine Wiener. You are champions, one and all.

This book was written for those who reach deep and for whom artful passion is limitless.

PROLOGUE

Madison Square Garden, New York City, 1996

"Steel Eyes! Steel Eyes! Steel Eyes!"

Twenty thousand obsessed fans chanted in three-four time in the arena. The forty thousand feet formed a sort of tribal percussion, banging and stomping; but backstage it all rolled up into an unorchestrated din.

"Steel Eyes! Steel Eyes! Steel Eyes!"

The rhythmic syllables reverberated until the two words merged into one, the same way that the past few cities had begun to blur together.

All but one band member fidgeted through their last-minute backstage ritual, and that was the iconic Steel Eyes herself. Sitting quietly in her intricately jeweled mask and costume, she breathed deep to beckon all of her emotion upward into her throat and down into her hands. She worked it like a snake charmer luring her cobra hypnotically upward, glad the whole time that it was the snake charmer's very last stop on the tour. She was tired.

After the show, she and the band would have their intimate meal across town, in the private back room of La Maschera on the Upper East Side. During their final late-night meal on the road, Steel Eyes would pretend that every thought for the past month wasn't about going home. Goose bumps chilled her at the mere thought of finally waking up in her own bed, gazing out at the greenish New Jersey ocean, knowing she could just sleep and eat and then eat and sleep some more.

"Yo! Steel Eyes, get ready, we're on in five, sweetie," JJ said as he twirled his drumsticks.

Calmly, Steel Eyes peeked up at him from behind the outrageous painted and jeweled mask. A cross between Catwoman's mask and cat-eye glasses from the 1960s, the dramatic elongated cobalt eyepiece flared out beyond the stunningly gaunt cheekbones.

With her sparkling, smoky eyes adorned with swirls of color, the chameleon-like gray morphed to blue, sometimes green, depending on the lighting. This was the mask of anonymity, the face of fame. The Steel Eyes mask was as famous as the face beneath it wasn't, and except for a chosen few, no one knew Steel Eyes's true identity. She liked it that way. She needed it that way. Steel Eyes never could have existed otherwise.

Deep breath in, exhale, she told herself.

Without the mask, she was invisible—an ordinary person, really, and she got a kick out of that. One night after a show, a rabid fan had pushed her out of the way to get closer to the stage door, unaware it was she who he was waiting for.

"Helllooo. Steely, where are you, girl?"

"No worries, JJ. I'm right here," she said confidently. "Where's Hunt?"

"Probably making sure everything is perfect for you, as usual."

Steel Eyes nodded. "I *am* a lucky girl." She and Hunt had history, and they had trusted each other with their lives since way before all the Steel Eyes madness.

"You look like you're a million miles away...even with the mask."

"Don't fret, JJ, I'm just a little tired, but I'll be fine once we're out there. We're here to rock!"

"Wrong," he snapped. "We rocked in LA. In New York, we kick ass!" He rolled his eyes at her. "Did you really just say 'Don't *fret*'?"

Steel Eyes stretched her celebrated sinewy fingers and smiled up at him from her chair.

"Your glitter is blinding me."

"Almost time to go to work, J."

"Play that screaming guitar now, and I promise we'll explore the universe later," he said when he patted her shiny shoulder.

Steel Eyes filled herself with stillness until she could no longer hear the stomping out front. She was fully present, her hands warm and ready. Temporarily there would be no painful past, no fairy-tale future, no thoughts of the woman she knew so long ago and had never forgotten—the woman who had made her into Steel Eyes without ever even knowing it. There would be only joy; the joy of playing every song she ever wrote for her. So what that it just happened to be her freakin' hit list.

"One minute, everybody," JJ said.

In one minute she would storm that stage, pour grace into every measure, and with God-given grit in her hands, she would ravage her pimped-out, whore-red axe Ruby; and she would do it before twenty thousand *rock voyeurs*...again.

She got up, adjusted her guitar strap, and positioned Ruby up against her, just below her breast, right where she wanted her to be for that very first note, that single droplet in a torrent of inner anarchy, raining down in one searing-hot, orgasmically melodic, grunge-laced note.

A cruel mistress to the ebony and mother-of-pearl fretboard, she would let everyone watch it happen. She wouldn't give a fuck about her vulnerability because nobody paid those big bucks to watch her do it. The rock voyeurs paid the money to watch *Steel Eyes* do it. And Steel Eyes always gave them their money's worth.

On her third breath, she flashed the trademark Steel Eyes smile, broad white radiant light framed by sumptuous lips.

"JJ," she said. "Is my game face on straight?"

He pulled back to examine far beyond the hard mask, the hair, and through the layers of stardom until he was gazing into her own eyes and not Steel Eyes's. "You know once you take that stage you'll magically forget about your old flame for a while."

She and JJ joined the others, everyone taking their usual places…again.

Steel Eyes didn't tell JJ that her old flame was at *this* concert. "Let's go out with a bang, guys," she said.

Melanie, the bass player, was all pumped up. "Saving the best for last," she yelled. "Last show. Yeah, let's make some memories!"

Contrary to JJ's statement, Steel Eyes had never told him that her inspired performances were the ones where she was infused with the memories of the woman she had simply never been able to forget…well, not in this lifetime anyway.

"Mel, remember we're doing that minor third dip in the second verse of 'Somewhere Like You.'"

"Just like last time, little sister." Mel winked at Steel Eyes. "Don't be nervous, I've got this. I got it, yeah, baby…let's go, let's go. I got it!"

Above the mob in the darkened arena, neon laser images of the distinctive Steel Eyes mask flew and floated, igniting the chain of events known as the Steel Eyes Flies Tour. The crowd's thunderous applause greeted the band when the house lights sank to their final shade of black, and the blue gels on the stage lights rendered Steel Eyes's already blue mask an impossible shade of cobalt.

A deep, frenetic boom of Melanie's bass guitar set off an explosion of Emphatic Rock; that unique space between classic rock and jazz that Steel Eyes had defined and made famous with her sexy fingers and unrepentant longing.

The drums *pop-popped*, punctuating the intoxicating *wah wah* of Rich's rhythm guitar. The instruments climaxed into a synchronous crescendo, where they smashed head-on into Steel Eyes's first note.

That one magical metal note. Her every organ screamed with visceral devolution down to each infinitesimal cell when she played that note. She executed it perfectly, milked it for all it was worth, and let it gut everyone who heard it.

"Hey, New York! How are ya!" she screamed into the mic.

Her fingers but a blur to the untrained eye, she unleashed the first hurricane of signature lead guitar licks that had made her into a worldwide brand and phenom. Steel Eyes haunted and provoked. That was her job, after all; that was her passion. Crowds roared in multiple languages and guitars screamed. It was just another day at the office for a woman who had been abducted and held hostage by fame. Fame that circulated in her blood like a poison.

The faster you move, the faster it consumes you, she thought.

That was her last conscious thought before she vanished through what she called her Transcendent Gateway. She slid across the stage on her knees in a steel-string-bending blur, all at her calculated whim, abandon at her command. She drowned out her feelings by playing harder, and the voyeurs were already on their feet. Her body rocked back and forth in time to her spectacular band, and she jumped when she played the high notes, her sparkly long hair swirling around her. She was everyone's picture of the quintessential rock star.

* * *

The shots rang out just before the end of that show. At first, Steel Eyes thought one of the amps had blown. She saw the crowd stampeding toward the exits and heard the screaming. Chaos had erupted.

Crack. A burst of excruciating pain and heat spread from her chest down her arm. One security guard ripped Ruby from her. The size of a tank, her bodyguard tackled her. Buried beneath him, she became faint, teased in and out of consciousness after her head hit the floor. She touched the liquid oozing from her scalp and saw the blood on her hand—felt it in her hair. Steel Eyes struggled to see beyond the stage, not knowing in that moment of burning delirium whether what she saw was fantasy, or a trick of the lights…or was that really the love of her life rushing *toward* the stage?

"Get the damn medics now!" someone yelled.

The tank named Jean Claude carried her backstage and she heard someone else say, "Easy, lay her on the couch."

Steel Eyes faded out for what felt like a few seconds, but when she opened her eyes, she was strapped to a gurney and squinting from the harsh light inside the ambulance, with only her knit under-mask on her face.

"That's it, honey…open your eyes for me. We're almost at the hospital," the paramedic said. "Follow this with your eyes."

Steel Eyes groaned as he continued swinging the penlight back and forth.

"Stay with me. I need you to stay awake. Okay?" he shouted. "Can you tell me your name?"

"Steel Eyes," she mustered.

"No, your real name," he said.

"Not on your life."

She tried to focus on their faces, but her vision was blurred and the stark white lights sliced through her retinas.

"I'm here, Steely, I'm right here." Hunt's velvety voice floated through her mind when he squeezed her hand. She tried to respond but could not move.

A surge of energy coursed through her veins. The poisonous fame was circulating fast now. Her heart pounded and fluttered, and she couldn't catch her breath. A movie played in her mind— it rolled in an instant. But in that instant, for the first time, she saw how she got here, right from the very beginning.

"Let the ER know we can't stabilize her!" the paramedic yelled.

Blood loss, she thought.

Out of all the fragments of sound, a quiet voice rose inside her head—a woman's voice; *her* voice. As Steel Eyes drifted out of consciousness, she heard it say, "Don't go, baby, don't go."

But that was *then*, and *then* was a long time ago.

PART ONE

CHAPTER ONE

1982

Some people meet for the first time and have a drink. Some have drinks and then sex, and some...just skip the drinks. Alex Winthrop was flexible—although this time, something was *different*.

She felt this girl enter the store before she even saw her. She felt it on her skin the way a canvas would feel a brushstroke if it could, and every follicle on the back of her neck stood and chilled her.

"Can I help you find your size?" Alex asked the girl rummaging through the shelves stacked with trendy blue jeans. She practically had to shout over the screaming guitars on The Allman Brothers song "Whipping Post," which she had blaring through the speakers.

"Twenty-eight, extra long," the girl answered. "Dressing room?"

Alex pointed to the back of the little store on Fourth Street, just off Seventh Avenue in the beatnik-turned-hippie evolution of Greenwich Village in Lower Manhattan. To her,

Conflicted or not, Alex had the sinking feeling that she could never get enough of the girl with no name. Certain of it, she tried anyway. As she stroked back the girl's silky, long hair, she realized it wasn't quite as long as the last time. Alex grabbed a handful of it, gently pulled back the girl's head to expose her neck, pressed her parted lips against it, then gorged on the skin. The girl moaned and didn't stop her.

Alex's eyelids burned against her eyeballs every time she closed them. To her, this was totally unavoidable, moronically inescapable but tragically hot, and Alex wanted it—all of it, all of her. And she wanted it now. The girl's body felt different than she remembered, more womanly...hungry.

Alex felt the heat of the woman's inner thigh against her hand. They kissed tenderly, but the passion was no less intense.

The girl's deftness, the sensation of her hand on Alex's thigh as she reached down and in, made Alex shiver the way she had every time she'd thought of her, which was every day since their encounter.

"Who are you?" Alex breathed into her neck when the girl fell limp against her.

The woman answered with a passionate kiss.

"You leave first," she told Alex.

Counting the word *funeral*, Alex had now garnered four whole words and none of them were a name. To her dismay, the girl never turned around—not even once to acknowledge her for the rest of the flight. Their eyes didn't meet again until a few hours later when they waited on opposite sides of the baggage carousel in Los Angeles.

Alex's limo driver came through the arrivals door and relieved her of her carry-on full of camera equipment, and then he waited for her suitcase. Alex used the opportunity to approach the girl.

"I have a limo picking me up. Can I at least offer you a ride?"

Deliberately not looking at Alex, she answered wryly, "I don't take rides from strangers."

Alex grinned. "Too late for that. My name is Alex...I live here now, in LA," she said as she scribbled her number onto a cocktail napkin and handed it to her. "You can usually reach me at this number, unless I'm photographing or I'm in the darkroom. Just leave your number on my answering machine."

The girl finally looked at her. "What do you shoot?" she said, stuffing the napkin into her back pocket.

"People. I have an eye for people...so are you going to tell me your name?"

The girl reached across Alex for her suitcases, and her breast grazed Alex's arm as she yanked her bags from the carousel. "Next time," she answered.

"Wait," Alex said, a slight air of desperation in her tone. "How do we know when and where the next time will be...or if it will ever be?"

As the girl turned to leave, she met Alex's stare directly and squeezed her hand. "Thanks for the dance, Alex. I never saw you coming, and I think it's better if you just watch me go."

"But what if I want to ask you on a date, Whatever-your-name-is?"

The girl smiled. "You're dangerous for me, Alex. We're dangerous...like 'crash and burn in a can whose aerosol melts the ozone layer' kind of dangerous." And just like that, she left.

Alex Winthrop had never been handled before, but she knew what being handled looked like, and it looked like her, standing there in the middle of the LAX baggage claim with her jaw hanging open, her hand on her hip, and a scoff stuck in her mouth. And as the imaginary camera zoomed in for her close-up, in her mind, somewhere, everywhere, feverish samba music spilled out into the streets.

Maybe she had finally met someone who not only intrigued her, scared her even, but who had actually crawled under her skin a little—and then a little more. Neither prospect felt comforting. Suddenly, she wondered who had died.

The chauffeur signaled that he was ready, and she mindlessly followed her Louis Vuitton luggage to the car.

"Welcome home, Miss Winthrop."

"Hey, Charlie, thanks for picking me up."

"Pleasure's mine. Hop in. I'll get you home as soon as traffic allows."

"I feel like I just left for New York."

Charlie laughed. "You did. I'll bet you spent most of the past seventy-two hours either in traffic, in the air or in a line."

With one foot perched on the threshold of the limo door, Alex glanced up and saw the girl boarding a hotel shuttle. The logo on the back read *Hilton*. Charlie waited for Alex to get in, then closed her door and got behind the wheel.

"It's a Friday afternoon all right," he muttered. "Get comfortable, this is going to take a while." He then raised the partition between them. The limo inched its way out of LAX toward West Hollywood as Alex remained oblivious to her surroundings. She cranked up the radio and lay back with her eyes closed as Chaka Khan's "Ain't Nobody" diffused through her little airtight cocoon.

I shouldn't have let her go like that. What was I thinking?

Maybe this was love, maybe it wasn't. Then again, Alex Winthrop had a lot of euphemisms for sex.

CHAPTER TWO

Three hours later, Will rapped on Alex's car window a second after she careened into the last empty parking space at the Corral.

"Willy! You scared me."

"I love to surprise you, sunshine. Your timing is perfect."

The LA Friday traffic crawl had left Alex barely enough time to drop off her cameras, get ready and leave for the party.

"Happy birthday, Will!" She hopped out of the car, hugged her pal and kissed his cheek. "And what a beautiful night."

"I picked a good one for the party."

Moonlit, cool nights such as this, with the wind tossing Alex's auburn waves in every direction, were meant for tearing through Laurel Canyon with the top down and the music blasting. Her red TR6 convertible had meticulously banked the narrow, two-lane, hypnotic snake from West Hollywood to the San Fernando Valley.

"You're the only one I would leave my photos for tonight, Will."

He slung his arm over her shoulder as she swiped a dose of gloss across her lips and tossed her hair back into position.

"You're not done with that project yet?" he asked as they strolled through the Corral's parking lot toward the entrance.

"We can't all be brilliant artists like you. Besides, I just got back from New York. I had an interview for an internship with Sonja Savarin for next year."

He stopped to face her. "Wow, Alex, Sonja Savarin, that's pretty freakin' impressive. I have a good feeling about that internship. I just know you're going to get it."

"She was very nice to me, but I don't think I have that kind of talent...not like you."

"You're wrong. You're as good as me and better than anyone about to graduate with you. Trust me, you wouldn't be Maurice van Bourgeade's protégé if he didn't think you were worth it. You're not just any trust-fund baby, baby. I've known you long enough to say that you're the kind who works harder than she has to, to prove herself."

Alex got quiet.

He laughed. "Remember when we lived in New York? You worked at that clothing boutique because you wouldn't ask your parents for money or tap your trust fund to buy all that darkroom equipment."

"True." Alex flashed back to the girl from the dressing room...and now the airplane.

"What I'm trying to say is that you got where you are because of your talent and drive."

"Sometimes I forget that," Alex said.

Will lightened his tone. "Of course, the downside is that you're so talented, you get myopic at times and forget about the people around you. But I still love ya."

"You're a good friend, Will. Thanks."

He smiled at her. "Come on, Alex, let's go celebrate."

Alex eyed the couples twirling and two-stepping across the wooden dance floor as she and Will entered the Corral Country and Western gay bar. She wondered if *the girl* liked to dance as much as she did. Alex liked the sound of all the boots shuffling atop the sawdust, sliding in time to the hit "Lookin' for Love" from the movie *Urban Cowboy*.

"Well, are you just going to stand there?" She knew the voice well.

Alex snapped out of her trance and turned toward the group of familiar faces. "Hiya, guys. Will, I knew you were talented, but who would've guessed that you're this well liked!" She eyed the row of full shot glasses lined up on the bar.

"A whole bunch of us from school are here. Come on, we're doing shots," said Greg, Willy's boyfriend *du jour*.

"Make mine a shot of Perrier," Alex said.

Willy stared her down. "You're kidding, right? It's Friday night, we're young and hot and livin' in LA, and your problem would be what exactly?"

"Just a Perrier, Willy. I still have miles of photos to proof, all strategically positioned to stare at me when I walk through the door tonight," Alex lied, although she hated having to do it.

"Stick-in-the-mud," Will mumbled as he reached out to get the bartender's attention.

Alex wasn't really in the mood for a party. She wanted to be home alone finishing her project on people and thinking about the woman from the boutique, and now the airplane.

I could replay it all in private if I was home. Jesus, I've had sex with that girl twice in two years and I don't even know her name! If there were a pill to make me forget her, I'd take it.

Everyone else looked as though they were having a good time. She smiled and made small talk with her classmates, occasionally glancing longingly at the door, counting the swollen minutes until she could make a graceful exit.

"Birthday dance!" Will grabbed Alex's hand and yanked her onto the dance floor.

"You're one helluva two-stepper," Alex said on their third sweep around the sawdust.

"You're not so bad yourself!" At the end of the next dance, he twirled her and swirled her like a swizzle stick.

Her mouth as dry as the sawdust on her boots, Alex reached for her Perrier. As she lifted it toward her lips, there was an instant, a nanosecond when her eyes locked with blue eyes so electrifying, so dazzling that she could actually see them across the room in a darkened bar. She caught the bottle just before it slipped through her fingers. Those eyes appeared to be in a spotlight, or more accurately, they seemed to be spotlights themselves, darkness and light redefined without a sliver of space to spare.

Where's my camera when I need it?

On second look, she realized the reflection of light on those eyes wasn't what made them so spellbinding—instead an infusion of light seemed to be coming at her from within them. Their eyes met, and the blue pair fixated on Alex when they saw her looking back.

Alex had to look away, if for no other reason than to make certain she could break the spellbinding stare, and then she realized she had to look again. They were right there waiting for her, and Alex's body instantly responded to the fixed gaze. Indeed, this moment had imprinted upon Alex's mind, just as if she had actually photographed it.

Strange how life flips on a dime. That thought made her smile, and the smile made Miss Electric Blue Eyes smile back. For an instant, Alex was able to let go of her thoughts of the girl on the plane. She crossed the bar with what was left of her Perrier, her hand trembling manageably at about two point three on the Richter scale. Alex recalled what Will had said. *"We're young and hot and living in LA. And your problem would be what, exactly?"*

She finally had the answer. *Not a damn thing.*

Beneath the tilted brim of the black cowboy hat, the siren leaned against the bar, her striking gaze locked on Alex's self-assured stride.

Always the photographer, Alex's mind had already snapped three rolls of imaginary film...of those insanely blue eyes. Dazzling. They were too intimidating for a lesser woman to look into, and Alex seized the opportunity to stare back. *She should never have to stand anywhere alone...especially on a sawdust floor.*

Alex unapologetically crossed the divide. "Hi."

"Hi, I'm Maddy."

Suddenly off balance, Alex wasn't sure which leg to lean on. She dismissed her thoughts of *the girl* and instead wrapped herself in the consolation prize of Maddy's visual embrace; this magazine cover in tight jeans, boots and a cowboy hat.

"Come dance with me…" Maddy paused, apparently waiting for Alex to complete the sentence.

"Alex," she said.

Maddy took her hand and led her out to the dance floor, where their feet danced the two-step and their eyes seduced each other. Alex's heart raced when Maddy took her hand, but she wasn't sure it wasn't an aftershock from the woman on the plane. But this didn't feel dangerous, or as the girl had said, like "crash and burn in a can." This warmth and connection flowed naturally, and if she was on the mark, it was about to become a lot more connected and decisively hotter.

Maddy followed Alex back to her place after they managed a graceful escape from the Corral. They barely made it through the door before their hands were all over each other. And though it wasn't in an airplane lav, the sex was just as hot and decidedly more comfortable.

They dissolved into each other over and over to the sound of their sweat-soaked bodies gliding. Alex's thigh muscles stung and quivered as she straddled her, anchoring Maddy's arms to the bed with her shins. The blue eyes beneath her invited her closer as Maddy kissed the inside of Alex's thigh. When Alex closed her eyes she flashed on the girl from the airplane. Only hours before, she had braced herself on Alex's thighs, unable to speak.

Deep, and deeper still into the night, Alex and Maddy's passion never wavered. Raw and demanding, Maddy had managed to erase the imprint of the blonde from Alex's body by the time Alex passed out against her.

When Alex awoke, she rolled over and sighed, drinking in the sight of Maddy's disheveled dirty-blonde hair strewn across her pillow, watching her breathe so peacefully she had to strain to hear it.

Maddy lay on her stomach with her head turned to the side. The comforter and sheet had ensnared her foot, leaving an uninterrupted line along her shapely tanned leg, over the gentle slope of her naked ass, past the contour of her breast. The full-body profile appeared virtually flawless to Alex, even in the morning light, as though that soft skin had never been touched. She smiled, knowing otherwise.

Morning would have to come in stages, Alex decided. First, the gorgeous, naked body as the art form, then the piercing blue eyes whose stare had made her shiver. But both at the same time would have overwhelmed even a photographer who could tame anything she could fit in a viewfinder. Alex wondered if she could ever get past those eyes, and then she reached onto the floor to grab the nearest 35 mm Nikon.

Silently, she peeled herself away, and standing naked in the hushed morning light, she photographed peaceful slumber suspended in beauty. She had a hunch this girl wasn't just a once-every-two-years stand. Wrapping herself in a silk kimono, she lumbered toward the coffeepot.

When she returned, she sat on the bed next to Maddy, holding two cups of steaming-hot coffee.

"Mmm." Maddy stirred when she breathed in the aroma.

Alex waited, and though she knew it was coming, still she couldn't reconcile the blueness of Maddy's eyes, nor the way they nested in the sultry almond-shaped stare. Now, in the light of day, those eyes were fucking blinding her with clarity.

"Good morning, Alex," she whispered, her naked form magnificently tangled in the sheets.

"Good morning. I made coffee."

Maddy smiled and uncoiled her body, semimodestly keeping the sheet wrapped around herself as she angled to lean against the pillows. She wiped the sleep from her eyes, took the coffee, and Alex climbed in next to her. Maddy blinked herself awake a few times before taking note of her surroundings.

"Whoa, Alex, how did I miss all the photos hanging everywhere?" Her laugh was velvety and easy on Alex's ears.

Alex kissed her bare shoulder and then looked into her eyes. "I think we both had something more pressing on our minds when we got here last night."

She watched Maddy take it all in.

"Photographer?"

"I'm trying to be."

"No, honey, you already are." Maddy's sleepy gaze surfed from one photo to the next, eyeing each one with the piercing stare that had disabled Alex from the start. Alex fidgeted, reached over and turned the stereo on low. Sly and the Family Stone's "Everybody Is a Star" played in the background.

Maddy took another sip of her coffee and looked over at Alex again. "You're not just sexy, you're brilliant." Then she leaned in and kissed her.

"Thanks for the compliment, but you take sexy to a whole other level."

Photography was the last thing on Alex's mind at that moment, except for the photos she had taken of the slumbering porn star just minutes before. She glanced over at the far corner of her cool and darkened bedroom. For the first time since she had arrived home, she noticed her answering machine. Under the stray clothing thrown on top of it, it kept blinking and blinking, a sure sign of a lot of missed calls. She wondered if one of the messages was from *the girl*.

"Wow, your answering machine sure is blinking a lot. I just got one of those things too. It's state-of-the-art...with a remote beeper that blares into the receiver. It lets me hear messages when I'm away, but I still can't get the damn thing to work every time."

Alex nodded and silently walked to her desk. She hit Play.

"You have fifteen messages," the disembodied voice said.

"Popular girl," Maddy said.

"I was away." Alex gestured toward the Louis Vuitton suitcase still parked in front of the walk-in closet. "When I got home yesterday, I grabbed a shower and left so fast for my friend's party at the Corral, I never thought to check the machine. I guess I'm still not used to having one of these things. I've never had this many messages before."

Maddy stood. "I'm going to use your bathroom while you check them."

Messages number eight through fifteen all sounded the same.

"Alex?" She knew the voice well, but it was frail, devoid of its usual spryness. She heard tears, and sadness, and bad news. That's when Alex's night with the insatiable and sexy Maddy came to a mind-numbing halt.

"Oh no," Alex said remorsefully when Maddy returned. "I'm really sorry, but I have to take a shower and go."

CHAPTER THREE

Phyllis van Bourgeade silently stared out the limo's window nearly the whole ride before uttering a sound.

"You live with a man for forty years and you think you know him." She shook her head in disbelief. "You would think I might have known that he was about to drop dead, Alex."

Alex snickered. She couldn't help admiring Phyllis's sense of humor on perhaps the saddest day in her sixty-plus years. "I'm sorry, Phyl."

"Don't be. It's one of the reasons why Maurice felt so close to you, you know."

"What do you mean?"

"Your sense of humor. Your ability to stare down the hard things and show them in a new light. The core of your photography is what Maurice called 'reframing'...and he said you were a master at reframing things through a lens that no one else could see until you put one of *your* pictures in front of them. 'This will set her apart from her generation,' he said.

That's why he worked you hard…because he expected great things from you."

Alex listened as she rode with Phyllis in the first limo behind the hearse. The car slowed. Gravel crunched beneath the tires as the procession loped into a shadowless mass of monochromatic gray—the hallmark of all cemeteries independent of the amount of sunlight.

She squeezed the widow's hand gently for support. "Phyllis, I've been trying to find a way to say this since I got to the house this morning. I don't feel comfortable taking pictures at Maurice's funeral."

"Listen to me, dearie. Maurice is…was a famous man. You are his protégé, close friend, and you're like a member of this family. So who do you think I trust more to take a few tasteful shots to release to the press…some schmuck or you?"

Alex cringed. "Geez, when you put it that way, Phyllis."

"It'll be fine. Everything…will be…just fine." Phyllis patted Alex's hand as she sighed.

The limo stopped, and the chauffeur offered Phyllis his hand when he opened her door. Alex got out on the opposite side and walked to Maurice and Phyllis's daughter and her family as they approached.

"I'm overwhelmed by your loss, Chantal," Alex said. "If there is *anything* I can do for you, I know you'll let me know."

Chantal nodded, trying to smile, but instead she sniffled and embraced Alex. "Thanks for riding in the limo with my mom."

"Of course. Where is your brother?"

"His flight didn't arrive until three this morning, and he didn't sleep a wink. He went straight to the mansion and saw to the details for the shivah. I'll tell you, Alex, that man is our rock." ·

"Where is he? I want to offer my condolences."

"He's here somewhere, but you'll have time for that once we get back to the house."

Alex nodded respectfully, hung her Nikon around her neck, and melted into the far side of the growing crowd. As people gathered, Alex stood far enough away to be inconspicuous, relying on her Nikon lenses to get up close. She panned the expanding crowd of mourners in her viewfinder, her depth of field distorted by the grayness.

From their expressions, Alex gleaned that some people attended simply out of respect for the icon. Others, however, showed real grief at the passing of the man himself. For now, she would express her sadness through her lens, for Phyllis's sake, and later she would indulge in the sobs that choked her. She continued clicking.

When the rabbi began the eulogy, Alex surreptitiously shifted to the other side of the crowd. Once again she scanned the faces through her lens, snapping away at true life, wondering how anyone would ever find *anything* of value, anything but grief in these photos.

Perhaps you gave me too much credit, Maurice. I don't think I'll ever be able to "reframe" this.

She wiped the teary blur from her eyes with her sleeve for the millionth time and focused. There would be no color today; no Ektachrome for the gracefulness of its ability to capture movement; no vivid blues or greens or reds. No, not today. There would be only black, white and every shade of gray that the light would allow Alex to bend.

Maurice had loved the raw honesty in her photos—he had told her as much. And if indeed he was watching over this ordeal, she wanted him to be proud.

She realized that her eye had passed something while she was lost in thought, then swept the camera back across the rows of faces she had just viewed. There it was, and *it* was a she. A beautiful and emotionally raw girl with red eyes puffy from crying, the long hair a little stringy, the clothes and the body language plain and unassuming.

It's the girl from the plane.

In her mind, she heard the girl say "funeral" when they were in the airplane lavatory, never in a million years guessing this funeral was the one she would attend, that this girl knew about Maurice's passing before she did. The arm that surrounded her, the shoulder she cried on belonged to Maurice and Phyllis's son.

They look like they know each other pretty well. Alex was confused, wondering what the connection was, and then she fired off a dozen or more candid portraits of the sultry girl with the sad monochromatic gray eyes, the girl who had turned Alex's insides to water. Twice. She could barely take her eyes off her, noting how different *this* girl acted compared to the steamy-hot girl she had met.

Turning toward a different grouping of people, Alex forced herself to keep photographing. She glanced back at the girl and felt remorse for invading what looked like a private and tender moment. Right then, she vowed not to share the photos of her with anyone. But inside, she knew that once she was alone in the darkroom, she would scrutinize the girl's every expression in an attempt to know her more; to have her picture, to have her, forever.

The service was shorter than Alex would have expected, and longer than she would have liked. As she meandered back to the limo, the hair on the back of her neck stood on end. She jerked around to look behind her, expecting to see someone standing there. Instead, her gaze drifted through the mourners and landed in a beacon of gray. Within seconds Alex Winthrop fell in love, again, but she managed to reach the limo without the girl who had rejected her noticing her.

By the time Phyllis got back inside the limo, Alex had managed to pull herself together.

"Phyllis, you're almost as white as your hair. When was the last time you ate something?"

Phyllis thought for a moment and quietly looked at Alex, confused. Alex opened the limo's fridge, pulled out a bag of orange slices, and opened it for her.

"That should give you a little lift until we get back to your house, and you're going to eat as soon as we get there."

Phyllis's head nested on Alex's shoulder as lightly as a sparrow, and she quietly wept as Alex tried to console her.

"It's going to be okay, Phyllis. I promise I'll always be here for you. Always."

The limo tires painstakingly crunched more gravel as they rolled toward the exit. Alex watched the slow-motion movie of people hunched over and walking to their cars, consoling one another, trying too hard to be cheerful. Their ages spanned generations, affirming the enduring effect of Maurice's photos and the lives they had touched.

She noticed a few people exchanging business cards, a testament to the timelessness of celebrity-funeral networking. The mourners returned in waves toward their Beemers and Benzes, and the movie stars and dignitaries to their bodyguards and limos. She recognized a few friends from school, some of Maurice's colleagues, and collectors to whom she had been introduced over the past few years. But one girl wandered back alone, apparently deep in thought, her arms wrapped partially around herself to keep warm. Her sultry gaze was fixed on the ground, and the breeze tousled her long hair.

"I must pull myself together," Phyllis said as she sat upright. "I have the rest of my life to grieve, and I don't want to use it all up right now." She took her compact out of her purse and powdered her face. "What are you looking at?"

"Phyllis, who is that girl over there?" Alex pointed to her.

"That's Kenna Waverly. She's so grown-up I almost didn't recognize her. She's part of our family."

"Y-your *family*? How are you related?"

"We're not blood relatives. Maurice and her father served in the French Resistance together in World War II. Our families were very close, and they lived next door to us at the old house. Maurice and I just adored Kenna, and we treated her the same as Chantal."

"I've never heard either of you speak of her."

Phyllis shook her head before continuing. "So sad…she was orphaned when her parents died in a car accident. We were her guardians, of course, and she lived with us for a few years—well, until she turned eighteen, and then she moved to New York. She calls, but I haven't seen her until today. Such a free spirit, that one. Poor baby never got over the shock of losing both her parents so young. It was very hard for her, and as much as we tried to make her a home, she knew her childhood had ended the night she received the phone call from the highway patrol." Phyllis took a sip of water and cleared her throat. "I wonder how she knew about Maurice."

Alex turned her attention back to Phyllis. "Phyl, it's not like Maurice was some *shlub*. I'm sure it made the news."

Phyllis chuckled. "You're so WASP-y...and it makes me laugh when you use Yiddish words."

"Did I say it wrong?"

Phyllis shot Alex a crooked smile and a wayward glance. "Maurice would be proud." She noticed Alex watching Kenna. "I'll introduce you to her when we get back to the house. She'll be there."

Alex blushed and looked at Phyllis. "No, today you will go home and let all of us take care of you."

Phyllis waved her off as if she were a pesky gnat. "Life is meant for love and adventure." In a dramatic voice she imitated old-time stage actresses. "Grab it by the balls...or whatever. You go live it!"

"I mean it, Phyllis, and don't piss me off. Maurice gonna be watchin' you, girl."

Phyllis smiled. "Keep practicing and maybe one day you will finally wake up black."

"Hmm, black *and* Jewish," Alex said. "That ought to go over really well at the Main Line blueblood family Christmas party."

"And gay, dearie, don't forget that. Let me *reframe* something for you, Alex. In a hundred years we'll all be dead and no one will give a flying—"

"Phyllis!"

"Well, excuse me, but I'm a little pissed off myself today. It's not easy being the second wife."

"What?" Alex said.

"Me and them. It was always me and *them*."

Alex looked at her. "Who is 'them'? The public?" She let it go when the chauffeur lowered the partition and interrupted.

"Mrs. Van Bourgeade," he began, "your son wanted me to remind you that he'll be arriving after you."

"Thank you," Phyllis said.

The loss of Maurice's earthly presence made Alex listless—as if someone had sucked the air out of the limo. They rode the rest of the way in silence. Eventually the chauffeur made the lazy right turn into the grand semicircular driveway of the Bel Air estate, where valets and volunteers waited to show people the customs before entering the shivah home—the place where all the mirrors would be covered for the next seven days, where no music would play. Friends and family would visit to ensure that Phyllis and her family would grieve amply and begin their healing process.

Alex glanced over at the torn black ribbon the rabbi had pinned to Phyllis's chest. Everyone would know this meant the loss of an immediate family member. Alex wished she had one too.

Within a couple of hours, the mood at the house shifted to something easier, lighter. She wasn't surprised that the girl from the plane never showed; the girl who appeared and disappeared faster than a trick at the famous Magic Castle. Instead, Alex studied the people who had come to pay their respects to Phyllis.

All in all, not a bad way to grieve, Alex thought, *what with the food and stories of the old days, and best of all, the pictures that accompany those memories.*

Grieving slowly gave way to a sort of celebration of the man's life. Maurice van Bourgeade never needed a narrative for his pictures unless someone was blind. His internationally acclaimed photographs always told a story somewhere between its beginning and the end, and although the beginnings and endings weren't always on film, they were always self-evident.

Like Maurice, Alex knew it made Phyllis happy to remember the stories the way she had told them, and the pictures the way he had taken them. The photos, however, Alex would view in private at another time, and she would take in the breadth of Maurice's messages that he had said only she could grasp in their entirety.

She was grateful when Phyllis's nieces came to sit with her.

"Would you excuse me, Phyllis?"

"Go, Alex. I don't need you to hold my hand."

Alex smiled. "I thought you were holding mine," she said and then left.

She had needed a bathroom break almost since they had arrived at the van Bourgeade estate. Running up the grand stairway, she aimed for the bathroom that was hers when she had stayed over to work with Maurice. She knew the other guests would be directed to the bathrooms on the main floor, and she could not wait a moment longer.

Before going back downstairs, she assessed herself in the mirror while washing her hands. "You look wiped out," she said to her reflection. She hastily exited the bathroom and ran smack into someone with a vicious head bump.

"Ow, ow, ow…shit," the girl groaned as she cupped her head in her hands.

"Ow, ow…I'm so sorry," Alex said, rubbing her own head. "Here…let me take a look at that." As she gently tilted the girl's chin upward, the sultry, smoke-colored eyes ensnared her, froze her again. Alex did her best to hide it.

"I'm so sorry, and I hate to break it to you, but I think I gave you a shiner." The girl grimaced when Alex lightly touched her cheekbone. "You need to get some ice on that."

"I will."

"By the way, this *is* the next time, and you told me that the next time we met you would tell me your name."

"Kenna."

"Your eyes are so red and puffy, Kenna. Are you all right?" Alex loved saying her name, but moreover she was glad just to *know* her name.

"I'm so sad. Really, really sad. Maurice was a second father to me, Alex."

"I can't believe he's gone. Listen, there's a guestroom right there." Alex pointed to the second door on the right. "Wait there while I go get us both some ice."

"No, that's okay, I can go get it myself."

"Yeah, but I have an *in* with the caterers…it'll be the *good* ice, I promise," Alex pleaded.

Kenna tried to smile but yielded to "Ouch" instead. "Damn, that stings."

Alex led her to the guest quarters, opened the door and showed her to the overstuffed chair. "I insist. I'll be right back… Kenna," she said as she left.

Running down the grand staircase, she mumbled imperceptibly. "A head bump! A fucking black eye? Real—ly? You couldn't have just walked up to the girl and asked her name?"

CHAPTER FOUR

Alex got into her car and yawned until her eyes watered. By the time she left the mansion she was dog tired, sad about Maurice, and still uneasy about Kenna. With the convertible top down on a canyon-cool Southern California night, she wound her way east on Sunset Boulevard toward West Hollywood, her auburn locks flying in the breeze.

Lost in thought, she hadn't noticed the only other car that pulled up next to her at the red light on the desolate stretch of Sunset Boulevard.

"It's a beautiful night," the driver of the Bentley convertible said so that Alex could hear.

Stunned, Alex smiled at the famous actress behind the wheel, and she needed a second to respond. "Yes, it is."

The actress stared directly into Alex's eyes in the glare of the not-too-distant streetlight, and then she stared at Alex in the way that so many women had in her young life—so *many* women.

"It's always better to share a full moon in Aries with someone." The actress smiled and then added, "Don't you think?"

Alex realized she was about to shoot herself in the foot—as soon as she managed to get the foot out of her mouth. She said it anyway. "I suppose it depends on who the someone is."

"The someone would be me."

Alex smiled. "Sorry, I honestly wish the timing was better. Have a good full moon in Aries." The light turned green, the Triumph strained for a quick shift into second gear and Alex cranked up Bob Seger's "Hollywood Nights," blasting it through the speakers. In her side-view mirror, she watched the Bentley turn onto Beverly Glen Boulevard.

When she turned off the car outside her hillside guesthouse midway up Sunset Plaza Drive, the first silence of a brutal day crashed so hard in Alex's head, she could feel where she and Kenna had head-bumped. *I can't believe she just took off without even saying goodbye. Why is this girl always running away from me… and why do I feel compelled to chase her?*

Alex pondered the question and then acquiesced to the fact that she wouldn't sleep without some kind of answer or closure. She remembered that Kenna had boarded the Hilton shuttle at the airport, but she couldn't afford to guess how long she would stay there.

She fired up the Triumph and headed back down the hill. "Kenna Waverly." *Jesus, I've earned the right to at least know her name after two years. I must be crazy for doing this, but if I don't do it right now, that girl could be gone by morning and I may never see her again.* She hit the gas.

Alex left her car with the valet, too tired and preoccupied to make anything of the car she kept glancing at in her rearview mirror for most of her ride. Nervous, she strode through the lobby, picked up the house phone and asked for Kenna's room.

"Hello?" Kenna said.

Alex paused. In that instant she called herself crazy and considered hanging up. "It's Alex. I know it's late and it's been a long and difficult day, but we need to talk."

"How did you know where to find me?"

"I'm in the lobby. Please."

Kenna hesitated. "Room 703."

Riding in the elevator alone, Alex wondered what to say, unsure of what she wanted to hear. Her center of gravity defunct, she shifted her weight back and forth, right to left. One glance in the lobby mirror was enough to scare her, but she couldn't have cared less. Her pulse pounded with every floor the elevator climbed, and by the time she found the room, she had a little trouble catching her breath.

When Kenna answered the door, Alex traded her inner turmoil for that first look. That instant told her all she needed to know—that this is where she wanted to be, no matter how she looked or how tired she was, even in the wake of how hard the day had been. Being compelled to know this girl with the odd name rendered Alex incapable of following any law but gravity—the gravity that pulled her toward Kenna.

Alex wanted to be near her, and it wasn't about the sex. She didn't quite know why being with Kenna was more important to her than sleep, food or her adored photographs. At that moment, Maddy wasn't a second, or even a third thought.

Kenna pulled back the door all the way, and her lazy wave was a centripetal invitation that pulled Alex into the room.

"Thanks. I know it's late and we're both pretty tired," Alex started.

Kenna nodded.

"How is your eye?"

"Not too bad…as long as I don't blink or smile." Kenna opened the minibar. "How about something to drink?"

"Perrier?" Alex sat on the upholstered chair by the window.

Kenna took visual inventory of the tiny shelves, reached in and walked to Alex holding a can of club soda. "This is as close as I can get."

Alex opened it and took a good long drink.

"So, what did you want to say?" Kenna cinched the belt on her plush terry robe and sat on the edge of the bed that had already been turned down. The delicately wrapped chocolates were still poised on the pillows.

Alex flicked away her bangs and looked into Kenna's eyes. "Look, I'm just going to be honest with you because I have no other angle." She exhaled the hard sigh of a gambler waiting for dice to land. "I have thought of you every day for two years, and then yesterday, there you were on the plane, and again at Maurice's funeral." She took a swig of the soda. "I find what I feel for you overwhelming to say the least."

"Fate," Kenna concluded.

"What about it?"

"Do you believe in fate, Alex?"

"I don't know. I believe what I feel."

"What is that, exactly?"

"The same thing you feel, Kenna."

"How do you know what I feel?"

"I don't know *how*. I just know that I do. And I think you know it too." Alex moved to sit next to her. She took Kenna's hand and stroked it gently, for the first time really noticing the hands that had touched her in a way no one else ever had. "I just want to know you."

"And therein lies the potential difficulty, Alex."

"Meaning what?"

"For starters, I can tell we're from different worlds. But more importantly, I was willing to let us be, and you weren't. For me, we were two random points in time and a wonderful memory."

Alex smiled a sad grin. "For the record, Kenna Waverly, you'll never be just two random points in time for me. Two years ago in that boutique, I felt you before I ever saw you. So, getting back to your question, yeah, maybe I *did* believe in fate...then. I just didn't know it until today." She stood, and before she left, she added, "I had no right to ambush you tonight, I know, but I couldn't let you disappear out of my life without letting you know how I feel. If nothing else, thanks for being honest." Her eyes welled up, but she wasn't about to be rejected and at the same time act like an idiot in front of this girl. "Good night, Kenna, and I guess...goodbye."

Alex fought back tears as she aimed for the elevator, anxious to get home and bury her head under her pillow. She was reaching for the elevator button when Kenna called out down the long hallway.

"Alex! Don't go. Please."

Alex turned and started back toward Kenna, her speed increasing with every step until the door to room 703 closed behind them. Kenna reached out for her, and Alex took her into her arms for the very first time. They held each other until their erratic breathing finally slowed and became synchronous.

"Lex, will you stay with me tonight?" Kenna whispered into Alex's neck.

"Did you call me Lex?"

"Yes, why?"

"I like it."

For hours they lay in bed holding each other while the night faded away. No words could have approximated or augmented the sensation of just the two of them, being who they were, together, next to each other. For the longest time, neither uttered a sound, and then Kenna snickered.

"Care to share?" Alex's voice was as soft as the dimmed lights.

"I find it baffling that we've had sex, twice, in places that were public, small, cramped and mostly upright. And here we are, alone in this big, comfortable, clean bed, fully clothed, and I'm so content just lying in your arms."

"It wasn't just sex, Kenna, it was hot sex…and even so, you mean something to me despite the hot sex." Alex leaned over and gave her a lingering kiss. When they separated, Kenna placed her head back on Alex's shoulder and sighed.

"What did Phyllis tell you about me?"

Alex didn't want to breach any confidences, but she wanted to be honest with Kenna. "She told me you were orphaned when your parents had an accident, and for a few years you had lived with the van Bourgeades. That she loves you like her daughter."

"That's all?"

She also told me your father and Maurice had fought together in the French Resistance during World War II." Alex thought better of it but told her how she felt. "She didn't tell me how you dealt with being orphaned or what you did when you left the family and moved to New York."

"Is that something you want to know?"

"I could be coy and say something like, 'Well if you want to tell me...' but truthfully, yes, I do want to know about that, and so much more. It means something to me to know."

"Have you ever had the feeling that no one gets you?"

Alex stroked Kenna's thick, straight hair. "I grew up that way. Thankfully, I have an older sister who gets me. Without her, I don't know where I would be."

"For me, life is just easier alone."

"Maybe you could be alone *with* me, and then one day you'll wake up to find you're not alone at all."

Kenna sighed. "I can't believe Maurice is gone. He really was a father to me, and I feel so bad for Phyllis."

Alex choked back the lump in her throat. "I'm going to miss him too. Don't you find it strange that it would be his funeral that reconnected us?"

"That's an understatement. Today Phyllis asked me if I wanted to move into the mansion."

"What did you say?"

"I told her I'd think about it."

Alex's heartbeat quickened. "Really?"

"Yes," Kenna whispered.

Alex wasn't sure where the conversation ended, but she was pretty sure it fizzled in the middle of a sentence when they both passed out from the sheer exhaustion of emotional overload.

Kenna awoke first and watched Alex sleep, taking note of every line on her face, the rhythm of her breathing, the warmth of her skin. In a fraction of a breath, she knew that everything she would ever need was lying next to her.

Alex was still holding on to her when she awoke, feeling exposed, then realizing that sleeping next to Kenna superseded any sex they might have had.

"Good morning." Kenna propped herself up on an elbow and softly kissed Alex's lips. "You're beautiful when you sleep, and beautiful when you wake up."

Alex felt anything but beautiful, but she took the compliment silently and rolled her head into Kenna's shoulder. In a muffled voice she asked to use the shower, and Kenna told her she would order breakfast from room service.

By the time Alex returned, Kenna had enough coffee for ten people alongside plates of rolls, fruit and omelets.

"Are we expecting company?"

Kenna laughed. "No, silly. You give me the best appetite I've ever had."

"But we didn't do anything."

"You're right," Kenna said, pulling the stem off a strawberry. "But who needs anything when you can have everything?" She bit into the strawberry and on the swallow, she added, "I suppose this would be a good time to tell you. I was up early, and while lying next to you, I decided to move back to Los Angeles."

Alex smiled. "Does that mean you'll finally stop running away from me?"

Kenna stood, took Alex's hand and led her to the bed.

While making love to Kenna, Alex hoped with all her might that Kenna had been wrong when she said that together they were "crash and burn in a can" dangerous.

CHAPTER FIVE

Kenna Waverly signed a short-term lease and moved into the little apartment on Norton in West Hollywood a few days later. A throwback to the flatlands of early West Hollywood, the apartment complex resembled a simplistic matchbox. Still, it was clean, safe and most importantly, it was available at the right time and price. She felt more comfortable here than at the van Bourgeade mansion but was close enough to keep an eye on Phyllis.

Kenna arrived with the only worldly possessions that mattered in the backseat of the compact car she had rented. Leaving everything but Sweet Jayne in the car, she carried the guitar across the threshold first and leaned the case against the wall. The second and last trip from the car consisted of a suitcase, a duffel and a small bag of groceries.

She stashed the perishables in the fridge before divining the location where she and Sweet Jayne would pass the time. The padded rattan couch felt just right. For as long as possible, she would ignore her full suitcase in front of the chest of drawers in the elevated sleeping area of the large studio.

Dark clouds had loomed all morning and finally let loose into a thunderstorm by the time she got down to the business of playing music. Sweet Jayne was the only constant she had ever known in her young life, the only thing she had ever loved that hadn't been ripped away from her. Wherever Jayne was, was home. Kenna was playing her favorite Brenda Russell licks when a knock on the door interrupted her. Holding Sweet Jayne, she peeked through the peephole. A tall, nerdy guy waited on the other side. He knocked again and Kenna answered.

"Hi, I'm JJ and you must be my new neighbor."

"Hi, JJ. I'm Kenna." She leaned Jayne against the wall and shook his hand.

"Yeah, I heard your guitar and thought I should tell you that you moved into the right building. Out of the fourteen apartments, half of us are musicians. Some of us do a friendly jam here on Wednesday nights in Melanie's apartment downstairs. Why don't you bring your guitar and sit in with us tonight?"

Kenna hesitated. "I don't think so...I'm pretty shy about playing in front of other people."

"Well, don't be. We're all levels and styles. I'm a drummer, Melanie studies at Bass Institute and everyone else just likes to have fun. Seven o'clock, apartment nine. Be there."

Kenna laughed. "Okay, but no promises to play. See you later...and hey, thanks for stopping by."

Of all the instruments Kenna had ever loved, she adored none more than the random orchestration of a thunderstorm that could drown out a symphony. Not even Brenda Russell or the guitar work of The Allman Brothers' Duane Allman or Dickey Betts could move her as much. She lay back on her new bed, conducting the orchestra, thunderclaps the punctuating percussion to the steady, melodic downpour.

It sounds like the intro to "Riders on the Storm" by the Doors.

The rain overflowed its gutter, and the continuous tapping of the drops as they pelted the shrubs below Kenna's window lulled her to sleep.

* * *

When she opened her eyes, the thunder had abated, twilight had dug in and it was almost time to make some music. She showered and changed her clothes before leaving with Sweet Jayne to find apartment nine.

"You must be Kenna," said the woman who answered the door.

"You're Melanie?"

"That's me." Melanie's gargantuan afro, silver jangly bracelets and big rings made Kenna feel so plain with her straight hair, simple blue jeans and T-shirt.

She looks like a queen, Kenna thought as she took in the breadth of her host.

"Well, don't just stand there, girl, come on in and show us what you got."

Kenna followed her into the small living room that was already littered with cords, a couple of amps and some percussion instruments. Kenna's eyes focused immediately on the conga drums.

"So you like the congas," JJ said when he saw her eyeing them.

Kenna nodded and shyly followed Melanie to the corner where the musicians had stowed their cases.

"Let me introduce you to your neighbors," Melanie said. "This here's Johnny on rhythm and lead guitar, Gringa on keyboards, Rich plays bass and guitar, and the rest, if they're not gigging or taking a lesson, might come later."

"Hi, everyone. Thanks, Melanie."

"Call me Mel."

"I don't have an amp," Kenna said, "but I do have a pickup in my acoustic."

"No problem," Johnny said. "You can plug in with me. You play rhythm, right?"

"I can," Kenna replied, taking Sweet Jayne out of the case, "but I prefer lead."

Mel turned to her. "How you gonna do that on an acoustic guitar with all this metal hangin' over you, girl? Here." She reached into the closet, pulled out a Fender Stratocaster and handed it to Kenna.

Kenna swallowed hard, hesitated for a second, then wondered what she had gotten herself into. She gently placed Sweet Jayne back into the case, swapped out the guitar straps and tuned the Strat. She had barely finished when JJ set a killer beat on the conga drums. Rich swung his guitar to his side, picked up the maracas and joined the Latin percussion section. Melanie hopped on to their train with a direct, no-nonsense bass line. The keys tapped out salsa, and Kenna found her voice. It was in her fingers the whole time.

All my new neighbors needed to tell me is that I was invited to a juerga!

The Latin jazz party was on and Kenna was all over it. She let loose with some lightning of her own, and the next two hours flew by like a sheet of day-old newspaper on a windy city street. After they'd finished playing, Mel called out from the kitchen as everyone packed up their instruments and recoiled their cords.

"Coffee's done."

"Thanks, Mel," Rich said. "She makes great coffee, Kenna. We all hang out after we play and drink a cup. Take a seat."

Kenna sat in the corner and listened as everyone else talked, noticing how small everything looked in Rich's big hands. His billowy light brown curls framed his oval face and softened his strong, thin nose.

Mel just dazzles, Kenna thought, *with or without an instrument.*

"You're awfully quiet without that guitar in your hands, Kenna," JJ chided.

She smiled at him, both hating and loving the fact that she was a loner.

"Kenna, you've obviously studied. Where did you learn to play like that?" Mel asked. She sipped her coffee.

"Guitar has been the only constant in my life, so I'm not really sure how to answer that." She caught an exchange of glances between JJ and Mel.

"You're too young to say that," JJ said.

She flashed on her mother's face and continued. "You guys are certainly amazing. I wasn't sure if I could keep up."

"Yeah right." Johnny rolled his eyes.

"I loved playing with you, girl," JJ said.

Kenna blushed. "You're very encouraging."

"So you're going to come play with us again, right?"

"Sure, Mel." Kenna placed her cup on the table and yawned. "I'd love to hang out, but I just moved in today and I'm beat."

"Say no more," Johnny said. "See you around, kid."

Kenna bristled at being dismissed like that but hid it. "Thanks again, everyone, it's really great meeting you."

"I'll see you out," Mel said as Kenna retrieved Sweet Jayne's case. Opening the door for Kenna, she whispered, "Don't mind Johnny, he's just jealous because you wiped the floor with him. You know how it is, girl. We can count the number of female rockers on one hand...thanks to guys like him. You know what I'm sayin'? Like all we should do is front the band and look good."

"Thanks, Mel, that means a lot."

When Kenna got home, she fell back onto her bed. Between the thunderstorm, and the raging beats whose notes had surfed on the cool night air, the silence in her apartment disquieted her. She tossed the guitar picks from her pocket onto the dresser and placed the scrap of paper with Alex's phone number in her wallet.

What am I going to do about her?

* * *

Kenna slept through most of the morning before the phone woke her. "Hello."

"How's the new place?" Alex asked.

"It's cute. Most importantly, it's furnished." Kenna yawned and stretched.

"Thanks for leaving your new number on my machine. I called you last night but there was no answer."

"My neighbors invited me over."

"Are you busy?"

"Busy waking up." Her eyes closed again.

"If you give me your address, I'll pick you up and take you to breakfast."

"Hmm, tempting. I'm pretty hungry." She remembered the measly groceries she had bought, which consisted of bread, peanut butter, coffee, and cream for the coffee. "Okay." Kenna gave her the address, zoomed into the shower, and ransacked her suitcase to find something that wasn't overly wrinkled.

By the time Alex rang the bell, Kenna had managed to pull herself together. "This is pretty much the whole apartment," she said when Alex entered.

Alex took it in in a glance. "Very cute, but it doesn't look like you."

"What do you mean?"

"Don't take this the wrong way, but you have an edge about you. And this apartment is, well…cute."

"So you're saying I'm not cute?"

"No. I'm saying you're…beautiful." And right there was the look—the smoldering affect that catalyzed the combustible karma between them. Every time. An affinity as feral and visceral as back-alley heat drew them together. Savage, breathless, they were at the same time the hunter and the prey. This was their dance. It was where they lingered and it defined them.

Kenna lowered Alex onto her bed and straddled her. She rhythmically pushed her body into Alex's, sensually exposing her round, firm breasts. She stripped off Alex's shirt and then her pants, kindling the hunger within her.

Denying Alex the right to reach for anything but her own asynchronous gasps, Kenna took her in the way she played her guitar—with splendor and abandon. Raw emotion was there for the taking, and Kenna took it; then she gave it back to Alex tenfold.

Kenna held her there until she was done with Alex, heightening the stakes with every stroke, leaving nothing behind—nothing.

"I can't wait anymore," Alex said with jagged breath.

"Then don't."

Alex rolled on top of her. "You are so going to pay for making me wait."

Kenna's grin was devilish. "You can *try*."

Two hours later, Kenna's shower and makeup happened all over again. As she locked up on their way out, she said, "This had better be some *big* breakfast, Lex."

"Are you kidding me? I'm so limp you might have to spoon-feed me," Alex replied.

The little garden apartment on Norton Avenue had an open walkway where some of the apartment windows had a full view of the comings and goings of anyone who lived there. Alex had parked her Triumph right in front of Maddy's friend's window, and Maddy just happened to be there for lunch. She watched as Alex opened the passenger side door of her car and waited for a woman to get in.

Maddy frowned. Alex didn't look at her that way. "Well, well," Maddy said to no one. "What am I going to do about this?"

CHAPTER SIX

"Harder." Maddy issued the plea with what uneven breath she could muster.

For months, Alex had gazed deeply into the electric-blue eyes beneath her; reckless on her part considering how much her feelings for Kenna had grown. In the heat of Maddy's passion, Alex tried every trick she knew to push the thought of Kenna away.

She drove Maddy closer toward the edge of abandon, owning the moment. Alex couldn't refuse her when she was locked in that stare. Temporarily able to relinquish her recurring visions of Kenna, she gave herself fully to the woman in her bed—almost.

Maddy continually reached out with a graceful devotion, a surrender that captivated Alex and kept her coming back for more.

Alex rolled to Maddy's side, her breath erratic and shallow.

Maddy flung her arm over Alex's chest. "You're amazing," she whispered through her dirty-blond hair strewn across her face. She buried her head under her pillow.

The exiled thoughts crept back into Alex's mind. *How can I feel this much for two women who are so different?*

Conflicted, she wanted to feel wholeness with Maddy, but she could only feel guilt. She felt dismantled, like a camera missing its lens, or worse, a lens without any focus. Being unable to savor their moment made her feel broken.

"Hey," Maddy said, lifting her head to look into Alex's eyes. "Are you still with me?"

Alex smiled. "What kind of question is that?" She sighed and turned on her side to face Maddy, gently removing the hair from Maddy's eyes before kissing her.

They dozed off in each other's arms, sated and spent from hours of lovemaking that had begun at the front door and made it only as far as the living room floor, then had moved to the shower until the hot water ran cold, and finally into Alex's bed.

An hour later, when Alex's eyes opened, the dread crept in. The dream that woke her was more like a breathless nightmare. She had introduced Maddy and Kenna and it all blew up in her face. She couldn't allow both of these relationships to continue on a course that was leading to something potentially meaningful with both women. Going down this road, with Maddy having been in the picture for the past several months, was already a guaranteed disaster for all three of them—and it had to stop. She had to let Maddy go, and this was the moment to choose that without looking back.

She loved Kenna, heart and soul.

I can't promise you anything, Alex. Kenna's refrain repeated in Alex's head in an endless loop that she couldn't unhear.

Why not? was always Alex's lament.

Maddy stirred and Alex braced herself, wondering how to tell a woman she thought she could fall in love with that it was over—that through no fault of Maddy's, Alex wanted to be with someone else.

She wouldn't tell her that she was hedging her emotional wager on an unstable girl, not yet a woman. A girl whose definition of the word *future* went no further than the mere concept of dessert after dinner, maybe not even as far as the dessert itself. A girl who could, and would, move on at the drop of a hat and leave her devastated; a girl Alex simply could never resist.

I love Kenna and I want to be what she needs. I have to break this off with Maddy right now.

"Maddy," Alex said softly, gathering her courage.

Maddy placed her mouth on Alex's and kissed her in a way that tortured Alex, that made her second-guess herself for the thousandth time in five minutes. She was speechless as Maddy pulled away, her mind racing with ideas of how to begin the conversation. But Maddy spoke first.

"Alex, I've been keeping something from you."

Alex perked up. In a cowardly moment she hoped Maddy was about to blow her off, tell her that she was seeing someone else.

"Oh?" she said.

"I've been working on getting an exhibition of your work into Gallerie Motek."

Alex propped herself up on her elbow. "Again, please?"

Maddy smiled almost to the point of gloating. "I didn't want to say anything about it just in case it fell through. You know that Motek rarely shows unknown artists."

Alex went silent, but the space filled with distant thunder. If she'd thought she was conflicted before, she realized she'd had no concept of conflict until this moment.

"How...when?"

"Remember the day when you gave me your apartment key to pick up your camera lens and bring it to you at the school's darkroom?"

"Sure."

"Well, I also took your portfolio and copied your key so I could put it back before you got home. Anyway, after I dropped off the lens for you..."

"You said you had an appointment," Alex recalled.

"Yeah, that was the appointment."

"You took my portfolio without asking me? And you made a copy of my key?"

"Yes. I'm sorry, but I wanted to surprise you...to get you an exhibit in the most lauded gallery in LA, woman. But there's a caveat. Since you're Maurice van Bourgeade's protégé, they are requesting a few of his relevant works. Preferably those that relate thematically to your work so that collectors can observe the influence. They suggested we go through Maurice's photos together since I know what they're looking for."

She took my work without permission! Stop changing the issue. Shit, how can I break up with her now?

Alex bristled. Right there she had her out. She could break up with Maddy for violating her trust and make an issue of the fact that Maddy had taken her portfolio, and she could make a clean break.

Then again, opportunities such as this would finally prove to her family, to her, that she didn't need their connections or her trust fund to survive. She could stand on her own with talent that spoke for itself. This chance would exalt or destroy her budding career.

"Why are you so freaked? I thought you would be over the moon about it." Maddy's tone shifted to apologetic. "I can call them and tell them I made a mistake, and it won't ruin any future chances you have with them."

"No. I mean, this is huge. I don't know how to thank you."

Maddy smiled and sensuously kissed Alex's neck before whispering in her ear, "Oh *yes* you do."

That's when it dawned on Alex that timing really *was* everything.

Hours later, Alex sat at a bar up in Trancas Beach. She had borrowed her neighbor's dog Harry for a run by the ocean, followed by a snack at a pet-friendly restaurant. Harry was as close to company as Alex could handle with all that she had on her mind. Preoccupied with the turn of events that even the endorphins from running couldn't neutralize, she took no notice of anyone when she and Harry entered the place and sat at an outside table.

"What a coincidence," said the waitress in an all-too-familiar voice.

Alex swallowed hard when she glanced up to see Kenna waiting on her. "What are you doing here?"

"I got the job yesterday," Kenna replied proudly. "What's your pleasure?" She winked at Alex.

No one pulls off adorable and sexy at the same time, Alex thought. *No one except you.* Her stomach churned with acid. She saw no way to escape the conundrum, causing her hearty appetite to instantly vanish. After the run and a day of making love to another woman, she ordered a shot of vodka, and in her mind called it breakfast, lunch *and* dinner.

Kenna returned and placed the shot glass on the table. "I called you a few times when I hadn't heard from you. Can I see you later?" she said.

"You called? Why didn't you leave a message?"

"I figured you were busy shooting or in the darkroom or something. So how about later?"

The guilt effected one colossal twist in Alex's gut. "Okay. I'll call you."

When Kenna left to serve her other customers, Alex downed the shot. For a second, she wondered what unique corner of heavenly hell this was.

Kenna returned and grazed Alex's hand when she placed the check on the table. The electricity that coursed through Alex from that brief touch rendered her fucking useless. She gave Harry another dog cookie, secured his leash to the chair and took refuge in the ladies' room.

About ten splashes of cold water on her face later, Alex heard someone enter as she wiped her face dry. The instant she glanced up into the mirror, Kenna spun her around and pushed her into a stall, kissing her passionately.

"You smell like a woman," Kenna whispered.

"Thanks, I am one," Alex dismissed her, even though she knew what Kenna meant. "Listen. About later…"

Kenna pulled back.

"I have a really important meeting tonight with a gallery about doing a show there. I'll call you after, okay?"

"Sure," Kenna said in a tone that was anything but. The word *sure* might as well have been the antonym. "I'm in love with you, Alex Winthrop," she blurted out. Her cheeks flushed as the words left her lips. She froze for an instant and then bolted out of the bathroom.

Alex stayed in the stall for the next three minutes, repeatedly flushing every conflicted emotion down the toilet. "I'm scum." Flush. "I'm an idiot." Flush. "No good!" Flush. More than having run out of self-loathing statements, she stopped flushing when she finally acknowledged how much water she was wasting.

When she exited, she tossed a fifty-dollar tip onto Kenna's tray, unwound Harry's leash and made her way to the car. On the way home she wished that Harry could drive so that she could hang *her* head out the window instead.

CHAPTER SEVEN

"Hey, Mel," Kenna called out when she entered Mel's apartment.

"You're early. I'm in the kitchen."

Kenna slid into her usual seat at the table while Mel finished her dinner.

"I have the Stratocaster all tuned up and ready for you," she said between bites.

"Thanks," Kenna said listlessly.

"You need to start thinkin' about getting you an electric guitar, honey. You know I dig you playing Sweet Jayne, love the acoustic sound and all." She pointed her fork at Kenna. "But in case you haven't figured it out, you are a lead guitarist. You seem a little down. What's going on?"

"Just preoccupied."

"It's that Alex woman, isn't it? She do something wrong again? Pardon me for telling the truth as I see it, but I don't like how that woman treats you. For months now, she's been comin' up short. You just say the word and I'll have a little talk with her."

Kenna smiled. "You're probably one of the best friends I'll ever have."

"I just want you to know I've got your back, little sister. I know you have mine too, so you can just admit that right now and we'll get it out the way."

"I admit it, freely. Hey, who's coming to play tonight?"

"JJ, Rich is playing rhythm guitar, Gringa, you and me."

"Johnny's not coming?"

"No, and I can't say we're all unhappy about that. You play better than him, you know all our music, and I can't understand for the life of me why you won't take his place when we gig. You'd make more in one night than working all week at that waitressing job. Just one weekend a month would pay your rent."

Kenna exhaled forcefully. "I told you, Mel, I'm not like the rest of you guys. I'm not a performer. Guitar is so personal for me that I'd freeze onstage."

Mel spoke softly. "This is about your parents, isn't it, honey? After they died, Sweet Jayne was all you had left." She paused. "I get it, I do."

Kenna heard the front door open and drifted out to the living room, relieved to withdraw from the conversation.

"Hey, Kenna," JJ said, playing with his drumsticks as though they were nunchaku. "What was that tune you were practicing earlier today?"

"Just a little thing I've been trying to write. Why, J?"

He stopped twirling the sticks. "Because it was fucking amazing," he deadpanned. "There are like three different musical lines in that piece that are just haunting. Couldn't get them out of my head all day."

"Play it," Rich said.

"No, it's nothing. It's not even a complete piece yet," Kenna said.

"Play it," JJ said, a little more sternly.

"Nah."

Mel strapped on her bass guitar. "Play the damn thing!"

"Okay, okay!" Kenna picked up the Strat, closed her eyes and started to play. Summer-orange warm, and sexy, the melody and harmonies smacked into each other as Kenna caressed the fretboard with her nimble fingers gliding up and down the guitar's neck.

Highs and lows smushed into each other like the first bite of a delicious peanut butter and jelly sandwich, sweet and savory all at once. The second part of the piece built in intensity and speed, and the music alternated between all-out jazz and full-on rock. It ended with sultry runs and bended strings.

When Kenna opened her eyes, Mel, Rich and JJ were gawking at her. They hadn't moved an inch.

Mel spoke up. "Damn, girl. What the hell is that?" Her phone rang. As she went to answer it, she added, "Would you guys please get her to replace Johnny?" She chatted for a moment, then hung up and said, "That was Gringa, she can't make it."

"Good," Rich said. "How about we work on Kenna's tune, just the four of us?"

* * *

When Kenna got home from the jam session, Alex had left a message on the answering machine that she had given Kenna as a housewarming gift. Over the months since, Kenna had saved a few cassette tapes of the *best* messages, the sexy ones, and then arranged them by date in her night table drawer. Late at night, when she hadn't heard from Alex for days, she would play an old message or two to remind herself how much Alex adored her.

She could tell by Alex's voice that she'd been smiling when she left this new message, telling Kenna to be ready at seven the following night for a romantic dinner.

Kenna fell back onto her bed and repeatedly pressed the Play button. She wondered if one of her music friends could put all the *good* messages on a continuous loop so she wouldn't have to keep rewinding to hear the voice that mattered most to her.

She sat up and grabbed Sweet Jayne. In her mind she heard the harmony Rich had played to her piece, and she loved it, so she reached for a pen and finished the song. There was already a growing portfolio by her bed—one she had hidden every time Alex came over. *I'd better start naming all the songs I've written for Alex.*

While leafing through the portfolio, she considered numbering them, but in the end decided it was a decidedly unromantic thing to do. She didn't quite know what to name the earlier songs, but this one, this one's title practically wrote itself. At the top of the page she scribbled, "Somewhere Like You."

She was playing the tune when her doorbell rang. "Yes, J, it's finished," Kenna said when she flung open the door.

"What's finished?" Alex said.

Kenna drank in the vision of Alex's sexy body leaning against the jamb—the emerald stare the door prize. She smiled and kissed Alex. "Just something my neighbor asked me to do. What a wonderful surprise. Come in." Kenna raced to gather her music portfolio and stash it in the closet before Alex could see it.

"So," Alex teased, "you *do* take your guitar out of the case."

"Her name is Sweet Jayne," Kenna said as she hustled to get Jayne back into her case.

"Named after the song 'Sweet Jane' by Lou Reed and the Velvet Underground?"

"Not really. It's Jayne with a *Y*."

"Why don't you play something for me?"

Kenna slipped her arms around Alex and pulled her close. "Because I'd much rather do this." They kissed.

Alex slowly pulled away. "I wanted to talk to you about something important."

Kenna gripped her and reeled her in. "Make love to me now, talk to me later."

Alex threw her on the bed. She ripped off her clothes and laid on top of her as she had done so many times. Their crude, animalistic dance was as fiery and unrefined as it had been the first time they had ever laid eyes on each other.

Kenna kissed her feverishly and let Alex take the lead, except for the incessant teasing she knew drove Alex insane. Resisting her at first, Kenna passionately drew Alex in and then resisted a little more until Alex pushed her through some gateway. A Transcendent Gateway, not unlike the one she passed through when she played the Stratocaster—the one that transported her to a place where sensation replaced thought and only her core self remained.

The heat of Alex's lips on her neck, her breasts and down her abdomen delivered Kenna to the only place she had ever been that made her feel safe. Unlike the rest of her life, in Alex's arms she knew who and what she was, she knew what she wanted and she knew how to surrender to it again and again. With Alex, she had learned that abandoning herself was the only way to find herself, and that in turn made her want to abandon everything else.

Alex pushed away her guilt. *How am I going to tell her about Maddy? She'll forgive me once she knows I'm breaking up with her... she just has to.*

Alex focused and gave everything she had to the one girl who knew what to do with it—who knew what to do with her— the only girl who had ever reeled her in and kept her there.

Hungry hours passed before they slept in a tangled heap, the wistful bodies of two stunning women who had spent all their capital, borrowed the rest and left nothing for themselves or for each other, ever.

* * *

The next day, Kenna hustled home from work to get ready for her date with Alex. She spent two hours soaking, moisturizing, and doing her hair and makeup. When the doorbell rang, she forced herself to count to ten before answering. She wanted to dazzle Alex, to make Alex want her more than even Alex knew possible. When she saw her expression, Kenna knew the moment did not disappoint.

Kenna's long shapely legs reached a mile longer than usual in the short, tight skirt and high heels. Her long hair was full and loose and wild. They kissed hello.

"Come in, honey. I'm just putting on the finishing touches."

"You look amazing and your makeup is gorgeous. Let me take some shots of you before we leave."

Kenna rolled her eyes.

"What?" Alex said. "You should know me by now."

"You're right. I *should*." *Why don't I trust you?* That feeling nagged at her, again. Still, she decided to let it go and have a romantic dinner with the woman she loved.

With the lid off the convertible, Alex took the long route up Pacific Coast Highway to Topanga Canyon. Kenna's eyes were fixed on the teal Pacific for most of the drive. As usual, Alex had The Allman Brothers tape blasting, and Kenna's ears tasted every note of Dickey Betts's and Duane Allman's guitars on the song "Whipping Post." Embedded in her mind since the first time that she and Alex had had sex in the boutique, the lyrics struck out at her whenever she heard them. The ones that stood out spoke of being lied to, being made to feel like a fool, the feeling of being tied to a whipping post.

They turned off into the canyon along with the end of the day, twilight now riding shotgun. The Triumph hugged the snaky turns in the layered hills. Measured light muted the colors of an arboreal canopy that jutted out from the pockmarked rock, shrouding the vegetation. In the distance, stenciled mountains shaped the early-evening skyline, and nature's discrete elements collectively succumbed to the homogenous night.

That fairy-tale drive inland from Malibu was special to them. Their late-night jaunts through the canyon always inspired Kenna to write music that would become yet another song about her love affair with Alex—the woman who had changed her illusion of life, from the way the sun set to the direction the earth spun.

Anchored by Alex's affection, she had discovered breathtaking passion to be a worthy sentinel for their deep love. For the first time since her parents had died, Kenna Waverly finally stopped drifting.

Alex held her hand. "You've been spending a lot of time with your neighbors. Do you just listen to them rehearse or do you try to play along?"

"Sometimes I play along." Kenna didn't know why she had never played for Alex or told her she was a proficient guitarist. Instead, she had used every opportunity to downplay her talent.

In the back of her mind she knew that if they broke up, it would be the one thing in her life Alex hadn't touched—unless the love songs she had written for her counted for anything.

Kenna continued. "There are some wicked good musicians in that group. They've played the Whisky, the Roxy, and they hope to open for a name band by sometime next year, but getting a recording contract is ridiculously tough."

"I'd like to hear them sometime. Maybe we could go to one of their gigs."

"Sure," Kenna said, knowing it would probably never happen. She filed that wish with all her other wishes that had yet to come true; the things Alex had promised and then forgotten. "You've been really busy, haven't you?"

"Yes, but nothing I can't handle. Why?" Alex downshifted.

"Because when I don't hear from you for days, I worry."

"Nothing to worry about, babe." The car turned into the small gravel parking lot on Old Topanga Canyon Road. "We're here."

Carved into the canyon stood a dreamy nook of a place. Alex leaned over and kissed her before they got out of the car. Kenna inhaled the fresh, canyon-cool breeze as twilight slipped behind the mountains surrounding the restaurant. They meandered toward the lilting music that flowed effortlessly from hidden speakers, and everywhere she turned, Kenna saw vivid hues of purple and fuchsia.

Seated outdoors where water cascaded from a fountain, they spent the first several minutes gazing into each other's eyes by candlelight. They never looked away when the waiter poured their wine.

Seduction itself, in its own nascent state, was never more quixotic than when their eyes met. That look silently confessed their craving for each other, the lingering abandon from the night before and all the nights before that.

"This place is beautiful, Lex. Are we celebrating something I should know about?"

Alex grinned. "Big yes. I got the Sonja Savarin internship in New York."

Kenna swallowed hard. "New York? I'm really happy for you, but not so happy for me."

"What do you mean? Kenna, I want you to come with me. That's the reason for this celebration…the part where you say yes. I'm sure there are plenty of places to wait tables in New York and you can make great money doing it."

"I'd have to really think about it."

"What is there to think about?" Alex asked rhetorically, not waiting for an answer. "Honey, you look so beautiful tonight. I can't wait to be alone with you," she added.

"Thank you." Kenna blushed, sure the color was lost to the moonlight. "I've missed you. I've missed you a lot, Lex, and so I need to ask you something."

"What is it?"

"You'll be honest with me?"

Alex nodded.

"Have you been seeing her the *whole* time we've been together?"

"What? Who?"

Kenna looked at her, narrowing her smoky-gray eyes until she could feel her stare turn to steel.

Alex fidgeted, hesitated before answering. "Yes."

Time and again Kenna had imagined this moment, had tried to brace herself for the worst. But she couldn't have conceived of how the brutal forthrightness of Alex's honesty would reverberate in her body. Shaken to her core, she wished she could get up and run away. Hide. Hiding always worked for her, and growing up in a family full of spies taught her to do it well.

Her mouth went dry. If she'd had any words, they would have been stuck in her throat. If only last night had never ended, then she wouldn't be sitting here suffering the hurt and humiliation that was about to blow her world apart.

"But, Kenna, we've talked about this. You told me commitment doesn't work for you. What were the exact words? Oh, yeah, 'I can't promise you anything, Alex.' How many times have you said that to me?"

Kenna's voice broke. "I was hoping you'd prove me wrong, Lex. I thought you had already proven me wrong."

"What? When?"

"Don't you remember the night of Maurice's funeral? In the hotel room when you said that I could be alone with you so that one day I might wake up to find I'm really not alone at all?"

"I remember."

"Are you telling me I've been in this alone the whole time?"

"No. I'm so sorry, baby. I don't know what to say, other than you're the one I want to be with."

"And she is committed to you?"

"Kenna, I just asked you to move to New York with me."

"That's not an answer, Lex. Did you check with your other girlfriend first? Did she turn you down or is she coming too?"

"No, Kenna, you've got it all wrong. I was going to break up with Maddy right before she got me into Gallerie Motek. I decided to wait until after the exhibition because I didn't want to embarrass her in front of her friends and business associates. My life is not like yours. It's complicated."

"Were you planning on bringing *Maddy* to the show too?"

"No."

"You could have turned down the showing."

Alex's glance darted away from Kenna's eyes and then back to face the music. "You're right, I could have, but I didn't."

Too wounded to cry, Kenna spoke softly. "So you're telling me that what we've experienced hasn't been…quite enough. That all of me is never really…enough. Excuse me, I need a minute alone."

She entered the restaurant and dug up some change from the bottom of her purse. Her hand trembled as she dialed Mel's number from the pay phone. "Mel, thank God you're home," she said when Mel answered.

"What's wrong, little sister?"

"I need you to come and get me…as fast as possible. I'm at the Seventh Ray in Topanga Canyon."

"I'm on my way, Kenna."

Fifteen minutes later she returned to the table. Alex had poured more wine and Kenna counted the minutes.

"K, I love you. I know you know that."

Kenna nodded. "Then you must love her too or you would have cut her loose."

"I want to be with *you*." Alex touched her hand.

Kenna flinched. "You *were* with me, so if that were true, we wouldn't be having this conversation."

"What do you mean by *'were'*?"

Kenna wanted to cry, but she sat quietly until she saw Mel's car pull into the parking lot.

"I'm sorry, Lex, I really am." She stared into Alex's eyes. "I called a friend to come get me, and I need to leave here right now before I say or do something that I can't take back."

"What?" Alex's expression was one of shock. "No. Don't go, baby. Don't go."

"Damn you, Lex," Kenna said under her breath. "Every time I look at you, all I can think is, 'Does she kiss her the way that she kisses me?', 'What does she have that I don't have?' and a million other questions that have one thing in common."

"What's that?"

"They all shatter my heart into a thousand pieces. Goodbye, Lex."

Kenna swept through the patio as fast as her mile-long legs and short skirt would allow, her long, flowing hair trying to catch up.

"Get me out of here, Mel," she said as she passed her.

When Alex got up from the table to chase Kenna, Mel intercepted her and stood firm.

"Stop right there, Alex. My little sister wants to go home now, and she called me to come get her."

"Who are you?" Alex asked.

"Honey, if you don't know your own girlfriend's best pal, maybe you should be askin' yourself the question you just asked me."

Mel had left the engine running, and Kenna was already in the car when she returned. Kenna's last view of Alex standing in the parking lot was one she hoped to someday forget. But in this moment, someday was unfathomable.

* * *

Alex left the food on the table and paid the bill.

I knew this would happen! Dammit, I should have never let things go this far...never.

Winding dangerously fast through Topanga Canyon, Alex banked every hairpin turn with her foot on the gas.

CHAPTER EIGHT

When Kenna opened her burning, puffy eyelids, she was glad to see she had finally slept for a few hours. The answering machine blinked from all the times she hadn't answered Alex's calls, and she'd been grateful when Alex finally gave up at five o'clock in the morning. It was only a matter of time before Alex would show up at her door, and Kenna did not want to be there when that happened. If she refused to answer, Alex would just let herself in with the key Kenna had given her, and she knew she would give in to Alex, again and again. She had been foolish enough already to want more from her. Her chest ached, and the reality of losing Alex made her tremble.

How could I have been so blind? If she really loved me, she wouldn't be seeing someone else! This will never work, and I knew it the first time I saw her. She's not good for me.

The avalanche of nagging thoughts wouldn't quit, and her apartment was too quiet for a Sunday morning. Waking up without Alex on a Sunday felt like a chemical withdrawal— painful enough for Kenna to learn the hard way that passion could not be assuaged or controlled. She was living proof.

Sunday mornings with Alex had always turned into Sunday night before they ever left the bedroom for any length of time. When they weren't making love, they were curled up in each other's arms, dreaming about the future, watching old movies and making plans. The world and the people in it were mere extras in their own little movie, in which *they* were the stars.

But Kenna knew it was over. At the same time, deep down, she knew it would never be over.

I just want to scream every time I think about her!

Dodging the hurt just long enough to wake up, she poured a second cup of coffee and phoned the one person who had always been there for her and whom she would always trust.

Hunter van Bourgeade answered his phone on the third ring, and Kenna sighed with relief. She loved Hunter's voice. The mere timbre of it had comforted her since they were kids. And Hunter knew the sound of Kenna's sigh.

"Hey, *Kenya*, is that you?" He laughed.

"*Kenya* is a country" was her usual reply, but not today. "What are we, still ten years old?"

"Hmm, it's a Sunday morning, and a very early one at that. Not like you, Wave, what's wrong?"

Kenna tried to answer him. She burst into tears.

"I'm on my way," he said.

Hunter got to her place quickly even though he lived clear across town. He hugged her the instant he came through the door. "Aw, Wave, you look like you just lost your best friend."

"It turns out hopes and dreams weren't such good friends after all."

By Hunter's third cup of coffee, Kenna had recounted the details of her breakup with Alex.

"You must be devastated. I've noticed how being with Alex has changed you this past year, made you more like the girl I knew a long time ago. Wave, I've never known you to feel this much for anyone since…"

"It's okay, Hunt, you can say it."

"Since your parents died. Even though I've only met Alex once, she is awfully close to the family. My mother has told me repeatedly how wonderful she has been to her since Dad passed."

"Then why did she lie to me from the start and break my heart? All this time and not once did she respect me or love me enough to tell the truth. All the while, she chased me, professed her undying love. She just neglected to tell me I wasn't the only one. I gave her more than I thought I had to give, Hunter. I gave her everything. Everything."

"Kenna, I want you to move in with me for a while." He gazed around the tiny apartment. "This place is so not you."

"Funny, that's what Alex always says."

"You have money, a lot of it. You don't need to be waitressing up in Trancas, and you certainly can afford a much nicer place to live. My mother still wants you to have your own suite at the mansion."

"I liked it here, and for the first time since you, I've made friends. I don't care about the money, Hunt. You know me better than that."

He smirked and rolled his laughing eyes. "I know, *Kenya*, that's why you have me managing your finances. We still have to talk about why you gave more than six months rent on this place to that animal rescue last month. Now get Sweet Jayne into her case and pack your stuff. We're going home."

On their way out to the car, Kenna slipped a note under Mel's door telling her where she was going and the number where she could be reached. It was way too early to ring the bell the morning after a gig.

Hunt pulled out onto Crescent Heights Boulevard, and Kenna caught sight in her side-view mirror of Alex's red Triumph turning onto her street.

"You'll be glad you did this, Wave."

"I already am."

* * *

Kenna refused to leave her room at Hunter's beach house for the first three days. Her clothes were all still in her suitcase, and the only unpacking she did was to take Sweet Jayne out of her case and spread her song portfolio out on the floor.

Hunter knocked for the third time in an hour. "Wave, you *have* to eat something."

Kenna didn't reply.

"Okay, I hope you're dressed 'cause I'm coming in."

When he opened the door, Kenna casually looked up at him from the middle of the floor, surrounded by piles of her sheet music. "I'm not hungry."

"I don't really care. You have to eat," he said as he sat next to her. "You look like hell."

"This is how musicians grieve. The refrain is direct enough: I keep wondering what I did wrong. How can someone profess their undying love, then treat you as though you're not enough?"

Hunter put his arm around her. "You are *more* than enough, and you deserved better. Come on, we'll take the dogs for a run on the beach."

She smiled. "You know I only run when something is chasing me...like that time Hamas made me when I snuck over the Lebanese border."

"Well then, the dogs will run and you and I will take a walk and catch a beautiful Malibu sunset."

"Not fair, throwing my most favorite thing into the mix."

"Yep, you've never been able to turn down an ocean sunset."

"Maybe we can stop in Trancas on the way back to pick up my last paycheck."

"Why, *Kenya*? You're just going to give it to some animal shelter."

"What's your point?"

* * *

Kenna was glad that she had listened to Hunter. The sunset had calmed her and the fresh ocean air had vastly improved her mood. She had even felt a little hungry. By her count, she hadn't eaten since before she had walked out on Alex up in Topanga Canyon, and that was three days earlier. Her jeans were already too loose.

The manager at the restaurant came out to the patio to speak with her when she, Hunt and the dogs sat down for a bite to eat.

"Here's your check," he said. "But without giving me any notice, you realize I can't give you a glowing recommendation."

"Don't be such a sourpuss, Mike. I had some major changes happen and I have to quit."

"Yeah," Mike said. "Don't expect the employee discount on your check."

Hunter laughed when Mike walked away. "How could you work for such a small-minded guy?"

"It was easy, really. Small, simple minds are easier to keep track of than intelligent, devious ones."

"True. So have you given any thought to what's next?"

Kenna sardonically pointed out that there hadn't been a *next* for her since she was fifteen.

"Listen, I have to fly to Europe tomorrow for a meeting with our *old uncle*," Hunter said in his quiet, serious tone. "Will you do me a favor and take care of the dogs...and yourself, please?"

"What's the mission?"

"Can't say yet."

Hunter took a swig of his beer, and Kenna intuited him like the planchette on a Ouija board. "But you might need me for a covert op."

"We might. I'll know more when I get there. I'll call you from London. We'll use our standard code on the phone."

Kenna nodded. "Whatever you need."

Hunt smiled his brotherly smile. "And the baton has finally passed to *both* of us—the next generation. *L'chaim*," he said before killing the last of his beer.

CHAPTER NINE

By the time the weekend rolled around, Hunter had been gone for a few days, and Kenna was uneasy because she hadn't heard from him. Any intelligence mission was dangerous by definition, but she had confidence in both of their tradecraft skills, having learned them together at such a young age. As if on cue, the phone rang.

"Hey, honey," Hunt began when she answered. "It's dreary here, but at least the Brits have nice umbrellas. In fact, it's raining now, and I'm in a phone booth looking for a place to buy one. I look like a drowned rat."

"Is there somewhere nearby where you can get out of the rain?"

"For the moment. You know, I think it might be a good idea to bring back some umbrellas and give them out as gifts... maybe just to our close friends."

"It's a beautiful day here," Kenna said.

"That's why I'm calling. I was counting on you to send some sunshine through the phone. Europe can be so gray, especially when you don't know anyone."

Kenna bristled. She counted the words, the pauses and the order in which they had occurred. Then she deciphered the remainder of the code in her head, something she'd had to teach to Hunter. So far, he had related to her that his dead drop had been compromised and he wasn't safe. He needed her to send him a new contact who could get him to a safe house, securely communicate intel and if necessary, arrange for a new dead drop.

As children, they had played the games their fathers had taught them every day after school until they had mastered them: the art of finding an object, doing it in shorter and shorter time frames, silent communication, physical training and keen tactical games. By Hunter's bar mitzvah, he knew his purpose was to follow in his father's footsteps, helping to secure a future for Israel.

Kenna's lack of attachment to things, combined with her naturally honed ability to assess and react quickly and accurately, made her an ideal tactician on any team. Her parents' sudden and violent death had thrown her into the haphazard tailspin that hadn't ended until she met Alex for the second time. She moved back to LA for Alex; now, she would likely stay for Mossad.

"I'm sorry," Kenna began, "but I think the dogs have to go out. Can I get back to you?"

"Sure," Hunt replied. "Can't have the hounds peeing in the bedroom, can we?"

Scrambling to the safe in Hunter's bedroom, she knew what she had to do. She had to go through the list locked in it and find someone who would serve as his point of contact. The numbers to the combination pad had been seared into her gray matter for as long as she could remember. She placed her right hand on the security pad where the scanner read her handprint, then opened the door.

Extricating her written instructions and the notes in Hunter's handwriting, she grabbed the keys to his car and drove to the address from where he wanted her to send the secure communication. An hour and a half later, she left the unassuming building in Hollywood, relieved that Hunter had already acknowledged receipt of the information.

On her way back to Hunter's house, she stopped by her little apartment in West Hollywood to fetch the few belongings she couldn't fit into her suitcase. Having already given notice that she was moving, she had one week to remove the last of her stuff, but she figured now was as good a time as any.

The tail of Alex's TR6 sticking out of her parking space was the first thing she saw when she arrived. Without slowing down, she cruised down the block, confident Alex wouldn't recognize her in Hunter's car even if she had been outside.

Her belongings would have to wait. Certainly, Alex was in the apartment at that very moment, scrutinizing whatever she could find that might lead her to Kenna. She hoped Alex would find the cassette tapes of all the sweet messages she had saved... and then choke on them.

For a moment Kenna pretended none of this drama had happened, that it was a usual Saturday night when she and Alex would begin their date that wouldn't end until sometime Sunday night. She ached for those delusional days when she'd thought she would have a future with the photographer who had chased her relentlessly—until she got her, that is. Telling herself she would have a lifetime of Saturday nights for fun, Kenna hit the gas and drove back to Hunter's to hide some more.

* * *

Soap in her eyes, Kenna jumped out of the shower to answer the phone. Monty, the lovable scruffy stray dog she had given to Hunt, licked the water off her leg as she picked up the receiver.

"Hello."

"Little sister, remember when you said you had my back?"

"Of course. What's wrong, Mel?"

"One of the billed bands at the Whisky canceled at the last minute and they called us to come play, but Johnny just walked out on the band. Honey, we *need* you."

"Shit, Mel! Shit! I don't perform, you know that."

"Little sister, you got to put your big girl panties on and help us out. If you don't, we're toast. We may not get this chance again. It's *the* Whisky a Go Go we're talkin' about."

Kenna took a deep breath. "I'm going to hate myself in the morning. Okay. Only for you would I do this."

"I'll bring the Stratocaster for you. Meet us backstage as soon as you can get there so we can go over the setlist with you."

When she hung up, Kenna flushed the sting from her eyes, dug deep down in her still-packed suitcase and pulled out the only trendy, low-cut top she owned. Blue jeans and boots would have to do. She made it down Sunset Boulevard and backstage to Mel, Rich and JJ in a little over an hour.

They gave her a crash course in the fine points of performance, including the setlist and their segues, and then Rich and Kenna practiced the timing for the guitar duets in the cover of "Whipping Post."

"Look at me, Kenna," Rich said. "This is just like all the months we've played together at Mel's. Forget about everyone out there and just look at us. We'll keep you on track, okay?"

Kenna nodded nervously. "I have to pee," she said, placing the Strat on the guitar stand.

"Well, hurry back," JJ said, "we're on in five."

Kenna ran down the back hall to the ladies' room. Adrenaline pumped through her body, causing her heart to palpitate. Her stomach cramped and her hands shook—all violent reminders of why she couldn't perform.

While holding back her hair as she bent forward, she thought of the legends who had played this house—Morrison, Hendrix and Joplin—and she wondered if, like her, they had puked into this very toilet.

She exited the stall, splashed cold water on her face and rinsed her mouth.

From the hallway, she heard JJ say, "You'd better be right about her, Mel."

"Just give her a chance. It'll be okay. I know it," Mel replied.

Racing back to the dressing room where the band was waiting for her, she spotted a glittery eye mask on a table. She grabbed it and put it on.

"What the hell are you doing, Kenna?" Rich said when she entered the dressing room.

"I'm thinking if those people can't really see *me*, then I won't really see *them*."

"Janis Joplin didn't wear a mask," JJ said.

"Sure she did," Kenna began, "it was called Southern Comfort."

"Get it while you can, little sister."

They took the stage together, and before Kenna was ready, Mel's bass notes popped out of the Marshall amp and punched her in the nose. JJ and Rich were already in for eight measures, and they all held their breath as they looked at Kenna to cue her.

Her first three notes were a little meek, but then Mel gave her the look that said, 'Come on, baby girl, show 'em what you got!'

Kenna closed her eyes and went to the place inside where everything made sense. The sounds of the other instruments made sense, the feel of the Strat made sense, the very *reason* for her hands made sense. Even the angst of her heartbreak somehow made sense.

Then her finger movements exploded. Like an airplane that had already taxied down the runway, they simply defied the gravitational pull of the earth.

Getting through the first piece wasn't exactly easy for her, but with each new song in the set, she followed Rich's advice, keeping her eyes on him, then Mel and then JJ. By the time their set was over, she realized she had actually survived performing.

Escaping evil people with guns in foreign countries is way less scary than this!

When they took their bows, the audience stood and cheered, and they weren't about to sit down again until this band played another tune. Mel, JJ and Rich glanced at each other, then at Kenna.

"Come on, Kenna," JJ said. "We've got one more trick up our sleeves. Your tune."

Kenna nodded.

Rich then started playing the piece Kenna had finally finished writing—the one they had all worked on that night in Mel's apartment. Kenna adjusted her guitar position, wiped the sweat from her pick, and with her first note, she finally came home.

Like all of her music, she had written the piece for Alex, and playing it now onstage with her eyes closed, she couldn't even hear the audience. She opened her eyes, and instead of focusing on Rich, she dared to look out into the house from behind the mask. She couldn't hear the audience because no one was making a sound. All eyes were on her as she played the last verse with raw passion.

Throughout the audience, people began to stand and clap. Some of them danced.

They like my song?

The audience whistled and applauded when they finished playing, and the band took their bows. Kenna ran off the stage first.

"I knew you could do it. I *knew* it," Mel crowed.

"Great job, Kenna," Rich said. "Listen! People are still clapping."

"Ha-ha, you're blushing," JJ chimed in.

Kenna handed him the Stratocaster and ran down the hall to the dressing room. She grabbed her purse and split out the back door without saying goodbye.

* * *

"Where did that girl go?" Rich asked as he, Mel and JJ entered the dressing room to pack up their instruments.

A man knocked as he entered the dressing room. "Hi, I'm Jordy Richards with Star Records," he said, taking his business card from the pocket of his sport coat and handing it to Mel.

"How can we help you?" she said.

"You guys really brought down the house tonight. I'm here to offer you the chance to cut a demo in our studio."

JJ dropped one of his nunchaku drumsticks. "Star? Seriously?"

"Seriously," Jordy said.

Mel stepped forward. "Hi, Jordy. I'm Mel and this is Rich and JJ."

"Good to meet you. Where is that smoking-hot girl guitar player in the mask?" he asked.

"We were just wondering the same thing," JJ said.

"If you're interested, call my office tomorrow and we'll set something up."

When Jordy left the dressing room, no one said anything for several seconds.

"I guess we'd better draw straws to see who gets to try to persuade Kenna," Rich said.

"Well, she did do this," Mel reasoned.

Rich stared at her. "Yes, and you were the one who convinced her so beautifully to do it."

"Aw, man, come on! Somebody else take a turn."

"You first, Mel."

CHAPTER TEN

Mel, JJ and Rich showed up unannounced at Hunter's door fifteen minutes after Kenna got home. She couldn't help but laugh when they rang the bell repeatedly.

"Come on in, guys. Anybody thirsty?" she said as she pulled open the door.

"Forget that, forget that!" Mel barged in first in a state of frenzy with her bracelets jangling above her head, as though she was waving off evil spirits.

"What are you guys doing here?"

JJ stroked his scruffy beard. "This is a performance intervention, Kenna."

"Huh?"

"You'd better brace yourself for this one, little sister."

Rich and JJ spit out the story of the Star Records guy and the opportunity to get a record deal, and the fact that he'd specifically asked for "the smoking-hot girl guitar player in the mask."

Kenna held up her hands in an attempt to stop the words from landing on her. "Oh, no! No, no, no. This was a one-time deal. I tossed my cookies before we went on tonight, and I almost fainted out there in front of all those people. If you're trying to kill me, there are easier ways to do it."

Mel lowered her voice and spoke calmly. "You loved how it felt."

"What?"

"You may have been scared shitless, but you loved it. I've never seen you look that happy. You owe it to yourself to do the demo, and you can decide after that whether you want to pursue it or not…but you owe your talent at least that much, little sister. Besides, there's no audience in the studio, so it'll be just like playing in my living room, only with better equipment."

"And headphones," JJ added. "You'll hear yourself and us so much clearer."

Kenna sighed and sauntered out to the deck to stare at the lights along the coast.

She didn't turn around when Mel followed her and leaned on the railing next to her.

"You realize, Mel, even just the thought of this scares the living hell out of me."

"I do, honey. You know I get you," she said softly. "But, see, that's where I think you got your priorities all fucked up."

Kenna looked at her. "What do you mean?"

"What you should have been afraid of was Alex, not the music."

Kenna's laugh broke the tension. "Now you tell me!"

"So is that a yes, my little sister?"

"I'll need a lot of help to pull this off, Mel."

Mel held out her hand to shake Kenna's. "You've got it, kid."

* * *

The next morning, Kenna awoke both excited about and afraid of her future—a future she had never considered.

Carrying her coffee cup and last Friday's Calendar section of the *Los Angeles Times* out to the deck, she sat and thumbed through the Arts section, as much to see what she had missed this weekend as to find a new way to spend an Alex-less Sunday.

Her pulse quickened when she saw the block ad for the exhibition at Gallerie Motek, featuring "the work of an inspired young photographer—Alex Winthrop, with photos by her mentor, the late, world-renowned photographer Maurice van Bourgeade."

As much as she tried, she couldn't get the exhibition out of her mind the rest of the day. She thought about it long and hard while she watched Monty and Louie run and play on the beach. Although she didn't want to go to Alex's show, she knew she needed to see the work; to see the connection between her surrogate father and the woman she loved.

"Come on, Monty and Louie. Time to go home."

Well, so much for an Alex-less Sunday, she thought as she performed a final check of herself in the mirror before leaving the house a couple of hours later. Dressed in a skirt, sweater and heels, her interpretation of 1980s styling forewent the era's most moronic trends.

The gallery was crowded when she arrived, allowing her to unobtrusively wander through the exhibit without seeing, or being seen by Alex. Transported instantly to her childhood when she saw her surrogate father Maurice's work, she smiled. She had grown up posing for and studying his pictures.

Kenna found herself standing before the section titled, "Then and Now." Maurice's and Alex's photos hung side by side according to subject matter.

Right in front of her was a photo of *her*. She stared at it and remembered the swing set in her backyard on her sixth birthday. Flanked by her parents, she looked so carefree, so safe, but she couldn't exactly remember what that felt like. Maurice had made her giggle, insisting she say the French word *fromage* instead of *cheese* when he had snapped the shot. Whole-body laughs like the one in the photo were long gone from her, not even a distant memory. That was the *then* picture. Hung next to it was the *now* picture Alex had taken of her in her apartment, just hours before they had broken up.

Kenna had never viewed herself in this way before—the way Alex saw her. Alex had captured the vulnerability in her eyes, and the full-body shot made her look wildly more beautiful than she'd ever thought she was. The lighting in the photo shone across one side of Kenna's face, the other side remaining a mystery, except for the eyes, which told one story to the world but a different one to herself.

Overcome with emotion, she turned toward the exit. In that instant, she locked eyes with a pair of the most electric-blue eyes she had ever seen. That's when the woman who owned them slipped her arm around Alex's waist and leaned in to plant a juicy kiss on her lips. Kenna wanted to rip the woman's lips off her face. Instead she bolted out of the gallery before Alex spotted her.

When she came home, her hand reached for the phone before the front door could close behind her. "Mel," she said when her friend answered, "when do we start rehearsal for the demo?"

"Wow, little sister, you almost sound like you want to do this."

I'll never be able to unsee the kiss that that slutty...slut...from... Slutsville planted on my girlfriend. My ex-girlfriend.

"Kenna, you still there?"

"Yeah, Mel. Can you go guitar shopping with me tomorrow?"

"Oh yeah! You ready to get you some real steel to match those eyes of yours, those *steel eyes*?" Mel laughed.

"I'm readier than you know."

"Okay, babe. I'll call you when I wake up."

* * *

Kenna barely slept. She spent most of the night out on the deck staring down at the city lights. An evening that had begun with thoughts of running away to lick her wounds had ended with the resolve of a pissed-off woman ready to change her life. Apropos to her lifelong training in both guitar and spycraft, she knew that to keep her balance, she either had to kick some bad guy's ass or play guitar like there really wasn't a tomorrow.

Mel met her at Strings and Things on Sunset Boulevard the next morning, where they spent two hours listening to various salesmen extol the virtues of the instruments that the staff liked. Kenna played every guitar that even remotely interested her but was dissatisfied with something about every one of them. Either the neck was too wide, or the action was too slow, or she didn't like the color, the tone, the wood. The list went on.

"I don't see anything here I want," Kenna said, matter-of-factly. "Don't you have any others?"

The salesman thought for a moment. "Hmm, let me check. We may have received a new shipment from Gibson this week. I'll go look in the back."

"He offered you a good deal on that used Strat," Mel whispered when he walked away.

"It's not what I'm looking for."

"What *are* you looking for, girl?"

"I'll know it when I see it, Mel." She mulled over the selection of hanging guitars until the salesman returned with a guitar box.

"Let's see what's in here," he said.

When he peeled back the lid, Kenna's eyes opened wide and her stomach growled.

"Jesus!" Mel said. "Does it come with sunglasses to keep you from going blind?"

Kenna removed the Gibson Les Paul Custom, limited edition color from the box and held it close. Guy musicians would have probably called the color "candy-apple red," but they would have been wrong. To Kenna's mind it was "whore-red," and decked out in the gold hardware, it was the guitar version of a Sunset Boulevard streetwalker, a hot one—on a Saturday night. A fitting pimpmobile, hot-pink fleece lined the case.

"I'll take it!" said Kenna.

"Don't you want to play it?" Mel and the salesman said at the same time.

"I don't need to. This is the one."

When they left the guitar store, Kenna clutched the guitar case with an exuberance she hadn't felt since she was fifteen, when she had met Sweet Jayne. Mel helped her load the Marshall amp Kenna had bought into her car.

"While you're on this side of town, how about we go to your old place and get the last of your stuff?" Mel said.

When they entered the apartment, Mel put her arm around Kenna's shoulders.

"I know you're sad, but now is not the time to think about it, little sister. Let's just get your shit and roll up on outta here."

Kenna nodded and silently gathered shoes from the closet and the outfit she'd worn the last time she had seen Alex. She tossed the outfit into a supermarket bag and handed it to Mel. "Give this to someone."

Mel nodded.

Kenna sat on the edge of what had been her bed and looked at the answering machine on the night table. She hit the Play button.

Alex had left her one last message. "I'm so sorry," she said. "I really do love you. *Please* call me."

Kenna met Mel's silent stare as Mel handed Kenna a picture Alex had taken of her. "I found this picture of you on the kitchen counter."

Kenna recognized it from the gallery exhibit.

Mel took the cassette tape out of the machine and held it up. "So what do you want to do with this, little sister?"

Kenna handed the photo back to Mel, gathered the last of her things, picked up her guitar case and walked to the door. Without looking back, she replied, "Toss them," and she left.

CHAPTER ELEVEN

The demo the band recorded landed them a contract, giving Kenna a studio to escape to every hour of every day for months while they rewrote, rehearsed and recorded her songs. The deeper she immersed herself in the craft of writing and making music, the less threatening the idea of performing became, but doing it without the mask wasn't even an option for her. Mel had been right when she had said that even though Kenna was scared, she indeed loved performance. More than that, she loved belonging to these three people who always stood by her.

The better part of a year had passed since Kenna and Alex had split up, but Kenna needed all of her concentration to not think of her every day. Her song portfolio had doubled in size during that time, and the record producers handily plucked out their favorite originals, helped with some of the musical arrangements and locked them in for the debut album and airplay.

Kenna insisted that no one know her true identity, including the record company executives, or she would quit. She and

Hunter had meticulously planned her route to and from the studio to protect her identity, and if it became necessary, a paparazzo didn't exist who could match her trained tactical skills for losing a tail.

Hunter had made sure her contract was ironclad regarding her anonymity, and the rest of the band was on board with the idea, knowing how Kenna's stage fright might cost them their big shot. The record executives liked how her talent, mystique and long legs would make them a lot of money.

Until they came up with a permanent identity for Kenna, she was known at the studio only by her alias, Steel Eyes, the term Mel had coined for Kenna's gray eyes, even though she now disguised them with blue contact lenses. Her mask was the latest incarnation of a work in progress. She and Mel had made the new mask look like painted-on steel—much more elaborate than the one she had found that first night when they had played at the Whisky a Go Go. It covered her face from her forehead to her cheekbones, and the eye openings were deceptively almond-shaped, giving her a completely different look. She was going to need something sturdier than this for the concert tour, along with a thin knit mask to wear underneath for comfort, or in the event that someone pulled off the outer mask.

All in all, the process was working for everyone. Before they wrapped up at the studio late on a Friday afternoon, Jordy Richards, the man who had discovered them, entered the sound booth, clicked the mic and spoke to them through the monitors.

"Take five, guys, I need a word."

"Be right in, we just finished," JJ said.

The four of them entered the sound engineer's booth.

"What's up, Jordy?" Rich said.

"We're at the point where we're getting ready to put the whole promotion together. Figure on six months of media blitz and airplay on all the top radio stations across the country, and then there'll be interviews, promotional events. So, tell me, which band name have you decided to go with?"

"We're not sure yet," JJ said.

"What about we call ourselves the Steel Eyes Band?" Mel said.

JJ thought for a moment. "I like it. It's edgy. Rich?"

"Works for me," Rich answered. "What about you, Steel Eyes? What do you think?"

"Whatever you guys want is fine with me," she answered.

Jordy chuckled. "I have to tell you…I've worked with a lot of musicians and bands, but I've never seen a band where everyone always gets along so well, without any ego trips. Keep that up and you guys will be unstoppable."

"Cool," Steel Eyes said. "Anybody hungry? I'm hungry."

"Me too, little sister. Come on, fellas," Mel said to Rich and JJ, "I'll make some pasta."

"Oh good," JJ said.

"Guys, guys," Jordy said, "you can afford to go out and get a good meal now."

"But Friday is always spaghetti night at Mel's," JJ said.

* * *

Before she left LA, Alex went to see Phyllis van Bourgeade to say goodbye. They dined on the brick patio out by the pool. The cascade from the man-made waterfall soothed Alex with its splashes against the river rock. She had spent many a late night on that patio listening to the water.

She gazed around, unable to reconcile the serenity when she compared it to the elegant luncheons she had attended there, where Maurice had hosted only the most accomplished in their fields. Alex had been the only unaccomplished on the invite list. Maurice had introduced her to Sonja Savarin at one of those bashes. On that day, Alex would have been hard-pressed to even conceive that within two years Maurice would be gone and she would move back to New York as Sonja's intern.

"I'll miss you, Phyllis."

Phyllis smiled and passed Alex the plate of madeleines.

"Maurice would be so proud of you."

"I hope so. He's the reason I have this opportunity." Alex became sullen.

Phyllis reached for her hand across the table and patted it. "I have a little going-away present for you."

"No, Phyllis, that's not necessary."

Phyllis smiled. "Yes it is. I'll be right back."

While Phyllis was gone, Alex drank in her last sight of the grand surroundings, wishing she had brought her camera to remember the way it looked at that moment. The Italian cypresses stood vigil on high, the ghosts of her innocence hid behind the billowing bougainvillea, and her memories would forever be just that.

"I didn't wrap it," Phyllis said when she handed Alex the old brown leather case. "Go ahead, open it."

Alex unzipped the case and looked inside. "Oh, Phyl! Really? Are you sure?"

"I can't think of anyone Maurice would have wanted to have this more than you."

Alex removed the old Leicaflex 35 mm camera from the case and held it as close as her memories. "This was one of his most prized possessions."

Phyllis sighed. "And now it will be one of yours."

"I'll cherish it. Thank you. You know, Phyl, even though I'll be in New York, I'll always be here for you."

"I know, Alex. I love you like my own." Phyllis took a sip of tea. "On another subject, have you heard from Kenna?"

The question stung Alex like a hundred bees. "No, and I don't expect to."

"Neither of you will tell me what happened. I so wish it had worked out for the two of you...you were so good together. Honestly, Alex, I hadn't seen Kenna that happy since before her parents died."

The bee stings cut like a knife. "Promise me that if she ever tells you the story, you won't hate me."

"I could never hate you."

Alex's eyes turned moist. "I accept full blame for what happened."

"We all make mistakes, Alex. Go to her."

"I've tried, but she cut me off completely. I can't even find her."

Phyllis chuckled sardonically. "She's very good at hiding."

"So I've learned."

* * *

The following afternoon, Alex scanned the long airplane aisle. She stuffed her winter coat into the overhead compartment of her first-class seat and stared out the window. It would be a while before she could visit LA again. Pushing away the incessant thoughts of Kenna, she reminded herself that she had no room for anything but making sure she learned everything she could from Sonja Savarin over the next year. Her new apartment was ready and waiting, and when she wasn't working with Sonja, she would be busy not thinking about Kenna.

The weather was already getting chilly in New York, and the golds of autumn would be the last warm colors Alex would see until spring. Grateful that this opportunity afforded her a clean and permanent break with Maddy, Alex had made it clear to her before leaving that their relationship was over. Maddy was forced to let go.

After losing Kenna, Alex's photos had become her only solace. She reached into her case and pulled out her favorite picture of Kenna. It had been part of her Gallerie Motek show and was the only photo of any kind she had ever carried in her wallet. Alex didn't blame Kenna for not coming to the show, but she still wished she had.

Staring at the picture every day wasn't helping her get over the girl, but it was all she had left, thanks to her own stupidity. The day she'd gone to Kenna's apartment to try to figure out where she had disappeared to, she left a copy of the shot on the kitchen counter in case Kenna ever returned. Alex wondered if she had ever played the answering machine message of her apology, where Alex told her that she loved her.

It doesn't matter now, she told herself, and then she repeated the mantra.

Alex closed her eyes and pictured the second time she and Kenna had met, on an airplane just like this one. She would have given anything to have that day back, as well as the subsequent ones where she had been so careless. The hum of the airplane engines lulled her into a dreamless sleep.

The bump of the wheels hitting the runway at JFK woke her. After disembarking, Alex took a deep breath and plunged into the brisk night with her suitcase, camera equipment and a longing for the girl who, just a few miles from where she was standing, had once asked her for size twenty-eight jeans, extra long. Not sure if her eyes were watering from the cold or from the memory, she grabbed a cab to the Upper West Side of Manhattan and rode the whole way in silence. New York had always embodied aliveness and creativity to her, and in her mind she framed almost every scene she passed.

The next morning, Sonja Savarin couldn't have cared less that Alex was still on West Coast time. She had insisted that Alex arrive no later than eight a.m. As Alex entered the studio, she debated whether or not to just pour caffeine directly into her eyes rather than down her throat.

"Good morning, Sonja," Alex said.

Sonja was moving umbrellas and lights around the set with her back to Alex. "You're late. It's eight oh two. Get me some coffee from the breakroom, please. I will say this once only—light with two sugars."

Alex smiled, but inside she rolled her eyes. She returned with the coffee while it was still hot enough.

"We are shooting a fashion layout this morning. One of these shots will be the cover for *Vogue Paris*. I want my cameras lined up over here, and lenses there. Familiarize yourself with all of it, because once I get going, I want what I want when I want it." She pointed to the specific locations. "Look on the floor for the markers for portrait lights and umbrellas. Yes?"

"Uh, yes."

"Good." Sonja sighed and almost smiled. "I suggest if you need coffee, which I assume you do between jet lag and the fact that for you it is five o'clock in the morning, you had better get it right now and be back in ten minutes. Yes?"

"Yes." Alex tried to suppress the yawn until she was out of sight. She gulped half a cup of black coffee, quickly poured another and gulped it too in order to make sure she was back a minute early.

Busy trying to memorize where Sonja liked everything, she was struck by the fact that this woman who had been so nice to her during her interview was proving to be a drill instructor. But Alex understood the need for perfection, and she decided right then that if the woman asked her to clean the floor with a toothbrush, she would do it.

By eleven o'clock, Alex had completed the tasks Sonja wanted done before the *Vogue* photo shoot. While she finished adjusting the tripods and lights, the door on the far side of the loft opened. Alex immediately stopped what she was doing and glanced into the dressing room.

The supermodel Silvana stared sharply into Alex's eyes with a look born only to royalty—the expectation of servitude. She was flawless in her presentation, a classic and timeless beauty.

"Silvana," Sonja said, "meet Alex. She's my new intern. Joseph," she yelled, "come out here. You need to fix the makeup for this lighting. It's wrong!"

When Joseph didn't answer, Sonja mumbled something and left to find him.

Alex helped Silvana up onto the set, carefully lifted and positioned her white gown on the divan, then took readings on her light meter in three different spots.

"Sonja's new intern, huh?" the raven-haired beauty with the caramel-gold eyes said. Her accent was Middle Eastern.

"Yes. Have any advice for me?"

"Get lots of rest. You'll need it."

Alex adjusted a light umbrella. "Funny you should say that. I flew in late last night from Los Angeles. In fact, for me it's only eight in the morning, and I've been here for hours."

"Poor thing," Silvana said. "You should ask Joseph to give you the eye cream he uses on the models when they look tired."

Alex glanced at her, and from the corner of her eye, she caught Silvana checking her out.

"Fine," Joseph said, a little exasperated as he followed Sonja back into the loft. "Yes, Sonja, I see what you mean about the jawline." Joseph fine-tuned Silvana's makeup as Alex pretended she was watching in order to learn. Glued to the vision of

Silvana's long, sexy neck when she tilted back her head, Alex imagined photographing her on satin sheets.

Sonja noticed Alex watching. "Alex, I'm ready. Hand me my Nikon, please. And when we take a break for Silvana to change her dress, I'll want all the cameras and lenses repositioned and ready for the next segment. Yes?"

The next three hours raced by. Alex absorbed every detail fastidiously and followed each command with precision.

"Beautiful, Silvana," Sonja said when they finished. "I can guarantee these pictures are going to come out gorgeous. Wait until you see the cover after the airbrushing. You'll think you're still nineteen."

"I'm only twenty-three, Sonja!"

"Yes, but *I* made you look nineteen!"

Alex retreated to the breakroom where Joseph was pouring his coffee.

"Done so soon?" he said.

She laughed. "Yes, but I had to leave the room because there was no space left between those two huge egos."

Joseph laughed too. "I see you're a quick study." He held out his hand to shake Alex's. "Welcome. I have a feeling we're going to work very well together."

CHAPTER TWELVE

By the time Alex made it home from her first day on the job, she felt like a sleepwalking, wet dishrag. While christening her new bathtub by candlelight, she put down her glass of wine to answer the phone.

"How was your first day, sis?"

"Rigor mortis is setting in as we speak, Dréa."

"That good, huh? I'm so excited we're finally on the same coast and only a couple of hours apart. That's probably like what...only ten zip codes away? When are you coming down to the shore?"

"If today is any indication, I'd say when the internship ends."

"Slave driver?" Alex's sister asked.

"That's putting it nicely. She hasn't discussed hours or time off yet. I think that might be because the hours will be whenever she tells me to do something, and time off is only necessary when you have to sleep, or die."

"Look at the bright side. It will help you tame your control issues." Dréa laughed hard.

"Stop. I do not have control issues."

"I rest my case."

"Dréa, if you loved me, you would come up here."

"Alex, we're not Jewish, I'm immune to guilt. Besides, I have a gallery showing of my jewelry and paintings in Philly at the end of the month. I still have pieces to finish."

"Congratulations." Alex snickered. "What are the odds that our family would have *two* black sheep?"

"That's why we understand each other…coming from the Mayflower people."

"You shouldn't call them that just because they don't understand the art gene."

"When are you going to get it, Alex? In the minds of high society, we're failures because we don't live that stoic life they seem so fond of. If we're not financiers, certainly we *should be* married to them."

Alex paused. She knew her big sister was right. "Thank God we have each other."

"I do that every day. Get some rest and I'll call you over the weekend, okay?"

"I miss you, Dréa."

"You sound just like when you were little. Miss you too."

When Alex hung up, her thoughts drifted to her day and the timeless beauty named Silvana. She took a sip of wine and sunk down into the tub.

I still miss her. Why isn't this feeling going away, not even a little bit?

The immediate peal of the phone interrupted Alex's thoughts of Kenna and brought her back to reality. She picked up the phone, wondering what Dréa had forgotten to tell her.

"What do you want now?" she said sarcastically.

"Since you asked, I want you to come join me at Sardi's," said the woman with the Middle Eastern accent.

"Silvana?" Alex said sheepishly.

"Yes, Alex."

"Sorry, I thought you were my sister calling back. I'd love to join you, but I'm soaking in my bathtub."

Silvana sighed. "Then perhaps you should just give me your address and we'll skip Sardi's."

Alex sloshed upright. She had no idea how to respond. If she said yes, would she suffer a Sonja shitstorm? Before she could stop herself, she heard her mouth give Silvana her address.

She hung up and bolted from the bathtub, smoothed her satin sheets and dried her hair before trying on almost every pair of jeans in her still-packed suitcase. Presentable was as far as she had gotten when the doorman phoned to announce that the world-class model was on her way up.

As excited as she was to explore the undeniable chemistry between them, Alex knew there was a place inside her that belonged only to Kenna Waverly. The doorbell interrupted her thoughts.

Alex caught her breath when she opened the door. Even without her camera makeup, Silvana was stunning, a true knockout, with enough mischief in her eyes to throw Alex off her game, and off her feet. The camel-colored cashmere coat brought out the gold in her eyes as she sauntered across the threshold, gently swinging a bottle of Perrier-Jouët champagne. Alex dove to keep it from crashing to the floor as Silvana let it drop.

"Come in. Sorry for the mess, but I haven't been here long enough to sleep, let alone unpack." Alex parked the bottle safely on the end table and turned on the small stereo.

"Hmm, I like that song, Alex. 'Kiss You All Over.'"

When Alex turned around, Silvana's gaze locked on hers. Silvana used the sexy music like a stripper auditioning for *Gypsy*. She kept eye contact with Alex as she undid the belt of her wrap-style cashmere coat. Careful to let it drop in slow motion, first she revealed one shoulder, then the other, allowing her straight, jet-black hair to trace its way down her back.

She wore only black lingerie over her milky complexion. The bustier extolled her sensuous cleavage. Alex visually traced the line downward to the garter belts that hooked on to her stockings and the thong between her slim thighs. To say that Silvana was just some girl wearing only underwear would have been tantamount to comparing the Sistine Chapel to some guy's graffitied ceiling.

Alex drank in the sight. "Stilettos. Nice touch, Silvana. A very nice touch."

Silently, the beauty took a step forward, wrapped her arms around Alex and kissed her.

Alex never had a chance.

* * *

By the time Silvana and Alex finally fell asleep, Alex had acquiesced to the fact that on top of her jet lag, sleepless first night and harrowing first day on the job, she would have to settle for a mere two-hour nap before going to work. She thanked God she was still young.

Seeing Silvana asleep on her satin sheets early the next morning, Alex thought, *That's exactly how I pictured her the first moment I saw her.* She thought about snapping a few tasteful shots as a personal gift but quickly realized she had to leave if she wanted to arrive at the studio before *eight oh two*, a time Sonja clearly did not favor. After anchoring a note under Silvana's bracelets on the night table, Alex grabbed her knapsack and headed out.

A long subway ride to SoHo later, she ran down Spring Street and up the stairs into the loft studio. Sonja had already hung some of the photos she had taken of Silvana the day before.

Without turning around, Sonja said, "Seven fifty-nine does not impress me."

Alex was out of breath, and Sonja turned to look at her.

"You look dreadful, Alex. You should go home and get some rest, yes? I won't need you for the rest of the day. And tomorrow we begin working on these photos."

"Are you certain there isn't anything I can do?"

"Tell Silvana I said dinner at my house tonight."

Alex's eyes opened wide. *Damn, how the hell does she know?*

On the subway ride home, Alex thought, *If Sonja didn't need me there today, why didn't she call to tell me?* Then it occurred to her that perhaps this was some warped kind of initiation, like a hazing.

When she opened the door to her apartment, Silvana was just waking up. Alex sat silently next to her on the bed. A golden-brown, sleepy gaze and a look as warm as Silvana's embrace came to rest on her. Leaning forward, Alex gently kissed her sensuous lips.

"Are you leaving for the studio?" she asked quietly.

Alex rolled her eyes. "No, actually I was already there, and Sonja sent me home after she told me how bad I look. Oh, and she told me to tell you dinner at her house tonight. How did she know you spent the night?"

"I told her before I left Sardi's last night."

Alex swallowed hard. "Oh no. Why didn't you tell me that?"

"It didn't seem important."

"I hope you're right. I don't want to jeopardize this chance to work with Sonja."

"You won't." Silvana smiled slyly.

"How do you know?"

"Sonja is my aunt."

Alex pulled a luxurious satin-covered pillow from the bed, put it over her face and screamed as loud as she could.

* * *

A week later, the proofs of Silvana's photos were approved for *Vogue Paris*, and out of those finalists, the editor chose the cover shot. Alex and Sonja had worked diligently and late into the night, perfecting every detail before they submitted the final art.

In an uncharacteristic gesture, Sonja took Alex out for cocktails to celebrate when they finished. They sat talking shop in a booth at the Oak Room in the famous Plaza Hotel. After taking a sip of her vodka martini, Alex gathered her courage.

"Sonja, if I had known Silvana was your niece, I would have never said yes when she called—"

Sonja held up her hand. "The fireworks between you and my niece are palpable, even to me. Besides, what's the big deal, Alex? In fact, you're a good influence on her. You work hard, you don't do drugs, you're well educated and very talented. I approve."

"That's very kind of you, Sonja. I respect you immensely, and I'm grateful for the chance you're taking with me, but I don't want anything to get in the way of our working relationship."

"Alex, I knew Maurice van Bourgeade for two, maybe three *centuries*. We had a few long talks about you. Everything from your talent, strengths and weaknesses, to your character. I'm not worried." Sonja finally smiled. "As a photographer, you know that the best shots come at the most unexpected moments, often from the most imperfect subjects. Some people call those moments flaws, Alex. I call them art. That's something you know too. It's why you're so good."

Alex's cheeks flushed. "Thank you, Sonja. Your confidence in me means so much. I haven't felt that since I lost Maurice, and I miss him every day."

Sonja reached out and patted Alex's hand. "Then let's make him proud together, yes?"

CHAPTER THIRTEEN

Her second winter in Manhattan left Alex cold. Photography was her sustenance, her bed and her only focus, but that did not mean she wasn't thinking about Kenna, even when Silvana wasn't off modeling in some exotic location.

Frigid February nights compounded by the endless barren avenues made her isolated and lonely, enough to spend them at the studio downtown. Having been promoted to Sonja's apprentice, Alex would spend her nights working and then sleeping on the studio's couch. Sonja had often found her in the morning buried under a pile of proofs.

On this particular morning, Sonja brought hot, fresh bagels for her. Alex awoke when she heard the key in the lock.

"Hi Sonja," she said, sitting upright and rubbing the sleep from her eyes. "Sorry, I guess I fell asleep waiting for some prints to dry."

Sonja scoffed. "You just want to be here before seven thirty to impress me. I'm impressed, now stop working so hard. Enough, yes?" She tossed the bag of bagels onto the couch next to Alex.

"Besides, you haven't been an intern for over a year, and you still act like one. Try to remember you're my assistant now and you're doing your own photo shoots. Impressive photo shoots."

Alex stood, stretched out the kinks and grabbed a stack of proofs. "What do you think?" she asked, handing them to Sonja. "I developed them from an old roll of film I found at about two this morning."

Sonja hung up her coat before thumbing thoughtfully through the contact sheets.

"Who is this intriguing creature, Alex?"

"Just some girl I used to know."

"I see more in these photos than just *some girl* you used to know."

Alex was silent.

"Who is she? It's a simple question, yes?"

"Maurice and Phyllis van Bourgeade's surrogate daughter, and, like I said, a girl I used to know."

"Why do you no longer know her?"

Alex sighed. "Because I was young and stupid, selfish and I didn't deserve her."

Sonja handed the photos back to Alex. "You need a little time off. Thanks to you, everything here is under control." She smiled. "Go visit your sister."

"A weekend? Really, Sonja?"

"Not just a weekend. A three-day weekend. Silvana's in Italy so you have no excuse. Now go, yes?"

Alex grabbed a cab uptown, packed a bag, and phoned Dréa to let her know she was coming. She made it to the train station in time to catch the ten twenty express to 30th Street Station in Philadelphia. Dréa and her Goldendoodle dog-son Chance picked her up, and together they drove an hour to the New Jersey shore.

Alex played with the radio while Dréa recounted in detail the gallery show her sister had missed.

"I sold twice as many pieces there as I did last year, and I met a CEO who wants to see slides of my work for a corporate project. Can you shoot some new slides of my paintings this weekend?"

"Absolutely. I'm so proud of you, Dréa. You're really making a name for yourself in the art world. I wanted to come to the show, but Sonja had me buried at the studio. We were up all night getting *Rocklandia* magazine's cover done right after the Grammys."

"From what I can see, the past year hasn't hurt you any. That last batch of photos you sent blew me away. Artist to artist, kid, I have a feeling you're going to be a star. Now you're out there under your own name photographing rock stars. Still can't believe you partied with the Stones."

"I just want to make a living doing what I love."

"You're already photographing rock 'n' roll royalty. Alex, if you're not careful, Mom and Dad are going to claim you as their own. Wait, go back to that song you just passed."

Alex dialed back a few stations. For an instant, she thought she recognized the gripping and unusual rock music. After listening for a minute, she said, "I like them. Who are they?"

"Who *are* they?" Dréa glanced at her. "Have you been living under a rock?"

"I wouldn't know. It's dark in a darkroom. You would think I'd know what's going on in the music scene, but really, *Rocklandia* just sends them…and that's how and when I get to know them."

"Their name is the Steel Eyes Band. They're taking the rock scene by storm. I saw them at the Trocadero in Philly last summer. I can't believe you haven't heard of them. I've had their album on my stereo since the day it came out. I've even copied it onto a cassette for my aerobics workout."

"I'd like to do a photo shoot to this music." The song was warm in Alex's ears, but the guitar was edgy and sharp.

"I keep forgetting to forget you!" The lyric mirrored the music.

The refrain stuck in Alex's mind. *I keep forgetting to forget you.* Each time the singer sang it Alex thought of Kenna. Reclining her seat, she closed her eyes and nodded out listening to the Steel Eyes Band's latest hit. She awoke to Dréa pulling into the driveway of her artsy bungalow on the bay.

"Have a nice nap?"

"I did. But I think I'm getting hungry."

"Good thing I cooked last night. Your favorite soup is in the fridge."

Alex sat up. "Sonja was so right about coming to see you. I feel better already. Is it okay with you if I go to the beach and freeze my ass off for a while?"

"I'll get some food ready for when you get back."

Alex bundled up and took Chance out onto the beach.

"The air smells so good, buddy," she said as she threw his ball for what must have been the thousandth time.

She shivered from the bite of a whipping wind and stared out at the solid gray horizon. *It's simply the illusion of a line that connects nothing to nowhere. I wonder where that leaves me? Without Kenna.*

"Come on, Chance, let's go." They crossed the sand. "I wonder what *she's* doing right now. Let's tell ourselves she's waiting tables somewhere up in Malibu and missing me. Yeah, Chance, let's say that." She dug her hands down into her pockets for warmth and hurried home.

After dinner, the sisters sat on the cozy couch by the fire and shared what was left of a bottle of wine. Snoozing, Chance provided Alex with a toasty footrest.

"How's the supermodel?" Dréa's tone leaked a tinge of distaste.

"You know her name," Alex replied. "What do you have against Silvana, anyway?"

"Well, that depends. You've been seeing her on and off for over a year now. Is it serious or not?"

Alex thought about it. "Yes and no. If you're asking me if we've talked about forever...she does, I don't. She's away for long stretches, and she knows I casually date other people. But having that freedom is partly what makes it so good between us when she's back in New York. I don't know what she does when she's gone, and I don't ask about it. Besides, what difference does it make if we're serious or not?"

"Honestly? I just don't see it long-term, Alex. Sure, I've seen how much she adores you, and hey, who doesn't want to walk around saying things like, 'Check it out…my girlfriend? Yeah, she's an international supermodel.'"

Alex snickered. "Okay, I'm sure I have never said that…and if I ever do, I can promise you I certainly won't say it *that* way."

The girls shared a good laugh as a stiff wind blew across the chimney, causing the fire to crackle and the logs to shed their embers.

"As your older sister, I feel it's my duty to tell you that you've been different ever since you broke up with that woman in California. She changed you, Alex. All kidding aside, I know you're crazy about Silvana, but I'd bet the house she can't hold a candle to that waitress in LA. I can tell, you know? Are you ever going to tell me what happened with that girl?"

Alex stared into the fire. "It's been over two years and I still can't talk about it. Every time I think about how self-centered and clueless I was, I just want to scream. Besides, I've moved on."

"Yes, I see that. An array of casual dates for when a gorgeous international supermodel who adores you isn't quite enough." Dréa took a sip of wine and observed her sister. "Oh my goodness, someone finally gave you a run for your money."

Alex didn't respond.

"*She* dumped *you*? Well, that's a first. If I didn't know better, which I do, I'd have to say by looking at you that you're still in love with her."

Alex nodded but she had no words, so she continued staring into the spiky orange, yellow and blue flames.

"I've never seen you like this." Dréa picked up her portable phone and handed it to Alex. "Call her."

"You don't understand…"

"I don't care what happened. Call her, right now."

Alex shook her head. "I don't have her number."

"I'll bet you know someone who does."

Alex looked into Dréa's eyes. She took the phone and dialed Phyllis van Bourgeade. After listening to Phyllis tell her about the family and her new mah-jongg club, Alex mustered enough nerve to ask about Kenna.

"She was here last Sunday for dinner. She didn't ask about you, Alex. I'm sorry," Phyllis said.

"It's okay, Phyl, I don't want to put you in the middle of anything, but do you have her number?"

"There isn't one. She's leaving LA tomorrow, and she'll be gone for months."

"Gone? Where is she going?"

"She rattled off a list of places, mostly in Europe."

"When you talk to her, please tell her I asked about her."

"Is that really all you want me to say, Alex?"

Alex sighed. "On second thought, don't say anything. There's no point in it now."

Alex disconnected and handed the phone back to her sister. "K doesn't even have a number because she's leaving tomorrow for an extended trip overseas. Have any other bright ideas?"

"Hey, it was worth a shot."

Alex finished her wine. "If it's all right with you, I'm going to call it a day. I haven't gotten much sleep lately."

Dréa stood and stretched, hugged her sister and walked to the stereo. She ejected the Steel Eyes Band cassette and handed it to Alex. "There's a stereo in your room if you want to listen to some music."

Alex nodded and took the tape. "Thanks, sis, see you in the morning."

Chance climbed the stairs with Alex, and she got ready for bed with "Somewhere Like You" playing in the background. That was the song she couldn't get out of her head, the one she listened to three more times before falling asleep.

I'm looking for somewhere like you.
Same familiar eyes,
Old familiar lies,
But I'd still live somewhere like you.

PART TWO

CHAPTER FOURTEEN

Kenna stood on the deck looking out over the Pacific.

Everything is so different now, she thought as she watched the skein of seabirds sail upwind.

When she was on tour, she missed Southern California as much as she missed the New Jersey shore. She glanced over her shoulder. Through the French doors, she saw Hunter take his seat at the kitchen table.

I don't know how I could have done all this without Hunter looking out for me.

"Hey," Hunt said when Kenna came inside.

"I really hope this tour goes better than the last one," she said.

"What are you talking about, Wave? The last Steel Eyes Band tour was a raging success." Hunter picked up the carafe of coffee and emptied it into their cups.

"I just meant that I want to hang out more seamlessly this time with Mel and the guys. And…I really wouldn't mind some female company."

"What about Brooke?"

"What about her?"

"You've been seeing her for six months. You don't think you could get serious about her?"

"No."

Hunt raised an eyebrow. "Well, that was succinct."

"It gets old having to break up with girls because of the whole anonymity thing. Always maintaining a distance so that when we finish in the studio and I go back on tour, they don't hate me."

"Where would you find the time on the road anyway?"

Kenna grinned. "If I found the right girl, I'd *make* the time. I can't see myself telling Brooke about Steel Eyes."

Now that the band was acclaimed worldwide, the past eight years had been fortuitous. By blending rock with various styles of jazz, the Steel Eyes Band had slammed into fame, claiming their niche with a string of hits that blurred the lines of music genres. They went on to win Grammys across categories every year but one since they had started.

Steel Eyes's penchant for Latin American rhythms and warm tones was ever-present in her songs. They ranged from hard rock to melodic ballads, always sung with distinction in Mel's resonant head tones and with Rich's airy vertical harmonies. Steel Eyes's signature guitar work was the only real part of her that everyone could see.

The touring schedule for the better part of a year was now more grueling than it had been when she was twenty-five, or even twenty-seven. Interviewed in every country on the tour, Mel, JJ and Rich would continually dodge questions about the anonymous megastar. The band reaped the heavy rewards of celebrity, while Steel Eyes, posing as Kenna, would slip out of the concert hall with her fans after every show. Anonymous in fame, anonymous by the lack of it, she was anonymous by choice.

The fans adored the band, the mystique and above all, the sizzling guitar. Steel Eyes loved the music, and fame was simply the price of admission.

"Did you pack all the blue contact lenses?"

"For the third time, Hunter, yes."

"I'm sorry, Wave, I just don't want to take the chance of anyone recognizing your gray eyes once you're in your Steel Eyes disguise. But at least now you'll only have to wear the contacts for up close appearances."

"I think you're being overcautious, but I do like how the new mask changes my eye color under the stage lights. On our other tours, my eyes got so irritated from constantly wearing those contacts. It's nice having a choice whether or not to wear them onstage."

Hunter rolled the suitcases to the door and did a final walkthrough. "It looks like we've got everything in order."

"I already miss the dogs, but your mom seemed happy to have them at the house while we're gone."

"She did, didn't she? They'll be good company for her."

The doorbell rang.

"Taxi's here, Hunt."

"What was the point of not letting me order a limo to the airport?"

The doorbell rang again.

"Incognito. I want to fly under the radar."

Hunt juggled the suitcases with disdain. "Next you'll insist on flying coach. I should just fly with the band from now on. They have all the rock star perks."

"Hi," Kenna said as she let the driver in to help with the rest of the luggage.

While riding in the taxi, Kenna wondered if Alex had stayed in New York and what she was doing. She stopped when she imagined with whom she was doing it. "Let me see the itinerary."

Hunter pulled the list from his briefcase and handed it to her. "What do you want to know?"

"When we'll be in New York."

"That's the last stop on the tour," he said. Then he seemed to realize why Kenna had asked. "Forget about New York. Alex Winthrop does her own big-time camera shoots now. And the day of your final concert, Sonja Savarin will be shooting you for *Rocklandia*'s cover."

Kenna smiled. She remembered it well. While she couldn't find it funny at the time, now, the memory of it made her want to laugh. Steel Eyes had frozen in her tracks when she had shown up for a camera shoot with the famous Sonja, only to find that Alex was her assistant. "Here," she said, handing Hunt the itinerary.

"What you should be thinking about is our side trip from Paris. We're lucky to have the tour as cover," he said so only she could hear.

Kenna looked at him, knowing he was referring to their meeting with their contact. Not that any mission was *un*important, but this one had great personal significance to them both. They were bringing a microfiche to a man named Menachem—the man they had only ever referred to as "Old Uncle." Maurice van Bourgeade had compiled the information on it with his dear friend and Kenna's dad, Sam Waverly. Upon his death, Maurice had willed it to Hunter.

Last night Hunter had told Kenna that Old Uncle had called to say it was time to see the contents of the film. Paris was the second stop on the tour, and they would see him next week.

"Now that you have me thinking about Old Uncle, I'm certain he was at your parents' house for the holidays when we were about four. Don't you remember? He brought his two children with him, a boy and a girl. The boy was a little older."

"I can't believe what you can remember, Wave."

"Yeah? I can't believe what I still can't forget."

"You mean *who* you can't forget. Starting now, you're touring. You're about to meet so many new people, and you'll have opportunities to find whatever or whomever you want."

She looked over at Hunter and whispered, "I still say being a rock star is scarier than being a spy."

"Wave, Alex is history…it's been eight years! Time to find something new."

She decided not to tell Hunt she still couldn't conceive of ever wanting anyone *more*. "I take it you've already mapped out the common area between our suite and the band's?" she asked.

"Like last time, you'll be able to get in and out of their suite from the adjoining suite, registered to *Monsieur* van Bourgeade.

As far as the venues, this time your ID says you're the band's private technical person. Meaning, you have access to everything and everyone. All hallways to and from the dressing rooms are watched by security, so you come in as plain and unassuming as you can, you exit the secure area with the band as Steel Eyes. Then it's back to the dressing room where you become *you* again and leave with regular personnel."

"You don't think security will figure it out?"

"No. You'll be coming and going. Like I said, they'll think you're the band's go-to tech, so you can go anywhere. Each individual has been heavily vetted, and as Steel Eyes's bodyguard and chief of security, Jean Claude will deflect any suspicion."

"And when they don't see Steel Eyes enter or leave the venue?"

"Jean Claude has that handled. He has told his staff that you enter and leave through a different location than the one they are in. They're forbidden to share information with each other."

"Don't you think that's a little unrealistic, that people won't talk? What if it were you and me? You don't think we would share that kind of info?"

"Trust me when I say they've all been *heavily* vetted."

Kenna nodded. "I do. I just want to be able to hang out with Mel and the guys, like in the old days."

"*Kenya*, you worked it out on the last tour."

"Yeah, but I still can't be seen with them in public."

"Well, this time next year you'll have just wrapped up this tour, and then you guys have a long hiatus before you go back into the studio. You'll be able to do whatever you want then, but right now, Wave, you need to keep your head in the game."

* * *

Three nights later in London, everything had gone just as Hunter had said it would, right down to the band being able to hang out in the suite and celebrate after their second concert.

"Hey, aren't we supposed to be partying like rock stars?" JJ said as they entered their five-star living room in the heart of London. "Mel, this is just like your old digs," he joked.

Rich laughed. "Tease all you want, JJ, but I'll bet you miss spaghetti night at Mel's old place as much as Kenna and I do."

"Thanks, Rich," Kenna began as everyone fell into the nearest comfortable seat. "It's nice to hear you use my name. Even after all these years, I still feel stupid sometimes when the press and the fans are screaming out 'Steel Eyes.'" She waved her hand to bat away the words.

"Little sister, that's our mystique, that's *our* edge, or to use the words of your people, our *shtick*. We know who you really are, and what makes you special is you've never forgotten. We're still a family...even though JJ, Rich and I get the limos while you stand out in the rain hailing a cab."

"Thanks, Mel. And I could never forget who I am when I get pushed around by fans trying to get close to you guys. I can't fault them; I'm your biggest fan. But I'm with Rich on this one—I miss spaghetti night."

Mel jangled her bracelets reaching for the phone. "Room service?" she said after she dialed. "Hi, would you please send us up five bowls of spaghetti marinara, Italian bread and salad? That's great. Yeah, and some table wine, nothing fancy. Thanks." Mel hung up and stared at Kenna. "Anything else, little sister?"

"No, that ought to do it." Kenna smiled.

"Tonight blew me away," JJ said. "It's so good to be back out there and promoting the new album. You really sizzled tonight, Kenna."

"Yeah? Thanks, but I think we all brought it tonight."

"During 'Forget You,' I thought my guitar was going to fly out of my hands," Rich said. "The lights and the sound, with all those people screaming...it was like a caffeinated adrenaline cocktail. I'm still buzzed."

"I dug the *hell* out of it!"

"Really, Mel?" Kenna said, straight-faced.

The band and Hunter shared a knowing laugh, and while waiting for the food, Kenna pulled Sweet Jayne out of her case. Leaning back on the sofa, she softly strummed a distinctive, undulating melody, and surely another upcoming Steel Eyes Band hit.

"Soulful, like Brazilian jazz...but like a love song," JJ said, picking up his sticks. His rhythm pushed the dreamy notes toward a hypnotic bossa nova beat.

"Where do you *find* these sounds?" Mel said. Then her clear, clean voice vocalized to it.

Mel's voice warmed the air in Kenna's ears. It welcomed her home in every foreign country. Cloaked in its timbre, Kenna discerned the influences of all the girl singers she had ever loved. With breathy soul, Mel had the perfect balance of air and tone. At times, like Rose from Sly and the Family Stone; the soft scrape of Brenda Russell floating on a line of *Ooie-ooie-oohs*, and the gritty fire of Merry Clayton singing backup for the Rolling Stones. The head tones and phrasing, however, were rich and distinctively hers. The notes broke in all the right places, sometimes like silk, sometimes more like coarse-grit sandpaper and then back to silk again. That voice inspired Kenna to write songs only Mel could sing.

Rich harmonized to Melanie's vocals, and Kenna sat forward, pulling Jayne in closer. She rocked gently to the rhythmic, seductive notes emanating from the guitar. They improvised continuously for almost half an hour before a knock at the door brought the tune to a halt. Hunt waited until the waiter left and then gave Kenna the all clear.

A minute later, as if choreographed, everyone took the facsimile of their usual place around Melanie's former kitchen table. The table they had shared every Wednesday and Friday night; the table JJ had helped Mel bring home from Goodwill on the roof of his junker over a canyon at rush hour; the table where a worldly yet naive Kenna Waverly couldn't have begun to imagine what was on the horizon or what this small group of people would come to mean to her.

Kenna raised her wineglass. "To destiny, and to family."

"You got that right, little sister." Mel glanced at Hunter. "What you smilin' 'bout, white boy?"

"You!" Hunt laughed. "All of you. Is this what it was like when you guys first got together?"

"Pretty much," JJ said. "Once we got Johnny out of the way. I still wonder sometimes if he'll create a problem for Kenna once he figures out she's Steel Eyes. Let's face it, there aren't enough women rockers of Kenna's caliber out there to confuse the bastard."

"Honestly, you give him too much credit. It's been years and he hasn't figured it out yet." Mel's bracelets jangled as she reached for the bread.

"Yep," Kenna added. "It all started the day I moved in, and ten minutes after I started playing, JJ knocked on my door. Except for Hunter, you guys are the closest thing I have to family, and I couldn't be *this* without you." Kenna raised her glass to make a toast. "Thank you for rescuing me, JJ. Thank you, Mel, for being the closest thing I've ever had to a sister… which is really great 'cause I get to have a sister who's actually a *sister*. To you, Rich, for keeping me grounded onstage, and of course you, Hunter, my brother."

"Hold on," Mel interjected. "If I'm your sister, and Hunt is your brother, that makes me and him brother and sister. Aw, damn, I'm going to have to protect his lanky ass now."

Hunt called her bluff. "I'm a lot tougher than I look, Mel."

Mel scoffed. "You wear expensive suits, Italian shoes that somehow *never* get scuffed—and what about those hundred-dollar haircuts? You come to my old neighborhood, I'm gonna have to watch your back is all I'm sayin'."

"I promise to do the same for you in Beverly Hills after ten p.m."

Mel laughed. "That is so sick, and unfortunately still true."

"Hey, what time do we leave for Paris tomorrow, Hunt?" Rich asked.

"The flight is at ten and you'll have the whole day and night off. The next day there'll be rehearsal time, sound checks and the show. But after that, you'll have the last Paris show, the VIP party and then a couple of days off. I'll let you know the sound check schedule after we get settled in."

"Hey, guys, let's do a little sightseeing tomorrow then. You coming, Kenna?"

Kenna felt a pang of regret. "Why do you always ask when you know we shouldn't be seen together?"

Mel patted her shoulder. "Because I don't ever want you to think I don't want you to go."

After their late-night meal, Kenna hugged everyone and went to bed. Lying in her darkened room, she picked up Sweet Jayne and played the refrain from earlier. She hummed some different melody lines, searching for *the one* that sounded right, *the one* that propelled the chords, *the one* that would haunt her. Some lyrics came along for the ride.

> *If I must believe in someone,*
> *It might as well be me,*
> *You had to stop the music,*
> *For the dance to set you free.*
> *So you made all the rules,*
> *And then won every game,*
> *Look where that has gotten us,*
> *I'll never be the same.*
>
> *From nowhere to now where*
> *From always to never*
> *We had it all*
> *You were so clever*
>
> *How much more could you take from me?*
> *You said I was your destiny*
> *When I found out*
> *It was too late*
> *You weren't destiny*
> *And I was fate.*

Kenna turned on her light, grabbed the pad and pen from the night table and scribbled the working lyrics. At the top of the page, the title read, "From Nowhere to Now Where."

CHAPTER FIFTEEN

Having checked into the Louis XIV hotel on the Right Bank in Paris, Hunter and Kenna set out in their rental car to pick up information from the dead drop that would instruct them where to meet Old Uncle. They drove across the Seine to the Jardin du Luxembourg on the Left Bank, Hunter slowing the car as they passed the Palais du Luxembourg on the Rue de Vaugirard.

Kenna spotted their handler's chalk mark on the pole. "It's a go," she said.

Hunt parked the Renault on the Boulevard St. Michel and they strolled arm in arm past the children sailing the miniature boats in the cement pond, beyond the old men playing *boules* until they reached the far side of the park, where the marionette Guignol and his cohorts had entertained children for generations.

Perched horizontally along the wrought-iron gate in the park's back corner lay a pen, indistinguishable to the casual eye. Kenna leaned her back against the gate, and Hunter retrieved the pen as he leaned into her.

"I've got it," he whispered.

Kenna pulled her ball cap brim down low over the top of her sunglasses, then crisped her collar to stay the steady autumn breeze that made the Seine feel closer than it was. They walked to the nearest exit.

Maddy? She spun around and pulled Hunter up against her. "Kiss me." She planted her lips on his.

He wrapped himself around her to shield her face and pretended to kiss her. Kenna waited before she let him go.

"What is it?" Hunt asked.

"Did you see the woman with the dirty-blond hair?"

"With the blue eyes?"

"Yes. I'm sure that was Maddy…Alex's *other* girlfriend? The girl that kissed her to spite me at her show in LA after we broke up?"

"You're certain that was her?"

"I did my homework. A girl doesn't forget a thing like that… ever."

"Especially you. I've been at this game too long to believe that someone you know in any way, near our Paris dead drop is a coincidence."

"What the hell could she be doing here, Hunt?"

"Only one way to find out. Get the car and meet me at the Gare du Nord in one hour." He pivoted to leave.

"Hunt, the keys!"

He tossed them to her and casually closed the distance between him and Maddy.

An hour later, Kenna pulled the car over on her second pass around the Gare du Nord train station and Hunter got in.

"Take the A1 autoroute toward Charles De Gaulle Airport. We're late," he said. He unscrewed the pen from their dead drop pickup. A rolled morsel of paper had replaced the ink cartridge, indicating where they would meet Old Uncle in Chantilly.

"Where did Maddy go when she left the *jardin?*" Kenna said as she drove north from Paris.

"She pulled a fast one at the Châtelet Métro stop with all those snaky underground tunnels. It's obvious this isn't her first rodeo. She managed to cross over to the other side and head back toward the Left Bank. I'm sure she didn't spot either one of us, though, and that's all I care about."

"Hunt, we have to know why she's here. If she wasn't there for our dead drop, what was she there for? Is it possible she's a friendly?"

"She could belong to anybody."

"I'm not touching *that* one. Jesus, what if Alex is in danger?"

"I'm sure she's fine. They broke up back when Alex moved to New York."

Kenna swerved onto the shoulder of the autoroute and slammed on the brakes.

"How do you know this?" she asked, incredulous.

"My mother told me a long time ago; Alex broke up with her when she moved to New York," Hunter said calmly. "Mom says she asks about you from time to time, has even referred to you as her ex."

"I have news for you; I'm not *her* anything. So you didn't think to share that tidbit with me at any point over the last... oh I don't know, couple of years? *Five* years? How about *eight* years!"

"I'm sorry. But in my defense, it's such a sore subject. Honestly, Wave, when it comes to Alex Winthrop, you get fucking crazy."

"I know. I know. You're right. Forget it. In retrospect, Alex didn't know what to do with me, so she ran...right to Maddy." Kenna slipped the car into gear and pulled back onto the highway. "Still, there is something about that girl that creeps me out, and the fact that she's here is setting off every internal alarm I have."

"Your instincts are usually right on the mark. I know you don't want to hear this, but I think it's too dangerous for you to continue this work. You should at least consider putting it on hold for a year or two."

"Why, Hunt?"

"Because you got the shit beat out of you in Istanbul? If you get hurt again, I don't know what I'd do. You've been lucky, and I don't think you should push it."

"Really, Steel Eyes is the perfect cover," she protested.

"As your business manager I can still travel with you, take care of business, and you can stay safe."

She thought about it and then spoke softly. "I'm not ready to give up the fight, Hunt."

Flanked by verdant forest twenty-four miles north of Paris, Chantilly conjured seventeenth and eighteenth century France. Its dense convocation of oaks stirred up images redolent of kings and carriages, of privileged French mademoiselles on parasol picnics, wooed by young men in the shadow of a château.

Kenna parked where the map indicated. She and Hunter got out and walked along the forest's edge until Old Uncle's vintage Rolls Royce pulled up beside them.

"Welcome, welcome," Uncle said joyfully as they got into the car. "I was beginning to worry."

"We had a slight delay, Uncle. Sorry."

Uncle looked back and forth between them. "I see. Pierre, take us home, please."

When they arrived, Kenna was struck by the magnitude of Uncle's eighteenth century château. History echoed in the marble foyer, casting its long shadow across a balustrade from the refined Age of Enlightenment. The baroque molding on the ceiling transported Kenna's imagination to a time when the literary salons of women like Madames de Stael and Geoffrin shaped France's Golden Age.

Old Uncle hugged Hunter. "I'm very glad to see you." They kissed on both cheeks. He then walked over to Kenna and embraced her. "You've grown up to be such a tall, beautiful woman, just like your mother with those startling gray eyes."

She hugged him back. "It's been way too long this time, Uncle. It's so good to see you too."

He stroked her cheek in a fatherly way and smiled at her. "Shall we go into my library? It's soundproof."

Kenna and Hunt shared a glance, and they followed him into the room with ceilings so high there were sliding ladders to reach the books on the highest shelves. The oversize windows were all outfitted with bulletproof glass, although they remained typically French with their vertical latches and oval handles. The fireplace was surely used in another era for Dutch oven cooking, but now roared with native oak.

"How about some true French cognac to chase away that autumn chill?" He poured it from a decanter on the bar and handed them each a snifter. "Please, have a seat."

Kenna sat, put the snifter on the table and extricated the microfiche from the hollowed-out, steel-reinforced heel of her boot. Uncle held out his hand as he hovered over her, and she laid the microfiche gently in his palm.

"You realize, the information we are about to share may change your feelings about a few things." He was staring down into Kenna's eyes.

"Like what?" Hunter said.

"You haven't seen this yet because of the atrocities your fathers and I witnessed in the Second World War. We agreed years ago that we would wait a generation, and whichever one of us outlasted the other two would share that information with the next generation."

"Speaking of children, Uncle, how are your son and daughter?" Kenna said matter-of-factly.

He laughed. "You really are the intelligence dream we always knew you would be."

"Who is *we*?" Kenna asked.

"Your parents, Hunter's parents, me and of course Mossad. You had only met my son and daughter once at the Van Bourgeades'. You couldn't have been more than three or four years old."

"But I remember clearly."

"Of course you do. My children are in Israel. My son is in the military, and my daughter made me a grandfather just last year," he said proudly. "My grandson's name is Schmuel, after your father, Kenna."

"*Mazel tov*," Hunt said.

"Little Sam, huh? Please tell your daughter thank you from me. It means so much."

Uncle smiled and glanced down at the tiny microfiche in his hand, then limped to the microform reader. The limp would forever remind her what sacrifices the Greatest Generation had made so that her generation could be born; so that she could become Steel Eyes. Old Uncle's story of being rounded up by the SS was not an uncommon one. However, like some Jewish people, he had been lucky enough to survive the atrocities of the camps.

This particular story told of an eighteen-year-old French Jewish boy named Menachem, who had jumped from a Nazi train, along with other boys and girls, as it sped its way toward Auschwitz. The Nazis had stopped the train and pursued them through the woods, firing upon them relentlessly. Of the eight Jewish children who had jumped, only Menachem and two others had survived, while the others were shot and left for the vultures.

Menachem had taken a bullet in his leg, and with the help of a beautiful Polish girl, they walked for two days behind enemy lines in Germany before a farmer took them in. The bullet had been lodged in his hamstrings, and the Polish farmer who removed it had gained his surgical skills from the animals he had raised and tended. The farmer stemmed the ensuing infection, and had it not been for him, Menachem would have had to have the leg amputated, or he would have just been another casualty of war. He married the girl after the war, but she died in childbirth, her delicate body having suffered one atrocity too many.

Meticulously, Uncle placed the fiche facedown between the pieces of glass and inserted it into the fiche tray. Adjusting the size of the image, he invited Kenna and Hunt to read along with him. The very first item was a letter from Sam and Dalia Waverly to their only child Kenna. Uncle read it aloud.

Darling Kenna,
If you are reading this, it means that we did not survive our mission. By now, you are much older and hopefully you have found your way past the tragedy that you so did not deserve. In the event this

*has happened, know that you were left in the care of those who loved
you as we did.*

*The Van Bourgeades are your family and will always be. Uncle
Menachem rescued us from behind German lines in World War Two,
and he is also part of your extended Jewish family. You can always go
to him. With this letter comes the responsibility of the reader, the last
of our trio, to tell you what really happened to us. By now, you are old
enough to know.*

The letter went on to say that her parents were assassinated
by people who wanted to see the demise of Israel during the
Cold War, and that due to her parents' efforts, she would always
have a home in Israel if she needed one. Uncle continued
reading from a list of people who would forever be in Sam and
Dalia Waverly's debt. The letter concluded with all the love
in the world the Waverlys had for their one and only precious
daughter.

Kenna chugged the snifter of cognac and felt it burn all
the way down. She moved to the château's nearest window and
stared out at blackness. Hunt came up beside her and put his
arm around her shoulder.

"It wasn't an accident," she said in disbelief. "Some bastard
killed my parents, and I want to know who it was."

"Kenna," Uncle began, "that's precisely why your father
had us wait so long to read this. He didn't want your life to be
saddled with anger and vengeance. Grief was bad enough. He
fought so that you would have a peaceful life, a good life."

Kenna turned to face him and spoke quietly. "I want the
sonofabitch who took them from me, Uncle. Who is he, or she?"

Uncle refilled her cognac and engaged her stare. "I don't
know."

Pierre, the chauffeur and valet, knocked and entered the
room. "Dinner will be served in five minutes," he said in French.

"Come, children, let's adjourn to the dining room."

Kenna's heart was heavy. She thought about it. Some
anonymous agent had deliberately killed her parents, leaving
her with the lifelong anguish of growing up an orphan. Here

she was, a trained Mossad operative, and she wasn't permitted to seek revenge? Where was the justice in that?

Uncle put his arm around her shoulder and walked her out of the library. "Something smells very good, and from the looks of you, you could stand to put a little meat on those long legs."

Dinner smelled delicious, but it wasn't until she started eating that Kenna's appetite returned. She burned so many calories during her shows that between being unable to perform on a full stomach and not wanting to eat much afterward, she struggled to keep her weight up while on tour.

"Uncle," Hunt began, "when we retrieved your instructions today at the Jardin du Luxembourg, there was a woman that Kenna recognized from Los Angeles."

"Who is she?"

"I don't know her last name, but her first name is Maddy and she has very blue eyes. *Very* identifiable electric-blue eyes," Kenna said. "She looks German. About five foot seven, dirty-blond hair and a pointed nose."

Uncle swirled his glass of wine and thought about it. "The ERR. Do you know of whom I speak?"

Hunter thought for a moment. "Einsatzstab Reichsleiter Rosenberg. They were the main Nazi agency that looted cultural art in Nazi-occupied countries."

Uncle nodded. "You know your history."

"How does that tie in?" Kenna asked.

"I knew a woman during the German occupation with electric-blue eyes and the pointy nose like you describe. She was one of our German assets. If memory serves, she was the wife of Heinz Messerschmidt, the Gestapo officer in charge of confiscated materials. Yes, I remember her."

"What became of her?" Kenna asked.

"I don't know exactly. Her job was to steal the lists of artwork and cultural items the ERR confiscated here in France...much of it from Jewish families. She then passed lists to the Allies. Investigators have used that information for years to track items and return them to their rightful owners."

"Uncle, what else is on that microfiche with Sam and Dalia's letter?" Hunt asked, breaking off a hunk of the fresh baguette.

"After dinner we'll have a look. But right now, you *must* taste the quenelles and have some wine from my vineyard."

Kenna took a long sip of the Sancerre. "Uncle's right, Hunter, you *have to* taste this wine."

Shifting the conversation to their everyday lives, they spent the rest of their mealtime catching up on the present, reminiscing about the past and telling a few good jokes. The spaces were filled with the art of eating a French meal, which was as significant, if not more so than the art of cooking it. When they finished dessert, they reentered the library and closed the door. Uncle pulled a big book off the shelf and handed it to Kenna.

"A photo album?" she said as she sat down and opened it.

Hunt brought Kenna a brandy and sat on the sofa next to her. "Who are all these people?" he asked.

"Have a look through there to see if anyone looks familiar to you. They are some of the assets and agents, past and present that we know about."

Kenna and Hunter studied the faces as they turned the pages. Many of the photos were old and in black-and-white. Midway through the album, at the same moment, they both spotted the color photo of a woman.

"The eyes and the nose, Hunt. They look just like Maddy's, don't they?"

Hunt didn't have to think about it. "They're so unusual that they're unmistakable. Uncle, have a look."

Uncle put on his glasses and concentrated on the face. "Her first name escapes me at the moment, but she is the one I was telling you about over dinner. Frau Messerschmidt."

"So she was on *our* side," Kenna said.

"Yes. She hated what her husband had done, and she was almost solely responsible for saving our cultural treasures."

"I wonder how she's related to Maddy," Hunt said.

"The resemblance is uncanny. I'd guess this is her grandmother," Kenna said matter-of-factly. "Maddy must be carrying forward some family business. How did Maurice fit into this?"

Uncle's smile was nostalgic. "For a while, Maurice and your father were that part of the military called the Monuments Men. They were fine arts officers attached to the armies whose job was, if possible, to find the art and the documentation about it when they invaded the German strongholds."

Uncle puffed on his extinguished pipe and continued. "After the war, as a famous photographic authority, Maurice examined certain artworks, often photographing them and documenting their provenance. He had access to confidential items from all over the world. While he compiled the items for various authorities and governments, he secretly copied everything, and then the intelligence agencies distributed that information to assets all over the world for recovery."

"Hmm."

"What are you thinking, Kenna?" Uncle said.

"In Los Angeles, Maddy's involved in the art world. Come to think of it, she was the one who got Alex Winthrop a photo exhibition at that gallery years ago."

Hunt chimed in. "The exhibition where Alex and Maddy went through all my father's photographs to choose the subject matter. That's just great."

"What if his catalog photos of stolen art were in with his things? Oh shit, Hunt. Maddy had access to your father's photo library and I'd bet she used Alex to gain access to your father's work. I told you she was a creep."

"If she's involved in any kind of black market art, this can't be good," Hunt said. "I hate to say it, Wave, but given her family's history, she could be perpetuating the sale of stolen art."

Uncle lit his pipe and drew in three quick puffs. "On the other hand, it's possible she's a provenance investigator—you know, trying to locate items and return them. Those people often work undercover. Then again, if she takes after her Gestapo grandfather, she could be a lot more dangerous than that. Who is this Alex that you mention?"

Hunter and Kenna glanced at each other.

"My ex-girlfriend," Kenna said dismissively. "She was Maurice's protégé."

"I see." Uncle digested the information. "Well, shall we have a look at the rest of the microfiche?" He located the next documents with Kenna and Hunt looking over his shoulder. They scrolled across the pages and scanned through the extensive photo archive of stolen art and the detailed descriptions.

"My dad was quite a guy." Hunt sighed. "I hope I'm half the man he was."

"Yes, Hunter, he was quite a guy, and I miss him, Sam and Dalia very much. But, children, as you have learned, life goes on because, quite simply, it must. Here we are together, and I am so happy to see you both. You will be receiving copies of some of these photos, and I would ask that you keep your eyes open for any of the stolen items. Their intrinsic value far outweighs the monetary value. To that end, you will need to break into an art vault in Paris to take photos to add to the ongoing catalog. You'll then leave the Minox film at the dead drop."

"Where's the vault?" Kenna asked.

"In the basement of an old church in the tenth arrondissement. The good news is there are no guards. The bad news is it's on a very quiet block around the corner from the police station."

"And the French authorities have never gone to examine the vault?"

"Perhaps, but they have no interest in recovery, and I'm not sure I trust what they say was...*or wasn't* there."

"I'll take care of it," Hunt said.

Uncle's grandfather clock chimed at eleven o'clock. "Oh my, look how time has flown," he said.

The three of them stood.

"Young man, you will give your mother my best and tell her it's her turn to call?"

"*Oui*. She told me to ask you to send some wine. Is that some kind of code?" Hunt teased.

"A gentleman agent never tells," Uncle replied.

They hugged, and Uncle's paternal grunt made Hunter smile.

"I suppose you had better get back to Paris before it gets any later, young lady." He kissed Kenna on the forehead. "You need to rest up for your show tomorrow night. Perhaps one of these days I will catch one of your Steel Eyes performances. I've heard such stories about them…" Uncle laughed heartily. "I would really like to see you do all those things I read about!"

"You know about all that craziness?" Kenna said, dumbfounded.

"Who do you think is providing private security for your tour?"

Kenna's eyes grew wide with surprise. "Uncle! Really?"

"We take care of our own, don't we?" He chuckled.

"Yes, we do." She smiled at him. "I would love for you to see the show. Hunt can arrange for you to watch from backstage."

"Aren't I a little old for your crowd? I haven't been to a rock and roll concert since the Beatles, and I was old back *then*."

"Well," Hunt said, "you're due!" He pulled two VIP tickets and backstage passes from his inside coat pocket. "Frankly, I was hoping we would get around to this."

Uncle took the tickets, a full smile on his face. "*Fantastique!* But remember, we can't have any personal contact. I'm too old to run from the bad guys, and I don't want to blow your cover."

* * *

Hunt drove leisurely from Chantilly back to Paris. Fourteen kilometers had passed before Kenna spoke softly in the hum of the darkened Renault.

"I want to know who killed them."

Hunter reached over, placed his warm hand over hers and said nothing.

CHAPTER SIXTEEN

The next night, greeted with applause from her adoring VIP fans, the magnetic Steel Eyes made her grand entrance to the VIP after-concert party from a private elevator. Close-up situations like these were the reason for the blue contact lenses and the altered voice. She cleared her throat. Her vocal coach had taught her well about changing the pitch and cadence of her speech in such a way as to protect her vocal cords *and* her identity. She had been doing it for so many years now, the subtly altered voice was as natural to her as her own.

Working her way across the room toward Mel, she schmoozed with her guests, shook hands and signed some autographs.

"Hey, Mel, great show."

"You too, Steely." They hugged.

Mel reached for the hand of the tall, wispy brunette standing behind her and pulled her a step forward.

"Steely, this young lady has been dying to meet you. Her dad is in charge of our European distribution." Mel batted her eyelashes at Steel Eyes, which in Mel nonspeak meant something approximating, *She has a crush on you.*

"Hello." Steel Eyes smiled as she extended her hand.

Starstruck, the girl stared down at it.

"It's okay, you can shake it." Steel Eyes laughed. "What's your name?"

With a frozen expression on her face and still no answer, the girl just stared at the hand.

"Her name is Cathérine," Mel said.

"*Bonsoir,* Cathérine."

Cathérine finally shook Steel Eyes's hand. "I'm sorry, I think I'm in shock," she said with a thick French accent. "I'm not usually this stupid…not even in English. *Usually.*"

Delighted, Steel Eyes engaged her stare. "Have a drink, Cathérine, it will steady your nerves. Mel and I have to go say hello to some people, but how about if we chat afterward?"

Cathérine shook her head. "No. Not if I'm still this stupid."

Steel Eyes laughed harder this time and then touched Cathérine's arm. "Don't leave, okay?"

Speechless, Cathérine nodded.

Mel and Steel Eyes carved a trail amid record producers, industry insiders, and French glitterati with the precision of a sushi knife, then they split up to work them in groups. Rich and JJ had already hightailed it out of there, and Mel wasn't far behind. The three of them were determined to sample the private after-hours clubs behind the Champs-Elysées. Steel Eyes escorted Mel to the door when she left.

"I'm off to meet the guys. You okay alone?"

"Sure, Mel. See you tomorrow." She turned to find Cathérine in the throng.

With the height of her boots under her long legs, it was easy for Steel Eyes to survey the crowd. She scanned the room twice, then she looked harder, about to give up right before she discovered Cathérine's solitary silhouette on the terrace. As Steel Eyes made her way across the room, she garnered two shots of Absolut Vodka from the bar.

"Jean Claude," she whispered in French to her bodyguard, "please see that no one disturbs us on the terrace."

"*Oui*, boss." Fair-haired and built like a Marine, Jean Claude emitted an aura of intimidation. No one got close to Steel Eyes unless he let them. He opened the door to the early twentieth-century stone veranda for her, and Steel Eyes sauntered through it.

Catherine turned when she heard the door open, and their eyes locked.

"Here, this one's for you," Steel Eyes said, handing her the shot glass of vodka.

"*Merci, Steeleyez. Santé.*"

Steel Eyes loved the sound of her name in the heavy French accent; all one word, the emphasis on the word *eyes*. Steel*eyez*.

"*Salud*," she replied. They clinked glasses and downed their shots, reacting with the contorted faces of two people who were clearly not used to doing this.

Steel Eyes placed the empty glasses on a table and then joined Cathérine, who was leaning on the railing.

"Magnificent," Steel Eyes said as she surveyed the City of Light. "The eroticism of Paris inspires me down to my soul."

Cathérine grinned and glanced over at her. "That is exactly how I feel when I listen to your music, Steeleyez. By the way, I'm so embarrassed about how I acted earlier."

"Don't worry about it. A lot of people get that way when they meet me and…want to know a little secret, Cathérine?"

Cathérine chuckled. "A Steeleyez secret? Sure."

"The secret is…I still don't understand why people freeze up around me. I'm just a guitar player. Let's face it, it's not like I've cured cancer or saved all the homeless pets in the world."

"Don't sell yourself short, Steeleyez. You inspire people to do those very things; you've inspired me." She nodded emphatically. "Oui, it's true. And you donate to animal causes around the world…I read it in—it might have been *Paris Match* magazine."

"Thank you, that's very kind of you to say."

Silent, they stared out toward the amber-lit, tree-lined Champs Elysées.

"So, Cathérine, what do you do here in Paris?"

least the lap dancers were honest about who they weren't, barely honest about their own attraction for the client. But for Alice—whose hot breath she loved feeling on her for days after their encounters. She knew Alice wasn't her name.

Alice wanted Kenna, enticed her with every *disallowed* move the strip club. "I'm not supposed to do this," Alice would whisper, each time. Then she would perform some new act of seduction on Kenna, simulating what sex with her would be like Kenna would simply let it happen—teasing Kenna relentlessly until Kenna finally reached out for her and gave Alice what she wanted.

Kenna treasured how Alice's slender and muscular ass felt in her grip when Alice straddled her and pressed her round, naked breast to Kenna's mouth. Wordless, grinding, with hot, erratic breath on Kenna's neck, Alice knew how to win. Then Alice would move in for the kill shot with two words only. "Touch me." Every girl Kenna had ever touched wanted her to do it again.

Men were kicked out if their hands so much as left the couch.

As dark as the VIP room was, Alice and Kenna still gazed into each other's eyes when Alice was on her knees staring upward, pressing her lips against Kenna's thigh. What Kenna really wanted was forbidden…but she fantasized about it anyway— the one time they had almost kissed.

Sometimes Kenna just had to have her. Still, she wouldn't allow it to go beyond the strip club. At those times, she tossed an extra hundred on the table afterward instead and left. Alice was the only one who could make Kenna feel anything at all, and they both knew it.

But this was totally different. To Steel Eyes, Cathérine's sensuality felt like a rush of heat every time their eyes met. She reached forward and gently stroked back Cathérine's bangs. In that moment, she could imagine their lips meeting, sizzling in the way her fingers melted the strings of a Spanish guitar when she played a Brazilian samba in the dark.

Cathérine leaned closer. "And if I were *agitée*, Steeleyez?"

"I'm a bartender at Agitée. In Engl...
"restless"...written in the feminine because...

"Agitée," Steel Eyes repeated. She sp...
agitée, Cathérine?"

Cathérine turned to face Steel Eyes, the...
her dramatic black bangs across her viole...
instant they were alone on the veranda, Stee...
was about to break the biggest and baddest ru...
someone home as Steel Eyes. This would be o...
time in three world tours she had done it. But s...
didn't have *this* girl, now, right now, she feared...
survive her loneliness. Her raw connection with C...
urgent, and even if it was only for one night, she...
needed to keep feeling whatever this was.

Steel Eyes didn't expect this. Normally, if she wa...
company, she would do that as Kenna Waverly; just...
who happened to connect with some other girl. Then t...
the strip clubs—the intimate lap dances with Alice's h...
on her neck as she straddled Kenna, wanting *her* too...
for an instant, Kenna could taste that passionate anim...
core self. Always paying triple the asking, always accepti...
artful reality of their deceptive illusion, always respectin...
fractured touch and the women who served it to her—one...
at a time; sometimes even to a Steel Eyes song.

But Cathérine came out of nowhere, and she had made S...
Eyes laugh with her unpretentious, self-deprecating attitu...
and warm wit.

Usually, when she met women as Kenna Waverly, sh...
would tell them she was a music tech for the Steel Eyes Band
and that she'd only be in town for a few days. It got messy.
Women pressed her for personal Steel Eyes information and
even introductions. The fact their attention was so focused on
some mythical character when the original was in their bed
proved more disingenuous than she could bear, so she told them
whatever lies were convenient. Kenna had never kept even one
of those rock voyeurs' phone numbers. Those experiences left
her emptier than the strippers did.

"Then I would ask if it would wreck your image of me if I stepped out of character."

She shook her head.

"I really want to kiss you, but for obvious reasons I can't do that here. Would you like to spend some time with me at the penthouse? It's quiet there, and we can be alone. Your decision, no pressure."

Cathérine nodded.

"I'll go inside first and go upstairs. Wait a few minutes, and then go to Jean Claude, that man just inside the door. He'll escort you there."

"Okay."

CHAPTER SEVENTEEN

Ten minutes later, Jean Claude knocked on the penthouse door and Steel Eyes opened it.

"*Merci*, Jean Claude," Steel Eyes said as she basked in Cathérine's sultry stare. Jean Claude nodded, leaving Cathérine at the door.

"Please, come in."

Steel Eyes watched Cathérine cross the threshold and slowly gaze around the penthouse with the three-hundred-and-sixty-degree backdrop of Paris staring back at her.

"You are right. It's very quiet up here."

"It's even quieter after you've been onstage rocking out in front of thousands of screaming fans." Steel Eyes poured them each a shot of vodka and returned to Cathérine, who had wandered to the bank of long, narrow windows facing the sparkling view of the Place de l'Étoile—"the Star." Whether the twelve spokes of streets began or ended at the star's hub, the Arc de Triomphe glowed at its center.

"I love your view," Cathérine said as she took the glass.

"There are a lot of them. Take your pick."

Across the Seine stood the illuminated Eiffel Tower. To the east, the glowing roofs of the Opéra, the Madeleine and Les Invalides.

They both downed their shot and set the glasses on the table.

"There is so much here I would like to show you, Steeleyez."

"Show me, Cathérine."

Steel Eyes turned Cathérine to face her, gazed into her violet eyes and leaned into a mutually hungry, lingering kiss. The flame of exploration ignited by the meeting of their lips migrated to their hands, then radiated through their bodies into a full embrace. That first kiss lasted forever and ended too soon.

Cathérine stopped kissing Steel Eyes's neck just long enough to ask, "How does this work? Do I remove your mask?"

"Do you want to?" Steel Eyes whispered in her ear.

Her breathing uneven, Cathérine buckled under Steel Eyes's hot breath on her neck. "I wasn't prepared for that…is it a trick question?"

"No."

"So if I say yes, then I get to take off the mask?"

"Exactly."

Cathérine sensually traced Steel Eyes's lips with her fingers, stroking her gaunt cheekbones. Gently, she peeled off the hard stage mask only to find the knit under-mask beneath it.

"Do I get to remove that one too?"

"No."

The kissing intensified, their breathing hard and irregular. Cathérine pulled back slightly and spoke as she thought it through.

"I can make love to your body, but not your face?"

"You can still gaze into my eyes." Steel Eyes smiled seductively.

Sizing up the rock star, Cathérine lingered in her stare. "It's a little kinky actually, and God knows a world better than our handshake."

Steel Eyes dimmed the lights, put on the bewitching Astrud Gilberto singing to Brazilian bossa nova in Portuguese and English, then took Cathérine's hand and led her to the bedroom.

Cathérine sauntered to another bank of windows for a different perspective of the Paris nightscape. "I would never imagine you to be the soft music type, Steeleyez. After all, *you* are a rock star."

"There's a lot that no one would ever imagine about me, Cathérine." She wrapped her arms around the sultry French girl and took one step closer to the carnal revelation that would free her, that would quell her demons—that would, in the end, inspire her to play. Though she remained the woman everyone wanted to meet but would never know, at least for a little while, someone *would* know her—all of her. For just a little while, she could pretend to be in love. Maybe she could even fall in love.

Standing behind Cathérine, she breathed in the woman's scent of Chanel, her lips touching the back of Cathérine's neck, not quite kissing her, not quite *not* kissing her. Cathérine reached behind, slipped her hands onto Steel Eyes's hips and pressed against her intensity. They swayed to Astrud's "Meditation"— the guitar and the voice perfect lovers; the violins, the bed in which they made love.

Cathérine whispered, "*Chérie*, before I give myself to you, I need to know, do you have a girlfriend...or perhaps several?"

Steel Eyes chuckled and answered softly in her ear, "No, and none."

"Really?" Cathérine exhaled, pressing her neck into Steel Eyes's lips. Steel Eyes paused with her arms around Cathérine as they silently took in the splendid view, Cathérine leaning back against her.

"I know...I'm such a great catch, it's hard to believe I'm single," Steel Eyes teased. "Why do you want to know?"

Cathérine ejected a sigh. "Well, we'll see how things go... but I may want to apply for the position...or *all* the positions."

"Careful, I like a lot of positions." Steel Eyes turned Cathérine to face her, swept her in, and while they kissed hard, Steel Eyes tenderly caressed her back with her seasoned hands.

The heat of Cathérine's milky skin on her fingers as she unzipped her dress made Steel Eyes shiver with buried longing. Cathérine let it fall to the floor and stepped out of it, her thong the only barrier to her nakedness. Steel Eyes lowered her onto the bed, then took her time undressing in the slanted streaks of moonlight as they staggered through the old panes of glass.

Cathérine gasped when the rock star slid her naked body on top of her, their alchemy boiling like an elixir ready to be drunk. Cathérine's smaller breasts pushed against Steel Eyes's larger round ones.

"Oh God, you're gorgeous. You should perform naked."

"I'm about to."

Steel Eyes stroked the sides of Cathérine's hips, lightly at first, then she gripped the other woman and pulled her hard against her own body, as though Cathérine were both the guitar *and* the note that would push her through the Transcendent Gateway.

"I feel like I'm dreaming." She stroked Steel Eyes's thick hair. Cathérine groaned and arched her back in a sacrificial offering to the rock goddess's altar as Steel Eyes kissed her breasts and stomach. Steel Eyes teased her with her mouth, then the curve of their bodies as their heat connected.

"Your hands are magnificent," Cathérine whispered as Steel Eyes slid inside her. "Take me, Steeleyez."

She did.

Out in the world, Steel Eyes was unreachable, untouchable. But here, naked except for the mask and Brazilian jazz, every cell in her body longed for this girl. Here and now, she ached for Cathérine's touch.

Steel Eyes reached into her night table drawer, took out a small bag of toys and laid it on the bed. She smiled at Cathérine and unzipped the bag. "There might be something in here you'd like."

Cathérine rolled on top of Steel Eyes and kissed her everywhere, lingering, luscious kisses that transported the rocker to heights she now only wrote hit songs about and vaguely remembered, to heights she hadn't experienced in a very long time. Too long a time.

Just when Steel Eyes thought Cathérine had moved on, she would go back to the places the woman in the mask had responded to most. Her warm and talented mouth harnessed Steel Eyes until she surrendered to it, and then surrendered to it again. Cathérine pulled out the strap-on from the bag Steel Eyes had placed on the bed.

"I'm starving for you," Steel Eyes breathed when Cathérine moved between her legs.

Cathérine commanded her, first with her violet stare. "Strap me to every crevice inside you and crave me, Steeleyez. Do it!"

Steel Eyes pulled Cathérine inside her. Glistening beads of sweat trickled down Steel Eyes's cleavage. With each fragmented breath, she succumbed deeper to Cathérine's will, until, breathless, she had no will of her own left.

"Cathérine…" Steel Eyes expelled the name from the precipice of her breath as the last drop of her longing escaped.

Spent, they lay in the quiet, holding each other, Cathérine stroking the long hair, then the sinewy hands that had ravaged her deep and late into the night.

"Close your eyes," Steel Eyes said softly. "Are they closed?"

"Oui, chérie."

Steel Eyes silently peeled off her under-mask in the sanctuary of darkness, took Cathérine's hand, and after kissing it, she placed it gently on her cheek. She craved the sensation of this woman touching her most private part—her face.

Cathérine caught her breath the instant her hand touched Steel Eyes's skin, and Steel Eyes breathed in the scent of abandon.

"Keep your eyes closed, Cathérine. You want to know what I look like; let your hands show you."

Cathérine traced her features so delicately that an unnoticed tear escaped from a completely naked Steel Eyes. To have a lover touch her face *and* Steel Eyes's face was unprecedented.

"*Tu es si belle.*"

"Sorry, I don't understand."

"I said, you are so beautiful."

"As are you. I wish we could stay like this, then go out for breakfast at a cafe...stroll along the Seine...hold hands in the Marais. I hate that night is abandoning us. I hate it."

"I would say *oui* to that date. What is stopping you?"

Steel Eyes sighed. "Fame."

"It's a big price to pay, Steeleyez."

"*Oui, chérie*, and the price has only gone up since we met." Steel Eyes slipped the under-mask back over her face, rolled on top of Cathérine and passionately kissed her, etching the moment deep into her own memory.

"May I ask if we'll see each other again?"

"If you only knew how much I want that. I just don't know how. Would you give me your phone number in case I can figure it out?"

"That depends, Steeleyez."

"On what?"

"If you're asking me just to be polite—you know, to not hurt my feelings—then the answer is, absolutely not. If, however, you're asking me for real, then *oui*."

Steel Eyes snuggled against her. "I'm asking for real."

Cathérine's voice turned light and playful. "May I have a souvenir of our night together?"

Steel Eyes clenched her jaw, her voice a little taut. "What kind of *souvenir* do you want?"

"One last kiss."

Steel Eyes's jaw relaxed and she smiled in the dark. "You won't remember the five thousand other kisses?"

"Yes, but I want to remember the next one...just in case it's the last one."

Cathérine left shortly before dawn. Steel Eyes fell into the deepest sleep she'd had in years until someone banged on her door a few hours later.

"Hold on." She wrapped herself in a robe and wiped the sleep from her eyes as she padded to the door.

Hunt stormed in. "Are you out of your fucking mind!"

"What are you talking about?"

"You brought a girl up here? As Steel Eyes?"

"I'm not discussing this with you," she said quietly. "It's none of your business."

"It's *exactly* my business, and it's *your* business too."

"Calm down. It's healthier than obliterating my loneliness with alcohol or drugs."

"If you wanted company, we could have arranged something for you as Kenna Waverly, but certainly *not* as Steel Eyes. What were you thinking, Wave?"

Kenna yawned. "I was thinking, 'Oh I ought to do this so that Hunter can make my life hell.' As for an *arrangement*, you know that only leaves me feeling empty. This girl was different."

"Oh?"

"I had no intention of being with anyone, but when I met Cathérine at the party, I *felt* something. I actually felt *something*. There was a real connection, even if it was only for one night. Hunt, I haven't felt that connection in a very long time. You know how long. Not since Alex. One night with this girl was a lifetime compared to the six months I dated Brooke in LA."

"You're serious."

"Yeah, I am." Kenna ran her hands through her hair. Cathérine's scent was all over her. It hung on her skin as her own. "I'm going to shower now, get some coffee and use my day off to walk along the Seine and think...*alone*."

"Fine," Hunt said. "I'm just trying to protect you. It's what brothers do."

"I know, and I love you for it, Hunt. But this time, it's my call."

Kenna returned to her bedroom and washed the fake color from her hair until her natural ash color came through. Before she left for the day, she made an entry in her road journal.

I'll fall in love with you and be your inspiration
You can fall in love with me and be my salvation
Through the night

In the City of Light
For those few precious hours
You were the love of my life.
We may never know
But I'd bet it to win
That we both went somewhere
We've never been.

CHAPTER EIGHTEEN

Later that afternoon, Kenna was lying in bed smoking a cigarette, staring at the ceiling when Mel tapped on her door using their secret knock.

"Come in, Mel."

"Where have you been all day, little sister?"

"Out walking. Thinking. I started out at Père Lachaise Cemetery to pay my respects to Jim Morrison, then spent the rest of the time walking along the Seine, thinking of a certain girl."

"I *heard* you had company last night."

"I did. How did you find out?"

"I thought Hunt was gonna burst a blood vessel in his head when he told me."

"Yeah, well, she was worth it."

"You don't say. Hmm, I've never heard you say that before."

Kenna glanced over at Melanie, whose smile was about to rupture. "What, Mel?"

"I'm glad you asked," she said as she plopped onto the bed next to Kenna. "I met the sweetest guy last night...*Michel*. He has no idea who I am. He bought me coffee and a pastry in one of those cute little cafés on the Left Bank. Coffee and a pastry! I can't remember the last time a guy bought me a Danish, or whatever the hell they call them over here. I'll tell you, it beat the hell out of the LA groupies who try to impress me with those fancy restaurants and lines of cocaine."

Kenna laughed. "You're acting like a teenager."

"I feel like one. I think I'm going to use the day off before we leave Paris to see him on the way out the door."

"You realize that Paris *isn't* a store, right?"

"I like this guy. He doesn't know anything about our world. It's been so long since I haven't had to question a guy's motives. I like being liked for myself. I thought of you today and how nobody knowing who you are really does make your life more real."

Kenna jabbed Mel lightly in the ribs. "Yeah, but you get all the perks."

"I thought you didn't care about that stuff."

Kenna sighed. "I don't."

"So are you going to tell me about the girl? She must be one of a kind if you were willing to take that big a risk."

"Cathérine. *You* introduced us."

"No shit? The sexy, shy French girl? Well, I'll be damned. How did *that* happen?"

"Exactly the way it was supposed to." Kenna grinned. "I wanted to crazy glue myself to her by the time she left."

"Really?" Mel was intrigued. "Who are you and what have you done with my little sister? This is not like you...at all."

"Tell me about it. She reminded me of everything I've apparently forgotten; what it's like to laugh with someone, to adore them and feel adored; what it was like with Alex."

"Do you realize that's the first time you've ever compared anyone to Alex?"

"I compare *all* of them to Alex. Cathérine's just the first one to set a new standard."

"Jesus, you're in trouble, girl."

"If I find her tonight, I'm afraid you might be right."

"You'd better think this through, Steely. I mean it."

Kenna fully understood Mel's less-than-subtle use of her alias. "Don't worry, Mel, I will. Where have JJ and Rich been all day? I haven't heard from them since before they left for the VIP party last night."

"When I saw them last, they were partying in their suite with a load of people—mostly hot girls."

Kenna scoffed. "I'm glad they're having a good time, but why is it okay for the guy rock stars to whore around while we would be trashed if we did that?"

"I know. It's so unfair. But people expect male rock stars to be dogs. And since there ain't a whole lot of girl rockers out there, I guess people don't know what to do with us."

Kenna thought of Cathérine and sighed. "So what are you doing tonight?"

"I have a date with Michel. He's taking me on a boat cruise down the Seine."

"Romantic."

"What are you going to do?"

"I think Kenna Waverly is going to visit the bar where Cathérine works. I need to see if there's any real connection or if I have to let it go. I envy you right now. You can go be with Michel, and I can't even be me with anyone but you, the guys and Hunter."

Mel placed her wrist on Kenna's forehead.

"What are you doing?" Kenna said.

"Making sure you don't have to call a doctor for that raging fever."

"Oh…I have a fever all right. But the only cure for it might be just beyond my reach."

"Little sister, I want you happy. Go get the girl. Go *get* the girl."

Kenna smiled. "The limb I've been clinging to could snap if I don't, Mel."

"I know," Mel said softly. "You know I get you…I *so* get you."

"You always have."

Two hours later, stripped of Steel Eyes, Kenna left the hotel. Her long ash-colored hair, devoid of sparkles and spray-on fake color, was pulled back into a ponytail. She wore tight jeans, camel-colored boots, a V-neck Harrods of London ecru cashmere sweater and a slightly beat-up leather jacket. Her eyes were gray again, not the cerulean Cathérine had stared into during her final raging climax.

Kenna had looked up the address of the gay girls' bar named Agitée. Strolling past the taxi stand outside the Hotel Louis XIV, she took note of the upscale stores on her way to the subway. She entered the nearest Métro station like any other Parisian out for the evening. It felt good to be an *anybody* instead of a somebody. She stopped in one of the Métro tunnels to listen to a guitar player, placing the equivalent of a hundred dollars in francs in his guitar case amid the coins.

"*Merci beaucoup, madame!*" the musician said.

The Métro train door closed behind her, and she took a seat. She watched the teenagers in front of her hold hands and trade loving glances. The ebb and flow of Parisians as they came and went became rhythmic by the second stop. She liked the visual trail of the large advertisements as they sped away behind her.

*Oslo, Stockholm, Amsterdam, Antwerp, Berlin, Zurich, Milan, Barcelona, Nice, Rome, Rio and Buenos Aires, Sao Paolo...*she thought. *How different would my life be with Cathérine waiting for me after every show?*

With all Steel Eyes's wealth, she still couldn't afford the thought.

Is it really so much to ask, to find love, to be happy, to want?

Her claim to Steel Eyes was born from the heartbreak Alex had caused her. It would be only fitting if being Steel Eyes allowed her to meet the *right* woman. In some ways, she felt she had been robbed by her extreme talent. Then again, it had made her into who she was, and had Alex never happened, she might have never found her true self. For that she would always be grateful.

Life is some kind of crazy experiment, she concluded as she exited onto the Avenue de l'Opéra. Reading her directions in French as she walked along the avenue, she didn't know why she hadn't told Cathérine she spoke French—fluently.

Too many compartments, she thought. *Kenna Waverly, Steel Eyes, Mossad...fuck.*

She spotted the small blue neon sign on her right when she turned onto the narrow, near-ancient cobblestone street. Even in the damp evening chill, her palms felt sweaty, her body tightened. Standing there, she realized she hadn't been nervous about a woman in so long that she had forgotten what it felt like. This was the first time since Alex.

Stop second-guessing yourself. Go in there right now!

Before she could back out, she opened the door and walked down the steps into the warm, low-lit bar. A bar that a couple hundred years earlier was likely a wine cellar, now catered to a decent-size crowd. Off to the left, past the stone archway, she saw a little room with a few tables and a small dance floor. Intimate enclaves of women sat around tables and chatted convivially in the front room. Kenna spotted an open barstool and squeezed in.

Cathérine was clearing off a table when she spotted her, and Kenna watched her when she walked behind the bar, tasting her every move with her eyes. A bartender startled her.

"*Qu'est-ce que vous voulez boire?*" the bartender asked.

Kenna ordered her Perrier in French, in her real voice. For the next thirty minutes or so, she used her tactical prowess to cruise the girl she had come to see. Cathérine was cordial to everyone and overtly pursued by young, cute girls. Every once in a while, she made eye contact with Kenna. The eye contact soon became more frequent, lasting longer each time.

Dammit, is she flirting with me? Was Steel Eyes that disposable to her?

With a heavy heart, she picked up her Perrier and wandered into the little room with the dance floor, where she sat at an empty table. While most of the patrons remained in the other room, she watched an older couple slow dance, wondering if she would ever have the luxury of growing old with someone.

Cathérine entered the room, and her piercing bedroom-violet eyes locked on Kenna's as she approached her.

In French, Cathérine asked her if she lived in the neighborhood. In the voice unfamiliar to Cathérine, Kenna answered her in perfect French. "No, I'm here visiting. Why do you ask?"

"You seem familiar to me, but I can't place you," Cathérine replied. "How did you come to find our quaint little bar?"

"A girl I met told me about it. I'm only in Paris for a few days."

"Well, Paris is a great city with lots to do."

Kenna decided to put her to the test. "Perhaps you can show me around, or have dinner with me?"

Cathérine smiled with a dreamy, distant look in her eyes. "Tempting, but I'm afraid my mind is on someone else."

"Your girlfriend?"

"I'm not sure what she is." Cathérine's tone was deadpan.

Kenna hoped that look belonged to Steel Eyes. It took every last bit of her self-control to not reach out and grab Cathérine. But she reminded herself that doing so as Kenna could conceivably land her in jail for assaulting a "stranger."

"Are you certain we've never met?" Cathérine asked.

"Maybe in another life," Kenna said.

"No. I'm pretty sure it would be this one...I can only keep track of one life at a time."

Kenna laughed. "Lucky you." *I could love this girl.*

Cathérine reached toward Kenna's face with a napkin. "You have a smudge of dirt on your face. May I?"

Before Kenna could answer, Cathérine was gently rubbing her cheek with the napkin. She stopped abruptly when she touched Kenna's cheekbone and stared sharply into her eyes... her *gray* eyes.

"There. It was nice to meet you...what is your name, anyway?"

"Kenna. What's yours?"

"Marie."

Kenna froze. *What?* She almost stuttered when she said, "Nice to meet you too, *Marie*."

Kenna walked briskly to the Avenue de l'Opéra and hailed a taxi. Within minutes she was knocking on Hunter's door.

"Come on in, Wave. I'm surprised to see you here. I thought you went out tonight."

"I did. But I came back because we need intel on someone, now."

"Who?"

"You're not going to like this at all. The girl I was with last night. When Mel introduced me to her, I was told her name was Cathérine and that her father is in charge of our European distribution."

"That would be André Bernard. I know him. You slept with André's daughter?"

"Yes, but that's not the point. Cathérine told Steel Eyes where she tends bar, so tonight I went there and met her as Kenna."

"What's the problem? She didn't recognize you, did she?"

"I'm not sure, Hunt. But that's not what freaked me out. She introduced herself as Marie. The girl has an alias."

Hunt scratched his head and stood. He took a few silent steps and looked at her. "Call her at the bar as Steel Eyes. Tell her you want to see her and that you'll send a car for her. See if you can get her up here so that Jean Claude can search her apartment. In the meantime, you'll have to get into character."

"I'm so disappointed…I hope I can pull this off."

Kenna went back to her room and wanted to cry. *Don't jump to conclusions.* When it came to spycraft, Kenna was a rock. When it came to women, not so much. She dialed the number to Agitée and asked for Cathérine in English.

"One moment," said the girl who answered.

"Yes, Steeleyez," Cathérine whispered when she picked up.

"How did you know it was me?"

"Because with you, I am Cathérine. To the rest of the world I am Marie."

"What? Why?"

"One would think I wouldn't have to explain a separate identity to you of all people. But it's no mystery. My name is Marie Cathérine and everyone calls me Marie. With you, I wanted simply to be Cathérine."

Steel Eyes laughed. "You're right, I can understand that perfectly. Is there *any* chance of seeing you tonight…now?"

"I thought you'd never ask."

"I'll send a car to pick you up."

"I want to go home and change my clothes."

Cathérine gave Steel Eyes the address and told her she would be ready in an hour.

As soon as she hung up, she went to Hunt's suite.

"I just hung up from talking to André," he said. "I told him that Steel Eyes wanted to send something to his daughter but needed her name and address. It's Marie Cathérine."

"Sorry, Hunt, false alarm."

"With what we've seen, Wave, suspicion is our life preserver."

"You realize that it's you, not me, who invited a girl home with Steel Eyes tonight, right?"

"Yes, I do. After tonight we're even, and you're done playing with fire."

She turned to leave his suite, then looked back at him. "No, Hunt, this girl is about to *light my fire*."

"*Light My Fire*? Really? Are you channeling the Doors?"

"Yep. I had a long talk with Jim Morrison today at Père Lachaise Cemetery."

In her transition to Steel Eyes, Kenna took a few shortcuts with her disguise. She quivered at the thought of another night with Cathérine. Wearing her under-mask and blue contacts, she sprayed the temporary color on her hair, forewent the sparkles and dressed in black jeans and a blue silk pullover to bring out her eyes.

Room service had already set the table with fine linens and food. Large silver-covered servers reflected the glow of a dozen candles, their domes amplifying the candlelight. With the rest of the lights in the room dimmed, the candles were the brightest among them. When the doorbell to the penthouse rang, Steel Eyes counted to ten in the time of five before answering.

"*Bonsoir*, Cathérine."

Cathérine entered, her sexy gaze panning the elegance, the candles, the care and detail Steel Eyes had used to create the romance she stepped into. She dropped her purse and coat where she stood and closed the space between them.

"Every breath since I left has belonged to you," she said before she planted the kiss of the decade on Steel Eyes's smoldering lips.

Steel Eyes pulled her in, and they sank to the floor where they made exquisite love, right there, below their sumptuous meal. Soft Brazilian music permeated the air, candles glowed and the three-hundred-and-sixty-degree panorama of Paris enveloped them. By the time they tasted the food, it was colder than the sweaty champagne bottle that bobbed in the tepid ice bucket.

They didn't bother to sit at the table gazing into each other's eyes by what light was left from the dripping candles. Instead, they brought the candles and food down to the floor and fed each other. Their sighs and moans were those of lovers who knew more than they could ever explain, to themselves or to anyone else.

Steel Eyes wanted to tell Cathérine to rip the under-mask from her face, but she held it in, doomed to keep Cathérine in the compartment where she had placed her. If she had met her as Kenna Waverly, this conflict wouldn't exist. Then again, she *had* met her as Kenna, but Cathérine's faraway attitude demonstrated how Steel Eyes had already ruined any chance for Kenna. One more reminder of how Steel Eyes could only win when she lost.

They ordered champagne with strawberries and fresh whipped cream. By midnight, with Paris nibbling at their feet, they found themselves in the large jet tub, drinking champagne, feeding each other the strawberries dipped in the cream. By far, the best part for Steel Eyes was staring into each other's eyes by candlelight, forever owning a piece of the other.

"I need to ask you something and I want you to be brutally honest with me, Cathérine."

"Okay."

"Do you still want to apply for the position of girlfriend?"

Cathérine's eyes opened wide. "What do you mean *still*? I distinctly remember saying that I *might* want to apply for the position."

"I know you must think that I do this with women all the time. The exact truth is, I've only ever done this once before, a long time ago during my first tour, and that was just a one-night stand."

"And I'm a *two-night* stand?"

"No."

"Why me?" Cathérine asked with the slightest tinge of Parisian arrogance.

"Honestly, I think you could be, you might be...*the one*. And I really want to have the opportunity to find out."

Cathérine stroked Steel Eyes's face and sighed. "How would we do this?"

"I don't know. Whether we do it or not, I really, really want to know how you feel about me. Not Steel Eyes. Me. You can be honest, baby; tomorrow I'm in Berlin."

Cathérine dipped a strawberry in the cream and fed it to her while staring into her eyes. "I fall more in love with you every time I breathe." She smiled. "But I have an important question. And this one is a deal breaker. Would you *ever* take off that mask?"

Steel Eyes laughed hard. "Yes. Gladly!"

"How would it work?"

"I would ask that while I'm on tour, you come with me."

"When would I see you? You perform, you do interviews, you hide your identity. Where would I fit into a world where I can't be with you when you're...this? And on tour, aren't you always this? I mean, do you ever go out as whoever you are?"

Steel Eyes became painfully quiet until after Cathérine kissed her. "You're right. I'm sorry. Whatever we feel for each other would be shattered piece by piece until you were lonely and miserable. I could never do that to you." Steel Eyes sighed hard. "I want you to know...if I ever had the chance, I would fall in love with you."

Cathérine kissed her exactly the way Steel Eyes wanted to be kissed and then got out of the tub. She put on the terry robe and held up a towel for Steel Eyes, wrapped it around her, held her close and inhaled the fantasy of one more night, of one last time.

Naked, they slipped between the sheets of the big warm bed and filled every precious second they had left, passionately declaring all the moments in time that stood still, just for them.

By the time they kissed goodbye, all that remained of Cathérine was the poignant scent of Chanel and another hit song: "If I Ever Had the Chance (I'd Fall in Love with You)."

If I ever had the chance,
I'd fall in love with you,
In the City of Light
If just for one night
You were the love of my life.

All through the night
In the City of Light
You fell in love with me too.
The moment we met
I knew
I'd always remember you.

If I ever have the chance
It's true
I'd love to fall in love
With you.

CHAPTER NINETEEN

Weary from almost a year on the road, playing to audiences whose languages they couldn't speak, the band cleared customs at JFK in New York. On the limo ride to Central Park South, the Steel Eyes Band minus Steel Eyes relished the privacy to discuss the end of their tour.

"It feels good to be back in the States," JJ said to Rich.

"I'm with you, brother. I can't wait to play our last show and go home. After spaghetti night at Kenna's shore house, I'm catching the flight with you back to LA."

"What's on the agenda, Hunt?" Mel asked.

"Kenna's already at the Plaza suite. I think you guys should get settled and rest up. Tomorrow's going to be hectic. There'll be mountains of press, so count on pictures and interviews, then you'll need to go to the Garden for the sound check and the concert. I managed to schedule the interviews for the front end, so after the concert you can just get out, go eat and then crash... for real."

"Hey, Hunt," JJ began, "I'm kinda glad Kenna's not here. I've been a little worried about her since Rio. She hasn't quite been herself."

Hunt nodded. "Yeah, I've noticed that too."

"So have I," Mel said.

"We're all tired," Rich said, "and she was like this by the end of our last tour. She'll bounce back once she has a month off."

"True," Hunt said.

When the limo stopped in front of the Plaza Hotel, the paparazzi began clicking their way to the next magazine cover shot. First Hunt exited to fans screaming from across the street, and Mel, Rich and JJ stopped to wave to them before they bolted into the hotel.

Right on cue, the concierge ushered them into a private elevator set to stop only at their floor. Once upstairs, Steel Eyes's private security would stringently maintain their privacy.

* * *

Kenna stood across the street watching the pandemonium from between the horse-drawn carriages poised to take tourists for romantic rides through Central Park.

"What's going on over there?" she asked a female fan.

"Are you kidding?"

"No."

The hipster chick scoffed. "It's Steel Eyes!" she said, rolling her eyes.

"Oh," Kenna replied. Then she left and walked a block to buy doughnuts for the gang.

"I'm sorry, miss, but you can't use that elevator," the concierge said to her when she entered the Plaza.

She flashed her special Steel Eyes Band personal security ID and rode the express to the suite.

"Hey, girl!" JJ was the first to see Kenna enter. They hugged.

"What's in the bag, Wave?"

"All your favorites...chocolate-frosted, maple-glazed, jelly..."

"Enough said, little sister." Mel reached into the bag and came up with the powdered doughnut. "Damn, I miss these things when we're abroad!"

"Me too."

"Me three."

"Me four."

"I'm so glad you guys made it on time," Kenna began. "How was your flight?"

Rich wiped the jelly from his doughnut off the tip of his nose. "Oh man, there were groupies everywhere when we got out of JFK."

Kenna laughed. "You should have been in the crowd across the street from here when your limo pulled up. We have some crazy-ass fans. Did you hear them doing the Steel Eyes chant?"

"No," JJ said. "We entered the hotel just a few seconds after we got out of the limo. I thought the fans only did the chant at the concerts."

"Not in New York, J."

"Are you okay, little sister?"

"I'm fine, Mel. Why do you ask?"

Kenna saw JJ glance over at Hunter. "Hunt, you want to tell me what's going on?"

"We're just all a little concerned about you. You haven't been yourself lately."

"Truth? I'm tired, but I'm excited to perform our last show here at Madison Square Garden. I can't think of a better place to end the tour."

"You're happy to end the tour within driving distance to your house at the Jersey shore," JJ teased.

"That too," Kenna said. "Honestly, I can't wait to wake up without this grueling schedule hanging over us."

"See," Rich said to JJ, "I told you she'll be fine. For the record, I'm tired too."

Mel chuckled. "I can always count on doughnuts to help get me over the finish line."

"Me too," Kenna said. "And guys, don't start with the 'me three, me four' stuff again."

Hunt winked at Kenna. "Well, now we won't have to."

* * *

Alex raced to open her apartment door in time to answer the phone. "Hello."

"Alex."

"Sonja? You sound terrible. Are you all right?"

"No, it seems I have a touch of the flu. There is no way I'm going to be able to do my photo shoot tomorrow."

"Who gets the flu in the summer?"

"Apparently, I do."

Alex sat down. "Do you want me to try to reschedule it?"

"No, Alex. It's yours." Sonja coughed.

"What's the job?"

"Steel Eyes. It's for *Rocklandia*'s cover."

"Steel Eyes? Are you *kidding* me?"

"No. My misfortune is your opportunity."

"What? No, Sonja, I could never do the job you could do. It doesn't get any bigger than this."

"You'll shoot it the way *you* see it. I've already told *Rocklandia* I was too sick. You've worked for them enough to know they love your work, and they know your reputation for shooting to Steel Eyes's music. The Steel Eyes Flies Tour ends after tomorrow night's concert, so think of it as the photo shoot of a lifetime. You have the exclusive."

"I'm glad there's no pressure." Alex exhaled forcefully, trying to tame her racing pulse. "You really think I can do this? I'm so nervous."

"Alex, you've been shooting famous rock musicians for years. You're known for it. Why should Steel Eyes be any different?"

Because...she is, Alex thought. "Okay, what time and what do I need to know?"

Alex jotted down all the information, took a shower and grabbed a cab for the ten blocks to the studio. Her lenses needed to be spotless, and she wanted to get there in the morning ready for the shoot. After setting up, she returned home in time to get a decent night's sleep, but her adrenaline had other plans, waking her every couple of hours.

The first time she awoke, she lay in the dark, remembering when she had assisted Sonja in her Steel Eyes shoot, right after the band's first tour.

I was such a rookie back then. Steel Eyes's only words to me were hello and goodbye. But I caught her checking me out. We had some kind of connection. I know I didn't imagine it.

Every time she closed her eyes, she pictured the amazon rock star goddess posing not for Sonja, not for *Rocklandia*, but for *her*. By the time she fell asleep, she had at least twenty different schematics for lighting, positioning and shutter settings. Ideas and themes flashed through her mind.

In the studio by eight o'clock the next morning, she cranked up Steel Eyes's latest CD while tending to every detail, even though Steel Eyes wouldn't be arriving for a few hours yet. Preparing to meet her rock idol, she wondered what intimate detail she might capture with her camera, what personal moment that had never been visible to anyone else. What picture would Maurice have looked at and approved of? She heard his voice in her head.

"Tell a story in layers, from beginning to end, without ever having to shoot the beginning or the ending."

Steel Eyes's bodyguards arrived half an hour before she was due and cased the studio, then the side rooms. They issued the all clear by walkie-talkie, and a minute later, the freight elevator door opened. Alex teetered when she saw Steel Eyes, who in that moment almost knocked her over with those blue eyes and penetrating stare.

Steel Eyes's mouth went desert-dry when she saw Alex. Her first instinct was to run back into the elevator to hide. Beads of sweat gathered underneath her mask around her hairline. Trembling inside, she knew that even if she wanted to, she could not, under any circumstances, run away. She was stuck. As Mel had taught her early on, this was one of those moments when she needed to put her big girl panties on and deal.

What are the odds? Steel Eyes thought. Then again, she knew how good Alex was, and she wasn't surprised that her talent and ambition had gotten her this far over the better part of the last decade.

"Welcome, Steel Eyes, I'm Alex Winthrop. I'm sure you don't remember me, but I was Sonja's assistant on your *Rocklandia* photo shoot after your first tour."

Lex, you look beautiful.

Steel Eyes changed the register of her voice. "I remember."

Alex got chills when they shook hands.

Steel Eyes drank in the sight of her, breathed in the scent she had missed for so long. It was the first time they'd touched since the night she had walked out on Alex up in Topanga Canyon almost ten years earlier.

Alex had no idea what the woman behind the mask looked like, but she knew from that touch what they had both felt—electricity. Steel Eyes pulled her hand away, and Alex couldn't believe she had touched the hands that ravaged a guitar like no other woman ever had.

Steel Eyes couldn't resist rattling Alex's cage. "No offense, but I thought that Sonja Savarin was doing this photo shoot."

"Sonja is very sorry she can't do this, but she's down for the count with the flu. If it helps to know, she has every confidence I'll do the job right."

"Send her my best wishes to get well soon. Where do you want me?"

Of the now-thirty brilliant settings Alex had planned for Steel Eyes, she couldn't remember even one of them. She bolted to her table, picked up the sheet of paper where she had written them down and then regained her composure.

"I've had some thoughts about using light to bring out the steel-like colors around you, especially since your costume is silver. That way the cobalt on the mask will really stand out against the black-and-gray background. Then, I'd like to do a series with some silhouettes in black-and-white to get the true flavor of the 'steel' in Steel Eyes. So let's start over here." Alex led her to the set, where the umbrellas and lights had already been set up.

Steel Eyes smiled. "Are you playing my music to impress me?"

"Not at all. I happen to be a raging fan, and I always do my photo shoots to your music"—Alex adjusted a tripod—"which Michael Jackson did ask me about when I photographed him."

"Can I ask why my music?" Steel Eyes said as she let Alex position her. She sighed when she felt the heat from Alex's touch.

"Quite simply, it inspires me. I had never shot to music before I heard you." Alex walked off the set. "Your music is very personal for me."

"How so?"

"I can't explain it other than to say your lyrics are like the story of my life. I'll bet you get that from fans all the time." Alex took her place and focused her lens. "Okay, Steel Eyes, are you ready to make some magic?"

"Yes, Alex. Let's make some…magic."

"Relax and be yourself. I'll do the rest," Alex said before cranking up "Somewhere Like You"—Steel Eyes's first hit and the song she had written for Alex when they had broken up.

Alex focused on her subject in the lens and fired off shots the way Steel Eyes played sixteenth notes—accurate, fast and confident. At one point, the stare reflecting back at her was so intense, Alex stopped clicking, lowered the camera and absorbed it with her naked eye. They both lingered in that stare just an instant too long for the moment to be nothing, but much too short for it to be *something*.

Behind the camera, Alex was as relentless as Steel Eyes was with a guitar in her hands. Turning dials and clicking buttons, she filmed the shadows, the negative spaces and the highlights of Steel Eyes's persona. Like Maurice van Bourgeade, she saw the story she was shooting, knowing her subject had neither a beginning nor an end. Each shot was like a musical note—when strung together, they told a story. Beyond the lights, behind the look and the mask, Steel Eyes was simply another subject to tell a story about. No one else had yet conjured the alchemy of an Alex Winthrop portrait, not even Sonja Savarin.

"Keep it coming, Steel Eyes. The camera's loving you. Fantastic. Lean to the left, please…a little more. Look back this way. Hold it."

For an instant, during the last part of the session, Steel Eyes looked into the camera with an expression unfamiliar to Alex, a vulnerability she rarely saw in any of her famous subjects regardless of how forthcoming they were.

This aspect of Steel Eyes was raw and base, like a back alley with a broken streetlamp in a bad part of town. Alex's camera jumped on it for the few seconds it was visible before Steel Eyes yanked it back, reining in her emotions.

Alex's lens made love to the rock star for forty-five minutes, and she didn't want to stop shooting. She wanted to keep telling Steel Eyes's story, and from what she could see, a lot of story remained to be told, but she didn't get the chance.

Hunter's assistant, Brit, entered the studio. "Steel Eyes, we need to wrap this up soon. You have a sound check for the concert tonight," she said.

Steel Eyes glanced at the side door of the studio when it opened and Silvana entered.

"Hello, Steel Eyes," Silvana said. "*Rocklandia* told me that I could come say hi." She walked up to Alex and kissed her.

"Steel Eyes, this is cover model, and my girlfriend, Silvana." Alex cringed as she recalled the night Dréa had said, "Who doesn't want to walk around saying things like, 'My girlfriend, yeah, she's a supermodel.'"

Steel Eyes tensed up when she shook Silvana's hand. "Hello, it's nice to meet you. I'm sorry, but I'm on a very tight schedule."

"Of course. I know how that goes. Break a leg tonight."

"Thanks."

"I'll see you in the breakroom, honey. We're almost done," Alex said.

When Silvana kissed Alex again before she left, Steel Eyes had to look away.

At the end of the photo shoot, Alex escorted her to the elevator. "I think you're going to be very happy with these photos, Steel Eyes. It's been a personal honor to photograph you."

"Thank you. See you backstage with the press."

"*Rocklandia* gave my ticket away to some muckety-muck. By the time they told me about it, there wasn't a ticket anywhere to be found for tonight. But I wish you a fabulous performance."

"Brit," Steel Eyes said, "see to it that Alex gets a ticket in the press box and a VIP backstage pass."

Alex's eyes opened wide. "Are you kidding? Really?"

Steel Eyes entered the elevator and turned to face Alex. From behind her mask, her fake blue eyes devoured the sight of her. Steel Eyes's body still ached for Alex, and she needed to get out of there before she lost what little progress she had made over the last several years trying to forget her. Finally Steel Eyes answered. "Really."

On the elevator ride, she wondered how long someone actually had to be an ex before you fell out of love with them.

CHAPTER TWENTY

Throngs of pedestrians clogged the Midtown Manhattan crosswalks, affording Steel Eyes time to disguise herself while Jean Claude drove her back to the Plaza in the limo. Her wig concealed her sparkled hair, sunglasses covered her face, and the costume and mask were stowed in a travel case by the time they arrived.

She passed the front desk unnoticed, but she was distracted by the photo shoot; still, as always, rattled by the effect Alex had on her. Her stomach was as jumpy as the rest of her, and when she opened the door to the suite, Hunt was sitting in the living room.

"Hey, Wave, how did the photo shoot go? I tried to reach you on your mobile phone, but these new things suck with all the tall buildings around."

She stared at him.

"What? Did something happen?"

Kenna fell back onto the chair facing him. "Alex Winthrop," she said in disbelief. "Alex happened."

"What are you talking about?"

She sat forward. "Alex was the photographer."

Hunter sprang to his feet. "How the hell did that happen, and why didn't I know about it?"

"Sonja Savarin got sick, and at the last minute, *Rocklandia* hired Alex to do the photo shoot."

"Are you okay? 'Cause you don't look okay."

Kenna yanked off the wig and scraped back her long hair. "What do you think, Hunt? No, not okay."

"You think there's any chance she recognized you?"

"No. But there was a moment when I was staring down the lens of her camera and she put it down. Our eyes locked, and I thought she was going to kiss me. I swear, Hunter, I almost ripped off my mask and kissed her."

"Oh no. That is not good…especially when the person you do it in front of has a loaded camera and takes pictures for a living. What stopped you?"

"You know that supermodel…shit, what's her name? Silvana."

"Who *doesn't* know her?"

"She came into the studio because she wanted to meet Steel Eyes. Anyway, she strides right up to Alex, puts her arms around her and kisses her. She's her lover. I didn't need this, especially on the day of our last performance."

"Right now. You need to let this go *right* now."

"I'm tired. I can't compartmentalize my feelings anymore."

"I know, Wave. It's almost over. After tonight, you're literally home free and clear. Look, the massage therapist will be here soon for her appointment with Kenna. Go relax and get ready for tonight."

"What about the sound check?"

"Mel, JJ and Rich can handle it."

"Okay."

Alex's scent hadn't yet left Kenna's nostrils. That scent had been locked in her brain her entire adult life. Closing the door to her room behind her, she breathed it in deep. The stare Alex had given her just before putting the camera down when they were so close had made her pulse quicken. Now, she just felt hollow.

I've got to focus on the concert. She picked up the phone.

"Mel," she said when the other woman answered, "I need you to ground me for tonight, badly. I'm really scattered."

"We all feel that way. I'm coming in." Mel entered Kenna's room thirty seconds later. "What's going on, little sister?"

"Alex Winthrop replaced Sonja Savarin on the *Rocklandia* photo shoot today."

"*What?* No, let me rephrase…are you fucking kidding me?"

"I wish."

"That's such a bad joke. Do you think…?"

"No, I'm sure she didn't recognize me."

"Okay, let's process this real quick. That woman screwed you over, tore your world apart and I had to rescue you and help you put the pieces back together…some of which are still missing. Yet here we are again."

"That was a long time ago, Mel. She also made me into Steel Eyes."

"Maybe, but here's the big question. Was it long ago enough?"

"Where Alex is concerned, you know it will never be long ago enough."

"If you tell me you're ready to take off that mask and throw it all away for *her*, I swear I will have your head examined."

"You have the most unique way of cutting to the heart of the matter, as usual."

"So what's it gonna be?" Mel planted her hands on her hips. "You comin' to the gig tonight?"

"You know Steel Eyes never disappoints."

Mel chuckled. "If it helps any, just remember we're all coming to your house Friday for spaghetti night. Oh yeah and we're all staying over. How do you like that! Yep, like we don't see enough of each other."

Kenna hugged her. "Thanks for having my back."

"Always, baby girl. See you backstage."

* * *

Kenna's brown wig hid the Steel Eyes hair. Nondescript and devoid of makeup, she waited for Hunt to exit his bedroom on the other side of the suite.

"You ready to go?" he said, putting on his belt.

"Yes."

"What's that?" he said, pointing to the floor by the entryway.

"An envelope." Kenna went to retrieve it. "It's not addressed to anyone." She opened it and read it, then looked at Hunt.

"What?"

"It's from Old Uncle."

"Now? You've got to be kidding me. Can't it wait?" He took two hurried steps and she handed him the note. He quickly perused it and sighed. "I have to pick something up."

"I know, and no it can't wait."

Hunt massaged his forehead. "This is getting old."

Kenna raised an eyebrow. "No, it's not. We are."

"Smartass." He glanced at his Breitling watch. "There should be enough time for me to get the information from the dead drop and make it to the Garden by the start of the show. If not, I'll see you after."

* * *

Steel Eyes sat at the vanity in her dressing room, staring at the wall clock, wondering why Hunter wasn't there yet. She called his mobile phone.

Hunt was right when he had said these things aren't sophisticated enough to get a signal in Manhattan.

Her eyes were already contact blue, and she stared at the knit face cover on the vanity—her under-mask.

The shot glass of vodka sat to the right of the mask. Although she didn't drink often, and never before a show, she knew it would steady her nerves, something she had been unable to accomplish from the instant she had seen Alex. She turned up the stereo and listened to Dusty Springfield's velvety voice singing "The Look of Love." She smiled at the memory of Cathérine, saying to her that night in Paris, "I would never imagine you to be the soft music type, Steeleyez. After all, *you* are a rock star."

Steel Eyes reached for the shot glass. "Last show," she said, toasting herself in the mirror. Tilting her head back, she downed the shot.

She slackened the strap of the under-mask, affixed it to her face and was tightening it when Mel entered her dressing room.

"Here, let me help you with that," Mel said as she secured the mask. "Are you ready for tonight?"

Steel Eyes chuckled. "You ask that as though I have a choice. I'll be ready by the time I get out there. Here," she said, handing Mel the iconic outer mask, "help me center this thing."

The light from the round bulbs on the makeup mirror reflected off the swirl of inlaid cobalt-colored jewels on the mask. Their eyes met in the mirror.

"You okay?"

Steel Eyes didn't answer.

"Little sister, I want you to take all those feelings you had about Alex today and leave it all out there on that stage. You already own your power, so just take it back."

"That's how this all started, didn't it, Mel?"

Mel went silent.

"Okay, let's do it," Steel Eyes said as she stood and walked to the door.

When they entered the backstage area reserved for the band, Rich was finishing his warm-ups amid the stomping from the audience. Steel Eyes sat in a chair and adjusted her thigh-high boots.

"I swear I can hear the Steel Eyes chant for weeks every time we finish a tour," Rich said.

"Steel Eyes! Steel Eyes!" the audience echoed.

"Yo! Steel Eyes, get ready, we're on in five, sweetie," JJ said, twirling his drumsticks as though they were disconnected nunchaku.

Calmly, Steel Eyes peeked up at him from behind the outrageous bejeweled mask.

"Where are you, girl?"

"No worries, J, I'm right here."

"You look like you're a million miles away, even with the mask."

Steel Eyes wondered if Alex's supermodel would let her come to the show alone…which is exactly why she had given her only *one* ticket. Even after all this time, the sight of Alex ignited a compulsion to shred the notes she played. Alex inspired her to feel. It was visceral passion at its best, and at its worst.

Hunter and Mel were right. I need to channel that old shit into something I can use to dazzle the world, if just for tonight.

Comforted by the thought that Alex would be one of the twenty thousand voyeurs in the blur, her rock-animal instincts started to stir.

"Here, Steel Eyes," the tech said as he handed Ruby to her.

Holding Ruby concentrated the animal instincts; playing her sealed them. Steel Eyes performed her last finger warm-ups and focused her breath until she felt completely still inside.

"You ready, little sister?" Mel said, right before they took their places onstage behind the screen.

"Mel, remember we're doing that minor-third dip in the second verse of 'Somewhere Like You.'"

"Just like last time, little sister." Mel winked at her. "Don't be nervous, I've got this. I got it, yeah, baby…let's go, let's go. I got it!"

The announcer's booming voice resounded throughout the Garden. "New York, at Madison Square Garden for one night only, please give it up for the Steel Eyes Band!"

JJ pounded a *pop-pop* with his foot on the bass drum before his sticks made thunder on the drumheads. The frenetic boom of Mel's bass guitar slapped the beat; Rich's powerful guitar chords transported Steel Eyes, and it was time. The audience roared in adoration as Steel Eyes stormed the front of the stage and hit that one magical note—the note that was the key to the lock of her Transcendent Gateway. Every cell in her body responded to it.

"Hey, New York! How are ya!" she yelled into the mic.

She eyed her mark across the stage as she and Ruby danced toward it, the first spotlight shot designed to beam off her whore-red guitar and her impossibly cobalt mask.

Why am I still thinking?

She played hard.

Drown it out, drown the thoughts. There are no thoughts! Fuck her! Play harder!

Almost too fast to see, she unleashed the first hurricane of signature lead guitar licks that had made her into a worldwide brand and phenom. Precisely at that moment, she realized fame circulated in her blood like a poison.

The faster you move, the faster it consumes you.

Finally, she managed to vanish through the Transcendent Gateway. The one where thought did not exist, the one where all her feelings lay in a heap to be recycled and transformed into sound. She slid across the stage on her knees in a string-bending blur, drowning out the last of her thoughts by playing even harder. The voyeurs were already on their feet.

When she stood back up, her body rocked back and forth in time to her spectacular band. She jumped when she played the high notes, her sparkled hair flying around her, the picture of the quintessential rock star.

Alex is here and she's watching me right now! Stop thinking! Play!

Steel Eyes moved to the front of the stage while playing and pointed the head of her guitar down at the press pit, aiming it like an arrow at Alex. A corpus of staccato camera flashes ricocheted back at her.

One of those flashes belongs to Alex, but that's all that belongs to her!

Steel Eyes unleashed her next firestorm and stared down into the pit as she did it.

Is this version of me enough for you, Lex? Is it?

In time with the beat of JJ's solo, she walked it back over to Mel. His drums gave way to the counterpoint duet of Mel's bass and Steel Eyes's guitar. They played off each other, frying the stage, staring into each other's eyes while the audience howled.

At this point in their history, she and Mel were practically able to read each other's minds.

Mel's look said, *Come on, little sister, show 'em what you got.*

Steel Eyes smiled large and whipped the guitar neck back and forth while she hammered the notes. Her Cry Baby wah-wah pedal made them plead and cry like a human voice. When she glanced at Mel, Mel gave her the "you nailed it" wink.

Rich stepped forward and performed his guitar solo. Steel Eyes flung her guitar pick out into the audience and grabbed a fresh one, adjusted her strap, stepped on her effects pedal and moved to center stage in preparation for her trademark solo.

Crack. Something hit her and pushed her backward. Searing pain from her chest radiated down her arm and took her breath away. One of the security guys ripped Ruby off her body, and Jean Claude tackled her. When he scooped her up in his huge, muscular arms, she felt as light as helium in a birthday balloon. She saw Alex racing toward her instead of rushing out of the Garden like everyone else.

Lex! She wanted to call out to her, but she simply couldn't.

In and out of consciousness, she woke up for a minute in the ambulance, with the horrid light slicing through her retinas. She heard Hunt's voice and felt him squeeze her hand.

A quiet voice rose inside her head, a woman's voice, and it drowned out all the drama. It was Alex's voice, the last voice she'd heard before she lost consciousness…and she heard it say, "Don't go, baby, don't go."

CHAPTER TWENTY-ONE

"Hunt!" JJ called out as Mel and Rich followed him out of the hospital elevator. Armed security had brought the band to the hospital as soon as they finished giving their statements to the police.

Hunt raced toward them, his hair a mess, his eyes red from crying, dried blood on his clothes. "She's alive, thank God."

Mel hugged him hard and wouldn't let go.

"What sick sonofabitch would do this!" Rich slammed his fist into the wall. "How in the hell did someone get close enough to the stage to do this and not get caught?"

"Where is she?" Mel said. "I want to see her."

"You can't," Hunt replied. "She's still in surgery."

"Jesus Christ!" JJ raked his fingers through his hair. "Do you know the extent of the injury?" He tried to suck the words back into his mouth as he stared at Hunt's blood-covered shirt.

"The paramedics couldn't stop the bleeding in the ambulance. There was significant blood loss. It was everywhere. The bullet hit her in the left shoulder. The gunman missed his mark—he was aiming for her heart."

"How do you know?" JJ said.

"I know."

"Hunter, tell me she's going to come out of this alive." Mel was shaking, and he put his arm around her.

"I don't know, Mel." Hunt started to sob. Rich and JJ encircled them in their solemn embrace and cried with them.

As they all sniffled and separated, Jean Claude arrived with a keg's worth of coffee and a large paper bag.

"Here," he said in his French accent as they each took a container of coffee.

"What's in the bag?" Hunt asked.

"Doughnuts."

"Doughnuts," Mel said flatly.

"*Oui*. Before Steel Eyes lost consciousness, she said to me, 'Make sure they have doughnuts.' *Alors*, I brought you doughnuts."

"She knew it was going to be a long night," Mel said, shaking her head. "That crazy girl was thinking of us." She reached into the bag and pulled one out. "Chocolate-frosted… her favorite." She took the doughnut and coffee and sat in the dreadful fluorescent-lit waiting room across from the TV. While the sound was muted, large white print flashed on the screen. *Breaking News: Steel Eyes Shot During New York City Concert.*

The four of them sat and watched the footage of the pandemonium outside the concert as people ran out of the Garden onto Seventh Avenue.

Rich got up and turned the TV off. "I can't look at this right now, guys."

"Fine by me," JJ said.

An hour later, Jean Claude returned with a change of clothes for each of them. "*Voilà!*" he said. "Here are your clothes and the makeup remover you asked for."

They each took a turn in the bathroom cleaning up and changing. Hunt was the first to nod out on a vinyl love seat, propped up on his arm. As the night slowed to a painful crawl and their adrenaline waned, Mel, Rich and JJ followed suit, each of them curled up on seats that were uncomfortably small.

At three a.m., the surgeon entered the waiting room. "Mr. van Bourgeade?"

Hunt sprang to his feet, looking like a forlorn puppy. "Yes?"

"It was a little tenuous for a while, but she's a fighter."

"You have no idea how true that is, Doctor. How bad is it?"

Mel nudged Rich and JJ to wake them.

"It wasn't good. That said, it could have been a lot worse. Luckily, the bullet just missed her aorta and subclavian artery. However, it caused some damage to the axillary artery when it tore through the soft tissues. Thankfully, we have one of the best vascular surgeons, and she was able to stop the bleeding and repair the vessels. The neurosurgeon feels confident that he was able to repair some of the nerve damage. Of course, the next twenty-four hours will tell us a lot more, and it will take longer than that to assess the nerve damage in her left arm and hand."

Mel gasped and put her hand to her mouth. "No! No, no, no, not her *left* hand!"

"Let's hope for the best right now and not get ahead of ourselves, okay? She's alive and her vitals are good, all things considered," the doctor said softly. "We have her hooked up to everything she needs, and I promise she's receiving the best possible care."

JJ put his arm around Mel. "Can we see her?"

"You can peek into the ICU but that's it. She's heavily sedated and won't wake up until tomorrow, and I'm sure she'll need you then. Your best bet is to go home and get some sleep so that you can be here for her."

"Are *you* optimistic, Doctor?" Hunt said.

"For the moment. But I won't lie—the next couple of days are critical. She's in a private ICU right through that door."

"Thank you, Doc. Thank you for taking care of our girl." Rich shook his hand.

When the doctor left, they walked through the door and stood staring at Kenna through the window.

"She's as gray as her eyes," JJ said.

"Fluorescent lights make it worse," Rich added.

"You know how little sister hates bad lighting."

Hunt remained silent.

Kenna had been intubated to keep her airway open, and an IV was attached to her arm to sustain her. To the three musicians, the machines beat to a haunting, unnatural rhythm. They turned to leave for the hotel.

Hunt sat back down as the band walked to the elevator.

JJ turned around to look for him. "Come on, man, you heard what the doc said. Let's get some sleep and we'll come back in a few hours."

"I'm not leaving here," Hunt said, barely above a whisper. "I'm not leaving her side."

Mel, Rich and JJ stared at each other and then walked back into the waiting room. They flanked Hunter on the couch and covered themselves with the blankets one of the nurses had given them earlier. Leaning against each other, they closed their eyes and silently made their individual deals with God.

* * *

Alex Winthrop wandered out of the police station with a heavy heart, desperate to know Steel Eyes's status. No one could tell her if the woman had even survived. The thought chilled her to the bone, or maybe it was the breeze that blew off the Hudson River, right through her at three o'clock in the morning. The damp summer air slapped her awake as she stepped out into the avenue toward an oncoming taxi, her arm outstretched to flag him down.

"Bleecker and West Eleventh," she said when she got in.

The cabbie nodded and turned on the meter. As the taxi bounced and rattled down an all but abandoned Broadway, Alex tried to wrap her head around what had happened, glad she had already called Dréa and Silvana from the precinct to let them know she was okay. She would talk to them in the morning.

Steel Eyes shot! Jesus, how did this happen? Yesterday morning, all I wanted was to kiss her. Now, I just want to know she's alive. Someone at Rocklandia *must already be on the story. This is all wrong…why didn't I just kiss her right then and there!* She wiped the attraction from her mind when she thought of Silvana, but the pang of guilt didn't last long.

The NYPD had confiscated her 35 mm film and logged it into evidence, and she prayed one of those pictures might tell the story, maybe even find the gunman.

Alex had the door open before the taxi came to a complete stop and handed the cabbie a twenty for an eight-dollar fare. "Keep the change," she said.

She entered her apartment, turned on the shower and dropped her clothes in a heap on the bathroom floor. Bracing her arm against the tile wall, she rested her head against her forearm and let the hot stream of water pour down her spine and backside. It felt so good, so safe.

Repetitive flashes of the horrid event flickered in her mind every time she closed her eyes. With each flashback, she heard the screams, the gunshots. She saw Steel Eyes right in front of her bleeding out on the stage. It was all starting to register now, and it knocked the crap out of her. Finally, the sobs erupted and the shower washed them down the drain.

While she washed her hair, the photo shoot with Steel Eyes played over and over in her mind. *That first instant when our eyes met, there was some kind of crazy connection between us…I'm sure of it.*

Maybe it was the late hour combined with the unthinkable event, but Alex had to admit, at least to herself, that of all her celebrity shoots, the Steel Eyes shoot was her greatest accomplishment. She toweled dry and replayed the events of the concert again.

I was under the stage clicking away. I swear Steel Eyes had pointed her guitar directly at me. Why? Then, a minute or two later, that insane man came out of nowhere. He started firing, and it was all I could do to take cover, praying that no bullets would hit me. I ducked down and held the camera above me, pointed it in every direction and let the motor drive shoot until the film ran out.

The bodyguards had already tackled Steel Eyes when Alex peered through the bloody pandemonium to catch a glimpse of what was happening, but it was all she could do to stay out of the line of fire.

I ran toward her. What was I thinking! Must have been instinct.

She raked back her wet hair, momentarily forgetting about the butterfly closures on her face until the skin stretched and stabbed her. The bandage on her cheek kept the skin from splitting open again, and she had another one over her eye. She knew how deep the lacerations were by the constant throbbing. The medics had told her she might need stitches. Ready to fall facedown onto her bed, she thought better of it for fear of her bruised ribs and splitting open her cheek.

Morning came sometime around noon after a fitful and disturbed sleep. Alex checked her answering machine after she poured her coffee. "Ten messages!" She took the phone along with the cup of coffee back into bed, where she flipped on a nightlight in the dark apartment.

The disembodied recorded voice on the phone said, "First message."

"It's Dréa. Thank God you called me! Knowing you, it's probably noon…so get your ass up. I'm coming to get you and will be there soon."

"Next message."

Alex hung up. She didn't have the energy to listen to her messages. The familiar rattle of Silvana's keys in her deadbolt lock made her smile.

"Is your phone off? I've been calling you all morning!" Silvana rushed to Alex and kissed her. "I can't believe you wouldn't let me come over when you got home. Oh, sweetheart, are you all right?"

"Honestly, babe, I didn't get home from the police station until three thirty, and when I got here, I took a shower and went right to bed…I just woke up."

Dréa entered practically on Silvana's heels. "Jesus, Alex, it's like a tomb in here!" she said as she flipped on some lights and raised the blackout shades. "Hi, Silvana."

They hugged.

Not yet awake, Alex staggered toward her big sister and hugged her gently. Dréa held on a little longer.

"Don't smush me, Dré, my ribs are bruised."

"Let me see." Gently, she pulled up Alex's tank top.

Silvana gasped. "Oh honey, are you sure none of those ribs are broken? Half your back is already black and blue." She passed her hand lovingly along the bruises. "And you're all swollen. I'll get you an ice pack."

Alex turned around slowly, the corners of her mouth quivering.

"Come here," Dréa said softly with her arms outstretched. Alex resisted at first but then fell into Dréa's arms like a little kid with a skinned knee.

"It's all right, Alex, I'm here and I'm taking you home with me."

"Mom did good giving me you."

When they separated, Silvana's open arms awaited her. Silvana kissed her softly several times on her cheeks while she held the ice pack lightly against Alex's back. "Do you want me to come to Dréa's with you? I can reschedule my photo shoot," she said warmly.

"I appreciate that, Silvana, but don't worry, I'll be back in a few days. There's no reason for you to turn your schedule upside down. You have a very busy week coming up, honey."

"I love you, Alex. I'm sure everyone would understand."

"I just want to spend a little quiet time at the shore, resting."

Alex noticed Silvana hid her disappointment when she said, "Whatever you need."

"I'll call you tonight, okay?" She kissed Silvana lightly on the lips and watched from her bed as Dréa and her lover debated wardrobe choices while they packed Alex's overnight case.

* * *

New York City was an hour behind them, with Dréa's house about another hour and a half ahead. They hardly spoke a word, and Alex insisted on listening to the news station only. She turned off the radio when she figured out they weren't releasing any Steel Eyes updates. Finally, somewhere on the Garden State Parkway South, she said, "Why haven't you asked me about it?"

Dréa mustered a slow grin and glanced over at Alex. "Because there are certain things a big sister knows. And what I know about you is that when you're ready, you'll talk."

"What if you're wrong? What if I want you to ask me about it?"

Dréa's eyebrows arched with surprise. "Do you? Do you want me to ask you about it?"

"No, not really."

"Well, which is it? No? Or not really?"

"Not really."

"There were all these conflicting stories on the news, Alex." Alex tilted her chin upward and Dréa touched it softly. "Poor baby, your neck is black and blue."

Alex took her sister's loving hand from her face, squeezed it and then started to sob.

"Let's just get you home, kid, and I'll cook you a nice dinner."

"I don't know what I'd do without you, Dréa."

And just like when they were kids, Alex's big sister came through. She always came through. "It's all over, Alex. I'm here and it's going to be okay."

Alex stared out her window. "I won't be okay until I know if Steel Eyes survived. I *have* to know that she's all right."

"Is that why you didn't want Silvana to come?"

"Maybe." Alex paused. "But I think I just figured that out."

CHAPTER TWENTY-TWO

Groggy with heavy eyelids, Alex was glad to see daylight, thankful she hadn't slept through the entire next day. Chance had fallen asleep with his big orange paw on her leg, but he wasn't there when she awoke. Only seconds after opening her eyes, the nightmare came rushing back.

She steeled herself for the moment she would become vertical. Ensuring the walls were where she had left them, she planned a definitive one-hop shot back to the bed in case of gravity overload. Once the strategic moves and their contingencies were in place, Alex took the plunge. She tentatively swung her legs to the side of the bed and made it to her feet.

"Ow!" The rib pain stabbed her. She doubled over to get a shallow breath.

Aiming for the bathroom door, she sauntered gingerly toward the oasis. Water, lots of flowing, cold water splashing continuously from her cupped hands to her face. She barely managed to avoid the butterfly strips. Her eyes burned. She brushed her teeth and stared into the mirror. "Do you smell coffee? 'Cause I smell coffee," she said.

When Dréa heard Alex limping down the stairs, she turned around, wielding a pot of the aromatic elixir.

"Coffee. Yes, yes." Alex slid into a chair and held out her mug as far as her ribs would let her. As Dréa poured, she glanced at Alex, then set the carafe down on the table.

"How are you feeling, sis? You look like shit."

"Good to know I look better than I feel." Alex grunted as she shifted in her chair, took a sip of coffee and wrapped her tapered fingers around the cup.

"Thank God you called me before I saw it on the news or I would have already been on my way to New York. What the hell happened up there?"

"Everything including you is a bit of a blur right now... except for photographing Steel Eyes the morning of the concert. Where's the remote? I need to know if she survived. I had nightmares."

"The latest reports say she survived."

"Huh?"

"As far as I know, she was the only casualty. Her people put out a statement of their regret, thanking their fans for all the good wishes, but it's obvious they're playing their cards close to the vest."

"The NYPD interviewed me at length and confiscated my film for evidence."

"Why?"

"Because I was on the floor right under the stage. While the bullets were flying above me, I held the camera overhead. The motor drive zipped off I don't know how many frames, and the cops want to see if I inadvertently shot any evidence or clues."

"You did what! You put your life in jeopardy, Alex? What were you thinking?"

"It happened so damn fast, Dré, and everything was so distorted. At first, I must have been in denial...and then it was as if time moved in slow motion. But before I knew it, I was rushed out of there." She picked up the remote to the kitchen TV and was searching for a news channel when the phone rang.

Dréa answered it. "Hold on, Silvana, she's right here."

Alex smiled as she took the phone. "Hey, baby, I miss you. I *really* miss you."

* * *

The band had left the hospital around sunrise and returned to the hotel to shower and change and to bring Hunt another change of clothes. Hunter was peering through the glass at Kenna, who was still heavily sedated when a nurse approached him.

"Mr. van Bourgeade, there's a call for you at the nurses station."

Hunt followed her and picked up the phone. "Hello?"

"I have been trying to reach you since I heard, Hunter."

"Uncle?"

"Who else?" he said. "I've been so worried. I heard our girl's going to pull through, thank God. I already have a private facility set up for her."

"I'm worried too, Uncle. They said she's critical. She's so heavily sedated that she hasn't even opened her eyes yet. I don't know if it's a good idea to move her."

"Are you questioning my judgment?"

"No disrespect, Uncle, but yes."

"I understand, son. But I've already been in touch with the doctors, and we were able to safely figure out the transport. I know you're scared, but have faith, Hunter. She's one of the strongest people I've ever known."

"She's also one of the most vulnerable people you'll ever know."

Uncle sighed. "The best ones are. You'd better go…they'll be airlifting her in a while, and Hunter, we'll get her through this."

"Thank you, Uncle. I'll be in touch." Hunter knew not to question Uncle's wisdom. He had long ago earned Hunter's respect for the thousands of lives he had personally saved with judgment calls just like this one; just like the one that had saved Maurice and Sam, years before both he and Kenna were even a remote twinkle in a distant Milky Way.

Hunter made his way back to the ICU waiting room to stand vigil, where he found the band looking scruffy and sleepless, but clean.

"Here, Hunt," Rich said, handing him a bag with his clothes and a shaving kit.

"You guys made it back fast." Hunt made sure they were alone and then quietly closed the door to the waiting room. He set the bag on a chair and looked into each of their eyes as he addressed them individually. "Mel, Rich, JJ…"

"What is it, white boy?" Mel said lovingly.

Hunt sighed. "There's something you guys need to know."

"Oh my God," JJ said, "is Kenna…?"

"She's the same." He exhaled forcefully. "It's time I read you in."

"What does that mean?" Rich said.

"It means I'm about to tell you something that requires more secrecy than Steel Eyes's identity. First, you agree it *never* leaves this room."

"You're scaring me," JJ said.

"Are we understood?" Hunt was motionless and his expression was serious.

They all nodded.

He continued. "Steel Eyes isn't Kenna's only alias."

"Spit it out," Mel said.

"She's an operative for Mossad…Israeli intelligence."

JJ laughed spontaneously. "Are you trying to take our minds off—"

"*What?*" Mel said. "You mean like a…spy?"

"Intelligence officer."

"Are you out of your mind, Hunt?"

"No, JJ. The only reason I am telling you this is because there are people whose job it was to decide whether or not to fake her death after the shooting…to protect her. As it happens, they've decided to leave it up to public speculation for now, until they have her in a safe location. There's about to be a full-court press in the intelligence community to draw out both the person who did this as well as those responsible for the order.

We're moving her to a private facility for security purposes, probably within the next couple of hours."

Mel walked across the room. "Hold up. You said 'we.' That means that you're one of them?"

Hunt nodded.

Mel finished her thought. "You're telling us this because we're not going to be able to see her once you take her, are we?"

"I'm sorry, Mel, but you have to realize it's for her safety *and* yours."

"Fuck that shit! I'm not leaving my little sister. And I'm not leaving *you*, either."

"Hunt," Rich said, shocked, "you're one too?"

I owe them at least this much, don't I? Hunt thought. He knew the gravity of what he was asking of them, and his heart sank. While he wasn't authorized to read them in, these three people had been as much family to him over the past decade as they had been to Kenna.

JJ scraped his long hair back from his face with both hands. "This is incredible. Where are you taking her?"

"I can't tell you. I want to, but I *can't*."

"Well, how are we going to know how she is!" Mel said, standing tall, her hands on her hips.

"I'll call you every day, I promise. For what it's worth, remember that I love you guys, a lot, and you're *my* family too. Since this attempt on Steel Eyes's life, security will be all over you. I want everyone safe." He walked over to Mel and cupped her cheek. Gently, he wiped the stream of tears from her face and gazed into her eyes. "I love you, and I promise you, Mel, I'll make this right."

Mel nodded as she cried. Then she gazed into his eyes, disbelief written all over her face. "Spies? You gotta be fucking kidding me."

Hunt looked at Rich and JJ. "Nothing said here leaves this room, right, guys?"

"I have your back, man," JJ said.

"You need *anything*, bro…" Rich added.

"It's just for right now." He looked at Mel. "It won't be forever, Mel. As soon as it's safe, I'll make sure you see her. Okay, you guys had better get out of here before we're all reduced to a puddle."

"Not yet," JJ said.

* * *

JJ walked into the ICU and up to Kenna's bed. He stared down at her, then at all the tubes, listening to the machines' sallow rhythms. Gently caressing her right hand, he wondered if she could feel him, if she could hear him. He bent forward, kissed her cheek and whispered in her ear the only thing he could think to say. "We're on in five, sweetie."

CHAPTER TWENTY-THREE

Hunt entered Kenna's private room at the clinic holding a bouquet of daffodils and purple daisies, and a bag containing one fresh chocolate-frosted doughnut. "Good morning, Wave," he said as he laid the flowers and bag on the table. He went to her and kissed her cheek. "Your color is better today."

Lying at a forty-five degree angle in her hospital bed, she turned her head away from him and said nothing.

"How's the arm today?" he asked, as if he didn't notice her ignoring him.

"Fucking great," she replied without turning back to look at him.

"Wave, look at me."

"No."

"I can wait," he said dryly.

Finally, she met his stare.

"One step at a time. You're making tremendous progress. I know it doesn't feel that way, but you are. It's only been a few weeks; give yourself a break."

Kenna sighed. "The doctors say it could be a year before the peripheral nerves have healed enough to *guess* whether or not I'll play again. And it hurts like hell."

"You are going to come back from this, and I'm going to make sure that happens."

"Are you going to heal *for* me?" she said sarcastically.

"If I have to," he answered, determined.

Kenna shook her head. "Why do I still believe you when you say things like that?"

"Because, Wave, you know if there's a way to do it, I'll find it." He took the hairbrush from the vanity in the bathroom and returned to brush her hair. "I'm sure you want to look nice for Uncle Menachem. He's on his way from the hotel and should be here any minute. Do you need something for the pain?"

"I don't want any pain meds. They mess with my head. How are Mel, Rich and JJ?"

"Missing you like crazy. I talk with at least one of them every day, and they're all caught up. You'll be able to speak with them soon…we just have to wait until we have secure communication all the way around."

"I want to see Mel."

"You will. It's only been a few weeks, and we really need to make sure they're safe first."

"Hunt, you'd better make sure nothing happens to them." She issued the phrase as an order.

"I'm all over it, Wave. Whoever shot you wanted *you*, not them. If they had thought they could get to you through the band, they would have taken the opportunity."

The door to her room opened and Uncle walked through it. He smiled sweetly at Kenna, took an envelope from his topcoat and placed the coat on a chair. "You look good," he said to her. "Better than I expected." He kissed her on the forehead.

"It won't mean anything if I can't play again. Do we have any intel yet on who did this to me?"

Uncle pursed his lips and glanced over at Hunt. He pulled a chair over to sit next to Kenna's bed while taking in the sight of her left arm just lying there, already showing signs of slight atrophy.

"The Home Office is working on it. But I do have some information you may still be interested in."

"About what?" Kenna said.

Uncle took a photo from the envelope and handed it to her. "About her."

Kenna struggled to sit more upright as she stared at the picture. "Maddy?"

Hunt walked over to look. "You were finally able to locate her, I see."

"It seems she was very busy this past year, and, of all agencies, Interpol notified us. Who'd have thought they would have found her before we did? In any case, she was dealing black market artwork…even some cultural pieces. She brokered items that the Nazis stole. Two of the paintings were on Maurice's list."

"So she *did* use Alex Winthrop's photography as an excuse to gain access to my father's photo archives. I guess she takes after her Nazi grandfather after all."

"It might be in our best interest for you to discover a way to find out what access Maddy did have," Uncle said. "Maybe you could talk to the photographer."

"I have a better way, Uncle," Hunt said with a smile. "Mom's been looking for a new hobby. She'd *love* that assignment. Alex and she are still close. Mom even gave her Dad's Leicaflex camera."

"Well, they *must* be close if she did that. Don't sell Phyllis short. She was as good as Kenna in her time."

Kenna scoffed. "Maddy. That bitch stole my girlfriend and dealt in Nazi-stolen art! I knew she was a creep. A creep and a slut," she said irreverently.

"Wave, you wanna dial it down?"

Without even shifting to look over his shoulder at Hunt, Uncle said, "It's all right, Hunter, she has every right to be pissed off." He laughed fondly. "Is that the best you can do, Kenna? I've heard much worse in *my* time!" Uncle took her uninjured hand. "I have a suggestion that I seriously believe you should consider."

"What is it?"

"You know I have many years experience with these things, and before I say it, I want you to keep an open mind and realize that I'm making you an offer I believe will give you back your soul, if not your life."

She looked into Uncle's eyes and felt something she had almost forgotten—the loving, caring look of a father; like Maurice, like her father Sam.

"I think you should recuperate at my villa in Jamaica."

"Jamaica?" Hunt said.

"Yes. It's very private. Jean Claude will have security detail, and we can protect you there. Kenna, I have some of the very best professionals ready to work with you to come back from this. The doctor says you're fit to travel, so as soon as I receive word that everything is ready for you, will you go?"

"What do you think, Wave?"

"Can I sleep on it?"

Uncle sighed. "Your mother used to say that."

"Really?"

"Yes. Oh yes. I see more of her in you year after year."

"Jamaica." Kenna tried it on for size.

"When I call my mom to ask her to get the information from Alex," Hunt began, "I'll *gently* drop the possibility of going to Jamaica into the conversation."

Uncle smiled. "I hope you don't mind, Hunter, but I took the liberty of preparing her for that in case Kenna agreed."

"Mind, Uncle? I'm grateful! You know how Jewish mothers are."

They both turned abruptly in surprise when Kenna laughed.

"What? The bastard didn't shoot my sense of humor, you know."

When Uncle left, Hunt closed the door and sat in the chair by the bed. "So what do you *really* think about going?" he asked.

"I like the sound of it. Warm Caribbean water. Reggae. Will you come with me, at least until I get settled?"

"Of course, sweetie. I'll be anywhere you want me to be."

That night when Kenna fell asleep, she had vivid dreams, memories that surfaced from caverns deep in her limbic brain. She was a kid again, on holiday in Jamaica with her parents.

They had vacationed there so often that the highlights of those visits crammed into one colossal 'best of' dream reel.

They were having breakfast on the terrace by the ocean: ackee and saltfish, the Jamaican national breakfast of champions. Her mouth watered when she tasted the sweet, sweet pineapple known as *sugarpine*. In front of her, the blackbirds dipped their beaks into the table vases to get fresh water as they squawked, and the large plate before her overflowed with Jamaican naseberries, sweet sop and croissants.

"Here, sweetheart," her mother would say, offering her a bite of melon from her fork.

The early-morning sea called to her, impatiently waiting to wrap its endless turquoise body around her flesh, where it would shelter her from everything but itself.

Kenna awoke with a start, unable to remember the last time she had conjured her mother.

That was too real to have been just a dream.

Although she was awake, her mouth was still watering, and now she couldn't think about anything other than getting her hands on some sugarpine.

She liked the idea of having the warm sea to assist in her recovery. Uncle had been beyond generous with his offer, and she trusted him implicitly when he said he felt this would be the best thing for her. Suddenly tired again, she closed her eyes and fell asleep thinking about sailing on turquoise water, slowing herself down to Jamaican pace, where everything was "soon come," the Jamaican phrase meaning "right away." And a Jamaican *right away* was tantamount to "sometime before you die." *Nothing* moved fast in Jamaica—it was the law. She wondered if moving that slow made people live longer...or just made it seem that way.

Two days before she was scheduled to leave, Hunt arrived at ten a.m. as usual, but he was grinning like a toothpaste commercial. "You have a surprise...and you're going to love it." He said it singsong.

Kenna looked at him quizzically and then did the toothpaste grin herself when she saw the afro poking out behind him in the doorway.

"Mel!"

Mel came rushing in, ran to Kenna and hugged her uninjured side. They kissed each other's cheeks five times at least.

"Hey, little sister, you didn't think I was gonna let you roll up on outta here without seeing *me*, did you?"

"Damn, Mel…damn!"

"I'll let you have your girl time," Hunt said, smiling. "Be back later."

Mel pulled the big comfy chair up to the bed to sit as close to Kenna as possible. "How are you feeling?"

"Truthfully? Washed up, like I'm never going to play again. My left arm and hand are a mess."

"I know that's what you're afraid of, but I've known you for a long time, Kenna, and I've never seen you fight a battle where you took any prisoners, I'll tell you that much. Give it some time, baby girl. You'll get it going again. That left hand has already forgotten what most guitarists will never even learn."

"How are Rich and JJ?"

Mel laughed as she reached into her purse. "They send their love, and JJ asked me to give this to you." Mel placed the child's toy on the bed next to Kenna's hand.

"A monkey drummer?" Kenna laughed.

"Here," Mel said as she grabbed the toy and wound it up. The grinning monkey tapped his drumheads with his miniature monkey drumsticks. When he ran out of steam, Kenna sat him on her nightstand. "Have you and the guys talked about your next moves?"

"None of us want to move on to anything else. We talked about keeping the band together, and in the end, we all feel that we need a break for now. What happened to you really rattled us. Besides, the gig is meaningless without you."

Kenna's intuition told her there was more to this story. She prodded gently. "I get it, Mel, but I know you too, and I can't picture you sitting around your lovely home in the hills eating Cheetos and not playing out. You're the queen of the gig."

"I got a call from Jordy Richards. Evidently, the band Aid & Abet needs a bass player for their next tour, and they asked him to offer me first dibs."

"That's terrific! After all that Steel Eyes music, do you think you can warm up to the soul sound?"

"Shit…you know my middle name is 'Funk.' Besides, there's a certain balance to it. I mean if I went off to play with some other rock band, I'd feel like I was cheating on you all, but funk…yeah, I could make a clean start with some funk."

"Have you talked to Michel since all this has happened?"

Mel smiled the girliest smile Kenna had ever seen. "Are you kidding? That boy has been like a mother hen, callin' me all the time."

"Oh *ma chérie*, I am so worried about you," Mel did a bad imitation of Michel's French accent. "Anyway, he's flying in tomorrow, and I'm taking some time off to show him California. I really want to see if there's a chance that he and I might have a future together."

Kenna laughed. "There's that teenager again. Since the day you met that guy, even when he flew in to visit you on tour last year, you just turn to mush around him. It's very cute."

"Not to change the subject, little sister, but you and I have something we need to square up."

Kenna would have said, "What?" but she didn't want to insult Mel's intelligence. "There isn't much I can tell you, you know."

"Okay, I get that you're all tangled up in some spy shit, but why didn't you ever tell me? *Me?* I didn't think we had, or needed to have any secrets."

"This is not the time to go into a long diatribe on the subject, but suffice it to say, my job was to keep the world safe. I'm one of the 'good guys.'"

"Well, who didn't know that!"

"Mostly, I passed information, photos, and that's all I can tell you about. You, JJ and Rich were never in danger."

"I know, Hunt told us. We'll have the rest of this conversation when you're stronger, but we're not done yet." Mel shot her the 'I'm not letting this one go' look.

Kenna sighed. "I know."

Mel chortled. "My little sister is a spy. *Double-O-Steel Eyes.* Anything else I don't know about?"

"Listen, Mel, they're moving me in a couple of days to recuperate and do my rehab…in Jamaica."

"Jamaica? As in Jamaica, New York?"

"No, as in 'play me some reggae, mon.'"

"Then how will I see you?"

Kenna felt the tightness of loss in her already aching chest. "I'm going underground for a while, Mel."

"What's *a while*?"

Kenna didn't know if she didn't want to tell Mel the truth or if she just wasn't ready to face it herself. "It may take some time for us to see each other, but it *will* happen. Believe me, *they* know who you are and how close we are."

"Damn, I hadn't even thought about all the people whose radar I'm on that I don't know. I don't know how I feel about that."

"Look at the bright side, Mel. All these years we've had the best security in the world."

Mel glanced at Kenna's arm. "You sure about that?"

"There's not a doubt in my mind. Will you come visit me?"

"Yeah, *mon*. I'll be there as soon as you let me know I can come."

* * *

Two days later, the nurse wheeled Kenna to the exit, where she waited for Hunt.

"I got all your stuff," he said, carrying a big brown box. "Be right back." He walked outside the medical center where Jean Claude took the box from him, put it in the trunk and then opened the back door to the limo.

When Hunt wheeled Kenna outside, Jean Claude smiled a big, toothy grin.

"Jean Claude," Kenna began, "I believe this is the first time I've ever seen you smile. You're quite handsome."

"How could I not smile when I see your beautiful face? May I?" he asked as he bent forward to assist Kenna from the wheelchair into the car. "I am so happy to see you."

Once they were on the road to the airport, Kenna pushed the intercom button and then lowered the partition.

"*Oui*, boss?"

"I don't know how to thank you for saving my life."

"You can give me a little kiss on the cheek and rent me a sailboat in Jamaica."

Kenna laughed. "You've got it, *mon ami*."

Jean Claude laughed too. "Did you say, 'mon' or 'mon ami?'"

"In Jamaica, there's no difference."

"I'll see you both in three days," Hunt said. "Jean Claude has all the information and instructions, Wave, so he'll get you set up."

"I'm a little scared to be out in public and on an airplane."

"Monsieur Hunt, you have not told her?"

Hunt smiled. "Guess it slipped my mind. Uncle arranged for a private jet."

"Classy," Kenna said. Then she heard Uncle's voice in her head, from that night in his library in Chantilly, when he had said, *"We take care of our own, don't we?"*

CHAPTER TWENTY-FOUR

"Jean Claude," said Kenna as she sunned on the sailboat's bow.

"*Oui*, boss."

"You know, you've become an excellent sailor over this past year."

"I should hope so. A year is a long time to practice." He steered into the wind. "You should have brought your windsurf board."

"The wind is too strong way out here. It's still too hard on my arm."

"This is the best assignment I've ever had, boss. In fact, I've had thoughts about starting a charter business when you go back to...you know...your real life." The boat surfed up and over the face of a small wave. "Can I ask you a question?"

Kenna sat up and put on her hat. "Shoot."

"Odd choice of words, boss," he deadpanned. "Okay, I probably shouldn't ask, but I must. Why don't you play guitar anymore? I miss it."

Kenna stood and walked to the helm. "I can't."

"How do you know if you don't try?" he said warmly.

She repeated quietly, "I can't. We should probably head back soon. I want to make sure everything in the villa is perfect before the gang arrives."

"Sure, we can go now. But don't worry, the staff said *soon come* to everything on the list, meaning it will eventually happen." He laughed.

Jean Claude tacked wide and carved his own compass rose in the deep black water. The sails slackened, then became completely flat, and the boat rocked gently in the lapping waves as it crossed the wind. A minute later, the sails poofed full of ocean air on the other side of the craft, carrying them downwind toward home. Kenna tilted her head back to feel the salty spray surf over her warm face.

Veronica, the house supervisor, greeted her as soon as she got home.

"Everything is ready for your friends, Miss Kenna. What time do they arrive?"

"Soon come, Veronica," she teased. "They land in an hour." She fidgeted about seeing the band after so long, but there was no way she wasn't attending Mel's wedding. Technically, Kenna *and* Steel Eyes were still underground, making this scenario the best of all options. Mel was thrilled when Kenna had suggested that Michel and she have a sunset wedding on the beach in Jamaica.

Kenna smiled at the thought of how much Rich, Mel and JJ were going to love the reggae band she had hired. Hunt was flying in with them, and he and Jean Claude had coordinated so that Jean Claude could pick them up together at Sangster Airport in Montego Bay. At the last minute, Kenna decided to go with Jean Claude in the van she had rented for the occasion.

"This van will be handy for shuttling the wedding party to and from Quarter Moon, boss," he said as they passed the exclusive Quarter Moon Resort.

"I love that place, Jean Claude. It's changed so much over the years, but always for the better."

"Like us, boss!" He laughed.

"*Just* like us, Jean Claude!"

At the same moment, they spotted the eye-catching billboard just before the roundabout near the airport.

"I want to draw a mustache on her," Kenna griped.

Jean Claude sighed. "Ah, Silvana. I want to spread whatever lotion she's selling all over her. Such a beautiful woman."

"Sorry, *mon ami*, she bats for my team."

"Really?" he said, amused. "Hmm, lucky you."

"Yeah, lucky me." In her mind, Kenna painted the mustache on Silvana anyway.

Once inside the airport, Jean Claude and Kenna waited impatiently just outside customs. Only when Kenna noticed Rich's pale face did she realize how tan she had become.

"Little sister!"

"Hey, girl!" JJ yelled.

"Hey, guys!"

Rich came through the door first and swept Kenna off her feet. He gave her his best bear hug as he swung her around in a circle before he put her back on her feet. "You're a sight for very sore eyes!" he said. "And speaking of eyes, with your skin this dark, your eyes look positively dreamy. Hey, Jean Claude, good to see you, man!"

JJ was next. "Oh man have I missed you!" They kissed on the cheek with a loud *mwah*, and then Kenna messed up his much shorter but still scruffy hair.

"Mel." Kenna exhaled the name, and her eyes turned moist at the sight of her. Mel grabbed her and the two of them did the traditional "girlfriend dance"—holding hands, jumping up and down like preteens before their first date. "You're getting married!"

"I'm getting married!"

"*Salut*, Michel! Welcome to Jamaica…and to the family!"

"Hello, Kenna!" Michel hugged her, his soft black curls tickling her face as they kissed on both cheeks. "Thanks so much for hosting the wedding for us," he said with his sweet smile and charming French accent.

"Are you kidding? Missing this was not an option. You may be marrying Mel, but you do realize you get all of us in this deal, right?"

Michel laughed. "How did I get so lucky?"

"Geez, is there any love left for me?" Hunt was still the only person who deplaned in Jamaica dressed in a suit, even if he did wear it without a tie. He and Kenna hugged, stuck to each other like glue.

"You look good, JC!" JJ said.

"You too, JJ. *Mon Dieu*, you finally shaved."

Jean Claude gave Mel a kiss on the cheek. "Congratulations! You too, Michel. I remember the night you two met in Paris. *Bienvenue*. Okay, let's get the luggage into the van and go home."

"Thanks, man," JJ said as he patted him on his thick shoulders.

Kenna froze inside when she saw their instrument cases. JJ was surely traveling with his nunchaku drumsticks, ready to drum on *anything*. Getting into the van, she turned her attention away from the instruments and back to her friends. "You guys are *so* going to love the band I hired for the wedding. I have a special surprise for your walk down the aisle, Mel."

"Bring it on, little sister."

"I really like your new streamlined look," Kenna said, stroking Mel's tight-cropped hair—a sure sign that *nobody* would make it through the 1990s without a sleeker persona.

They were all so engrossed in each other that the half-hour ride to the villa took about five minutes.

Kenna led them into the beachside villa and oriented them. "The staff will show you all to your rooms, and don't hesitate… if there is anything you need, just ask. I'm pretty well stocked for this event. Oh, yeah, and *soon come* means 'maybe now, maybe later.'"

Mel shot her a look. As always, Kenna and Mel's silent communication was still intact.

"You have no idea, Mel, what it took to get real doughnuts made for you."

Mel did her little happy dance. "You have doughnuts?"

"Okay, guys, go get settled in while I hit the water," Kenna said. "See you shortly…on the veranda…for afternoon tea. Be there."

"She's living the good life!" JJ laughed as he grabbed his suitcase and followed Veronica to his bedroom.

Once everyone had disappeared into their corners, Hunt walked out onto the veranda and joined Jean Claude. They watched Kenna take off from shore on her windsurf board, sailing toward the horizon.

"How is she?" Hunt asked.

"The same. She *won't* play. I ask her why not and all she says is, 'I can't.'"

Hunt shook his head, watching Kenna's image diminish as she sailed into the distance on her Popsicle stick with the tall pink-and-aqua sail. "I hope that this is the kick in the pants she needs. Maybe with everyone back together, it will spark something in her."

Jean Claude put his hand on Hunt's shoulder. "I hope so. There are times when she won't even go listen to her local music friends play because she says it's too hard. She spends most of her time alone, windsurfing and swimming."

"It kills me to hear that, Jean Claude."

"It kills me to tell you, Hunter. Although it *is* making her strong again."

For Kenna Waverly, however, merely dreaming big was once a standalone act of courage. But a fair wind at her back on the ocean? Now that was living large. No one else was privy to how windsurfing had transformed her, had taught her how to be in the present moment, commanding the inner quietude necessary to master the forces of wind and sea. That was a private matter between her and life itself. She returned to shore and beached her board just as the gang was assembling on the veranda for afternoon tea.

The table had been set with linens and Royal Doulton china, and with the exception of the new chair added for Michel, everyone automatically fell into their usual place at the table. Like any family reassembled for a holiday or a special occasion, everyone had their special spot no matter the table, or the country in which that table found itself.

"Let he without cream pass the first scone," Hunt joked.

"Pass those tea sandwiches, please," JJ said with his arm already reaching for the triple-tiered serving tray.

"Kenna, you look like a mermaid that someone just plucked out of the ocean," Michel said. "A beautiful mermaid."

"*Merci*, Michel. So what do you think, guys? Tell the truth, do I look like me?"

Rich stuffed a piece of blueberry scone into his mouth. "No. You look better than you."

Kenna laughed and then spent the next hour listening to the details of their past year, since that horrible night that had changed the Steel Eyes Band forever—how Rich had finally become serious about studying piano; how JJ had taken up yoga and meditation after the shooting, which led him to meet an amazing woman he had been seeing ever since. The one thing they all kept coming back to was how much they all had missed her.

"I hope you all enjoyed your afternoon tea," Veronica said as she cleared the table.

"Gee, you think, Veronica?" Hunt said. "There's not even one cake left."

"I'll be back in a flash, guys. I have to wash off the salt," Kenna said. "Relax and make yourselves at home."

When she returned, everyone was on the veranda, stretched out on the loungers. Mel leaned back against Michel, his arms wrapped comfortably around her, and his curly black hair tousled by the sea breeze. JJ and Rich were drinking Red Stripe beer, Rich's bottle dangling from his hand as he slumped on his chaise.

"Come on, little sister, get your butt out here for the sunset."

A rush of warmth filled Kenna at the sound of Mel's voice, at the sight of these people she loved so dearly, together again and awaiting her.

No one uttered a sound as the honey-colored ball sank behind the black water, its streaks of orange and yellow reaching out like fingers hanging on to the puffy, muted clouds; as if the sun itself were attempting to delay the inevitable, reluctant to relinquish its hold on the hemisphere. With each passing minute, the sky lost its fight to repair its waning shade of blue.

Kenna smiled as she glanced over at their faces, each one of them more relaxed than she had ever seen them. *They just got here. Wait until they've been here for a few days.*

After dinner, Rich brought his guitar case over to Kenna, who went cold at the sight of it. He opened it teasingly and then held Sweet Jayne up in front of her. "Surprise. I thought you two must be missing each other by now."

Under the pressure of the moment, Kenna smiled graciously and took Sweet Jayne from him. "Thanks, Rich." It felt awkward to hold her again, like revisiting a childhood home as an adult, only to discover that it wasn't as grand as memory served.

Kenna carefully placed Sweet Jayne back in the case.

Mel clamped her tongue gently between her teeth and shook her head.

Rich glanced at her as a warning to not say, "Come on, little sister, show 'em what you got."

JJ sighed and passed a lit joint to Rich. After taking one hit, Rich retrieved Sweet Jayne from the case, leaned back and strummed softly.

Kenna smiled. "A ballad. Is this one of yours, Rich?"

"I wrote the music and Mel wrote the lyrics. It's called 'Astrology.'"

Mel picked up the vocals.

You look at the girls who look nothing like me
I simply look at you
No one makes me feel this way
You simply look away

If you knew how
I feel about you
Then again,
Maybe you do

I watch the night with sweet intent
Knowing it never comes true

Why do you like me
If I'm not your kind
Why do I bother
When the stars won't align
In my own world
It's magical fate
You'd better come get me
Before it's too late

Every night I swear you off
Release you from my mind
From out of nowhere
You sneak in
I swear it's the last time

Why do you like me
If I'm not your kind
How can I love you
When the stars won't align

I feel you so close
Even though you're so far
I can't hold you
So I hold a guitar

Why do I want you
If you're not my kind
When in the hell
Will these old stars align

It's taking forever
We've lost so much time
Talk to your stars, baby
I'll talk to mine

Kenna took a hit of the joint. "That was beautiful, guys. Just beautiful. Rich, maybe you should keep Sweet Jayne."

Rich smiled. "I don't think so, babe. That would make me a homewrecker."

* * *

The next day, while the caterers and decorators set everything up, the guys went out on the boat with Jean Claude. Kenna tended to Mel, taking her for a massage and spa services at Quarter Moon. She had even set up appointments for their hair and makeup, in essence doing everything a sister and maid of honor would do. By the time they returned home, they were so relaxed that Kenna had to take a nap. When she awoke, the last and most important thing on her list was to get dressed and get Mel down that aisle.

Mel peeked out from her room. "Oh my!"

Candles and soft lighting were everywhere, and the intimately arranged tables were set with fine linens, crystal and bone china. The deep mahogany furniture was soft on the eyes. A sea-breeze scent permeated the room, carrying with it the notes from the band warming up on the beach.

On the sand just below the veranda, tiki torches lined the bride's aisle, and white sashes flanked its length, draped on posts along with prehistorically large tropical foliage and bright-colored flowers. Set at an angle that would deflect the sun, the altar gave way to the most spectacular view of the bride, the groom and the sunset.

"Dig those guys, JJ," Rich said, looking down from the veranda.

"I'm digging it," he replied as he tapped out the reggae rhythm on the railing with his hands.

Veronica stood at the entrance to welcome the guests. It wouldn't be a big wedding party, but at least some family from both sides were attending. Michel's parents and twin sister arrived, immediately showing their relief when Kenna spoke to them in French. Mel's brother, parents, her aunt, uncle and two cousins arrived, and they all hugged Kenna, happy to see her again.

As the sun sank a little lower in the sky, Kenna rounded everyone up and had them take their seats on the chairs on the beach. Once the guests had settled in, she saw Michel stand at the altar, and the preacher gave her a thumbs-up. Kenna ran up the stairs to get Mel.

"It's time, honey. You look beautiful. Are you ready?"

Mel turned, her expression hopeful, fearful, happy. "I can't believe it's about to happen."

"You so deserve this, Mel. Michel is a doll and his family is wonderful, so I guess you'd better start taking French lessons."

"*Je parle francais, ma petite soeur.*"

Kenna roared with laughter at the accent but understood her perfectly. *I speak French, my little sister*, she had said. "Wow, I'm so proud of you."

"Kenna, who would have ever thunk it? While we're on tour in Paris, some guy who had no clue who I was just wanted to buy me coffee and a Danish. Something told me to say yes, and now here I am, a couple of years later getting ready to marry the guy!"

"Yes you are. And if nothing else, Michel *knows* you're a cheap date. Are you ready to go down the aisle with me to greet your handsome prince?"

"I hope so. I'm so nervous, my knees feel like water."

"Don't be nervous." Kenna straightened Mel's necklace lovingly and gazed into her eyes. She quoted the line Mel had said to her more often than not throughout her career. "Come on, baby girl, show 'em what you got."

As soon as Mel appeared at the top of the stairs, the reggae band started to play the Steel Eyes hit song, "If I Ever Had the Chance (I'd Fall in Love with You)."

"For real?" Mel whispered when she heard the first three notes. "I've never imagined this song done reggae style."

"For you, big sister, with a *slight* lyric change at the end," Kenna whispered back.

Kenna had arranged the music to be played Jamaican style, complete with a steel drum and a Jamaican music box, two acoustic guitars and a definitive reggae beat. She had changed the lyrics of the last line to fit the occasion.

The guests stood for the bride; they *oohed* and *ahhed* as Mel, never looking more radiant than in her strapless V-neck gown, sauntered down the aisle escorted by Kenna. The tasteful beads meticulously hand-sewn on the bodice of the wedding gown glistened in the crepuscular sun, cradled as it was in the horizon's bosom.

In a thick Jamaican accent, the sun-worn, craggy-featured front man sang:

If I ever had the chance,
I'd fall in love with you,
In the City of Light
If just for one night
You were the love of my life.

All through the night
In the City of Light
You fell in love with me too.
The moment we met
I knew
I'd always remember you.

If I ever have the chance
It's true
I'd love to spend my life with you.

At the end of the ceremony, the preacher joyfully proclaimed, "I now pronounce you husband and wife. You may kiss the bride."

Cheers of joy erupted, and everyone clapped and hugged as the reggae band began to play the Bob Marley classic "One Love."

Cocktail hour could have passed for a beach party, with everyone smiling, celebrating and dancing together barefoot. White-jacketed waiters served rum punch and hors d'oeuvres, and the tiki torches swayed to the evening Jamaican rhythm. When the musicians took their break to set up inside the house for the dinner music, Kenna watched her friends from the veranda.

Who would have ever guessed that JJ's knock on my door ten minutes after I moved to West Hollywood would have led to all of this!

She stared out at the ocean and thought of Alex, wondering why she *still* thought of Alex, why she had never stopped thinking of Alex, not even after all these years. Then she thought of Cathérine and wondered how things might have turned out differently if after that last tour she hadn't been shot. Glancing at her watch, she counted the time difference, and pictured Cathérine tending bar at Agitée at that very moment.

"Miss Kenna," Veronica said, "would you like us to seat the guests now?"

Kenna nodded. "Thank you, Veronica. Is the champagne ready for the toast?"

"Soon come, we've been keeping it cold," Veronica replied.

Once everyone was seated, Kenna stood. "First, I would like to welcome you all to *me yard*. For those of you who don't speak Jamaican, that means welcome to my home. For over a decade, Mel, Rich, JJ and Hunt have been my family, and now, thanks to Michel, our family is finally growing. In our little apartment building in West Hollywood, four scruffy young people came together, and their fate was inextricably linked to an unimaginable destiny. I know I speak for all of us here when I say"—Kenna lifted her glass—"to Michel and Mel, may they have a lifetime of togetherness, great, *great* love, and an embarrassment of riches...including little nieces and nephews for JJ, Rich, Hunt and me to spoil. I *love* you, guys!" She repeated the last part of the toast in French for the benefit of Michel's family.

"Here, here!" JJ said. "To Mel and Michel!"

* * *

For the next few hours, the food flowed like wine. The reggae melodies drifted softly through the room, champagne corks popped, the candlelit bubbles bouncing and sparkling, and Kenna was grateful to have them all together again, under her roof. As the guests danced, she checked the time and then disappeared into her room.

She picked up the phone, hesitated, then dialed the country code for France and punched in the number for Agitée. When the bartender answered, she asked for Cathérine, in English, and then waited.

"Oh my God, is it really you?" Cathérine said.

"*Oui, chérie,*" Kenna replied.

"I am so thankful you really *are* alive. So many reports said you weren't, and I have been so terribly worried about you. My sweet, sweet Steeleyez."

"Thank you, Cathérine, that means so much to me. The press would eat me alive if I came out of hiding, and I'm not ready to deal with it. I apologize for waiting this long to call you. I guess I'm calling because there is something I have wanted you to know. Something I very much need to say."

"*Oui?*"

"I still think of you, Cathérine…and you meant something to me. Actually, you meant more than *something* to me." Kenna twirled the phone cord over and over.

Cathérine sighed into the phone. "I missed you so much that I could barely eat or sleep for a month after you left Paris. But it forced me to really look at my life and what I wanted. Steeleyez, you changed me. You changed what I thought was possible for me, and for that I will always be grateful. And you… are you okay, my love?"

"I'm still healing, although I don't know if I'll ever play again."

"No, no, no. *Chérie*, you have to. You can't give up. Please, for me."

Kenna changed the subject. "How is your life now?"

"I'm happy. I have a girlfriend. I mean, she isn't *you*...but she isn't bad."

Kenna laughed, which instantly reminded her of what had attracted her to Cathérine in the first place. "If this is what you want, then I'm happy for you. I wish you the very best, Cathérine. Always. It's good to hear your voice."

"Wait, Steeleyez. There is one thing."

Kenna smiled. "'If I Ever Had the Chance'? Yes, chérie, I wrote it for you and we recorded it while on tour."

"I knew it! Thank you...so much. It's a beautiful song, and every time I hear it, I am filled with love, filled with...you. I promise to listen to it always...and remember."

"I know I'll think of you too, Cathérine."

Kenna sighed heavily, and when she placed the phone back on the receiver, she rested her fingers on it delicately until she could let go. She returned to the party as it was winding down. Mel and Michel's families drifted out in pairs, ready to go back to Quarter Moon.

From inside the house, Kenna stopped to watch as Michel and Mel swayed to a slow dance, on the veranda, in the moonlight, in love.

One by one, Hunt, JJ and Rich joined her.

"They look so happy," JJ said.

Kenna looked over at him. "From what I gather, you're next."

"Would you help me pick out the ring, Kenna?"

She slipped her arm around his waist. "You have to ask?"

PART THREE

2003, Seven years later

CHAPTER TWENTY-FIVE

Kenna and Hunt flashed their VIP backstage passes and went directly to the after-concert party. JJ and Rich were cornered, posing for pictures with producers' friends, fulfilling their obligations with their public smiles. Mel was giving an interview to the press.

"Not much has changed in seven years, huh, Wave?" Hunt whispered.

"Everything has changed," Kenna replied, looking around.

"Everything or just you?"

Mel saw Kenna first and signaled the guys.

"Sorry, folks, that's all for now," JJ said. "Hey, Kenna." He gave her a hug. "I'm so glad you and Hunt could make it."

"She flew in just for the concert," Hunt said.

"You guys were *spectacular* tonight," Kenna said. "You still blow me away."

"Give me some sugar, Kenna!" Rich leaned in and they hugged.

"So, little sister, any of this coming back to you?"

Kenna panned the room, overwhelmed. "How did I ever do this?"

"Oh, come on," JJ began, "nobody did it better than you."

"Aren't you just a *little* tempted?" Mel teased.

"It wouldn't matter if I was, Mel. I don't have *it* anymore."

"Kenna!" Michel came racing up to her and they kissed on both cheeks.

"Michel, it's so good to see you." She looked at Mel. "Okay, where is she? Are you hiding my goddaughter from me?"

"More like holding her hostage...but only until she's thirty, then we'll let her date," Mel said. "But she'll get over having to stay at home tonight as soon as she sees you in the morning. You *are* coming over tomorrow, aren't you?"

Kenna smiled and quoted Mel. "I was planning on seeing her before I *roll up on outta here*."

"Do you really have to go right back to Jersey?"

"She does," Hunt replied. "We have an upcoming fundraiser for Wanted! in Philly. Do you guys have any idea how many strays our no-kill shelters have saved over the past seven years?"

"Don't say it, Hunt," Kenna warned.

"Why not?" Rich said. "I want to know the good that my tax-deductible donations do."

Hunt answered for her. "She says it makes her think of all the ones that couldn't be rescued."

"On a personal mission to save them all," Rich said.

"If you ask me," Hunt said, "she sees that glass as half-empty."

Kenna rolled her eyes. "How many times do I have to say it, Hunt? Whether you see the glass as half-empty or half-full, there's still the same amount of stuff in the glass!"

"That's my girl," JJ said.

"I'll be back in LA after the holidays," Kenna said, "and by then you'll be on hiatus and we'll have some time to spend together, right?"

"Absolutely, little sister. You'll be here for Dalia's birthday party?"

Kenna smiled, remembering when Mel had asked her if they could name their daughter after Kenna's mother. "I can't wait."

"Yes," Michel blurted out, "we're renting ponies for the occasion, and all the little kids will get a ride and a picture."

"You two are so delightful, it gives me hope. Look, I know you have to still make the rounds, so go do your thing, and I'll talk to you this week from home."

"Great to see you, Kenna. Miss you!" JJ kissed her cheek and then shook Hunt's hand. "Later, bro."

Kenna threw her arms around Rich's neck and whispered in his ear. "Why isn't Karina here?"

He whispered back. "JJ and she have some marital issues, but don't worry, they're okay." Rich kissed her cheek before leaving. "Love you, babe."

Kenna nodded and turned to Mel. "What's really going on that I don't know about?"

"Honestly, I think we're getting old. Karina would like JJ to be home more. As for me, I've been a rock star. Now I want to stay home, bake cookies and host play dates for Dalia. JJ's hoping it's just a phase." Mel laughed so hard it brought tears to her eyes. "Listen, I had a thought, and you can say no."

"What, Mel?"

"How about we come out to visit you this summer and hang at the Jersey Shore for a week?"

Kenna's eyes lit up. "Really? *Two* whole weeks? I'll bankroll Dalia down the Ocean City boardwalk. Do you have any idea how many times you can play Whack-a-Mole for twenty bucks? Then there's custard...you know, soft serve ice cream, and we can go on the roller coaster and the Ferris wheel...and the spinning teacups! Salt water taffies."

Mel shook her head. "You spoil my kid rotten."

Kenna smirked. "What is the point of having kids, dogs or lovers if you're not going to spoil them? Besides, Dalia is the closest thing my mother would have had to a granddaughter. She's her namesake, and my goddaughter. For me, it doesn't get any better than that."

Mel laughed. "Yeah, you remember that when I ship her off to you during the terrible teen years. So I'll see you in the morning?"

"Definitely."

After Hunt and Kenna were back in the limo, he waited a few minutes before saying, "Don't you even miss it a little bit?"

Kenna's voice was low and soft. "Sometimes I miss it so much, it physically hurts."

"Then what's stopping you? You know Mel, Rich and JJ would bring you back in an instant."

"They are so good, Hunt. So fucking good. Watching them onstage tonight, I realized I wouldn't be able to keep up with them anymore. It's been too many years since I've played."

"Sure you could, Wave. You just need to focus...and to start playing again."

"No, what I'd need is to start over, from scratch. And for that, I don't just need skills, Hunt. I need inspiration."

"Okay, fine! I'm dropping it," he said. "On a different subject, I spoke to Mom today. She said she had spoken with Alex Winthrop. Alex asked for you, wanted to know what you're doing now, how you are."

Kenna's grin was resigned. "Yeah? That's nice to know."

"Wave, what is going on with you? It's like you've just given up."

She looked into his eyes. "Is that the same thing as giving in?"

* * *

The next night, Kenna stood on her New Jersey deck with a glass of wine and the New Steel Eyes Trio album playing on her stereo inside. A late-autumn gust cut through her long hair and nipped at her neck, making her miss the warmth of Jamaica and reminding her that Jamaica seemed so long ago, because it was.

She sipped the wine and did a final proof of the invitation to the upcoming winter fundraiser for Wanted!, her organization of no-kill animal shelters. For the past seven years she had found great solace in salvaging the permanently lost and unwanted—herself being the exception.

The isolation of winter was settling deep into the bones of the New Jersey shore, carving the meat of summer beach towns down to their skeletons. It was the time of year when the barrier islands became ghost towns, and the houses hushed, no beach chairs or boogie boards to trip over as Kenna roamed the empty streets and beaches. Once all the seasonal visitors had left, and those who lived in the city no longer found time to visit their shore houses, the shore became quiet enough for her to think. That was how she liked it best. Even though the ocean wasn't blue and was only warm in summer, the energy there made her feel at least some sense of purpose. Shrugging off the salty chill, she stepped back inside the house and sat by her toasty fire where she finished her glass of wine.

It was almost time for her scheduled online meeting in the Steel Eyes chat room. She liked this new Internet thing. It was a way for her to be alone but also to be *with* people...well, one person in particular.

Kenna's screen name, "Steel Eyes Disguise" popped up on the screen as soon as she logged in to the chat room. Her online buddy "Eyes4U" called her "Disguise" or "SED," for short. Any minute now, Eyes4U would log on, and within minutes, as on every other "cyber date," they would escape to a private chat room, just the two of them.

Kenna watched the screen as all the regulars and a few newcomers chatted about everything Steel Eyes. They argued over which songs were the best ones, who they might have been written for and what great musicians JJ, Mel and Rich were. Over the past year, she had read all the comments, conspiracy theories and suppositions about Steel Eyes and her whereabouts. She couldn't believe some people out there still truly believed she had died after the shooting and that was why she had never made a comeback.

If it had only been that simple, she thought. An instant message appeared in the left corner of her screen.

EYES4U: Good evening, Disguise.
STEEL EYES DISGUISE: Hi, Eyes.
EYES4U: I've missed you the past few days. Where have you been?
SED: I had to fly to LA for a concert.
EYES4U: Let me guess...the New Steel Eyes Trio concert?
SED: Of course. They were amazing. AMAZING! Really.

EYES4U: I'm sure, but it's just not the same without the masked maven of music herself.

Kenna didn't know how to respond when Eyes said things like that, so she wrote what was expected of a hard-core Steel Eyes fan.

SED: You're right, but it doesn't mean they weren't awesome. I actually had a backstage pass.

EYES4U: You're just trying to impress me.

SED: And what if I am?

EYES4U: I would take it as a compliment.

Kenna smiled. Of all the times she had wondered what Eyes4U looked like, tonight she was more curious to know than ever. Eyes4U intrigued her, made her think and most importantly, made her smile…a lot.

SED: I'm blushing. For the record, I did miss you…even though I don't know whom I'm missing. Is that right, Eyes? Whom?

EYES4U: (Rolling my eyes) WHO cares, Disguise!

SED: So I can feel confident ruling out that you're an English teacher? Grammar notwithstanding, Happy anniversary, Eyes. Hard to believe we've known each other for eight months.

EYES4U: I know virtually everything…and virtually nothing about you. I sent you an electronic card to your email, but I'm still waiting for an answer to my question.

Kenna fidgeted in her chair, twirling the end of her hair like a teenager. "I want to kiss you all over, Eyes!" *No, you can't write that!*

SED: Are you really ready to ruin the fantasy?

EYES4U: That sounds a bit like the "glass half empty," if you ask me. Besides, we created this fantasy.

SED: But after all this time, what if when we meet we have no chemistry?

EYES4U: Impossible, Disguise. We already have that. You make me laugh.

SED: Why?

EYES4U: Because I just don't know how you can't see what's right in front of you.

SED: So…you're certain that we should meet.

EYES4U: I'll put it to you gently...Even Humpty Dumpty had to eventually fall on one side of the fence.

SED: Exactly! And just look at what happened to him. All the king's horses and all the king's men, Eyes.

EYES4U: Something tells me you're not as fragile as Humpty.

SED: Well, something could be incorrect. But I am warming up to the idea.

EYES4U: At least we're both crazy about Steel Eyes. That's a start. After all, I am her most devoted fan.

SED: You must be, since she hasn't released a CD in almost a DECADE! Maybe she can't make a comeback because she really is dead.

EYES4U: Don't say that. You'll see, she'll come back and it will be unforgettable. Better, if that's even possible.

SED: You sure have a lot of faith in someone who just left her fans hanging.

EYES4U: You really need to stop popping those pessimist pills. And I'm not giving up any time soon on the subject of meeting. (Just thought you should know.)

Kenna laughed and finally admitted to no one else that Eyes4U had given her back her smile, but more importantly, she gave her the joy that made her want to smile.

SED: I like your persistence. It's good for me.

EYES4U: So is that a yes to meeting?

Kenna froze and then typed.

SED: I'll let you know, but I have to make a business call before it gets too late.

EYES4U: Tomorrow night?

SED: Out of town for five days for business.

EYES4U: Don't they have computers wherever you're going? You do realize you can log on from anywhere in the world, hence the name...Internet.

SED: Hey! I found YOU, didn't I, Eyes? :-) Sorry, it will be all work, no play.

EYES4U: :-(Have a safe trip. BTW, where are you going?

SED: Europe.

EYES4U: Have a question for you. Honest answer please. Are you really that shy, or just afraid to meet me?

SED: *Are those my only choices?*

EYES4U: *Hmm, you really are a woman of mystery. I WILL figure you out, you know. Sweet dreams, safe trip…and come back to me soon.*

SED: *Until then.*

Kenna logged off with a grin that lasted for all of three seconds until she glanced at the clock. She cringed, knowing she still had to pack and get ready to catch her plane to Paris the next night out of Philadelphia.

Whoever Eyes4U is, she certainly has a lot of faith in Steel Eyes, Kenna thought. *A lot of faith in me.*

CHAPTER TWENTY-SIX

While perusing the intelligence Hunt had given her regarding this upcoming operation, an ancient urge stalked Kenna like unsuspecting prey. It lurched out from the shadows in her room and eclipsed her view with deadly silent stealth. An instantaneous shiver made the fine hairs on the back of her neck stand up.

Buried in its shallow grave and resurrected in that moment, the urge to play guitar effaced her thoughts. She wondered if that's what inspiration felt like for her *now*. She had forgotten the feeling. While she could remember being inspired, she couldn't conjure the actual sensation.

Most times, her desire to play guitar was so encumbered with conflict that she would shrug it off for the sake of her temporary sanity. Until now. This wasn't one of those times. Something Eyes4U had said about Steel Eyes resonated with her. It picked at her.

You'll see, she'll come back and it will be unforgettable. Better, if that's even possible.

Kenna admitted to herself that even though her relationship was online—and worse yet, with someone she had never met—that didn't mean she didn't *know* Eyes4U. And somewhere in that knowing, she realized that she had finally found her long-lost love—inspiration.

Eyes4U inspired her, had kept her coming back almost every night for months. She turned her attention back to the dossier but couldn't concentrate on it and then abandoned it on her desk.

She climbed the stairs to the darkened third level of her beach house and opened the door at the end of the hall. The room was as silent as it was dark. She flipped on the light switch and peered into the dimly lit music studio. At this point it had become a ritual—turning on the light and staring at the deadly silent amps and instruments, the gleam of the lights as they bounced off Steel Eyes's gold, platinum...multiplatinum records that hung on every wall. She never seemed to notice the Grammy statues—the music had been its own reward. The Grammys only served to remind her of what fame had cost her.

As usual, she turned off the lights without entering, wondering what it would really take to walk across that fucking threshold, plug Sweet Jayne into the goddamn dusty Marshall amp and actually turn the sonofabitch on. There was just one little problem: she had abdicated Steel Eyes long ago. Subconsciously, she flexed and extended the fingers of her stiff left hand.

Tonight wasn't the night to find her courage. She would need it tomorrow for a mission that would be dangerous enough without any distractions. Reverently, she closed the studio door then removed her duffel bag from the hall closet and packed for her trip.

From Paris, she would take two trains into Germany and meet her asset in Hanover, one of the many cities famous for Europe's *Kristallnacht*—the epic burning of more than a thousand synagogues and the incarceration of more than thirty thousand Jewish people who were then sent to the death camps. The looting of their possessions by the Nazis was a stain on the pages of European history—a stain Kenna was determined to help wipe clean. The soul of her assignment was the recovery of some of those stolen items, but more personally, it was to dole out justice to those who had perpetuated the black market sale of stolen Holocaust items for over half a century.

In Hanover, her contact would then drive her into Berlin so she couldn't be tracked. Hunt had asked her if she wanted him to come with her, but she had declined, telling him to stay in LA and visit his mother. "Give Phyllis my love, Hunt. Tell her I'll see her as soon as I can," she had reminded him.

Tired, she hastily packed her duffel.

Eyes4U is worth losing a little sleep for.

As she finished up, she remembered what had drawn her to Eyes4U in the first place. They had met in the Steel Eyes chat room one night when Kenna had been curious to know what people were saying about Steel Eyes herself. That first night, someone named SurferDude69 had trashed Steel Eyes's talent and spread rumors that she was either dead or close to it from drug addiction. It took everything Kenna had not to defend herself.

And then, riding up on her white keyboard, Eyes4U had come out of the ether to save the day and to defend Steel Eyes from SurferDude69. Kenna had watched the heated exchange between them on her screen, the insults flying so fast she had to scroll backward several times to follow the conversation. In the end, Eyes4U had eviscerated SurferDude69, virtually saying everything she would have said, if she hadn't been so afraid to attract attention to herself.

As "Steel Eyes Disguise," sometimes just plain "Disguise" or "SED" for short, Kenna had been chatting with Eyes4U almost every night for the past eight months, starting that very night.

Kenna set her alarm clock for noon and turned off the light. The late-night wind off the ocean whipped the striped canvas awning outside, the cold threatening to breach the pale gray walls. Kenna buried herself under the fluffy down comforter and passed out seconds after her head hit the pillow.

Heinz accelerated to what seemed like a thousand miles per hour to pass a Volkswagen.

Overkill, Kenna thought.

He steered into the right lane and eventually slowed down to the resolute one hundred and thirty kilometers per hour. "From what I know, she's as dangerous as anyone in the art underworld. Are you sure you don't want to rethink your strategy?"

"If I wasn't sure of my strategy, Heinz, I wouldn't be here."

Is he trying to cajole me into changing my plan? She knew enough to not trust anyone with anything more than they already knew. Besides, her friend and fellow operative Jocelyn would be her handler for this operation, and Kenna would see her at the Berlin safe house.

"*Ja*, your reputation precedes you. I don't know if you saw the addendum in the file, but intelligence added to the list. Evidently they've located some of the Cezannes and Manets that Adolf Eichmann looted. We think Messer will be brokering at least two of them, but we don't know which ones. There's also artwork by German impressionist Max Liebermann."

"That's a sad story, Heinz."

"I don't think I'm familiar with it. Tell me."

"The story goes that when the Nazis were closing in on the German Jews during the Holocaust, Hitler outlawed them from making a living, getting medical care, buying food… in effect, every dehumanizing thing he could do. It's said that Liebermann's widow was forced to trade his paintings for food and medicine. What works remained, the Nazis looted. As for the Manets and Cezannes, and even some Monets, Jews took them from their personal collections to pay off Eichmann to secure their survival. Once he possessed the art, he herded the owners off to the gas chamber anyway. It's time their families got those back and had some peace, don't you think?"

Heinz shook his head. "It's still hard to believe sometimes," he said remorsefully.

"For me, it's harder to forget it than it is to believe it. Trust me, I've tried. If you don't mind, I'm going to close my eyes for a while."

"Good idea. I'll wake you before we get to the safe house. You'll need to be in the warehouse before ten p.m."

Kenna nodded, balled up her scarf for a pillow and reclined the seat, trusting that her situational awareness was on duty even when her conscious mind was not. She awoke a good forty minutes before they arrived in Berlin and rode the rest of the way in silence, taking inventory of her surroundings, concentrating on every detail of the upcoming operation.

For any mission where the stakes were high, whether storming the stage as Steel Eyes or going for the jugular of an international criminal, her preparation was the same. These situations demanded an extreme state of inner stillness that was inversely proportional to the event. The greater the stakes, the more intense the calm and focus. Like windsurfing, it required being completely in the moment. This was the only way to survive anything this big, this dangerous, alone.

When they arrived at the safe house in Berlin, Kenna first examined her cadre of weapons. While waiting for her handler Jocelyn, she checked the sights, examined the individual rounds, then loaded each magazine clip meticulously. Uncle had insisted that if she wouldn't let Jocelyn accompany her to the warehouse, that at the very least she allow Jocelyn to brief her in Berlin.

Roughly five years her junior and a few inches shorter, Jocelyn possessed a life-preserving combination of crude animal instincts and lightning-fast reflexes. Dressed up or down, her timeless European features and demeanor opened any door she cared to walk through, like the ones of French ambassadors around the globe. Known for her keen attention to detail and operational judgment, she had climbed the ranks of Mossad quickly. In the end, that's what reinforced Kenna's decision to go it alone in the warehouse. She knew from experience that if Jocelyn sanctioned the operation, every detail had been turned on its edge beforehand.

While she had yet to tell anyone, Kenna had already decided that this would be her last mission. As sharp as she still was, she knew that *almost* as fast and *almost* as agile could cost her her life.

"Anything you're not completely clear about, Kenna?" Jocelyn asked when she finished the briefing.

"I'm good to go, Jocelyn."

"On another subject, just between us, I have the personal information you asked for." She smiled slyly. "Steel Eyes's French girl Cathérine?"

"Yes?"

"She's good. She and her lover live a pretty standard life from what I can see. They own the bar named Agitée and they have two children. Why did you want to know?"

"Just looking out for an old friend."

"I'll wait to hear from you before I dispatch the cleaners," Jocelyn said. "If anything goes wrong, call me immediately from the car phone."

Kenna nodded. "Of course. You're the only person here I know and trust. Thanks for everything, Jocelyn. It's good to see you. And tell Uncle I send my love." They hugged.

"He worries about you as much as he worries about his own daughter. Just watch your ass in there tonight. If *anything* doesn't feel right, promise me you'll abort and you won't go all superhero on their asses."

"You can tell Uncle that I promise."

Kenna took a shower, meditated, then picked at a light meal that was delivered to her. Slightly hungry was the best way for her to approach an op. It afforded her the ability to remain wide awake but without her stomach growling. A growling stomach, she had learned long ago in Istanbul, was loud enough to give away her position.

She arranged her tactical gear, clipping one holster at the small of her back, strapping one to her right ankle and nesting the third at her shoulder. A nostalgic smile graced her lips while she secured all three weapons, remembering her childhood lesson in holsters.

Maurice van Bourgeade had shown her and Hunter how he and Sam had carried their handguns as members of the French Resistance during the Second World War, or as Maurice had referred to it in his native French, *La Deuxième Guerre Mondiale*.

Although many names were associated with this particular carry method depending on culture and the era, Maurice had referred to it as the *clown carry*. In reality, it was a string holster, used when behind enemy lines. Its purpose, should a partisan have to dump his weapon, was to not get caught with a holster. The objective, although well intentioned, was not without risk of a partisan shooting off his balls. The upside was that the string holster, if applied properly, would indeed keep a firearm from dropping down a pant leg, should the carrier have merely shoved it into his waistband without being secured.

The design was a simple cord, double looped to hang on a belt loop. The free end of the loop provided a nest for the gun's barrel, which the wearer then tucked into his waistband. Kenna was glad she had holsters. She fine-tuned their positions.

With her handguns in place, she brought along the sound suppressor, should silence prove life-preserving. In her vest pockets she carried two smoke bombs to obscure an assailant's vision long enough for her to get away. Two pairs of plastic hand restraints lay flat in the breast pocket opposite the silencer. Since no one was coming to get her, she forewent communication tools. With Maddy in tow, she'd make her way to the southern end of the park where a car waited for her. The keys would be in a magnetic holder inside the wheel well, and on the seat she'd find a winter coat to cover her gear.

Having memorized the warehouse blueprints and the layout of the industrial park, she closed her eyes and walked through them in her mind one last time. Night had long since fallen.

She pulled her straight, ashen hair into a ponytail, over which she would wear a black watch cap. Dressed in black thermal gear, she glanced at her watch, confident she would be able to pull this off. It was time.

Heinz's Mercedes decelerated to a crawl. Kenna exited low as it crept through the adjacent property in first gear. She crouched and headed for her designated entry point about twenty yards away. The monochromatic industrial park blended easily into the night. With its block-like, nondescript repetition of concrete outbuildings, it was desolate enough to remain devoid of people and cold enough to hopefully remain absent of stray cats—another variable.

The security guard was an older man whose belly was no smaller than an eighth-month pregnancy—only in his case, the baby was made of knockwurst. His station was two buildings farther away, on the opposite side at the security gate, where he mostly napped and watched television.

Indistinguishable from each other, especially in the coal darkness of a wintry Berlin night, the buildings were just beyond the fence. Kenna scrutinized her surroundings and then, as planned, she slipped through the southern edge of the park where the chain link had been benignly separated from its bottom frame. She shimmied diagonally through the narrow opening and hugged the buildings' shadows, then surreptitiously edged past the first two warehouses. She hung a right before the third one, careful to avoid any offending shards of light.

The fine, freezing drizzle pelted the desolate and creepy buildings. Hearing it reminded Kenna of the sounds of summer—of shaved ice being poured into a snow cone cup on the Atlantic City boardwalk.

Even though she was a trained spy toting three weapons, this was about as vulnerable as she had ever been with regard to uncontrolled variables; controlled variables were dangerous enough. Stealth and focus, her seasoned specialties, had allowed her to successfully remain anonymous as Steel Eyes for all those years. But this was different. Without Hunt, without Jean Claude, without Jocelyn, Kenna needed all her focus to be in the moment.

Every half breath was another blind step, each step like the click of a revolver engaged in Russian roulette. Embedded in each new shadow hid a potential assassin. For a fleeting second she wished she *had* played her guitar the night before she left New Jersey, and she promised herself that if she made it home, she would finally step across that mile-wide threshold into the studio and play.

Counting the steps from the edge of Warehouse Four to its center, Kenna located the fire escape and scaled it to the second floor without the slightest rattle. The handrail was slick, the metal beginning to ice over. The fingers on her left hand became stiff as the cold permeated her gloves. She swung off below the parapet. Pressed flat against the building, she surveyed the environs below and to the sides, taking note of every sound.

Car tires on slick asphalt. Raised pitch…not exactly in the distance, but not close, either. No sound coming from inside the warehouse as best I can tell.

The freezing rain fell more steadily, making it difficult to discern the sounds inside. Another uncontrolled variable.

Once satisfied that her immediate location was secure, she slid the glass cutter from her waist pack, drew a circle on the designated decrepit window, then yanked it out toward her to keep the glass from shattering.

Although baked in filth, with chains inside its rust-riddled frame, the inside latch of the old factory window opened easily. Kenna was grateful that this uncontrolled variable worked in her favor. Still, it was old and rusty, and she prayed the loud, frozen droplets pelting the warehouse windows disguised her movement. One less variable if someone was already inside.

She clutched the upper frame with both gloved hands and slid inside feet-first, then moved several feet to her left and took cover behind the first row of containers.

Closing her eyes, she envisioned the photos Heinz had shown her. The sealed wooden containers stood three deep per aisle, and two high with a twenty-foot space at the top. Silently she counted to twenty.

When she opened her eyes, they had mostly adapted to the darkness, enough that she saw the containers and some debris strewn about her. She was always looking for anything that might come in handy if she needed it.

The darkness was too thick to see the detail on anything. She pushed away the fleeting fear of not living through this to meet Eyes4U, reminding herself that staying in the present was imperative. In that very moment she realized she *did* want to meet her in person, and then she wondered if that had anything to do with wanting to play her guitar.

From her position on the second floor, Kenna had an excellent vantage point to clearly see Maddy when she would enter through the front door. She would watch to see which containers Maddy went to.

The plan is simple enough. While Maddy is occupied with her spoils, she'll be vulnerable and unsuspecting. I'll strike fast; if possible, from her right—disable her shooting hand.

Listening for the sound of any movement in the dark, she waited another minute, then crept toward the front of the warehouse.

Click.

The sound was faint. Her pulse spiked. Someone was there, in the dark, lying in wait. She stepped to the side of the container next to her and waited. If there was one thing being Steel Eyes had taught Kenna, it was the art of impeccable timing—a vestigial skill, or rather a fugitive she gladly harbored. The ambush would have to be thirty-second-note fast, maybe even sixty-fourth note.

A minute later, she was rewarded with a sound she knew in her sleep. In her mind, those three clicks painted the picture of a single military sniper rifle.

Good. I now have two advantages over this sniper. The element of surprise and a fifty-fifty chance he's lying prone. If I'm fast enough, forceful enough, he won't have time to turn and fire on me given the length of that barrel.

She wrapped her fingers around the handle of the Sig Sauer saddled against her lumbar spine and slid it halfway out of the holster as she padded toward the next row of containers. The sound of the sniper's movements landed so close to her ears that she quietly slid the gun back into its holster.

His *clicks* were too sharp, clear; not muffled enough to indicate a comfortable distance between them. She was closer to him than she'd thought.

Why is the sound so much clearer here? Open space? She listened harder. *Still can't rule out a second shooter.*

Complete silence.

I can't draw my weapon...he'll hear me. And I can't shoot what I can't see.

Three minutes passed before Kenna saw her next move.

She would pounce on him, mindful of *all* uncontrolled variables; his exact position, his size. Straining to see, she fixed her gaze along the impotent spray of jaundiced grime that passed for light. Slivers of outside beams rested near the sniper, enough that she could now make out his outline.

Perfect. She heard Mel's voice in the back of her mind. "*Show 'em what you got, baby girl.*"

Kenna had time to take this guy out before Maddy showed up, then her only focus would be to get Maddy into that car and back to the safe house. She would call Jocelyn on the way and hand Maddy over to her. The cleaners would recover the art later on, once the warehouse was secured. But several big questions remained: who was this sniper, was he the only one, and most importantly, what *else* didn't she know?

CHAPTER TWENTY-EIGHT

Kenna crouched beside a crate twelve feet diagonally behind and to the left of the sniper. Her presence was ghost-like, translucent—her focus the umbilical cord between thought and action. She centered her weight on the ball of her right foot, poised to ambush him in the dark. On the count of three she would take him out of the equation.

One. Two. What the fuck!

She heard the front door to the warehouse open about an hour too soon. This was all wrong. The lights to the first level came on, and Kenna saw the red dot planted on Maddy's chest.

"Maddy, gun!" she yelled, flying through the air. In an instant, she landed on the shooter, defocusing him. A volcanic floodgate of adrenaline erupted as she pummeled his head into the floor. "No you don't, asshole, she's mine!" She swung his rifle and sideswiped his head with the butt, hearing it *thunk* as all resistance ceased.

Maddy had turned on the upper-level lights. "Behind you!" she yelled—a moment too late.

A man wearing a ski mask smashed Kenna's head with the butt of his gun and charged past her. Maddy fired two shots in his general direction as she raced up the stairs, taking two steps at a time. When she reached the upper landing, the man she fired at was gone. Maddy glanced at her sniper who lay still at her feet, unconscious and bleeding profusely from his head wound. She took a shooter's stance and pivoted sharply in every direction with her Beretta pointing straight in front of her.

Kenna stumbled. She tried to lunge for one of the Maddys in front of her. Instead, she fell to the floor, flirting with fleeting consciousness and fuzzy vision.

Maddy yanked her onto her feet. "Come on, we have to get out of here." She supported Kenna with her free hand, keeping her handgun poised as she pulled her down the stairs. Maddy's car was still warm when she tossed Kenna into the backseat like a rag doll, jumped behind the wheel and peeled out. Her back wheels fishtailed on the glossy, ice-coated asphalt.

Kenna tried to sit up. She squinted to see through the jagged prisms cast by frozen crystals on Maddy's windshield. But when the back wheels of Maddy's car spun out, Kenna heaved all over the leather interior. *So much for new-car smell*, she thought, using every mind trick she knew to remain conscious. Her concussion had other plans for her.

Disoriented, Kenna awoke with her head throbbing. Her eyes opened one at a time. Instinctively, she pulled against the flex handcuffs that now cinched her wrists to the wooden arms of a kitchen chair. The figure who sat across the table from her might have been fuzzy, but the piercing blue eyes were not. She gasped for air and spotted a blurry version of her Sig Sauer lying on the table between them.

At least she's not pointing it at me. As far as Kenna could feel, Maddy had relieved her of all her weapons.

"What are you doing here?" Maddy asked in the calm register of a seasoned agent.

Kenna didn't answer.

"We don't have time to play games. Why are you following me?"

"Because you broker art stolen by Nazis, from the people they gassed in the chambers. Tell me, Maddy, what kind of demon seed do you have to be to do that?"

"I *might* take off your restraints as soon as you hear what I have to say."

"I don't really want to hear what you have to say." Still nauseated by the nasty head bump, Kenna dry-heaved to the side of her chair.

Maddy continued. "Not that you're in a position to make demands, but believe me, you'll want to hear *this*. First I want to know who you're working for."

Kenna chuckled sarcastically. "Who am I working for? I'm here on behalf of the people the Nazis murdered. I work for *those* people."

Maddy stood, walked to the side of the kitchen window and barely separated the blinds to peer at the street below. The blinds flipped back into position, and she sauntered toward Kenna, grabbing a bottle of water from the fridge. She twisted it open and tilted it for Kenna to drink. Several seconds passed as Kenna emptied it.

"Try to keep that down, would you? Since you saved my life, Kenna, I guess I owe you something, so I'll go first. I'm not brokering stolen art. I've been in deep cover for years trying to stop it. I'm MI-6."

"*What?*" Kenna said, incredulous. "You expect me to believe that coming from the granddaughter of *Nazi* Herr Messerchmidt? The man Adolf Eichmann trusted with *the* list of stolen artifacts?"

"Yes," Maddy said, unfazed, "coming from the granddaughter of his *wife*, who stole that list *for* the Allies. Why would I have saved your life from those goons tonight if I was who you think I am? Besides, weren't *you* there to shoot me too?"

Kenna recalled the photo of Maddy's grandmother that Uncle had shown her and Hunt years ago, when he had related the story of Frau Messerschmidt, the wife of the Gestapo officer who had secretly obtained lists of Nazi-looted items from her husband, then passed them on to the French Resistance. Because of Maddy's grandmother, agents worldwide had recovered many of those items after the Second World War.

Maddy smirked as she cut the plastic restraints from Kenna's wrists. "We're on the same side."

Kenna wobbled a little when she stood and used the nearest wall to guide her first few steps while she tried to process the information. "MI-6? Seriously?"

Maddy retrieved a bottle of water for herself, tossed Kenna an ice pack for her head and sat back on a kitchen chair. "It's true. Your turn."

Kenna had monitored Maddy carefully from the instant her vision began to clear. Even though it could be faked, her micro expressions, respiratory rate, the consistent diameter of her pupils, and other objective signs told her that chances were Maddy was telling her the truth.

"Mossad," Kenna offered.

"I know," Maddy said, exhaling a sigh.

"Then why did you ask me?"

"To see if you'd tell me the truth."

"If you're MI-6, then why was Interpol tracking you?"

Maddy stood and leaned against the counter. "Because if I wasn't on a list *somewhere*, then my cover would be blown. Trust me, you don't want to blow your cover in a network that would just as soon shoot you in the head and take the artwork for free."

Kenna blinked to further clear her vision. "And Alex Winthrop? What was *that* about?"

"I don't know if we have time for the wayback machine. Let's stick to present tense."

Kenna stared directly at her. "No, let's not. Alex Winthrop?"

"Strictly business. I liked her. She was smart, hot...we had a good time, but like I said, for me it was business. I needed to see Maurice van Bourgeade's photo archives to compare them with my grandmother's lists as well as those from England. I'd had actionable intelligence about a shipment making its way from Saudi Arabia to be auctioned at Sotheby's, and we had to act fast. Provenance forgeries were epic at that time. Maurice's archives held the most comprehensive and meticulously compiled information, and among other things I needed to know which provenances were suspect. As his protégé, Alex had access to them. I had targeted her for months. The timing couldn't have been more perfect for my cover when Maurice van Bourgeade unfortunately passed away. I was ordered to accelerate the process, so I put together Alex's first big gallery showing. But leading up to that, you were in the picture more and more, out of nowhere. Where the hell *did* you come from?"

"A Greenwich Village boutique dressing room...*and* an airplane lav."

"She loved you, you know. Even though she was with me... she was thinking of you."

Kenna was thankful that Maddy had finally come into clear view. "I can't believe how wrong I had this story, and for all these years." She paused, looked into Maddy's ridiculously, impossibly blue eyes and then decked her with a solid left hook.

Maddy coughed and tried to catch her breath as she stared up at Kenna from the floor, a steady stream of blood leaking from her bottom lip.

"*That's* for stealing my girlfriend! Damn, you didn't even *love* her."

Maddy had regained her ability to breathe, but she still didn't seem ready to get up from the floor. "Do you feel better now, Kenna?"

Kenna extended her hand and pulled Maddy up onto her feet. "A little," she conceded. "So now what?"

"Now we'd better ask someone to get us the hell out of Berlin. Obviously, my cover's blown."

"You have any idea who those guys were in the warehouse?"

"The one you nailed is a known sniper." Maddy walked into the bedroom, her voice trailing off but still audible. "I was supposed to meet with an art agent later tonight. I've finally closed in on one of the largest black market art rings between the Balkans and South America. My guess is he sent those two to eliminate the middleman—me." Maddy reentered the room and laid a file on the coffee table in front of Kenna. "Have a look at this."

"What is it?" Kenna asked as she sat on the sofa holding the ice pack against her swollen skull.

"Open it. I know if the situation were reversed, I would want to see this."

Kenna saw a photograph of the sniper she had fought in the warehouse. She rifled through the classified document, and by the time she closed it, she knew that Maddy had answered a very important question for her.

"You know?" Kenna asked.

"About you, Steel Eyes?" Maddy chuckled. "Yes, I know."

"So this sniper"—Kenna glanced down and read the name—"Darius, is the one who tried to kill Steel Eyes. Who does he work for?"

"Whoever pays him. So to answer your next question, no, I don't know who hired him to shoot Steel Eyes. The word is that whoever did needed to take out a certain Mossad agent, and what better way to do it than in an arena of thousands?"

"If you had told the press Steel Eyes's real identity, you could have made a lot of money…and you could have made my life hell."

"I'm not in it for the money or to make your life hell. Besides, I figured I owed you one for getting between you and Alex. I thought about revealing your alter ego to her, but I could see how she regretted losing you. Telling her would have only added salt to the wound. Were you really going to shoot me tonight?"

"I wasn't going to shoot you, Maddy. I was going to bring you in to face charges. I was moving toward the front of the warehouse when I heard the sniper in the dark. I was one second away from ambushing him when you came through the door. I saw the red dot on your chest and pounced."

"Thank you for saving my life." Maddy thought for a second. "Pretty impressive, considering how long you've hated me."

"How could I have been so wrong? If I hadn't saved your life, you wouldn't have been around to save mine, so I guess we're even."

"Kenna, somebody set up either one or both of us. Who was your contact here?"

"The guy who drove me to Berlin from Hanover introduced himself as Heinz. Midforties, about six foot one, black hair, ice-blue eyes, strong jaw, pockmark on the right side of his neck."

Maddy went to the kitchen table, opened the portfolio she had left there and returned with a photo. She handed it to Kenna.

"That's him. Who is he?"

"MI-6 thinks he's a double for what used be the East German Stasi, and that he brokered illegal arms in the Middle East during Operation Desert Storm."

"You're right. We have to get out of here. Where are we, anyway?"

"The MI-6 Berlin safe house, so we're okay for now. The phone is secure."

Kenna thought immediately of Jocelyn, who by now knew that something had gone wrong when Kenna didn't check in. Kenna trusted her. "I know just who to call. She'll be able to get us out of Germany."

Maddy nodded. "You can tell her that my alias is Maura Binstock."

Kenna placed the call and turned back to Maddy after hanging up. "She'll pick us up at Alexanderplatz in one hour, but I won't know about my ID until we get there. I can't take a chance going back to the safe house where I was earlier."

Maddy picked up the phone. "I should call my handler. On second thought, I think I'll wait to call home." She put the phone back on the receiver. "Who knows where the leak was, and our combined intel might just keep us alive. Our best bet right now is to stick together and fly as low as we can." She smiled. "I could tell by your punch how much she meant to you."

"I *almost* don't hate you right now."

"Good luck with that."

"We have one more piece of business, Maddy."

Before Maddy could say *What?*, Kenna stood and landed a body shot—not nearly as hard as she could have.

"What the hell was *that* for?"

Kenna smiled, gratified. "The first punch was for stealing my girlfriend. The second one was for deceiving her. You used her."

"You're right. Are you done punching me?"

Kenna mulled it over. "I think so. For now. Maybe this trip did have some highlights after all."

"You mean other than punching me out?"

Kenna pulled out her miniature silver Minox spy camera, slid it open, then carefully photographed everything in the file on the sniper known as Darius. When she finished, she exhumed the tiny roll of film and hid it in the steel-reinforced, hollowed-out heel of her boot.

Maddy watched her. "Who do you think you are...James Bond?"

"Maurice used the Minox countless times and left it to me in his will."

"We need to leave for Alexanderplatz soon. How is your head?"

"I have a headache but my vision is clear, and I'm not nauseated anymore. Oh, sorry about puking all over that nice Mercedes."

"It's a loaner, and I've already ditched it. Take a winter coat from the closet...you look like a cat burglar."

Kenna scoffed. "You calling me a pussy?"

CHAPTER TWENTY-NINE

Dréa Winthrop let herself into her sister's beach house with her key. The house was still except for a muffled, incessantly pounding beat.

"Of course," she said, climbing to the third floor. Year by year, the small workspace had expanded until a dedicated studio and darkroom filled the entire floor, leaving Alex to move her bedroom down one flight. Dréa knocked on the darkroom door. "Are you in there?" she called out over the loud music.

Alex lowered the volume. "I'll be out as soon as I finish hanging some photos."

"Take your time. I'll put on some coffee."

"Make mine hot chocolate?"

As the coffee finished brewing, Alex bounded down the back stairs into the kitchen. She gave Dréa a big hug and ruffled the furry neck of Dréa's dog Beau. The dog responded with a slurp on her cheek.

"Wow, Alex, you sure look happy. What's up?"

"I had an epiphany."

Dréa set the mug of hot chocolate in front of her baby sister, poured herself a cup of coffee and shot her a glance.

"The other night it occurred to me that it's time I do a retrospective on Steel Eyes."

"Why now, Alex?"

"It came to me…just like that. The next morning, I pitched the idea to *Rocklandia* magazine and they went for it. I've been in the darkroom for two days pulling shots that were never published, and they were some of the best of all. You're going to dig them." Alex sipped her hot chocolate.

"It's been what…seven years since she disappeared? Died?"

"Disappeared."

"You have proof of that?"

"Well, no."

"Either way, that issue is going to sell an awful lot of copies."

"I'm not doing it for that reason, although I'm sure *Rocklandia* is. I'm doing it as an homage to the greatest woman rocker of our era. Top fifty rock guitarists of all time…and the only female."

Dréa drank some coffee and then snickered. "Do you think you'll *ever* stop being a Steel Eyes groupie?"

"Not anytime soon."

"Alex, I know you keep avoiding the subject, but your fortieth birthday is coming up in a few months. Let's have a big party. You can invite all your famous New York friends, and between my house and yours, we'll have plenty of room to put some friends up for the night."

"No."

"Why?"

"I don't need a party."

"Yes you do!"

"No I don't."

"*Yes you do.* You've been single ever since you broke up with Silvana. In the past couple of years you've become…"

"Quiet?"

"That's not the word I would have used, but okay, let's say quiet. What's up with you?"

Alex looked around. "I'm content here. I spent a lot of years with Silvana, and you know that wasn't always easy. Here, alone, I feel like I can think, like I can create again."

"That's because ultimately she wasn't right for you. I told you that a year after you got together. But that doesn't mean the right woman isn't out there. Maybe she's looking for you as we speak."

"Maybe," Alex conceded. "But I don't need a party."

"Yes you do!"

"What time is the reception for your exhibit tomorrow night?"

"Real smooth subject change. Seven o'clock. Hey, can you get there early to help me out?"

"Absolutely. I can't wait to see Mom and Dad try to explain your work to all their Main Line friends."

"They don't have to. I've already sold pieces to two of them for their shore homes and I have one on commission."

"When I spoke to Mom yesterday, she told me how proud of you she is, Dréa."

"Really? I wonder if she'll ever tell me."

"I think they're finally getting that just because they didn't understand our talent, it didn't mean we weren't talented."

"Did you know that they display your *Rocklandia* magazine covers in the house, Alex? They're proud of you too."

"They're softening with age."

"They're impressed with your success. And so am I."

"I have you to thank for that." Alex downed the last of her hot chocolate and looked at her watch. "I need to get back into the darkroom and change my developer. The color isn't right." She grinned. "Hey, it's like the old days...I'm on deadline. See you tomorrow...lots to do before then."

Alex stood and kissed Dréa's cheek and pet the dog on her way out. She poured the last of the hot chocolate into her cup and climbed the back stairs.

Dréa heard the muffled Steel Eyes music bouncing through the walls and waited another minute before entering Alex's study. She shuffled some papers on the desk, knocking the computer mouse by accident. The screen awoke from sleep mode.

"Nifty," she said under her breath. Alex had not signed out of her email account. Dréa compiled the list of email addresses and hit the Print button. Only the addresses printed without an accompanying list of names. "A surprise party, Alex. That's *just* what *you* need." When the list finished printing, she stuffed it into the pocket of her winter coat, called the dog and locked the front door on her way out.

CHAPTER THIRTY

"Over there…at two o'clock," Kenna said.

Maddy followed her lead and got into the car.

"You okay?" Jocelyn asked Kenna while driving away.

"Other than the fact that someone's going to need to wake me if I fall asleep tonight?"

"Is the concussion that bad?"

"It wasn't good," Maddy said from the backseat. "She heaved a few times, had blurry vision and the knot on her head is probably the size of a baseball by now. On the bright side, I can tell you her left hook is still pretty solid."

Jocelyn hung a right. "Your papers are in the glove box. I was able to retrieve them from the safe house."

Kenna pulled out the documents and looked them over. "Has there been any chatter about tonight?"

"No, it's been quiet, which is why Uncle and I have decided your best bet for getting out of here is to do it right now, before anyone has a chance to put the pieces together or come looking for you. I figure that will happen as soon as the guy who hit you contacts his people."

"He was wearing a ski mask, so I'd be hard pressed to give you a description," Maddy said, "other than the fact that he's about five nine with a stocky build."

Jocelyn glanced at Kenna. "It's a shame you have to travel in the shape you're in."

"Speaking of that," Kenna began.

"Maddy, hand Kenna the bag on the floor."

"Thanks, Jocelyn, I owe you." Kenna pulled out the change of clothes Jocelyn brought for her and started stripping.

"As soon as I know our safe house is clear, I'll get the rest of your things and send them to you. In the meantime..." Jocelyn pulled the car into a poorly lit parking lot and killed the headlights "...you'll drive this car back to Hanover and you'll follow the directions on the map for parking. I've reserved a double cabin for you both on the train to Paris under both your aliases. You'll be the only ones in the compartment, and there's staff to serve you so you can stay inside. Here are your tickets. Take the bag I brought for you. There's another change of clothes, toiletries, cash...well, you know the drill. Once you're in Paris, Uncle's driver will pick you up outside the Gare du Nord. Do you remember what he looks like?"

"Yes, of course. Then what?"

"That's above my pay grade. They'll take over from there and get you home safe and sound." Jocelyn smiled and leaned over to hug Kenna. "I'm glad you're okay. Until next time, my friend." She turned around to address Maddy. "You're lucky my friend here has lightning reflexes and that she vouched for you."

"Don't I know it?" Maddy replied. "Thank you for getting me out of here, Jocelyn."

Jocelyn looked into Maddy's eyes and then at Kenna. "It's a long train ride to Paris, so don't kill each other while you're sequestered in that cabin."

Kenna scoffed. "We're past that. We are past that, right, Maddy?"

"For now. Besides, Jocelyn, under different circumstances I'd rather stay right here tonight."

"Hmm, well then, have Kenna give you my number in Paris."

"I will," Maddy flirted back.

"Excuse me, you two…I've got guns, a concussion and spooks trying to kill us."

"That reminds me, Kenna. Remember to throw your gun from the train before you hit the border. Until next time, dear friend."

Kenna squeezed her hand, and when Jocelyn left the car, she slid over into the driver's seat, waited for Maddy to get into the passenger seat and took off toward the autobahn.

"Pretty girl, what's her story?" Maddy said.

"Forget it, I'm not giving you her number," Kenna said softly.

Maddy laughed. "I think it's safe to say that women are a subject we should avoid for now. Are you getting hungry?"

"It wouldn't matter, we're not stopping."

"What if I have to pee?"

"Find a cup or hold it."

"You're serious."

Kenna veered onto the autobahn and hit the gas. They rode in silence for the first half hour.

"You should stop to get some ice for your head."

"We'll be in Hanover in under two hours. I'll get it on the train."

"Whatever happened to Steel Eyes?"

"What do you mean?"

"Why is it that she never came back?"

Kenna glanced at her, stalling to think of an answer. "She had more important things to do."

"Things like bringing me to justice?"

"Don't rub it in."

"I happen to be a Steel Eyes fan. I wish you'd make a comeback."

"Yeah?"

"Yeah."

"Well, I wish *you'd* shut up."

CHAPTER THIRTY-ONE

The overnight train from Hanover to Paris ushered in a peace of mind Kenna had never expected to gain from the disparate pieces of her personal puzzle. She had finally slain the demons who had once owned her. Even though Alex had betrayed her, Maddy was no longer a wound.

By the time the train pulled into the Gare du Nord, the weight of Kenna's past with Maddy had dissolved. They had boarded the train in Hanover with a bilateral truce and exited as founding members of an exclusive sorority. Few women could even fathom what they had done, what they knew and had seen…who they had been. Maddy was her ally, not her enemy. The old adage still rang true: "All is fair in love and war." One-on-one, Maddy was good company, tending to the details so Kenna could rest.

"Here," Kenna said, handing her a piece of paper just before they disembarked.

"What is it?"

Kenna quoted what Maddy had said at the Berlin safe house. "I know if the situation were reversed, I'd want to see this."

Her expression serious, Maddy took the paper. She unfolded it, read the one word and the number beneath that name, then smiled. "What changed your mind?"

"That's *not* my blessing. It's just Jocelyn's number, and I swear, Maddy, if you hurt her…" Kenna kissed her left fist "…Miss Left Hook will find you."

Maddy feigned fear. "Oh, no, not Miss Hook. Stop worrying. Are *you* the same person you were all those years ago?"

"No, I'm not. But just because I've changed, that doesn't mean you have."

"I never want to meet Miss Hook again…I'll be good. Something tells me Jocelyn can take care of herself."

"Come to think of it, you'll be in worse shape answering to her than you ever would be answering to me. Maybe I'll just wish *you* the good luck."

Before parting ways in Paris, they would meet with Uncle. He would personally make certain Kenna had immediate arrangements to fly back to the States and that Maddy would securely reenter Great Britain.

Outside the Gare du Nord, Kenna instantly recognized the vintage Rolls Royce whose driver still wore a chauffeur's cap.

They met with Uncle briefly in the car. Kenna was elated to see him, but for the first time she noted a slight tremor in his hand—he looked older. She closed her eyes and tried to picture what her parents might look like by now, but even her vivid imagination couldn't envision them as anything other than youthful and vibrant. Then the odd thought struck her that in a few years she would be older than they had been when they died.

"Our agencies are aware of the security breach and are cooperating to find the source of it," Uncle began. "Darius—the man you knocked unconscious in the warehouse—was found dead."

"I didn't think I hit him hard enough to kill him, Uncle."

"You didn't, Kenna. When the cleaners arrived, there was a bullet hole in his head. He was shot from behind at close range."

Kenna and Maddy glanced at each other.

"Jesus, we got out of there just in time," Maddy said. "Do you have any clue who assassinated him?"

"Not yet," Uncle said. "In any event, it's in the hands of the chiefs and the backdoor politicians by now, and what's important is that you both arrived in one piece and have safe passage home."

Kenna kissed his cheek. "I don't know what I would do without you."

"Nor I, you," he replied with his fatherly smile.

Glad to meet Maddy, Uncle related two stories to her about her grandmother's bravery during the Second World War. "I met Frau Messerschmidt on two occasions to receive her information. Looking at you brings back memories of your grandmother; your eyes are exactly like hers. She was a good woman, Maddy," he said. "Like you. Fearless and determined in the face of treachery."

"Thank you. It helps me to have that to hang on to in times of failure."

"From what I've learned"—Uncle chuckled—"your prime minister certainly doesn't think you're a failure."

"You know him?" Maddy asked. "He knows of me?"

"Yes to both. You'll be meeting him in London. Offer him my best wishes. Kenna, I hear Phyllis isn't doing so well."

"I'll be in LA next month, and I've already planned to spend time with her."

"She misses you." He patted her hand. "It's not easy being an orphan, is it?"

Kenna did not answer. She was afraid that, as with her music studio, if she ever walked through that door again, there'd be no way to *un*walk through it...ever.

"Take care of yourself, Uncle. I love you."

* * *

Kenna trudged through her front door, climbed the stairs, stripped and ran a steaming bath for her aching body. She stood naked in front of the full-length mirror.

So this is what almost forty looks like.

Her gaze drifted to the display of scars that landscaped her once muscular and smooth left shoulder. Unconsciously, she flexed and extended the fingers of her left hand, glad that someone had shot the bastard who had done this to her and changed her life. As hard as it was to imagine, she needed to retire from operations, at least for now.

She eased into the hot water inch by inch. It was too hot, in the exaggerated way that warm feels hot when coming in from the cold. In all manner, Kenna Waverly had finally come in from the cold.

Groaning as the hot water soothed her, she thumbed through the entertainment section of last Sunday's *Philadelphia Inquirer.* A small ad in the bottom right-hand corner of the page drew her attention. It read: "Musicians and artists welcome at the Fort. First and third Friday open mic night. Arrive early to network and meet other players. No need to bring basic amps, mics etc. Seven p.m.'"

When Kenna finished her soak, every hour of her long journey to and from Europe finally consumed her. The knot on the back of her head still hurt like hell.

Christ, even my shoulder aches from pouncing on Darius. What I should do is go to bed.

Upstairs, outside her lifeless studio, she stared at her hand on the doorknob before turning it. This time she bravely stepped across the threshold without looking down.

Her multiplatinum records sizzled on the wall in the glow of the dimmed spotlights. She surveyed the room from right to left before committing to another step, then plugged in a Fender amplifier and turned it on. In spite of herself, she had dutifully maintained her guitar collection.

"You're still a hottie." She stroked Ruby's neck. The sensation of her fingertips touching the strings felt less than familiar. Then she reached for Sweet Jayne, hugged her to her body and said, "Welcome home, baby."

Music has always been my escape...so when did I become its prisoner?

She selected a cord, plugged in and tuned up. Warming up gently, she noticed how her fingers were no longer nimble, how slow and heavy they felt when she played the scales and chord progressions. Still, she hit most of the notes first time out.

Too many mistakes!

They frustrated and defeated her. Her left hand hurt, and certain angles caused stabbing pain in her left wrist. The doctors had told her repeatedly that there wasn't anything they could do to help her.

This sucks! I suck!

She wiped down Jayne's neck with a guitar cloth, hung her back up in the guitar closet and yanked the amp's cord from the wall in silent protest.

Bone-tired, she lay in bed for a half hour, wondering if she could ever become a great guitarist again. The question gnawed at her until she was too restless to sleep, replaying in her mind those moments when as Steel Eyes, she would storm the stage with Ruby strapped against her. For an instant she conjured the sensation of playing with abandon and passion.

Hell, I'd settle for good. Even adequate seems unlikely right now. But for the first time since I was shot...I want to play.

She remembered how Mel had said to her often that she owned being Steel Eyes—that being onstage was Kenna simply taking back the power she had given away to Alex. How many times had Mel said to her, "You already own it, little sister, so just take it back?"

Then she realized she had never had to choose greatness before. It had chosen her. But if she *really* did want it, then she could choose that choice *right now*.

After pulling on her sweats, she trudged back up the stairs, pulled out Ruby and plugged her in. Red and still shiny, that guitar had *channeled* Steel Eyes, embodied the Steel Eyes story, such that she wondered if by now the guitar could play itself.

This is the most refined magic I've ever known. She tuned Ruby. *When I make music, Ruby makes magic; fucking bitch knows how to make magic. She knows this! And she makes me magical.*

Kenna stepped into the recording booth and cued up The Allman Brothers song "Whipping Post."

Aah, Greg, Duane and Dickey. Home. She tilted Ruby's neck up and hit Play to jam with her favorite band.

She held Ruby close, her sinewy fingers attacking the fretboard with a rusty soulfulness. And like skydiving, it came back to her in a lick. Like skydiving, she knew that if it hadn't, she would simply crash and fracture into a thousand barely recognizable fragments. While her hands were not as young and as fast as Steel Eyes's, they were wiser, and in their care, the notes were now sacrosanct.

Once she started to play, she *couldn't* stop. Anger…no, rage and passion, longing, crashed into each other as she played her own songs until there was nothing left of her. The Transcendent Gateway finally beckoned her, and all she wanted to do was answer its call. She had begun to block out the pain in her hand after the first ten songs, and that had to have been at least twenty takes ago for each tune.

Spent and pale, when Kenna turned the doorknob to leave the soundproof, windowless studio, she winced at the pain in her wrist and at the affront of daylight smacking her in the face, assaulting her through the skylights in the cathedral ceiling.

"Fuck *me*!"

It was seven in the morning. She had played right through the night.

Numb from exhaustion, she closed the blackout shades in her bedroom, fell facedown on the bed and didn't surface until every depleted reservoir in her body filled and replenished her at her core.

CHAPTER THIRTY-TWO

Whoever said obsession couldn't be a good thing! Kenna was lost in thought while waiting for Eyes4U's typed words to appear on her computer screen.

The past several weeks had proven fruitful. With the exception of her short jaunt to LA for her goddaughter Dalia's sixth birthday party, and time spent with Phyllis van Bourgeade, who was recovering from knee surgery, Kenna lived in her music studio. She only left it to prepare food, which she then ate while mixing new guitar tracks in the recording booth. For days at a time she acclimated herself to naps on the studio sofa rather than sleeping in her bed.

EYES4U: I take it you're working late again tonight?

SED: Yes, but it's a good thing. Except that it limits my time with you.

EYES4U: I've missed us lately. Is that okay to say?

Kenna smiled. She couldn't tell Eyes how she had started playing again. Nor could she casually mention that facing death in a Berlin warehouse had made it crystal clear to Kenna that she *needed* to play again, and that in order to do that she needed to be inspired; that it was Eyes who had inspired her. And she knew that the death of Darius, the man who shot Steel Eyes, ignited in her the need to reclaim her soul. Taking back her power from him was like taking back the power she had naively given to Alex. Suddenly, all roads led her back to Steel Eyes.

SED: *More than okay. I feel the same way. But it's important that I finish what I've started.*

EYES4U: *Understood. I'm pretty fanatical about my work too.*

SED: *Which is...?*

EYES4U: *I've told you, Disguise, I'm an all-or-nothing girl. Full disclosure or none at all.*

SED: *I know, but that doesn't mean I can't try.*

EYES4U: *Let's see, you've ruled out English teacher, anything medical, chef, spy...*

SED: *Okay, you win*

EYES4U: *I'll have won when we meet face-to-face. Oops, I have a kitchen timer going off. See you tomorrow? Say yes.*

SED: *Yes, yes, yes. Stay warm.*

With years of dust wiped away, the equipment lights flickered in the studio. Kenna had almost told Mel and Rich that she had started playing again when she saw them at Dalia's party in LA, but the timing wasn't right. She needed to know deep down that she was physically capable of playing. Presently, the thought of taking the stage with her dear friends and former bandmates was intimidating, daunting—the kind of daunting that made her stomach rumble the way it had right before her first performance at the Whisky all those years ago, when she had tossed her cookies in the ladies' room. She'd never forget that jumbled emotion of self-doubt and fear; the fear of failing, the fear of succeeding—that sense of doubt even doubting itself. The jarring recollection caused acid to bubble into her esophagus.

Tonight was the night. She stuffed the scrap of paper with the directions to the Fort in Philadelphia into the pocket of her jeans along with some guitar picks. Her vintage black Stratocaster would be her date for the event. As much as she hated to admit it, the Strat was lighter and therefore easier on her left shoulder, and she had grown accustomed to playing it with its double cutaway shape of the body. Even if she could bring the famous Gibson Les Paul Custom, Ruby just felt so heavy now.

Kenna's warm breath puffed like smoke as the old Porsche set out for the long pitch-dark drive to the city. She could make it in an hour if there was no black ice on the roads. Thanks to modernization, she had to slow down twice for deer forced to forage on the Atlantic City Expressway.

An hour later, the old Porsche engine rumbled in the bone-chilling February night as it idled at the red light on Frankford Avenue in the Mayfair section of Philadelphia. When the light changed, Kenna made two more turns into a ghost of a neighborhood that had seen better times, but not in a very long time. What was once a thriving blue-collar neighborhood with kids playing ball in the street—and the hoopla of block parties every summer, was now a spate of boarded-up row houses, each with its requisite playpen plot of grass. Sandwiched between the Latino Church of Inner City Rehab and a hoagie joint, the narrow one-way street had succumbed to dilapidated industry.

Cold. Bitter, biting, freaking arctic-cold wind splayed flesh and sliced through to the bone with its East Coast winter blade. Kenna glanced at the clock. *Seven on the nose. Might as well be the middle of the night it's so dark.* The Porsche's left rear wheel spun out on the dirty city ice. Around the next curve, the top floor of the decaying warehouse shone like a battered tanker on an otherwise boatless sea.

Kenna drove around the block twice before trusting her vintage Porsche to a neighborhood that hadn't been safe since the Rolling Stones had followed the Beatles across the pond. But in that warehouse two nights a month, scattered among the novices, some of the area's best musicians schlepped their instruments up the concrete stairwells with the broken and dirty windows to claim their birthright—the Philly Sound. Tonight, Kenna Waverly would be one of them.

"Maybe I don't really want to do this," she said to the idling engine before letting it sputter to a halt. "Maybe I'm just in love with my car heater." The stillness around her amplified the quiet. Immediately, the frigid air permeated the old metal and sucked out the heat. Pulling up her collar against the gelid night air before she could rationalize her way back home, where a homing device named the remote control beckoned, she extracted her beat-up guitar case from the passenger seat. With her breath trailing off in swaths of cold-smoke, Kenna hustled toward the dissonant screeching melodies that spilled out into the desolate industrial neighborhood.

She paused on the second landing to rest for a minute. *I swear this used to be easier. Where's a roadie when you really need one!*

What she witnessed when she finally reached the top floor startled her as her gaze drank it in. Well lit and, more importantly, warm, this place was where musicians and artists collided in a panoply of creativity. Hipsters, Goths, misfits like her—artists expressing themselves. She breathed it all in, deeply.

For an instant, she felt just as much of a hunger to be young again like them as not to be. The point was that she was finally hungry—hungry enough to come here in the bitter cold to eclipse her darkened shadow. She knew of no rule that put a limit on the age of a rocker...as long as they were *men*. In her time, the role of rock star had been exclusively a boys' club— well maybe with the exception of a few like Janis Joplin, a forever member of the Twenty-Seven Club—a designation she was grateful to have avoided.

What chance would she have now? The Gen-Xers were already old in the eyes of the Gen Ys and Gen Zs...which didn't bode well for a woman who came from a generation that didn't even have a letter designation.

Kenna pulled off one of her lined leather gloves, and propping up her guitar case against the table in the entrance, she smiled back at the young volunteer who greeted her at the Check In sign. She blew three short warm breaths into her fist to loosen up her fingers, took a name tag and scribbled *Kenna* onto it.

The cacophony of instruments tuning up was no worse than the sound of kids playing in their garages after school...which she assumed most of them did. But unlike Kenna they were the regulars, the core artists who braved *every* winter night to come out to play just a song or two with, and in front of, their peers, not caring a lick about pesky details like stage fright or bad tuning.

"Here you go," the volunteer said, handing Kenna a card with a number on it. "Your number is eighteen. Go to the right of the stage when number sixteen is on and hand the stage guy your card. You're playing alone, right?"

Kenna froze. "I thought there was an area where I could meet some musicians to jam with."

"Oh…sure. All the way to the right there's an area for soloists to network…but they're *mostly rockers* tonight." His tone reeked of *Aren't you a little old for this?*

Kenna glared at him when she picked up her guitar case. "Over to the right, you said?" *Fucking kids!* Then again, she remembered a time when her guitar case didn't feel *this* heavy. *Fucking kids!*

Crossing the warehouse, she looked at a ceiling so high that the room felt spacious even filled with people. She surveyed the art hung on the walls, the objects on display for sale. Magnetized by the cobalt-blue in an abstract painting, she stopped to admire it.

"I'm the artist. May I answer any questions about the piece?" a woman in her forties said. She had billowing brown waves and a smile that made Kenna feel welcome among all these kids.

"I'll say one thing for you. Your sense of cobalt is the most *cobalt-y* I've ever seen. It reminds me of a summer storm over the ocean."

The artist laughed. "Cobalt-y?" She pointed to the card on the wall next to the painting. "Did you notice the title?"

Kenna glanced at the card. "Summer rain. Well, I guess that says it all. You're asking five hundred?"

"Since you're from my generation, make it four fifty."

"You've got a deal. Problem is, I drove here in my Porsche, and if I take it with me, I'll have to leave my vintage guitar, which I could never do. Can I pay you tonight and pick it up another time?"

"Sure, hon'. Where do you live?"

"Down the shore."

"Me too!" The artist wrote her private home number on the back of her card along with her address. "I'm in Longport."

Kenna laughed. "So am I!"

"I'm Andréa, but you can call me Dréa," the artist said. "Such a small town and we had to come all the way into Philly to meet."

Kenna shook her hand. "Kenna." She peeled five one-hundred dollar bills from her wallet and handed them over.

"Thank you," Dréa said before handing her a fifty and putting a Sold tag on the piece.

"I'll be in touch, Dréa, but right now I have some demons to tame."

Dréa leaned in to share a secret. "I call them *kids*."

Kenna laughed, picked up her guitar case and wandered into the musicians' pit.

Over by the sidewall, she spotted an area full of musicians in varying stages of preparation, and the closer she came, the more she could feel their eyes on her. She breathed an imperceptible sigh, flashed the Steel Eyes smile and submerged.

"Hello," she said.

There was no response to her presence at all. She was fucking invisible; old and invisible.

"Hey," she said, louder this time, refusing to be intimidated by a crowd with a heavy Converse sneakers vibe.

"Hi," said the twentyish, scruffy, dark-haired boy holding the Fender bass by its neck. He reminded her of a young JJ. "I can't see your name tag."

"Sorry, haven't had the chance to put it on." She held out her hand. "I'm Kenna. Lead guitar."

The young man sized her up with a disbelieving grin. "Lead, huh?"

She could practically read his mind. "*Some old chick with a beat-up guitar in an old beat-up case.*"

"Put it there, Kenna." They shook hands. "I'm Rex, bass player."

Kenna glanced at the instrument still in his hand. "Yeah, I gathered."

Rex gawked at her the way most men did, especially when they saw that broad, sexy smile framed by the gaunt cheekbones, long hair and stunning gray eyes.

"So, Rex, how do I find some players who need a lead?"

He placed the bass on a guitar stand and turned to the crowd behind him. "Yo, Jack, Primo, come here."

Kenna figured Rex was the guy to know.

"Listen up, guys, she's a lead guitarist looking for a band."

"Hi," Primo said, sporting the same general look that Rex, and now all the people in the circle, were giving her. Most of them turned back around to their groups without so much as a nod.

She unzipped her leather jacket. Her long legs were wrapped in molded-on jeans, and a guitar charm dangled into her cleavage framed by the V-neck sweater. The kids stared at her as though she was a parent who had just invaded their space or embarrassed them in front of their friends. Kenna sucked it up, but her momentary shiver wasn't from the cold outside—it was from the realization that this would be the first time she would play in public since that fated night when she had been shot...almost a decade before.

The only way I can fail is to not play. I can do this. I've played to the biggest audiences around the world.

"Hi!" said a girl with blue hair as she walked up to Kenna. "I'm Deidre...singer. I mean, I'm Deidre and I sing. What's your talent?"

"Lead guitar player, singer." Kenna smiled and shook her hand. "What do you like to sing?" she asked as she unpacked the Strat and plugged it into her Boss tuner.

"Steel Eyes," singer said.

"What?" For a second Kenna thought she had addressed her as Steel Eyes, then realized she was just answering Kenna's question.

"I love to sing Steel Eyes music. I sit in a lot with Jack, Rex and Primo. They're great at Steel Eyes covers."

Oh yeah. I've got cover bands. A band of sweat emerged around her hairline. *Pressure, yes; hot flash, hell no!*

"Can you play any Steel Eyes music, Kenna?"

"Yes, but I haven't played most of those leads in a long time. It's old music." She wasn't lying.

Primo turned to her. "Warm up. We're on in ten minutes. What's your name?"

"Kenna."

"Okay, Kenna, we're playing 'Somewhere Like You.' You *do* know that one, don't you?"

Kenna's mouth went dry. She nodded, put her head down and spent the next nine minutes doing warmups and the lead guitar licks from the song.

"Hey, Primo, this oughta be interesting," Jack said. "Have you ever rocked out with anyone *her* age before?"

Kenna pretended not to hear them.

Primo peered over Jack's lanky shoulder. "She can't be that old...she's still good-lookin'."

"Yeah," Jack said, scratching his day-old stubble. "Killer smile."

Kids! Screw it, I've got bigger fish to fry tonight!

Trying to subdue the adrenaline, Kenna realized she wasn't this nervous the times she had played at the Grammys. *That was so last millennium.*

"Come on," Singer said, "we're up next."

When they took the stage, Kenna positioned herself across from Rex where she could watch his changes on the bass guitar. The song required the bass and the lead guitar to be in exact sync. She had written the music on Sweet Jayne and then arranged it in counterpoint to show off Mel's skills.

Rex did the lead-in, Primo hit the bass drum right on time, and eight bars later, Kenna joined them. Singer hit the notes with a style reminiscent of Mel but with a unique twist on the harmonies. Kenna liked it. Two minutes later it was time for Kenna's solo, and she realized she'd forgotten to bring the Transcendent Gateway.

All eyes were on her as she hit the first section of the solo.

Fuck, fuck, fuck!

She tried to pick it up again, but the other musicians had to fill in for her. She flubbed it, missed the timing, hit the wrong string. The acid bubbled into her esophagus *again*. When the song ended, she saw the look Primo gave Rex and wanted to run off the stage.

Wait a minute! I wrote that music. Instead of running away to hide, she decided to let all hell fly. "'Whipping Post,'" she called out and began the lead-in. Rex's bass jumped on the notes, and Primo attacked the eleven-eight timing. Kenna closed her eyes as the sound of her metallic strings first heated up the stage and then *fried* it. She jumped when she played the high notes and bounced back and forth as she burned them into the old fretboard. Singer slammed the gritty parts with vocal precision, and when Jack wiped out on the swell of Kenna's guitar wave, he retreated to a solid rhythm on his guitar. By the end of the song, Rex's bass and Kenna's lead had whipped "Whipping Post."

"Yeah!" Primo yelled as he hit the last beat.

"Fuckin' A!" Rex said, offering Kenna a high-five with his pick hand.

A crowd had assembled by the stage, their applause a sign that even those nasty little pricks from earlier couldn't deny her.

"Hey, Kenna," Jack said, "can you play 'Miles from You'?"

Kenna nodded. She'd written that tune so long ago, its howling lead and the shadow of emptiness it left behind were pure Alex. Kenna figured that was the reason for her futile reflex to always try to nail the notes to air. Her face flushed. Singer smiled and patted her on the back.

She played the first line to the song, and before she knew it they were through the hardest parts, the musicians on full-scale alert to keep up with her. When the song ended, Kenna hurried off the stage and over to her gear as though someone was about to steal it. She got the Strat into the case without performing her fretboard-cleaning ritual, threw on her jacket, picked up her case and bolted. She stopped on the frozen second-floor landing with the punched-out windows to fish out her car keys and to switch her guitar case to her other hand.

"Kenna!" Singer said, shuffling down the steps. "Wait up."

"Singer, you need to get a coat on."

"I would have if you hadn't run out of there. Where are you going? The whole place is talking about you. You can't leave!"

"Gotta go."

"Here, take my number." Singer pulled Kenna's hand out of her coat pocket and wrote on the back of it with a pen she whipped out of her boot leg. "Promise you'll call me!"

Kenna laughed. "Okay."

"No, I mean it!" Singer said, her hand on her hip.

Singer's insistence reminded her of Mel, and that made her laugh again. "I promise, Singer."

* * *

When Singer got back upstairs, Primo and Rex were waiting for her.

"Who the hell *is* that woman anyway…and how come this is the first time we've seen her? Fuck, when will we see her again?" Primo asked, perplexed.

Singer just smiled.

CHAPTER THIRTY-THREE

When Kenna awoke, she watched the blotchy gray clouds hover over the suspended animation of a beach town in winter. She made coffee, lit a fire and stared down at the blurry number written in ink on the back of her hand. She stretched out her arm until the numbers were far enough away to see them clearly and then picked up her phone.

"Hi, Singer," she said when the woman answered. "This is Kenna, from last night."

"Hey. The Fort was buzzing after you left."

Kenna chuckled. "And that's a good thing?"

"Are you for real? I mean, how is it I'd never heard of you before last night? You're wicked, woman!"

"Even though I botched the Steel Eyes song?"

"Well, Steel Eyes leads aren't exactly easy," Singer said sympathetically. "I think you more than redeemed yourself with 'Miles from You.'"

"Do you have a car?"

"Yeah, why, you need a ride?"

"No, I have an offer for you. I have a great music studio in my house down the shore. I loved your voice and wanted to know if you'd like to come down and do some songs with me. I'm in Longport."

"Just say when…I'm already there!"

"Anytime you like."

"Give me your address. I can be there in a little over an hour."

When Kenna hung up, she raced upstairs into the studio and dug out several boxes. First, she packed up the Grammy statues. In the next box, she stacked her multiplatinum records, in the third, fourth and fifth she organized all the other gold records and then stashed the boxes in her bedroom closet. Lastly, she took down all the photos Steel Eyes had taken with every A-list celebrity and dignitary.

As soon as the Steel Eyes memorabilia was gone, the doorbell rang. Kenna flew down the stairs and opened the door.

"Singer, glad you could make it. Come in and get warm. I have a fire going."

Singer was shorter than Kenna and more curvy than lanky. She sported short, cropped hair and softly rounded features. Her dark eyes formed a stunning contrast against whatever the unnamed shade of blue her hair was, and she exuded the edginess of a generation that actually had a *letter* designation.

"Do you have any coffee?" Singer unraveled her scarf and dropped it with her full-length, black wool coat on a chair, revealing a different shade of blue sweater over black jeans and thick outdoor boots. She kicked off the boots and put on a pair of flats she took from her messenger bag.

"Yep, made it about ten minutes ago." Kenna led her into the kitchen.

"Smells good."

"It's Jamaican Blue Mountain."

"I've never had it."

"Then you're in for a treat," Kenna said as she placed a plate of rolls on the table.

Singer poured a cup of coffee, walked into the living room and gazed at the high ceilings and art-filled walls. She surveyed every piece, taking in the lithographs, the acrylic paintings and finally the sculptures. "Wow, this place is amazing, Kenna."

"Thanks. So...you wanna hang out by the fire first to warm up?"

Singer beamed. "Where's that studio?"

Kenna led her upstairs and down the hall.

"My god! You have a sound booth?" Singer said when she entered the room. "I don't know what to look at first! Hey, is that a vintage Hammond organ? Wow, look at that PA...and all the amps. Jesus, how much equipment do you have?"

"I've definitely collected a few things over the years, Singer."

"Do you have any guitars?"

"I have a few of them, why?"

"I can play rhythm. Not like you, but I can play."

Kenna smiled. "Excellent." She walked into the guitar closet and returned with a Martin acoustic. She plugged it into an amp, tuned it and handed it to Singer. "Here, this one looks like you." She adjusted the microphone she had already set up for Singer's vocals.

"And a vintage Martin," Singer said as she took the guitar from Kenna.

"If you stick around long enough," Kenna began, "everything becomes vintage. So what would you like to play?"

"I loved how you played 'Whipping Post' last night. Let's do that one again."

"Okay." Kenna took her white Les Paul from the guitar stand and sat on a stool facing Singer.

Singer began to play the chords and stopped.

"Something wrong?" Kenna said.

"Let's sing it together, Kenna."

"I don't think so. You're really good and I'm only passable as a singer."

Singer rolled her eyes. "So what! Who cares? Come on, if I can play guitar with you, then you can sing with me."

Kenna laughed. "Okay, point taken."

After their fifth rendition, Kenna set the Paul on the guitar stand. "Singer, can I run something by you? I need the opinion of a good musician."

"You think *I'm* good?" She laughed.

"I think you're terrific. Your sound is so fresh."

"Thanks. What do you want to know?"

"I've been working on a new sound, but it might be too mellow. Can I have the Martin?"

Kenna used her unique style to strum the bronze acoustic strings, their tone bright like sunlight—she made them ring. She swayed into the lazy beat and set down a melody that Singer took off with. She vocalized with Kenna's guitar until she uncovered the innermost harmonies.

"I love your voice, Singer. It's airy and clean," Kenna said when they'd stopped. "You surf over the notes like Sarah Vaughan."

"Your music is beautiful, Kenna. It's dreamy and creamy, and I want more of it."

"Let's work on it right now. You ready to write a song?"

"Really? No kidding? You want to write with me?"

"Hell yes!"

"Right now" lasted the whole afternoon and into the evening. By the time they took a break, they had their first versions of a song with the working title "What Goes Around." The only common thread to Steel Eyes's music was that Steel Eyes wrote it. But no one would ever guess it or believe it. Soft like velvet, there wasn't a hint of jazz or hard rock in its style. The simple and direct melody flowed with a sweet temperament devoid of the edginess that had defined the Steel Eyes era. The choruses and rests embraced two-part vocal harmonies.

This new style was a Steel Eyes counterrevolution—by all counts, a coup. Kenna's music had at last surrendered to the sultry melodies that colored her innermost self.

They recorded several versions—fast, slow, and arrangements with the emphasis in different places.

"Take a seat, Singer," Kenna said when they were done. She cranked up the playbacks and joined Singer on the couch.

"Oh, man, this place is great! Seriously, Kenna, where the hell have you been hanging that none of us have ever heard you play before last night?"

Kenna laughed it off. "I haven't played out in a really long time. Wait a sec, Singer. First off, what exactly *do* you call that shade of blue in your hair?"

"It's my own creation—aquamarine mixed with indigo violet," she said proudly. "Thank you for the best day I can remember." She stared into Kenna's eyes and brushed the side of Kenna's leg with her hand.

Kenna flinched.

"I'm sorry...seems I got the wrong message?"

Kenna smiled warmly. "It's okay."

"You're not attracted to me."

"Quite the contrary. I'm just kind of involved with someone. Besides, I'm too old for you." Kenna thought of Eyes4U, the woman she had never seen; the woman whose voice would be that of a stranger; the woman she almost never stopped thinking about.

"I should have guessed you weren't single."

Kenna squeezed Singer's hand. "I'm starving. How about you?"

"Yes! How long have we been at this anyway?"

"I have no idea. That's why there are no clocks in here. For me, music is timeless."

"Is there anyplace to get something to eat around here?"

"Come on, I'll buy you dinner if you come with me to pick up a painting I bought last night to hang in here." Kenna pointed to the wall that now looked so clean without her past hanging around.

Later that night, after Singer had left, Kenna hung her new painting in the studio, covering the places where Steel Eyes's photos had hung. She cranked up the takes she and Singer had recorded and stared at the abstract painting. The cobalt reminded her of Steel Eyes's mask, and if she weren't so lazy, she would have dug out the mask to compare the two—the mask that would surely now look back at her with a vacant stare, a vacancy she now entertained filling.

Feels like it's getting late. She thought of Eyes4U and raced to her computer to make their usual online date on time.

EYES4U: *How was your day?*

SED: *I had a great day. You?*

EYES4U: *Not as great as your day sounds, but not bad. My sister was bugging me to do something I didn't want to do. You know how that goes!*

SED: *Not really. I'm an only child, and my parents died young.*

EYES4U: *I'm sorry, I didn't know. What made your day so great?*

SED: *A new friend came over and we played some music. Sang, played guitars.*

EYES4U: *A new female friend?*

SED: *Yes.*

EYES4U: *Is she cute?*

SED: *Yep. Very.*

EYES4U: *Should I be jealous now?*

SED: *I have too much invested in you to look anywhere else, Eyes.*

EYES4U: *You really mean that?*

SED: *I do. Springtime is almost here. Why don't we meet then?*

EYES4U: *You're serious! You're ready?*

SED: *I will be by the time the days get warm.*

EYES4U: *That's months away.*

SED: *You're angry.*

EYES4U: *Just impatient.*

SED: *It's going to take a while to finish the project I've been working on all winter, and then I'm all yours.*

EYES4U: *Well, when you put it that way, how can I say no?*

SED: *Maybe we should start planning our meeting.*

EYES4U: *Sorry, I'm calling it a date.*

SED: *I'm still a little scared about the attraction thing…thinking you may not be attracted to me.*

EYES4U: *It goes both ways, Disguise. My risk is just as big as yours.*

SED: *Thanks, that doesn't help. Besides, I'm already attracted to you.*

EYES4U: *I'll bet you're as beautiful as your words. Your insecurity is showing again.*

SED: *Yeah, how about that? Does it drive you crazy yet?*

EYES4U: No. You drive me crazy. Almost forgot, I have a project that I'm working on, and for the next couple of weeks my time is not my own, so it looks like we'll be hit or miss.

Kenna breathed a sigh of relief, knowing she needed as much practice time as possible.

EYES4U: By the way, have you seen the new issue of Rocklandia *magazine?*

SED: No, why?

EYES4U: They just published a whole Steel Eyes retrospective. All never-before-seen photos.

SED: What?! I have to go get my copy from my mailbox RIGHT NOW!

EYES4U: Enjoy, babe. Miss you.

SED: Miss you more.

* * *

Kenna raced outside and tore open the flap to her mailbox. She dropped everything but her copy of *Rocklandia* onto the table by the door and sat by her fire until the chill subsided.

Steel Eyes's full-body shot stared back at her from the cover. Clad in steely silver with her cobalt mask, on stage with that fierce "come fuck me" expression and her hair flying around her; playing Ruby, bending strings while in midair. Kenna read the title out loud. "The Steel Eyes Retrospective by Alex Winthrop—with never before published photos."

"Whoa." Kenna stood and teetered, dizzy. Glancing at the fire, she resisted the impulse to toss the magazine into the flames and watch it ignite. Instead, her hands trembled as she poured a glass of pinot grigio and ambled out to the deck. It was so late into the winter night, she swore she could see the quiet, and she wore it like her unrequited love. The silence unnerved her.

Damn it's cold out here. She made a futile shrug to shake it off. The dizziness subsided more each time the cold wind smacked her face, and now the fire beckoned from inside.

She curled up on the couch in front of the fire with the issue of *Rocklandia*, the glass of wine and the bottle within easy reach.

An article accompanied the photos, written by a guy who had interviewed Steel Eyes several times.

This guy writes like he wants everyone to think he knew me. Putz.

Two glasses of wine later, she was glued to the photos, each one capturing Steel Eyes in a way she had never seen herself.

"You always could see things in me I never saw, Lex." She stared hard at the backstage photos of her and Mel laughing, and Rich and JJ clowning around. They all looked so young. An old longing crept through her like the memory of Alice's lap dances. "Right here. I remember what it means to lose when you win. To be lost *and* found at the same time."

Oh my God. I never thought it would happen...but it's time.

Then she remembered how she and Alex had wound through Topanga Canyon in Alex's Triumph convertible, The Allman Brothers pouring through the speakers.

She flipped to the photo that Sonja Savarin had taken of Steel Eyes with Alex. "I devoured you with eyes that would forever be able to conjure Topanga." She raised her glass to toast Alex's picture. "And here I sit all these years later doing just that." She downed what was left in her glass. "You remember, don't you, Lex...when I thought I was the love of your life?"

The fire crackled, and small bits of bark succumbed to the embers. Kenna pulled the cashmere throw over her and nestled her head against the sofa pillows. As she drifted off to sleep, the empty wineglass dropped from her lazy grip, and Alex's photos stared up at her from her lap. The headline still read the same when she awoke.

Kenna padded to the kitchen and put on a pot of coffee after she had showered and dressed. Caressing the hot cup in her chilled grip, she got online and purchased a plane ticket to LA. The second cup of coffee kept her company through the packing process, during which she tucked the recordings she and Singer had made inside her carry-on.

Mel picked up her phone on the third ring. "Hey, little sister, can I call you back? Dalia and I are unloading groceries."

"Don't bother calling me back, I'll be at your house by dinnertime. Can I crash there?"

"Auntie Kenna's coming to surprise us, Dalia!" Mel yelled so loud that Kenna had to pull the phone away from her ear.

"Gotta catch a plane, Mel, see you tonight."

CHAPTER THIRTY-FOUR

Coffee cup in hand, Kenna stood on the porch and watched Dalia playing outside the luxurious Bel Air home. She set down the cup.

"Good morning, my beautiful goddaughter," she said as she stepped into the California sunshine.

"Auntie Kenna. You surprised us!" Dalia ran into Kenna's arms, and Kenna lifted her off the ground and swung her in a wide circle as they kissed each other's cheeks.

"That's because I miss you so much. I just had to come see you." Kenna gave her a huge squeeze before setting Dalia's feet back on the ground.

"Daddy's taking me to the zoo this morning."

"Lucky you. You have such a good dad."

"I know." She hugged Kenna again. "See you later," she said before she ran off.

Kenna walked back to the porch, picked up her coffee and sat on the padded wicker chair. Mel joined her.

"She's incredible, Mel."

"How did a scrappy chick like me get so lucky?"

"She's a lot like you."

Mel grinned. "Yeah? I don't see it. She's daddy's little girl for sure. Her French is really good. She corrects me all the time." Mel watched Kenna drink her coffee. "Are you going to tell me what this little surprise visit is really about?"

"I'm playing again."

"Get out. Really?" Mel smiled.

"Really."

"And how long has this been going on?"

"Since the fall."

Mel's eyebrows arched. "What! You've been playing for months and you haven't told me…us? I thought your hand still hurt too much to play."

"It did…it does sometimes. But I'd had enough, Mel. The demons were screaming so loud they wouldn't leave me alone. And then something happened."

"What?"

"I became inspired."

"What's her name?" Mel chided.

Kenna smiled at the familiar trust, at the best friend she so missed every day. "I swear, I got over missing my Steel Eyes persona, but I've never gotten over missing you. As for her name, I don't know actually. But I turned a real corner when I went to an open mic jam in Philly a couple of nights ago."

"Ha! *You* went to an open mic? Steel Eyes doing an open mic…that's rich!"

"I did. That's the first time I've been on a stage since the night I was shot."

"And no one even guessed?"

"Well, I did manage to fuck up the first guitar solo to 'Somewhere Like You.'"

"Oh no you didn't!"

"Hand to God. Fucked it up royally."

Mel laughed so hard that tears came to her eyes.

"Did pretty good with The Allman Brothers covers, though, and I ripped 'Miles from You.'"

"I can't believe it. Tell me you played 'Whipping Post.'"

"Of course. But what I wanted to say was that I met a young lady there…"

"Oh no, girl problems."

"No, not at all, strictly professional. She's young, but she's got a great edge, a fresh voice, rhythm guitar talent…which is not as strong as her vocals."

"And?"

"I've been writing new music. Nothing like what I used to write. I brought a tape that we cut in my studio that I'd like you to listen to."

"*Your* studio? The one with all the Grammys and gold records?"

"I obviously hid all that stuff."

"She doesn't know?"

"Has no idea."

Mel sized up her old friend. "Well, let's go give it a listen."

* * *

JJ, Rich, Mel and Kenna were already playing Steel Eyes's new music in Mel's studio when Dalia burst through the door with Michel at her heels.

"Hi, Uncle JJ!"

JJ parked his drumsticks and stretched open his arms. "There's my star!"

Dalia raced to him and sat on his lap while he pounded the bass drum pedal with his foot, which always made her laugh as she bounced up and down on his pedal leg.

"Why is he getting all the love?" Rich said.

Dalia ran to Rich and hugged him.

Michel laughed. "Wow, it looks like old times! Babe, you want me to order some pizza?"

"Pizza!" Dalia yelled.

"No." Mel smiled. "I think we're due for one of our old spaghetti nights."

"Spaghetti night!" Rich and Kenna said in the same instant. Suddenly, for that moment they were all young, broke and in

Mel's apartment on a Friday night, pooling their resources for spaghetti and sitting for hours around that old beat-up kitchen table.

"Spaghetti night!" Dalia confirmed.

Mel laughed. "*The* Dalia has spoken. Spaghetti it is."

Later, with only one noodle left on her plate, Dalia kissed her parents and her uncles good night. Kenna tucked her in, sat on the bed, read her a story and waited before returning to the band.

She could hear Mel, Rich and JJ talking downstairs.

"I'm all in," Mel said. "Bringing Steel Eyes back for a reunion concert would be spectacular."

"I agree," Rich said.

"*Bonne nuit*, everyone. I'm going to bed," Michel said as he leaned over to kiss his wife. "Good night, *chérie*."

"*Je t'aime*, Michel."

"I love you too."

Kenna left Dalia sleeping and ran into Michel in the hallway.

"She really misses you, you know," Michel began.

"Mel or Dalia?"

"Well they both do, but I was talking about Mel."

"Is she okay, Michel? Are you guys okay?"

Michel smiled. "I can't speak for her, but I still think we're a match made in heaven."

"From what I see, you have nothing to fear, *mon ami*. That girl is still head over heels for you."

"I'm glad you're here, Kenna. It's good to have the family back together. *Bonne nuit*. See you in the morning."

"*Fâites de beaux rêves*, Michel."

He leaned in and kissed her cheek. "Sweet dreams to you too."

Kenna rejoined the band.

"So this is really big, Kenna," Rich began. "I never thought you'd ever have a change of heart."

"I just needed time and inspiration. What do you think, guys? One night...in New York at the Beacon."

"I'm in," Mel said.

"Me too," JJ said.

"I'm there." Rich smiled. "This is gonna be fantastic. How do we get it set up?"

"I already have Hunt working on it, just in case you all said yes."

"You'll need to stay out here for rehearsals, little sister. You down with that?"

"Absolutely. I've been practicing our stuff and I'm getting there."

"Except that you said 'Somewhere Like You' still needs work?" Mel asked.

Kenna nodded.

"I figure six to eight weeks of rehearsals," Rich said.

"I think you're right, bro." JJ reached for the pad and pen on the coffee table. "Let's make the setlist right now."

"I think we should open with 'Kiss My Axe' and end with 'Somewhere Like You,' like we used to."

"I agree, Mel. Thanks, guys, this really means a lot. A lot."

"This feels so good with all of us back together. We're going to bring down that house!" Mel jumped up and played air bass.

Kenna stood next and bounced around with her air Ruby. JJ pounded on the coffee table as though it was a conga drum.

Rich sat back and laughed. "Oh, this *is* gonna be good."

CHAPTER THIRTY-FIVE

A few months later, the first seventy-degree day hit the Jersey Shore. The crocuses had been in full bloom for two weeks, the sun had reclaimed its provenance, and the winter gray of the Atlantic had faded. Dogs roamed the beach with their people, and Dréa Winthrop had all the arrangements in place for Alex's surprise fortieth birthday bash.

Dréa had scheduled a full day for Alex at a local hotel's spa in Atlantic City to keep her away from home. The day concluded with hair and makeup appointments in the swanky hotel salon. Alex left there dressed for her supposed birthday dinner with her sister.

It was a solid plan. Meanwhile, the crew Dréa had hired toiled diligently at Alex's beachfront house.

"You look so relaxed, Alex," Dréa said when she picked her up.

Alex hugged her big sister before they got into Dréa's car. "What a great present. Thank you. I think it was your best ever."

"That's not your only present."

"No?"

"No." Dréa pretended to fish through her purse. "But first we'll have to make a detour back to your house before we go to the restaurant. I left my wallet on your kitchen table."

"Don't worry about that. I have my wallet."

"No, Alex, it's your birthday, you're my little sister and I'm not going to let you pay for dinner on your fortieth birthday!"

"Do you have to keep saying *fortieth?*"

"What do you want me to call it?"

"It's my *twenty-twenty* birthday…because I've never seen things this clearly before."

"Wax on, grasshopper. Just remember, next year you'll turn forty-one and no one will notice."

In ten minutes, they'd made it all the way down Atlantic Avenue to Alex's house in Margate.

"Gosh, is it me or are there a lot of cars down here?" Alex said.

"Maybe someone has company," Dréa said. She glanced at Alex, who wasn't leaving the car. "Honey, would you please run in and get my wallet for me?"

"Okay." Alex got out of the car and walked to the front door.

"Surprise!" Thirty women, most of them old flings and one-night stands, shouted in unison. Among them were a few faces that, thankfully, were just friends.

Alex's face flushed bright red and she gasped.

"Happy birthday, sis!" Dréa followed her inside and jumped up and down as though she had just delivered on the best secret surprise ever. Only when she looked at Alex's face did she see the sheer terror. But she had no time to ask Alex what was wrong. The feral pack of exes came barreling toward her sister.

"Hang on, ladies, we'll be right back!" Dréa pushed Alex into the kitchen and up the back stairs. "What is wrong with you, Alex?"

Alex scraped back her hair. "Dréa, what are all my old flings doing here?"

"Your *what?*"

"There are only maybe five women in that room I *haven't* slept with."

"You're not kidding, are you?"

Alex shook her head. "How did you contact all these people?"

"I stole your email list one night when you forgot to log out of your account."

"The Eyes4U account?"

"Yes, why?"

"That's the email address I give to women!"

"Oh…my…God!"

"What exactly did you say to get these women to show up?"

"I sent out a birthday party invitation that said: 'This girl is turning forty. But ssshh, it's a surprise party so you *must* reply to me, her sister, at my email address…' and then I gave them the party particulars."

"What do I do, Dréa?"

"Well, Sis, I suppose you'd better get down there and be as charming as hell."

Stunned, Alex made her way back to the party and plastered an unalterable smile to her face. One by one, women came up to her, came on to her, trashed her quietly, and when they were done raking her over the coals, they still had enough game to cruise each other.

The DJ cranked the music so loud it spilled into the ocean. Getting cozier with each drink, the girls danced and schmoozed.

All things considered, it isn't going badly, Alex thought.

For a while the crowd was almost civilized, until the liquor bottles emptied.

"I'll say one thing for you, Alex," Dréa began, "looking at all these women in such close proximity, it's obvious you don't have a *type*."

"See the brunette on the couch with the redhead?"

"Yes."

"Look at her expression. I think she just figured it all out. I should have known she'd catch on first. She's an analyst."

As the party amped up, that same expression crept across the room.

"And just when did you find the time to date all these women while you were supposed to be with Silvana?" Dréa said.

"I have been single for almost three years! Five or six of them happened when Silvana and I broke up the first two times, and then the blonde over there, she was my consolation prize when we broke up for good. And...you know what? You don't need to know this."

Alex cringed as she watched the conversation quietly make its way around the room. In her mind, it sounded something like...

"So how do you know Alex?"

"I slept with her...once!"

"Oh really? Me too."

And it was all out of her control.

Maybe it'll be okay. She took the bottle of pinot and poured a small glass, downed it and poured another. She almost choked when, while swallowing, one of the women clinked her glass to get everyone's attention.

"Hi, ladies, I'm Cary, and I would like to toast—or rather, roast—Alex. First off, welcome to the Hot Night with Alex Club. I'm certain you have figured out by now that we all have a similar story. This is mine. I met Alex on a Tuesday night at Slide in New York, and *our* first, and *only*, date lasted for forty-nine hours. But what a date it was! Happy birthday, lover!"

While all eyes were on Cary, Steel Eyes stood listening on the opposite side of the room, obscured by the partially open door. One of the women saw her and yelled, "Hey, a Steel Eyes look-alike!"

Alex pivoted on her heel. Her mouth agape, she deadlocked on the cerulean stare. Like their last photo shoot in the SoHo loft, the day Steel Eyes had been shot, her presence was intense and commanding—her stare unmistakable.

It is her! Alex knew it in an instant. *What?*

Steel Eyes froze. Then she took two steps into the room, grabbed the first bottle of vodka she saw and bolted out of the house. "No, no, no. This isn't happening, again!" she muttered.

"Play *loud* music right now!" Dréa barked at the DJ. "Loud! Now!"

The dance music blared and everyone danced...except for Alex.

CHAPTER THIRTY-SIX

Steel Eyes planted herself on the beach under the deck, cradling the *half-full* bottle of Absolut Vodka.

Eureka.

She couldn't wait to tell Hunt that she saw the *bottle* as half-full, finally realizing that in their age-old argument of whether the glass was half-full or half-empty, the fucking problem all along was the *glass*. Bottles didn't seem to be a problem—at all. In the shadow of the stairs leading to the beach, she tried to wrap her head around this...this *karmapocalypse*.

No way! Eyes4U is Alex Winthrop! The second shot of vodka didn't dull the refrain any more than the first one had. That certainly wouldn't do.

Lex? Out of the whole cyber planet, we live a mile apart? During our entire online affair, she's been one mile downbeach!

"Let me get this straight," Steel Eyes said to the bottle, "for over a year, I've been falling in love with the love of my life, who I've spent most of my adult life trying to forget." She couldn't help but laugh. "Now *that* is funny. Or is that so not funny? Big help you are." She cringed. The next shot of Absolut came into the mix, and it didn't even sting her throat this time.

She tried to focus on what had happened. *According to the blonde who was making the toast, that blonde...and every other woman there were all Alex's ex-flings? And where was the supermodel anyway? Duh! That was the long-term relationship Eyes and I had talked about online. So Silvana must be the woman Eyes had said she split up with almost three years ago.*

Although Steel Eyes might have been the only *non*-ex at the party, Kenna Waverly was not a *non*-ex. In theory, Steel Eyes could remain the exception for as long as she chose to stay behind the mask. Nevertheless, it was she who went catatonic at the sight of Alex. The blood drained from her face; the back of her head tingled; an ancient, worthless piece-of-shit backlash leveled her. She had raced out of there, snatching the vodka on the way. And now here she sat, in a daze. *That* wouldn't do either.

Mask-less, she wandered the beach for almost an hour. The waxing gibbous moonlight splintered the sea-foam crests and the waves licked the coastline just shy of her laden steps. *This* wouldn't do either.

Under the deck was decidedly safer than behind the wheel of her car after three shots of vodka and the sight of Alex. She hoofed it back to the beachfront home and slipped underneath the stairs again, trying to let the events wash over her, to settle into her bones. She downed another shot from the bottle.

Fate. Isn't that what we talked about so long ago? Kenna recalled that first conversation they'd had in the hotel room after Maurice's funeral, when Alex had said she *did* believe in fate because they had met.

Steel Eyes put on her mask and was about to down another shot when she heard the French doors to the wooden deck creak above her. Two sets of footsteps scuffed the planks.

Sounds like the party's over.

"My God, Dréa, what were you thinking?" Alex said. There was a pause.

"I'm *so* sorry, Alex. I totally fucked up."

Dréa? As in Andréa, the artist who painted the cobalt piece in my studio? Really? I've gotta move to a bigger town.

When Steel Eyes heard the wine pouring from the bottle to the two glasses, she seized the opportunity to down a shot. This time it stung.

"I never dreamed the email list I stole from you was your old dates and girlfriends list. You have every right to disown me, sis…but before you do…" Dréa gulped some wine.

Lex's sister? Really?

Dréa continued. "Tell me how in the *hell* does Steel Eyes fit into this? I mean that really was *her*, wasn't it?"

"I'm certain of it. I've spent years gazing into those eyes, staring at the face beneath that mask through the camera lens and in the darkroom. At first I thought you hired a look-alike, but when our eyes met, I knew it was her. Then it hit me. Steel Eyes Disguise was on that email list! And *Disguise* must be…the real Steel Eyes." She exhaled forcefully.

When she spoke again, her tone was remorseful. Steel Eyes still recognized the low, silky-smooth timbre; that feminine bedroom voice whose fluid register marinated her, especially when it had whispered words of devotion in the dark. She strained to hear over a set of crashing waves.

"Okay, Dréa…I'll tell you. About a year ago, late one night, I was curious to know if there was some kind of online chatroom for hardcore Steel Eyes fans like myself."

"Please, I know how you like this whole new Interwebby thing."

"Anyway, I found one." Alex sipped her wine for punctuation. "I was watching the conversation when someone started to bash Steel Eyes, so I rushed to her defense. After that person left the chat room, a private message came up on my screen from someone named Steel Eyes Disguise, congratulating me for putting that idiot in his place."

"So how did this turn into you cyber-dating the most famous international anonymous woman rock star who's ever disappeared?"

Steel Eyes smiled. *I like her.*

"I'm getting to that," Alex said. "So Disguise, for short, and I developed this relationship online for the past year. It's been an onscreen affair, and I fell in love with her. I actually fell for a woman I've never met. We chose to not share our identities...or photos...until we meet. We've never even talked on the phone. I can't tell you *how* I knew I fell in love with her, I just know that I fell in love with her words. Oh Jesus, I fell in love with Steel Eyes! I'm such a loser."

Dréa waited as Alex downed the last of her wine and then poured her another glass. "Yeah well, at least you know why she didn't meet you before now. She didn't want you to know who she was! But with her reunion concert in two days, she can finally come out of hiding. Crazy. This is so crazy. So just to recap—you fell in love *with* your idol while unknowingly chatting *with* your idol *about* your idol...for a *whole* year. And... you already know each other professionally."

Alex scoffed. "The odds of this happening don't even exist yet."

If you think those odds are high, Lex...I have a bet that'll blow your mind.

Alex downed her wine and held out her glass. "More, please. Damn. Did you notice how fast Steel Eyes bolted when Cary roasted me? I'm so embarrassed."

"Well, sis, not to make it worse but, *no one didn't* notice. Maybe it's just fate."

"No, I have to take full responsibility for this one. I blew it, Dréa. I blew it that day of the Concert Zero photo shoot when Steel Eyes and I almost kissed, then Silvana walked in; and I blew it again tonight. You know, as short a relationship as it was with Kenna in LA, here it is almost twenty years later and I've never gotten over her. Honestly, I made peace that I'd never be totally over her—had finally accepted that I haven't loved like that since. Then this year it all changed. I really thought that whoever Steel Eyes Disguise was, I had found what I've been looking for."

Steel Eyes let a handful of sand filter through her fingers.

"Maybe the wine has me confused, but I could swear I sold a painting to someone named Kenna this past winter. The blue abstract. I don't know, my brain hurts."

Sounding lost in thought, Alex continued. "Steel Eyes had every right to run as far and as fast as she could in the opposite direction tonight. I deserved it."

"Why?" Dréa said. "Is it because, thanks to your sister, she finds out she is in a room full of *a lot* of casual exes? Or do you think it's more that she freaked out when she saw that her online love turned out to be you? Oh, honey…I wish I could get all that toothpaste back into the tube for you, but even the family size isn't *that* big."

Alex sighed.

"On the bright side, Alex, I did see a few matches made tonight at the party. Seems a few of your old flames found some new candles to light."

Alex chuckled. "I don't even want to know; I'm fried. Can we talk in the morning? I just want to go to bed."

"I don't want to leave you like this. I know you. You'll drive yourself crazy."

"I'll be all right…and I'm really not mad at you. It's karma, and my fault on *so* many levels. Honestly, what was meant to be…or not to be is out of my hands." She kissed Dréa on the cheek. "Promise me, Dréa, no more surprises."

"*Never* another surprise. Not even a tuna surprise. Try to get some sleep, okay?"

"Sure, right after I change my phone number and my email address."

Steel Eyes heard the door close and she breathed in the salt air. With the partygoers gone, the waves didn't seem to crash as hard as they had, but she still felt her insides gurgle with their ebb and flow. Alex's voice shocked her out of her fog.

"Who's there?" Alex said. "I can see you moving." A streak of moonlight hit something shiny, and Alex caught the reflection of movement under the stairs. The movement stopped. "*I said, who's there?*"

Steel Eyes parked the more than half-*empty* vodka bottle, twisting it down into the sand until it stood upright. One deep breath later, she crawled out from under the stairs with her mask still on, stood up and then brushed the sand from her clothes.

She looked up. "It's just me, Eyes."

Alex's mouth went chalk-dry when she saw Steel Eyes standing below her on the beach. "You came back," she said with a sultry sigh.

"Except for a walk on the beach, I never left."

Alex gazed at the masked rock star. "W-would you like to come up here?" she asked, not quite sure what pose to strike, which words to speak. She was suddenly thirteen again, tossing back her hair in a transparent attempt to evade her awkwardness.

"I would like that very much." Steel Eyes's voice was soft and unhurried. She maintained eye contact with Alex while slowly climbing the stairs.

When she reached the deck, she sauntered toward Alex. The only words that entered her mind were: *radiant, vulnerable... simply stunning.*

In all her former incarnations, Alex had never apologized once for being cool. She owned cool. Except, right now her breathing was shallow, her expression unhopeful and she couldn't qualify to rent cool, let alone own it. Too exposed to be this close to either Steel Eyes *or* Disguise, she broke eye contact, then took a deep breath and again met Steel Eyes's stare.

"Steel Eyes, I'm so sorry. I had no idea about this party... you see, my sister Dréa..."

Steel Eyes gently touched Alex's lips with her fingertips.

"It's okay, Eyes, that's not what I want to know."

Puzzled, Alex cocked her head to the side. She gazed longingly at Steel Eyes's sensuous lips, desperate to kiss her, for this and for every other moment she had ever craved the touch of the other woman's lips. Intimidated by the mere thought of it, she stood stone-like.

Steel Eyes continued. "Forget about everything else. I just want you to tell me how you feel about me, for real."

"I fell in love with you, Disguise...I *am* in love with you."

"But you don't even know what I look like. What if I take off this mask and the attraction is gone?"

"That won't happen. It's not even possible."

Steel Eyes smiled. "You sound so sure."

"Steel Eyes, I fell in love with you when we met years ago, and again anonymously in cyberspace during this past year. I mean, you never know, but right now the odds are looking pretty good, right? I didn't know it was you or what you looked like…and truthfully, I still don't care. I fell in love with *you*. Both of you. The fact that your music captures me in ways that are very personal for me only makes it more visceral. I *knew* you had survived…I *felt* it, even before you announced the reunion concert."

"How?"

"I felt you. I know that sounds weird, but it's true. You probably don't want to remember our photo shoot the day you were shot, but I fell for you that day too. There was something between us…a moment when I was photographing you in the SoHo studio. The way you stared into the lens, I had to pull away from the camera. I felt exposed by that look. It was so intense I had literally stopped breathing. That moment was magic for me. And while you may think otherwise based on the insanity you saw here tonight, I've only ever felt the presence of one other woman this way."

"The supermodel?"

"Unfortunately…no. As I told you online when we had that discussion, I loved Silvana very much, but looking back, she was in many ways the most fabulous consolation prize for losing the love of my life. But the way I feel…"

"What way, Eyes?"

"I knew about you in an instant—I knew about *her* in an instant too. I felt her enter the room before I ever saw her, and from the moment we met, I thought she was my destiny. It turned out I was just her fate. It was like your song, 'From Nowhere to Now Where.'" Alex recited part of the lyric.

How much more could you take from me?
You said you were my destiny
When I found out
It was too late

You weren't destiny
And I was fate.

Sprayed by salty air and a sobering confession, Steel Eyes's head began to clear. She tried to exhale the newly trapped tension from her neck. "Where is she, this woman you loved?"

"I don't know. It was a long time ago, a very long time. We were so young, and when it didn't end well, she disappeared. Can't say I ever blamed her."

"What happened?"

"To put it plainly? I was stupid. Maybe even afraid to feel that much."

As Steel Eyes listened, she paced to the far side of the deck and turned.

Older and humble looks so fucking sexy on you.

Alex's thick auburn waves now had layers of highlights, her eyeshadow was an alluring smoky-gray, and those lines in the corners of her eyes—the ones Kenna had always been a sucker for—were a little deeper, sexier. The lines that showed such warmth when she would laugh, and more so when she had said, "I love you."

"Eyes...what if I told you there was a reason that my music was personal to you? That I know what the reason is."

Alex stepped toward her and stopped about a foot away. "What are you talking about?"

Steel Eyes broke Alex's stare and glanced out toward the ocean. *It's now or never.* Her gaze drifted back to Alex. "What if I told you that those songs were written for you?" She peeled back the hard outer mask, hesitated, and then pulled off her under-mask.

Alex's wineglass dropped, and it shattered on the deck just ahead of local East Coast gravity time. "Kenna?" She could barely get the name out. Motionless, she forgot to breathe, and then she gasped for air.

With a lightning-quick reaction, Kenna caught her when Alex almost fainted, lowering her onto the chaise behind them.

"I think I'm okay." It took almost a minute for Alex to come to that conclusion. "Is this happening?"

"Did you mean it, Lex? Did you *really* love me?" Kenna knelt beside her so that no breath would be lost as the answer left Alex's lips. Alex turned her head away.

"Lex, look at me." Kenna gently turned Alex to face her. The instant their eyes met, Alex reached out and pulled Kenna on top of her, kissed her passionately. The kiss disoriented Kenna.

"Yes. I meant it. God, yes. I'm so sorry for ever losing you."

Kenna kissed her with soft lips, then passionately hard, like a prisoner torn between escaping or serving out a life sentence. After all these years, their bodies still fit perfectly. Kenna lifted her head so she could feel Alex's wine-stained breath on her cheek, so she could look into those emerald eyes, the ones that had changed her life in an instant, both then *and* now; the emerald color that had shaded every moment in between.

Kenna slowly peeled away and stood, looking down at her.

"Where are you going?" Alex asked.

Kenna held out her hand. "With you."

Alex took it and stood slowly, afraid she might faint. "I should have known it was you when I looked into your eyes at the photo shoots, and I should have known tonight. How could I not know? I'm guessing those blue contact lenses threw me off...and your voice was different...wasn't it?"

"Yep. Vocal coaches taught me how to do that."

Kenna gazed into Alex's eyes and pulled Alex to her. With their redemptive embrace, Alex's sensuous mouth landed on the lips that had long awaited her, their passion still familiar, still hungry. Ruined for anyone else long ago by the promise of each other, they lingered and kissed and touched; kissed until they were nearly breathless.

"It's *always* been you," Alex whispered.

"It's always been *you*!" Kenna smiled. "Let's go inside."

Kenna laid Steel Eyes's mask on the table as Alex led her by the hand up the stairs into the master suite. When Kenna crossed the threshold into Alex's sanctuary, she stopped cold. In a gallery-like display, Alex's collection of Steel Eyes concert and magazine photos stared back at her from every wall, each one framed and then positioned in the timeline of Steel Eyes's career.

Collectively, they told Steel Eyes's story, from beginning to end, without a beginning or an ending, just the way Maurice, Kenna's surrogate father, had taught Alex to do. The stark memories came flooding back.

Startled at the sight, Kenna let go of Alex's hand and slowly toured them, scrutinizing each one. "You've always had a way of seeing me that I never saw in myself." She pointed to one. "That's from Madison Square Garden the night of the attack?"

Alex nodded. "I have a question for you. When we were online that one night months ago and we talked about meeting in person, what made you change your mind and back out?"

"I kept thinking, what if I show up as me and she doesn't like me? I had already fallen for you so hard that after my experience years ago with, well, *you*, I was really gun-shy. So then I thought I could meet you as Steel Eyes because I *knew* you liked *her*, but since Steel Eyes was long assumed dead, what were the chances you would think I was really her? In which case, you would think I was just some wacko groupie. It was a no-win proposition for me. So I called my buddy Mel to talk it over with her."

Alex put the pieces together. "Oh my god, Kenna. Melanie… she's your bass player! Of course. That night up in Topanga when you broke up with me, it was *she* who came to get you, wasn't it?"

"Yes."

"I can't believe I didn't even know you were playing music back then. And not just playing…you were becoming Steel Eyes."

"No, honey. By the time we broke up, the only thing left of me was you. I became Steel Eyes when you destroyed my faith and ripped out my heart. You made me this. All the early Steel Eyes songs were written for you while we were still together, or breaking up."

"Fuck! How self-absorbed was I?"

Kenna smiled. "You really want me to answer that?"

Alex shook her head.

"So," Kenna continued, "when you and I had chatted about meeting, Mel convinced me I hadn't thought it through. If I had actually met you as Steel Eyes—even if you did buy it, I would have had to reveal my identity, which for security and legal reasons I wasn't allowed to do unless absolutely necessary. You do realize you're one of a select few who know my identity... and a handful of those are medical personnel who had to sign a nondisclosure agreement? Anyway, Melanie said, 'You'd do *all* that just to get a *date*?'"

Alex laughed. "Well, did you?"

Kenna hesitated. "Maybe. I admit I was insecure about meeting you in person after all that time we had spent online."

"So you crapped out and made Steel Eyes do your dirty work. That is so Kenna W."

Alex's breathing slowed when Kenna stepped forward.

"I swear I can feel your heartbeat from here, Lex. I still feel you in every cell of my body."

Alex gazed into her eyes. "Be sure to let me know if I miss even one square inch of you."

Kenna slipped her arms around Alex, pulled her close and let the gorgeous green stare baste her. Alex unzipped Kenna's jeans, then lifted her sweater over her head and tossed it onto the floor. She removed her own shirt and pressed up against Kenna, kissing her neck, then her lips.

Alex teased her in a whisper. "Dear Diary, I'm about to get it on with Steel Eyes."

Kenna and Steel Eyes draped her body around Alex.

"Dear Lex's Diary, turn the page already."

Their dance was subtler than it once was, but no less intricate. An electric shock with every caress, and every kiss, a meditation. There was simply nowhere left for either of them to go that didn't include them both.

From Nowhere to Now Where, Kenna thought. *Indeed.*

CHAPTER THIRTY-SEVEN

Alex awoke with a jolt during the night. She had reached out for Kenna in her sleep, but all that remained of Kenna was her scent. Wrapped in her kimono, Alex found her on a chaise on the deck, smoking a cigarette. Kenna didn't turn around when Alex opened the door, nor did she look directly at her when Alex sat on her chaise facing her.

Alex stroked her hand. "Are you all right, K?"

Kenna's gaze finally rested in Alex's. "I don't know. That's not true. No, I'm not."

"What's going on?"

"I don't know where to begin to have all the conversations we need to have, Lex. What woke me is knowing I can't sleep until we put some things to rest."

Alex moved closer to her. "I know. Do you want to go inside and talk?"

"I think I need to."

"Come on, baby." Alex took two bottles of water from the bar near the stairs, held Kenna's hand and led her back to the bedroom. She climbed onto the bed and leaned against a pile of pillows, but Kenna sat on the side of the bed, one foot on the floor.

"Where do you want to start, K?"

Kenna exhaled hard. "The promise of you. Your warmth. God, your skin on my lips. I've never known what I feel right now except with you. For years, it…you surfaced in my sleep… in dreams so real they jarred me awake, and I swear, Lex, in those first conscious seconds, I couldn't tell the difference between you…and the promise of you. For all these lost years, the dreams bled into my reality…they escaped into Steel Eyes's hit songs. And for what?" Kenna shook her head in defeat. "Just so I could keep the *promise* of you, the place that no one else ever filled, only because they weren't you.

"And you, Lex? In all those years, did you ever once stop to think about who I really was…*how* I'd loved you? I'm glad we had tonight, but I'm asking you to let go of me once and for all. I've had enough. As tempting as the promise of you is, the real you scares me. I finally get it. Until you let go, I'll never be free. I'm pleading with you—please let me go." Her chest heavy, Kenna couldn't catch her breath.

"What about the past year and our online relationship? Are you trying to convince me that you didn't fall in love with me too? I fell in love with you, again," Alex said lovingly. "What about our connection when I met Steel Eyes? I've been in love with Kenna, with Steel Eyes *and* with Steel Eyes Disguise, and they're all Kenna Waverly. I don't want to let go…I never did. I was really stupid, and young, and I'll apologize until the end of time if that's what it takes. I've always wanted you, I want you still, and while I may not be everything you want…"

"You never bothered to know me enough to know what I wanted. It was always about what you wanted. You not only sabotaged us, Lex, the kicker is, you did it with a woman who used you."

"What are you talking about?"

"Maddy Messer. But that's a whole other conversation."

"Kenna, I tried. You didn't answer my messages, my letters. You must have felt so betrayed. Rightly so. I want *us*, but not just on your terms."

Kenna felt the same wretched dread she had felt for all those years: waking up empty, discovering anew each time that Alex was not beside her, that whatever woman was, fell short in some way. Through no fault of their own, they just weren't…Lex.

Vivacious and artful, for Kenna, Alex's exquisite sensuality blurred boundaries. It abandoned rules until all that remained was raw expression. That's why her photos were so telling. Alex was *still* all of that, better at it than she had ever been.

"Lex, you're the only woman who's ever felt as wrong for me as you've felt right, right from the very start. And what do you mean by, 'not just on your terms'?"

"It means that starting fresh means getting to know each other again."

"You're missing an important part."

"What?"

"I did know you, and that terrified you. What's worse is, you were afraid of *us* and I've never understood why. You knew you were hanging me out to dry from the instant you pursued me… relentlessly pursued me, made love to me—Jesus, professed your undying love for me, all the while sleeping with someone else…the *entire* time. You owned me, you knew it and you used it. You used *me*." Kenna flicked her hair away from her face. "I've already woken up more than once to realize I've lived half a life because I fell in love with you. I won't live by default ever again."

Alex teared up.

Kenna cursed herself for craving Alex's touch even now.

I refuse to want you. Stop making me want you! She pulled on her jeans and cashmere sweater, still aware of Alex's veil on her skin, praying that the sound of Alex's tears would not haunt her dreams. Kenna sat on the edge of the bed and slipped into her boots that lay exactly where Alex had dropped them when she had undressed her. As Kenna's weight shifted to her left foot to stand, she felt Alex's warm hand on her back. The sensation sent shivers up, down, out to the tips of her fingers and toes. It felt every bit as good as she remembered.

"Don't go, baby. Don't go," Alex whispered. "Demons are what make *our* kind of abandon exquisite. And you, honey, are exquisite."

That touch. Kenna closed her eyes and swam in it, cleansed her wounds and redeemed her soul in it. She begged herself to not want Alex, but that was just never going to happen. To her, that was as futile as trying to defy gravity. Her body capitulated and her voice softened.

"Lex, the night I was shot, as I drifted out of consciousness from blood loss, I really thought my life was over. I felt my life force simply slip from my body. In that moment—" Kenna choked up "—those words, your voice saying, 'Don't go, baby. Don't go,' were the ones that kept me alive. It was what you had said to me the night I left you in Topanga Canyon."

Kenna didn't leave, but she still had not turned around to face Alex. The only thing she wanted more than to leave was to fall into Alex's arms the way she had all night, in the dark, shedding every layer until there was nothing left of either of them. But she was a grown-up now, and she needed more than that—if that even existed. She needed peace of mind. All her life, she had dodged bullets, love, fame, and she had done it all as an orphan. She had downplayed her talent and her power, instead consistent in her ordinariness. But it was Alex who unraveled those tangled parts of her, effortlessly. Now, the mere thought of losing Alex again caused a pervasive nothingness to spread through her hollow insides. She unsuccessfully raked back her long, flowing hair, tangled and falling down over her eyes.

"What's it gonna be, Lex? Are you going to let me go?" she said quietly. She wouldn't turn around, knowing one look from those seductive cat eyes would force her to cave in.

"Kenna, look at me."

She shook her head. "I am not going to look at you."

"Why?"

"Because that's how you always won."

Alex laughed. "Come on, work with me. K, how can I kiss you, how can I promise myself to you if you won't look into my eyes?"

"Are you promising yourself to me, Lex?"

"Are you turning around?"

Kenna couldn't suppress her laugh. "You're maddening... *really.*"

"Maybe you've been right about us all along, Kenna."

A lead weight replaced the hollowness in Kenna's chest.

"But I can't wait any more. Kenna Waverly, marry me. Marry me."

"Are you saying that to get me to turn around?" She slowly twisted, and Alex brushed the hair from Kenna's eyes, from Steel Eyes's.

"Steel Eyes." Alex scoffed. "How could I have listened to every song a million times, stared into that mask, done a photo shoot with you, for God's sake, *twice*, and still not have known it was you? All those years, I felt like those songs spoke just to me, of course never believing it, what with millions of other fans feeling the same way...never knowing that the reason they gripped me was because they told our story. I was a damn fool, Kenna. A fucking idiot. I ran from the one thing, the one person who had made my life the most interesting ride; the girl I fell in love with before I even knew her name. You take my breath away still, and I love you. I miss you."

Kenna reached out and touched Alex's face. "Well, you've had a long time to do something about it, and you never did. I've learned that while life is what we get without a choice, happiness only comes when we find the courage to live it." Kenna stared into those tear-filled, luminescent cat eyes. "Where was the courage, Lex?"

Alex stroked Kenna's hand. "I wonder how many times the earth has spun since our very first kiss. I know we can't get back the years we've lost, but we can move forward...together. Marry me, Kenna."

Kenna froze in the heat of Alex's touch, every cell in her body shocked out in that instant—she forgot to breathe. All the years of longing, craving and withholding love from every woman, praying one day Alex would come back to her. And here it was, the do-or-die moment. Was it really what she wanted with Alex after all, or was she just using Alex as an excuse for all those years to keep every other woman at arm's length?

"Say something, Kenna. Jesus, say *something*."

Silent, Kenna turned away, stood and walked to the bedroom door.

"No, Lex," she said. If she could only walk through that door it would finally be over. Done. Two steps in front of her and she could get free, begin fresh. She glared at the door's threshold, thinking it might as well have been the finish line of a marathon, some twenty-six miles from her toes.

"No? Why not?"

Kenna could hear Alex's tears move into her throat, and she turned to face her.

Her feet weighed a thousand pounds each. "I'm...afraid. I couldn't survive losing you again if it didn't work out." She measured her words. "I simply won't survive it. I've made it *this* far on the fumes of fame."

Alex stood and sauntered to her, still breathtaking, stunningly sensuous bathed in amber light with her kimono falling open. The sight of her took Kenna's breath away. Alex wrapped her arms around Kenna and placed her head on Kenna's cashmere shoulder. She whispered into her ear. "Where is *your* courage, K? You do realize I'm asking you for forever? Oh, baby, you're trembling again."

"Yeah I know...it happens every time I breathe you in. Like last night, years ago it happened at the photo shoot, the day of the attack. It happened every day for the first year we were apart."

Alex reeled her in tighter. "It's okay. I'm right here, and I've got you." Minutes hemorrhaged silently, forever gone from life and yet indelible, immortal. Kenna's trembling subsided. "Look, you have the Steel Eyes concert in two days. We've waited this long, so put all of this out of your mind for now. Just focus on the concert. I want you to be okay."

Kenna grabbed her, raked her hand through Alex's hair, and only when she saw total submission in her eyes did she kiss her.

"Whatever you want, K, however you want it."

"Will you come to New York with me tomorrow and stay until the concert ends?"

Alex got it. "You're thinking of the night you were shot, aren't you?"

Kenna nodded.

Alex pulled her in even closer this time and repeated, "It's okay, baby. I'm right here, and I've got you. I'll be anywhere you want me to be."

CHAPTER THIRTY-EIGHT

Alex had yet to arrive at the Plaza in Manhattan. Kenna checked into the room she had reserved under the name Cathérine Bernard, one of her old aliases. She was certain that Cathérine, her Parisian angel, would have felt comforted by the thought that she still used her name. Kenna had to scramble if she was to get to rehearsal on time.

A talented spy and chess player, Hunt had arranged an obscure enough location for her to rehearse with the band as Kenna. He had conveniently waited to leak the wrong information to the paparazzi, which put them clear across town as Kenna took a taxi in the opposite direction. New York allowed for any number of people on any given street at any point in time, making spotting the band a near impossibility, as long as they arrived separately.

Alex had promised to be at the hotel by the time Steel Eyes had finished rehearsal. Kenna hadn't told Mel, Hunt or the guys about the events of the past day, about Alex…about any of it. Mel was the only one who knew she had been having the online relationship, but Kenna wouldn't tell her friends about the unimaginable events of the past day until after the concert the next night at the Beacon.

They all had enough to worry about with the reunion concert. Kenna had had too much time to think and didn't know which made her more nervous—the rehearsal, the concert or coming home to Lex.

She picked up her cell phone and called Singer.

"Kenna!" Singer shouted when she picked up. "I can't believe you had someone deliver a Steel Eyes ticket to me *and oh my God a backstage pass!* Who the hell do you know that you were able to get us tickets? Hey, you want to drive up to New York together?"

"That's what I'm calling about, Singer. Here's the deal. I'm already in New York. I'll be backstage for the concert, so when it's over, just come backstage to the VIP area and I'll see you there."

"But how did…"

"I have to run. See you tomorrow, okay?" Kenna laughed when she hung up. Steel Eyes had every intention of introducing her to Mel and the guys. Along with Eyes4U, Singer was the breath of fresh air that had delivered Kenna back to the music, back into the studio and ultimately back to Steel Eyes. When she had left LA two days before Alex's party in New Jersey, rehearsals had been airtight, and they were all used to playing with Steel Eyes again.

Singer, you're going to flip out when I introduce you to everyone. You deserve a shot at the big time, that's for sure. She checked the time, scribbled a note for Alex and left the hotel for the rehearsal studio.

When she arrived, Kenna paid the cab driver and entered.

"Hey, girl!" JJ kissed her. "So are you ready for this? Are *we* ready for this?"

"Bring it, J! Hey, Rich, Mel!" She walked over to them. "You guys ready to get to work?" She hugged them both.

"Here," Rich said, "Hunt gave me Ruby for you."

"Great, thanks. Where is Hunt anyway?"

"He said he'll be here before we finish rehearsal, and then we can all go to dinner tonight," Mel added while tuning her bass.

Kenna thought of Alex and inhaled the thought. Inspired, she reminded herself to focus on the concert. Then she noticed that the lines to her compartmentalized life were finally beginning to blur. She was so ensconced in the music, the next two hours raced past her.

"Kenna, you sound terrific, even better than before. Wow."

"Thanks, Mel. So what do you think, guys? I think we're ready. We can go over the little stuff at the sound check tomorrow."

"Yeah," Rich began, "I think we should go eat and get back to the hotel. I'm a little jet-lagged and I want to crash early." He pouted in the way that made Kenna laugh.

"What, Rich? What's with the look?" she asked.

"We've always been simpatico…can't you read my mind by now?"

They locked eyes. "I *so* know exactly what you're thinking," she said.

"Well…you guys want to fill *us* in?" Mel asked.

"It's spaghetti night!" Kenna and Rich blabbed in unison.

* * *

Kenna stopped eating after her first few bites.

"What's the matter, Wave, you love spaghetti night. *I* love spaghetti night."

Mel chuckled. "Hunt, we all love spaghetti night."

"I guess I'm just nervous about the concert. It's my first performance in nearly a decade, my stomach is jumpy and I don't have much of an appetite." She monitored their reactions in a glance.

Whew, they bought it.

Alex was all around her. Again, she was the new paradigm through which Kenna viewed and sensed her world.

After dinner, she returned to the Plaza alone without consequence.

Illuminated only by candles, the glow of "Cathérine Bernard's" hotel room shone golden when Kenna opened the door. She breathed in the scent of flowers…lots of them, and the table had been set with two glasses and a bottle of Perrier-Jouët champagne sticking out of the ice bucket.

"Even candles can't hold a candle to the sight of you in a black lace negligee and stiletto heels, Lex."

Alex greeted her silently, and Kenna pulled the woman in the negligee up against her, kissed her feverishly. When they separated, Alex's expression was playful.

"K, all those years ago, when we broke up?"

Kenna stared at her. "October ninth."

Alex's eyes opened wide. "You remember the date?"

"You *don't*?"

"Well, that notwithstanding, what I do remember is that I never got to give this to you. That night, when I asked you to move to New York with me, you were supposed to say yes, and I was supposed to give you this. I've kept it all these years, hoping that one day I would have another chance. I'm praying this is that chance."

Alex opened the small box and held it out to her. Kenna hesitated for a moment in Alex's gaze and then stared down at the box. She was awestruck at the beauty of what lay inside—a diamond in a platinum setting with two trillians on each side of the large stone.

Alex engaged her stare. "Kenna Waverly, I loved you then, I've loved you ever since, I love you now and I will love you always. Please marry me already. Please?"

Kenna heard a tone in Alex's voice that she had never before heard, nor even imagined—humility. Instantly, she saw Lex in a whole new light, and humility looked as hot on her as humble and vulnerable had after her party.

"Yes!" Kenna had to scream it before her mind had the chance to censor it. She embraced Alex and kissed her. With barely enough space between them to breathe, she said it again. "Yes, yes, yes."

They kissed almost ten years worth before Kenna lost her breath.

Alex playfully pushed her onto the bed, and Kenna sculpted the outline of her body against the silk-and-lace negligee as Alex lay on top of her.

"Keep the heels on, Lex."

"Wait," Alex said. She removed the ring from the box and placed it on Kenna's finger as she draped her body over her. Then she stripped Kenna of her clothes and boots again. But, for the first time ever, she stripped her of her doubt.

Kenna kissed and stroked Alex's flesh with a hunger that had simmered for decades, perhaps lifetimes; a perpetual flame incapable of being extinguished, innately fireproof to anyone or anything that wasn't *them*.

"Take me right now," Alex breathed.

Kenna obeyed. With the ardor of a rock star, she exhumed Alex's soul with her adoring body and her gorgeous hands. Kenna caressed her breasts over the veil of lace, at first gently, then with a warm mouth that teased and prodded.

With uneven breath, they devoured each second. Every gesture a stroke of art, together they created a masterpiece. Alex groaned beneath Kenna, their synchronous bond throbbing, holding out for every stroke. Kenna held her there, making Alex reach for each morsel of sensation until she couldn't any longer.

Alex gasped. She wrapped her legs around Kenna and then pulled Kenna into her deepest self. "I need you now."

"Come to me, baby," Kenna said, and then she stripped Alex layer by layer, until they finally found their very own Transcendent Gateway. In that moment, Kenna realized she would never again have to transcend the gateway alone.

The tension in Alex's body reached its breaking point. Her muscles contracted hard as she kissed Kenna, pulling her in, thrashing until she fell limp in Kenna's embrace, every yesterday vindicated.

No one except Kenna had ever seen *this* Alex, and they both knew it.

Kenna lifted Alex's chin and gazed into her eyes when she felt the tears. "I thought this was supposed to be a happy moment," she whispered.

Alex caught her breath. "I never believed I would feel you again. It's overwhelming." Her mouth savored the taste of Kenna's skin as she kissed the scars on her shoulder. With the certainty that had once possessed her, Alex rolled her naked body on top of her. Kissing Kenna's sumptuous breasts, caressing her, she controlled Kenna with the flagrant abandon of her own body—the abandon Kenna had never forgotten.

She pushed Kenna beyond every boundary until Kenna surrendered to the sentient meditation that Alex had long ago given to her, had long ago promised to her, and then left Ruby and millions of Steel Eyes fans to fulfill.

After almost twenty years apart, in an instant, they reclaimed who they had always been and would always be together. From the first time their eyes met, this was their dance: to give all they had, to take everything the other had to give and to leave nothing, ever.

The exact shade of the room was finally pitch-black, its musical tone was silence, and that silence was finally at peace with itself. Drifting off to sleep, Alex's long, sexy leg entwined in Kenna's, someone's arm was somewhere, at the end of which was a hand that wouldn't, that couldn't let go, not even in sleep.

By the time morning came, they had a new life—the life they had longed for. The smell of all the fresh flowers had commingled with the scent of passion, and they awoke quiet, satiated and somehow ready for more. Stripped of the fear and the abandonment, they had finally returned to each other, and Kenna was struck with knowing that all it took for them to be together was to finally make peace with themselves. They would be unrecognizable to those two young women on that fated day when their eyes had first met in that Greenwich Village boutique—the eyes that now revealed lines that chronicled lives lived. But nothing was more beautiful to each of them than the other in this very moment.

Kenna stared down at the ring on her finger, bright and shining with the hope of a future to match.

Alex took her hand and admired how the ring looked on the hand of her one true love; the hand that ravaged a hot guitar; the hand that both commanded and redeemed her; the hand of her soon-to-be wife.

Kenna kissed her, taking note how the scant light cast its muted glow on the lines of Alex's face as she pulled away. *There's a song in there somewhere*, she thought. "Alex Winthrop, you are the most beautiful, sexy woman I have ever known. I can't believe it's finally our time. I love you. I just fucking love you."

Alex smiled. "I've been waiting for almost two decades to hear you say that again." She sighed and nuzzled into Kenna's neck. "Want to go have breakfast? Seems you've made me ravenous."

Kenna grabbed her muted cell phone off the nightstand. "Oh shit!"

"What?" Alex asked, alarmed.

"Guess what time it is."

"I don't know…ten, no, eleven o'clock."

"No, Lex, it's two o'clock in the afternoon! I have to get to the theater for sound check like right now!" She pressed a few buttons and flopped back on her pillow. "Okay, seems the entire band has been calling…I've got to go."

Kenna jumped to her feet and clumsily climbed into her clothes. She hastily kissed Alex and stumbled to the door as Alex observed and adored her every move.

"I'll leave a ticket with a backstage pass at will call. You *will* be there tonight, won't you?"

Alex smiled. "Are you fucking kidding me? Go, I'll see you later."

Kenna flew out the door and grabbed a sandwich on the way.

CHAPTER THIRTY-NINE

"Jeez, Kenna, we've been calling you all day," Rich snapped. "We still have to run through the last verse of 'Somewhere Like You.'"

Melanie was miffed. JJ leaned against the door to Steel Eyes's dressing room *not* twirling his drumsticks.

"I know, I know. I'm so nervous, I overslept. I'm *really* sorry, guys."

"Everyone stay calm. Let's get ready, do the sound check and have a great show." Rich waved his muscular arms in a large circle toward his body. "Come on, guys, group hug!"

Mel laughed, Kenna snickered and JJ rolled his eyes at how well they knew each other; how, even though Steel Eyes had left the band long ago, Kenna Waverly had never left the family.

Kenna took a deep breath. "I'm making a change for tonight's show…"

Melanie groaned. "You can't be serious, there's no time."

"Stop, Mel, this is an easy one. I promise. Just trust me, okay? I'm asking you to trust me."

"I've known you a long, long time, Kenna. You want to tell us what's going on?"

"Okay, Rich. Everyone relax. You don't have to worry about playing 'Somewhere Like You' tonight."

"But it's our encore," JJ started.

"Wait, J. Tonight I want to do the encore unplugged, alone. I want to perform 'Somewhere Like You' the way I wrote it…on Sweet Jayne, in my West Hollywood apartment."

Kenna's bandmates fell silent.

"*Why*, little sister?"

"You'll see." She couldn't yet tell them about Alex, as protective as they had always been after Alex had broken her heart. They were the ones who had picked her up off the floor of the bar where she'd gotten drunk after it had happened. Theirs were the shoulders she had cried on long after. They had held silent vigil by her side after she had been shot, when they didn't even know if she would live. "Trust me, okay? Now go get ready. I'll see you out there."

As the door to Steel Eyes's dressing room closed behind them, Mel looked at JJ and Rich. "Something major is up. Either of you have a clue what it is?"

"What are you talking about?" JJ said.

"You men are so oblivious. What the hell is up with her?" Mel's question hung in the hallway as each of the members of the Steel Eyes Band retreated to their dressing rooms to begin their arduous rock-persona transformations.

Kenna turned toward her mirror and began her transformation to Steel Eyes once again. She wondered how she could feel calm and nervous all at the same time. Noticing that something about her indeed looked different, she stared at her face in the makeup mirror, trying to detect just what that difference was. After a minute, it came to her. Her eyes were smiling, and she had a plan.

CHAPTER FORTY

After the sound check, Steel Eyes stood alone on the stage looking out into the empty, historic three-thousand-seat Beacon Theater. Flanking the stage stood two golden sentries, poised with their swords, tall enough that they appeared to reach as high as the second balcony, with yet another balcony above that. She had only ever seen them from the audience. The superior acoustics of the theater and even the sound check inspired her.

Inhaling all the past legends who had graced this very stage, she thought about the great shows she had attended there in her younger days, before Steel Eyes had been born. The Allman Brothers had captured her. But the show she would remember most fondly was the Carole King concert back in the day. She had given a ride to a young, long-haired, shy guy with round, wire-rim glasses whom she had met in her hotel elevator.

"This is my first time in New York," he had told her. "Is there somewhere in the neighborhood to get a good bite to eat?"

"There's a great place. My car is right outside," she'd said. "I'd be happy to drop you off."

On their short ride in her Mustang named Benjamin, she casually asked him about himself.

"I'm a guitar player," he replied.

"Cool," she said, "me too."

It wasn't until the concert that night that she realized the sweet guy was the guitar player who had fried the stage with his sizzling axe. That moment had inspired her to get serious about her music. That was the night that the classic song, "Will You Still Love Me Tomorrow?" became a favorite, second only to "Whipping Post."

The next time she would be on that stage was fast approaching. It would no longer be serene, so she drank in the moment and retreated to her dressing room.

A while later, she looked at the clock and saw it was almost time to take the stage. She listened for the stomping and the age-old 'Steel Eyes chant' in three-four time but didn't hear it. Times had changed in the past decade. Her original fans, like she herself had grown older, had grown up. The energy in the theater resonated differently now—it felt calmer. The Beacon was cozy compared to the stadiums, and she would, for the first time, be intimate with her audience. The thought both terrified and delighted her. Singer would be there. Alex would be there. Her family would be backing her up onstage.

Maybe it has all been worth it…because this is how it all shook out.

Butterflies were in her stomach, but at least she didn't want to puke; now *there* was a perk! And she thought perhaps she was calmer than she had expected because the largest part of her personal puzzle had finally been solved. The love of her life would forevermore actually *be* the love of her life. Then again, maybe it was all the hot, tawdry sex with Alex, the overtures of love in the flower garden of *Cathérine Bernard*'s hotel room; the stunning engagement ring she had hidden and peeked at several times, waiting for the moment when she would wear it, flaunt it, *own* it.

But now, it was showtime.

* * *

"Hey, New York, how are ya!" Mel screamed out.

The audience went wild. They were on their feet for the opening number, "Kiss My Axe." Mel and Rich sang the anthem, one of the most lighthearted and fun songs in their repertoire. It was an all-time favorite, and audiences around the world had loved screaming the refrain, "Kiss my axe!"

Steel Eyes bounced around with Ruby, but she had left the sliding-across-the-stage-on-her-knees-thing back in the last millennium. Their timing was perfect on every song, the four of them smiling, having a genuine blast with the same ease as during one of their old jam nights in Mel's little West Hollywood apartment.

The roar of the audience chanting "Welcome back!" at the end of the show was so loud that it caused the stage floor to rumble. Steel Eyes signaled the band to keep playing as she raced off the stage. She flew down the hall to her dressing room, where she had everything already set up. Adrenaline coursed through her veins so much that her hands trembled as she added to the makeup under the Steel Eyes mask. The cerulean contact lenses landed in the trash can, and she glanced into her gray eyes in the mirror. Tenderly, she hung the mask on the corner of the mirror and ran a brush through her long, sparkled hair.

"Well, it's now or never," she said, staring into the reflection of age and wisdom.

For the first time in all her fame, Steel Eyes was about to take the stage as Kenna Waverly. In just a few moments, the mystery would be revealed to the world, and forevermore, Steel Eyes's true identity would be known. Kenna Waverly no longer had anything to fear or anything left to hide. She was finally at peace with herself. Most importantly, tonight she would finally wear her *own* skin. Instead of Steel Eyes's silver costume, she would perform in a pair of jeans and her favorite French-knit T-shirt.

When Kenna Waverly sauntered onto the stage, Mel's jaw dropped, JJ lost his drumsticks, Rich stopped playing and they all stared at her.

Singer was the only one laughing. From the front row, Kenna heard her beautiful voice belt out, "Fuckin' yeah, Kenna. Go for it!"

Kenna's heart pounded, and she felt naked without Steel Eyes's mask to hide behind. She ignored Mel's open mouth, JJ's grappling for his backup sticks and the fragmented gasps from the audience as they began to realize what was happening.

She sat on the stool behind the microphone that was already set for her. When she nodded to the stagehand, he brought her the aged and worn Guild F-47 guitar with the spruce top. The name *Sweet Jayne* in mother-of-pearl inlay glistened along the fretboard. The theater fell deadly silent.

Kenna loved the feel of Jayne the same way she had on her fifteenth birthday when she had first played her. In an instant, she was fifteen again, only this time she wasn't afraid to perform.

She spoke into the microphone. "Hi, everyone. My name is Kenna Waverly, but you have always known me as Steel Eyes." The press clamored under the stage with all the lenses aimed at Kenna, their flashes of light streaking, pelting her.

"As you know, it's a Steel Eyes tradition to end our show with the song 'Somewhere Like You.'" The crowd cheered. "How about a huge round of applause for Melanie, Rich and JJ. Give it up for the Steel Eyes Band, who has so graciously agreed to let me do this."

The audience cheered long and hard.

When Kenna glanced behind her at the band, Rich and JJ were laughing. Mel shook her head in disbelief, and then gave Kenna the look she had given her onstage since their very first performance at the Whisky a Go Go—the look that always said, *Come on, baby girl, show 'em what you got.*

Kenna continued soulfully once the band left the stage. "I figured it was time to play this song for you unplugged, the way it was written so many years ago in my little apartment in West Hollywood...when I looked...well, like this. This is for Alex."

Kenna's steel strings rang out as clear as a harp in an angel's headphones. For the first time ever, her audience listened silently, reverently, giving her voice and her guitar the power they had once had, before she had let fear disguise it and let fame mutilate it.

I'm looking for somewhere like you.
Same familiar eyes,
Old familiar lies,
But I'd still live somewhere like you.

By the time Kenna finished the whole song, no one doubted Kenna Waverly was Steel Eyes. The crowd's roar of approval was one thing when she was the mysterious Steel Eyes, who strutted across the stage with her hot-red Ruby and the cobalt mask. But now they were applauding *her* and Sweet Jayne as Ruby finally got her long-deserved rest backstage.

She peered out over the darkened theater, realizing that *nothing* would ever be the same for her, forever. Her heart raced and her face flushed. She had to get off the stage. As the camera flashes blinded her, she leaned into the mic. "Thanks for coming! We love you, New York!" she proclaimed.

As Kenna Waverly made her way past the backstage crowd, everyone including the technicians, stagehands and roadies stopped what they were doing to applaud her, to bombard her with whistles and shouts of encouragement. They approved. She sent her security guy to get Singer in the VIP line and waited a moment for Singer to join her.

"Can we talk about it later, Singer?" she said when the girl arrived. Kenna laughed as Singer nodded, an expression of shock and delight on her face.

From behind the crowd, Alex waved Kenna onward, conveying to her that she was cleared by security and was following her through the backstage madhouse.

The band awaited Kenna's arrival in her dressing room, staring at her speechless when she opened the door. Singer followed her in, too stunned that the *iconic Steel Eyes*, was just her buddy Kenna, with whom she'd spent countless hours playing music and writing songs, ordering in pizza and watching old movies.

Reverently placing Sweet Jayne on the guitar stand, Kenna scanned each of their eyes before speaking. Mel, JJ, Rich and Hunt waited. As she searched for the words, the dressing room door opened and Alex entered. Mel and J were speechless squared. Hunt fell backward onto a chair, his mouth hanging open on its hinges.

"What's going on, guys?" Singer asked innocently.

"Singer, meet the band and my brother Hunter. Guys, this is that fabulous voice that you loved on my new demos."

But that wasn't the story Mel, JJ, Rich and Hunt were waiting to hear.

Alex was in as much a state of shock as the band. "K, what possessed you?"

"You, baby." She turned to face her band, who were still reeling in confusion.

"Little sister, are you having some kind of nervous breakdown?"

"No, Mel. I just felt like it was time to, well, come out. I don't want to hide anymore. I no longer need to hide. It's taken me almost my whole life to figure that out. I started hiding when I was orphaned, but I'm not an orphan anymore. I have you and Rich and JJ and Hunt...and—" she stared longingly at her lover "—and you, Lex."

Rich laughed.

"What's so funny?" JJ asked.

"I just flashed on our first gig together at the Whisky a Go Go. You remember, when Kenna found the mask to hide behind right after she tossed her cookies at the *thought* of being onstage. You've come full circle, Kenna, and I'm so fucking proud of you!"

"You can thank Alex for that."

"But it was because of her that you needed the mask in the first place!" JJ said, still protective of the lanky, long-haired girl on whose door he had knocked to invite to a jam session on that rainy Wednesday in LA.

"Well then, I guess it's poetic justice, J. Since you guys are the closest people in the world to me, you should be the first to know. Alex has asked me to marry her, and I've said yes." She opened the drawer to her vanity and slipped the ring back onto her finger.

"Jesus H. Christmas!" JJ grabbed Kenna and hugged her tightly. "Alex, at this point I could write a book about you. It's been a long time."

"Oh my gosh, little sister! You sure this time? Are you *sure*?"

"Yes, Mel, I'm sure."

"Then I should say...it's about goddamn time, you two! Welcome to the family, Alex. You *do* realize this is a package deal, right?"

"I should have figured that out that night in Topanga when you put me in my place," Alex said.

Mel chuckled. "Maybe not...that event, you turned her into Steel Eyes, and we've had one helluva run! You mind telling me how you got back together?"

"Mel," Kenna began, "meet Eyes4U."

Mel's eyes opened wide. "Your online...relationship?" She stared at Kenna in shock. "Unbelievable!"

"Your what?" Rich said.

Kenna glanced at Hunter. "Say something, Hunt."

In a daze, he looked up at her, then at Alex, then back at Kenna. "The comeback concert, the shedding of the mask...and now you and *Alex Winthrop*?"

Kenna could see he wasn't taking this well, at all. She stepped over to him and stroked his hair. "Although everything *is* different, Hunter, nothing has changed. I'm still me, and we're still us—the Steel Eyes Band. I just don't need to hide behind the mask anymore, which means I can *finally* cash in on some of those rock-star perks!" She roared with laughter.

"Wave. I don't know what to say." He stared at all their faces, finally realizing Singer was the other face in the room. He stared at Singer, then at Mel.

Mel smiled at him. "Well, you can start with congratulations, Hunter."

Hunt stood and gazed deep into Kenna's eyes, and even Singer knew better than to make a sound. He gently cradled

Kenna's left hand in his and glanced down at the ring. "You're blinding me," he said. "But I'm the best man, right?"

To Kenna, he looked like the insecure boy the moment before he had chanted his *Haftarah* at his bar mitzvah.

"Dude!" JJ said. "You, Rich and I are *all* the best man."

Hunter was still processing. "What possessed you to toss the mask, Wave?"

"The same thing that possessed me to wear it, Hunt. Alex."

"Okay." He acquiesced and wrapped his arms around her. "*Mazel tov*. You know I'm always on your side." He looked into Alex's eyes. "You'll be good to her this time?"

Alex stepped forward and hugged him. "There isn't *anything* that I wouldn't do for her."

There was a knock on the door, and Hunter stepped outside to speak with security. When he came back, he said, "You have a *pile* of photographers out there just dying to take pictures of the woman behind the mask."

Kenna glanced at Alex. "Sorry, Hunter, you'll have to tell them I've already given the exclusive to Alex Winthrop."

Alex slipped her arm around Kenna's waist. "Come on, baby. Let's go home."

"Fat chance that'll happen now that everyone knows what you look like," Hunter said.

JJ laughed. "Yeah, no more sneaking out the exit doors with the fans."

"Did she *really* do that?" Alex asked.

"After every single show," JJ said.

"Wait. I have an idea to create a diversion," Singer said. She took one of the Steel Eyes backup wigs off the mannequin and respectfully cradled the Steel Eyes mask, trying it on for size.

Kenna burst out laughing. "Go for it, Singer. You *know* you want to!"

EPILOGUE

Marie Cathérine Bernard carried the latest edition of *Rocklandia* magazine folded under her arm to the Sunday marionette show at the Jardin du Luxembourg in Paris's sixth arrondissement. She read the article about Steel Eyes and studied the pictures of Kenna Waverly, taken by her lover—the photographer.

While her children and their other mother laughed at the iconic marionette Guignol, Cathérine reminisced with startling clarity about the two nights she had spent in the arms of her lover Steeleyez. She had known, even back then, that the woman who had appeared briefly at Agitée and had introduced herself as Kenna after the first night of their affair was Steel Eyes.

At first she was thrown by the different appearance, eye color, voice, even the French fluency. But Steel Eyes couldn't have hidden the chemistry between them no matter how she had tried. Cathérine *knew*, and she had let Steel Eyes have her privacy anyway, never revealing to her that she knew, never betraying her to the press, or to anyone. Cathérine had never fallen out of love with Steel Eyes. She had simply chosen a different life. This life.

When the marionette show ended, Cathérine left the copy of *Rocklandia* on the bench, and on the way home, she bought her daughter Kenna the guitar she had been asking for.

On that same day, Maddy Messer was shot in London and left for dead. Thankfully, she was found in time by her lover and fellow spy Jocelyn, whom Kenna had introduced her to in Berlin.

After the small private wedding ceremony in Massachusetts, Kenna and Alex honeymooned at Uncle Menachem's villa in Jamaica, where Kenna had recuperated after being shot; where Mel and Michel had gotten married; where she was the last time she had heard Cathérine's voice, on the phone when they had said goodbye. The very place where Kenna had renounced Steel Eyes for what would become the better part of a decade.

Kenna watched the sunset from the couch on the veranda with Carole King's "Will You Still Love Me Tomorrow?" playing in the background. Alex came racing out from the living room with a copy of today's *Herald Tribune*. She opened to the full-page article and dropped it on Kenna's lap as she sat next to her, slinging her arms around her.

Kenna smiled when she read the first paragraph. "It's been my lifelong dream, you know."

"I know."

As a wedding gift to the rocker who had given so much to the world, both through her music and her philanthropy, donations poured in to animal sanctuaries all over the globe.

"K, if you had to do it all again, to go through all that you've been through…would you do it?"

Kenna stroked the breeze-tousled hair from Lex's emerald eyes and then kissed her until the sun fled the hemisphere.

Bella Books, Inc.

Women. Books. Even Better Together.

P.O. Box 10543
Tallahassee, FL 32302

Phone: 800-729-4992
www.bellabooks.com